WARSTRIDER

REBELLION

WILLIAM H. KEITH, JR.

AVON BOOKS • NEW YORK

"Hope Eyrie" © Leslie Fish, 1975; recorded by Firebird Arts & Music of Oregon, P.O. Box 14785, Portland, Oregon 97214-9998.

WARSTRIDER: REBELLION is an original publication of Avon Books. This work has never before appeared in book form. This work is a novel. Any similarity to actual persons or events is purely coincidental.

AVON BOOKS
A division of
The Hearst Corporation
1350 Avenue of the Americas
New York, New York 10019

Copyright © 1993 by William H. Keith Jr.
Published by arrangement with the author
Library of Congress Catalog Card Number: 92-97435
ISBN: 0-380-76880-1

First AvoNova Printing: June 1993

AVONOVA TRADEMARK REG. U.S. PAT. OFF. AND IN OTHER COUNTRIES. MARCA REGISTRADA. HECHO EN U.S.A.

Printed in the U.S.A.

RA 10 9 8 7 6 5 4 3 2 1

Prologue

There was Rock . . . and there was ››self‹‹, the former parting for the latter in the flux of powerful magnetic fields. A universe of rock subtly textured and diverse surrounded ››self‹‹ in a warm and comforting embrace that flowed around ››self's‹‹ shell with semimolten plasticity as it burrowed upward through the yielding strata. Behind lay the depths of Mother Rock; ahead, closer now, was the goal, a concentration of riches undreamed of, a magnetic anomaly tasting of deliciously, dizzyingly pure metals, ceramics, and hydrocarbon compounds.

››Self‹‹ could sense its universe in myriad ways: through density and water content and something that might be called the taste of silica, quartz, limestone, metal-sharp ores, and hydrocarbons; through the tug of gravity; through magnetic fields and the far weaker trickle of electrons within the Rock; through the life-giving heat of encompassing Rock and the dimly sensed "flavor" of remarkably concentrated metals now so close ahead.

Though ››self's‹‹ concept of time was not, strictly speaking, linear, it knew that it wouldn't be much longer now.

Dimly, ››self‹‹ remembered Self, a far vaster progenitor of ››self‹‹ now far below and behind the upward threading fragment. It shared Self's perception of the universe, of course, though it remembered only dream-vague slivers of its past life. Self's view of the universe was shaped by its evolutionary genesis eons past in the bowels of another world light-millennia distant, and by a harshly Boolean logic that perceived its surroundings in terms of yes and no, of Self and not-Self, of Rock and not-Rock. It did not, could

1

not, recognize the concept of other worlds. In Self's curiously inverted reality, Universe was an infinite sea of Rock, growing ever denser and ever hotter in all directions out from the Center, while at the Center itself lay a vast emptiness, the Chasm at the Heart of Creation. Self's former Selves, its predecessors that had vaulted the gulf from another world to this, had passed down memories of the crossing as frozen lattices of magnetic bonds between Self's subcellular, nanotechnic components, but those memories held images only of black emptiness and slow-dragging eons of time, and not of separate worlds or stars or the basis of astronomical theory.

Tunneling through rock turned plastic, ››self‹‹ was suddenly aware of near-vacuum, of a flood of radiation, of alien sensations that recalled the memories of the central Chasm. Breakthrough! Self had emerged in the emptiness at the universe's heart!

Disorientation swirled within the several parts of ››self‹‹, dizzying, mind-wrenching. This particular local expression of Self had never pierced the walls of the Great Cavern, and inherited memories were weak and fragile things compared to this new perspective on the world.

Analysis . . .

The vacuum was not absolute. There was matter beyond the cavern wall, a thin gas of recognizable elements combined in unfamiliar molecules. Oxygen was present, for instance, but as free O_2 instead of the usual SiO_2 or Fe_2O_3 of Rock. Self's knowledge of astronomy was nonexistent, but its understanding of physical chemistry was superb, its analysis of its surroundings flawlessly precise. ››Self‹‹ was bathed in electromagnetic radiation as well, energy in two separate frequency bands, one between 10^7 and 10^{10} hertz, and another between 10^{14} and 10^{15} hertz. It suspected that the gap between the two sets of frequencies was the result of absorption by the tenuous gas that blanketed this place.

Self/››self‹‹ lived by absorbing energy directly through shifting, nanotechnic surfaces, but the high-energy end of the spectrum was more than it was used to, or needed. Adjusting its surface to a dazzling, reflective silver, ››self‹‹

began to morph from the slender, streamlined shape used in through-rock travel to the more utilitarian, globular shape of an explorer. Tentacles flicked out, questing. Weapons formed, a precaution in case of attack.

But ››self's‹‹ *movements were painfully sluggish, slowed by the bombardment of raw data from eighteen separate senses. Reality was far stranger than second- and third-linked images of transmitted memory, imperfectly perceived, imperfectly understood. Emptiness clawed at* ››self‹‹, *the raw wonder and terror of the not-Rock Void at the Heart of Creation. And . . . and there were things here, things at once not-Self, yet, impossibly, they moved, reacted, acted in all ways alive . . . like Self, yet not. . . .*

And they were attacking.

Through fragmentary recollections of past encounters, transmitted to its progeny by Self, ››self‹‹ *knew of the not-Self things that could not be alive because they were not-Self, yet nevertheless seemed to have some alien, unreachable life of their own. Something perhaps twice* ››self's‹‹ *mass, something of intricate and literally incomprehensible form, was already probing the outer shell that protected* ››self‹‹ *with a barrage of various radiations. Something like a smooth-shaped rock penetrated* ››self's‹‹ *shell, then detonated.*

Hurt! Dysfunction! Appendages lay on the ground, uselessly writhing, now little ››selves‹‹ *of their own and independent of* ››self's‹‹ *control. Pivoting,* ››self‹‹ *brought weapons of its own to bear. . . .*

Too late! ››Self‹‹ *could feel its consciousness dwindling, lessening with each new, explosive impact.* ››Self‹‹ *was, in fact, a cascade of separate consciousness, of many* ››selves‹‹ *nested within one another. Dominant was* ››self‹‹, *but* ››self‹‹ *was the sum total of hundreds of separate Nodes, and each Node was composed of trillions of cells, some biological, some technological, and each capable of an independent, if limited, existence. Many Nodes working together made* ››self‹‹, *just as many trillions of* ››selves‹‹ *together composed the far vaster Unity of Self.*

Flame, a white-hot plasma, scorched the writhing tendrils and seared away ››self's‹‹ outer layers. Worse, the Adversary's own nanotech weapons had been loosed and were disassembling ››self's‹‹ molecular structure almost atom by atom.

Then ››self‹‹ was gone, replaced by the random gropings of the Nodes, those that had survived the explosion, at least. And under the deadly assault by radiation and flame and nanotechnic disassemblers, even the Nodes were beginning to dissolve. The memories of other places were gone now, as was any memory of ››self's‹‹ personal past or of the glory of lost Self.

And then, even awareness itself was gone.

The LaG-42 Ghostrider stood at the crater's edge. Within the Ghostrider's protective armor, Lieutenant Vincent Creighton, 3rd New American Mechanized Cavalry, surveyed the scene through the warstrider's senses, probing the milk-white haze above the disintegrating Xeno.

The Xeno was dead . . . and it was damned lucky Creighton had seen the thing when it first nosed clear of the ground. Xeno snakes were always a bit slow shapeshifting to combat mode, and that was definitely the best time to hit them. This one had been a Mamba, a big son of a bitch, and more than a match for a LaG-42 when it was fully morphed and ready for a fight.

Grimly, Creighton turned his attention from the crater to his surroundings, a densely forested hillside beneath an azure-green sky. The domes of Winchester, the planet's capital, glittered in the distance. Closer at hand, scattered pastiches of red and gold forest reminded him of New America . . . though the gauzy, mushroom-shaped trees of the Wilderland only remotely resembled the arboreal forms of either 26 Draconis IV or Earth itself. Eridu was a lovely world, one of the Hegemony's richest and most promising extrasolar colonies.

Or it had been.

Now that the Xenos were here, Creighton knew better than most that the world's eerie loveliness was doomed.

More of the subterranean monsters would appear . . . then more. Nuclear weapons would be used. Eridu would become a wasteland, her native ecology ravaged, her population herded into camps. The terraformers would have their way at last.

The thought filled Vince Creighton with a bitterness that left him, momentarily at least, unable to link fully with his warstrider. For several seconds, he stood motionless on the crater rim, concentrating on the largely automatic process of safing his weapons and reporting the Xeno kill over his tactical net. Then, finally, he was able to swing the big machine about and start it stalking back toward his base.

A gentle rain began falling an hour later, washing the milk-thick mist back into the ground, until little remained of the Xenophobe machine save blackened lumps of twisted metal.

Chapter 1

Nippon's ascendance to world domination during the twenty-first century was scarcely surprising. By stepping into the high-tech void left by the former superpowers when they abandoned space research in the late 1900s and early 2000s, Japan assured its preeminence in space manufacturing and materials sciences. These advances led directly to even greater revolutions: nanotechnic engineering, biocomputer implants, and ultimately, of course, to the K-T drive that gave Man the stars.

—Man and His Works
Karl Gunther Fielding
C.E. 2448

North, the glowing white thread of the Singapore Sky-el slashed vertically out of the sky, ruler-straight against the night. East, the full moon rose silver above the glittering pillar of its own reflection.

With a dwindling hum, the magflitter settled gently onto the teak landing platform beneath hovering glowglobes. A scarlet-clad attendant was at its side at once, sliding the canopy aside and assisting the slender young man from the vehicle.

"*Konichiwa,*" the attendant greeted him with a crisp bow, his Nihongo perfect though his features looked Malaysian or Indonesian rather than Japanese. He held out a book-sized facereader, its slick black surface drinking the glowglobes' light. "Identity, please?"

Dev Cameron extended his left hand, bringing the intricate pattern of golden wires and circuits embedded at the base of his thumb into contact with the reader. Somewhere beneath this mountaintop, the estate's computer would be scanning his interface and, through it, the cephlink plexus embedded between the hemispheres of Dev's brain, reading his service record and ID data.

The black surface of the reader flashed green. "*Domo arigato gozaimashte,*" the attendant said, bowing again, and Dev sensed, rather than heard, the marginal relaxation of unseen figures in the darkness outside the circle of light on the landing deck. Kodama's personal guard, no doubt, watching for uninvited guests. "Welcome to Lord Kodama's estate, *Chuisan*. A servot will store your vehicle. Please, this way."

He led Dev onto a curving, stone-walled path, around a garden of exotic night-blooming plants and up toward the estate proper. *Taisho* Yasunari Kodama's party had already been in full swing for hours, though guests continued to arrive as the night sky darkened overhead. The Admiral, a member of the Emperor's personal staff, was well-known for these affairs, and to be invited to one was not only an honor, it was considered a mark of special favor. For military personnel, at least, an invitation to Pulau Kodama indicated a rising career, even official Imperial notice.

Dev, tall, pale-complexioned, and unaccustomedly resplendent in the immaculate dress blacks of an Imperial army officer, stepped into the throng gathered on the veranda outside Kodama's imposing, sleekly modern hab. It was difficult to tell at a glance where outside ended and the building began, for walls and skylights were open to the night air, and dancing holographic sculptures shifted and interpenetrated in soft-glowing abstracts and geometrical patterns.

Hundreds of guests were already present, gathered in small groups for conversation and drinking, or swaying rhythmically in larger circles to the liquid ripplings and tone-shifting drips and plops of Hagiwara's water music. Attire, Dev noted, ran the gamut from full military dress with sword and honors to formal jackets or gowns to masquerade costumes to complete undress. Many of Kodama's guests, men and women both, were nude save for jewelry, richly ornate skin implants, elaborate masks, or headpieces. The military officers present were all Imperials, in army black or navy white, and all were high-ranking, *taisa* or above.

Which left Dev feeling unpleasantly out of place. He couldn't attend a function like this without surreptitiously checking from time to time to make certain that his tunic was clean, the folds of his arm cloak were hanging straight, and his gold braid aiguillettes were still secure on his shoulder. His rank of *chu-i*, equivalent to that of a Hegemony army lieutenant or a naval j.g., was startlingly junior in this gathering of *shoshos* and *chujos*, while the glittering civilians present included senior Imperial administrators, diplomats, well-known ViRdrama personalities, and even a few Hegemony governors returned to Earth from the frontier.

Still, the starburst medal at the throat of his blacks, the *Teikokuno Hoshi*, commanded a respect beyond that usually accorded the two cherry blossom pips of a *chu-i* on his collar tabs and shoulder boards. The Imperial Star had opened doors undreamed of just a year or two earlier. All things considered, Dev had done quite well for a *gaijin*—a non-Japanese—from the free housing warrens of BosWash.

A servant in a traditional kimono approached, bowed low, and offered him a sensphere.

"*Arigato,*" Dev said, accepting the crystal sphere. It warmed pleasantly against his interface, inducing an erotic tingle and a mild euphoria as he walked deeper into the crowd. An Imperial Navy *shosho*, a rear admiral, smiled and nodded back as Dev inclined his head in a polite bow. Yes, he'd come far indeed for a *gaijin*. Pride and the stimulation of the sensphere mingled, countering self-doubt.

Scanning the throng for a familiar face, he saw only strangers and had to suppress an irrational disappointment. Kodama's hab, after all, was huge, and he'd seen only a tiny piece of it so far. But he still wanted to know: had she come? The black pillar of an information kiosk caught his eye, and he pressed his way toward it through the crowd. Shifting the sensphere to his right hand to free his interface, Dev placed his palm against the cool slickness of the pillar, framing his questions: *Is Katya Alessandro here yet? If she is, where is she?*

Answers formed in his mind as the hab's AI consulted its memory, then scanned through the hab's many rooms, levels, and balconies. A map drew itself in Dev's mind. He was *here*, near the main entrance. She was *there* . . . through the main foyer and out on the north veranda.

So she had come after all. Maybe she'd changed her mind, then, about leaving Earth. He hurried on into the central core of Kodama's hab.

The entire island belonged to Kodama. Once, it had been given over to a sprawling warehouse facility, part of the far-flung Towerdown complex encircling the base of Earth's oldest sky-el space tower some one hundred fifty kilometers south of Singapore. Fifty years earlier, however, Kodama's father, himself a member of the Imperial Court, had purchased the island, then loosed a cloud of nanotechnic converters on the place, stripping it to bedrock and transforming the sterile ranks of storage towers into this palatial estate—a small city in one building, actually—clinging to a mountaintop above impenetrable, genetically nangineered jungle.

Though the Inglic word *hab* suggested a permanent habitation, Kodama rarely lived here, but it was a spectacular place for a party. The main foyer was like a cathedral's interior, the vaulted ceiling three stories overhead. Gene-tailored koi of fantastic shapes, miniature dragons and whales and indescribable monstrosities, swam in the stone pool beneath shifting patterns of holographic geometry. The walls were lost in stars, and the thronging thousand or so people in the room seemed to stand on empty space, with the vast, crimson-cored pinwheel of the galaxy turning slowly beneath their feet.

Following the map still outlined in his cephlink RAM, Dev made his way to the north veranda. Through a shimmering veil of liquid light, more dozens of people were gathered outside on a railed balcony overlooking jungle, silver beaches, and island-dotted sea.

"Excuse me," a woman's sultry voice said at his back. Her Nihongo had the crisp precision of someone using a downloaded RAM language implant. "Are you Devis Cameron? The one who destroyed the Xenos?"

He turned at the voice and found himself facing a cute Eurasian woman wearing sandals, a startling spray of peacock tail feathers as a halo about her lavender hair, and little else. An intricate pattern of loops and whorls etched in glowing gold descended from her right shoulder to her wrist, bright enough to cast shadows that shifted across her skin in interesting patterns as she moved.

"Destroyed them? No. I was with the team that first managed to talk with them, though, out at GhegnuRish."

The woman rubbed her sensphere against her cheek with slow, sensuous movements as she listened to him, but her violet eyes lacked any trace of comprehension. "I ViRed what you did out there," she said, her voice dropping to an intimate huskiness as she shifted to deliciously accented Inglic. "It was *wonderful*!"

The way she said the words triggered memory. Dev thought he recognized her now . . . a well-known erotic ViRdrama actress. He was a little taken aback. He was certain he'd enjoyed simming as her lover more than once—through a recjack linkage, of course—but he could remember neither her name nor the scenarios she'd played in.

"Just—ah—lucky. I was in the right place at the right time."

He didn't add that he'd stumbled into a hole in the ruins of a long-dead city on the DalRiss homeworld, fallen into a cavern deep underground, and there confronted the alien horror known to Man as the Xenophobes only because he'd had little choice. A DalRiss biological construct, a sheath of living tissue on his arm called a comel, had enabled him to touch some part of the Xenophobe's mind, enough to learn a little about what it was and how it viewed the universe.

"Oh, *no*," the woman breathed, her peacock feathers rustling, their eyespot patterns faintly luminous in the dim light. "You're far too modest. I understand that, because of what you did down in that *awful* cave, the Empire's won the Xeno war!"

"Well, let's hope so." Dev decided that it wouldn't do any good to explain reality to her. His brief contact with a Xeno world mind had taught him something about that enigmatic blend of biological organism and submicroscopic nanomachine. The war would be continuing for a long time to come, but he very much doubted that the girl was interested in Xeno life cycles or worldviews or that she'd believe him if he told her the truth. Looking past her, he thought he saw a familiar silhouette against the moonlight on the veranda.

"Uh, excuse me," he said, breaking away just as she took a step closer. "*Shitsurei shimasu*. There's someone over there I have to see."

"Hurry back, Devis. I'm looking forward to finding out *all* about Earth's greatest hero."

Some hero, Dev thought, with an ironic cock of an eyebrow. He'd been *scared*.

Katya Alessandro stood on the veranda, lithe and slender in her Hegemony dress grays, in sharp contrast to the gaily clad or disrobed people around her. The moon hung enormous, low in the east behind her. The night was clear, the white razor slash of the sky-el starkly visible from the north horizon, where it rose in splendor against the orange sky glow of Singapore's lights, clear to the zenith, where it dwindled and was lost among the stars.

"Hello, Katya," he said, walking over to her. "I'm glad you came."

She looked at him, an unfathomable expression locked

away behind eyes of ice. "I'm still not so sure this was such a good idea, Dev."

Katya's collar tabs proclaimed her a *tai-i*, an army captain, but her uniform was that of the Hegemony Guard, not Imperial. Once she'd been Dev's commanding officer in Alessandro's Assassins, A Company, 1st Battalion of the 5th Loki Warstrider regiment, the Thorhammers. Then they'd gone to the DalRiss worlds, and the confrontation with the Xenophobes on Alya B-V.

Like Dev, Katya had been offered an Imperial commission, but to his surprise she'd turned it down cold, preferring to remain with the Thorhammers. She looked more out of place here among all the Imperial white and black than he did.

Well, to be honest, he'd turned down the posting too, at first, but that had been before his sponsors at the Imperial Court had pointed out how valuable his firsthand expertise on the Xenophobes could be. Then too, there was the matter of his father. . . .

He smiled at her.

"I really wanted to see you before you left," he said. "And, well . . ." He gestured at the glittering crowd around them. "You don't turn down an invitation from Admiral Kodama!"

"Maybe you don't." Her words were cold. "This scenario isn't for me, Dev. Thank God I don't have to be part of it any longer."

"So? Why'd you agree to come tonight?"

"Because you insisted. And because I'm going up-tower in another ten hours."

"And then where?" He offered her his sensphere, but she refused with a curt shake of her head. Her dark hair was close-cropped at the sides, longer on top, a style that left the silver rings of the T-sockets behind her ears free. They gleamed in the moonlight as she moved.

"I'm leaving for the Frontier, Dev. My early out with the Hegemony came through. This is good-bye."

"I . . . don't want you to go. I thought we had something together."

An expression passed over her face, one of . . . was it weariness? Reaching out, she flicked the Imperial Star at his throat with her finger, the sound a tiny click of nail on metal. "I'm afraid *this* got between us somehow."

"It doesn't need to." He was surprised at how angry his own words sounded. "Things aren't as bad as you sometimes pretend they are."

"Come on, Dev," Katya said. "Look around you!" She gestured at the crowd on the veranda with a grimace of distaste, taking in glittering and perfumed Court parasites, a nude man jacked glassy-eyed into a pleasure sim, a half dozen bureaucrats in elaborate, 100-*sen-en* cloaks, and three women in the corner in an erotic embrace that must have been embarrassing to someone of Katya's rather provincial background.

He smiled and shook his head a little sadly. Katya had always been a bit uncomfortable in the *Shakai*, as the blend of culture, manners, refinement, and, she would say, the *decadence* of Japanese society was called. They'd had this discussion before, in more private places. He knew she felt as though the character of the Frontier worlds was being swallowed by the more relaxed culture of *Shakai*.

Dev quickly changed the subject.

"Please, at least tell me where you're going." He ground the sensphere against his palm implant with a deliberate, rolling pressure. The induced stimulation was already quickening his senses, adding extra dimensions to the gurgling tones of the water music, to Katya's musky scent mingled with the heavier odors of perfume and jungle and salt air. "Loki? New America?"

The 5th Loki, the Thorhammers, had originally been raised as a planetary militia, the 2nd New American Minutemen, and New America was Katya's homeworld. If she was really leaving Hegemony service, she would probably go back there.

"Away from Earth and the Empire," Katya said.

"I wish you'd change your mind."

"And I wish you'd open your eyes, Dev. I wish you'd see what the Empire is, what it's doing. . . ."

Dev shook his head slightly, eyes narrowing. Admiral Kodama probably wasn't in the habit of eavesdropping on his guests, but his hab AI was almost certainly keyed to pick up on certain words or phrases. *Rebellion*, say, or *Empire*. Just to be on the safe side.

"Arts and entertainment," he said softly, a veiled warning. The so-called civilized pursuits, techno-art and virtual entertainment, were the universally accepted safe topics for casual discussion.

"I've said nothing treasonous," she said, defiant, daring him to say more. "And they don't own my mind. Not yet. And admit it. The fact that you feel you have to shut me up proves just how bad things are getting—here on Earth, anyway."

Dev clamped down on an immediate, almost automatic retort. Arguing with Katya here and now would accomplish nothing, save, possibly, getting them a visit tomorrow from Imperial Security. They'd argued politics more than once before, and Dev found the whole subject tiresome. It had been the one source of friction between them since they'd arrived on Earth two months earlier.

He hated to see her leave, but he didn't want her to make trouble for herself. Earlier, when he'd first called her, he'd been unwilling to see her within the artificial intimacy of a ViRcom. It was on his insistence that she'd come corporally to Kodama's hab tonight at all. She'd wanted to say good-bye over the ViRcom, but he hadn't wanted to settle for Katya's virtual presence. He'd needed to see her, to *touch* her in person.

That was a mistake, he now realized.

"Things really aren't so bad."

"Are you saying that for yourself, Dev? Or for your father?"

"Leave him out of it!"

Shosho Michal Cameron had been an Imperial naval officer, one of only a handful of *gaijin* to be given a slot on the Emperor's staff. Later, however, in command of an Imperial K-T drive warship, he'd destroyed the sky-el on Lung Chi to keep the Xenophobes from reaching an evacuation fleet at synchorbit, an act that had doomed half a million civilians and five thousand Imperial Marines still on the planet's surface. The elder Cameron had been disgraced by that action and later had committed suicide. Only recently, after Dev's encounter with the Xenos at Alya B-V, had he been officially and posthumously rehabilitated.

"You're wrong about the Empire, you know," Dev went

on, his voice pitched scarcely above a whisper. "Except for the odd insurrection or two, they've kept Man at peace for better than three centuries. The Core Worlds are prospering, the Frontier worlds are as free as they can be—"

"Good God, Dev, why don't you link in and switch on? The Frontier has just as much freedom as the length of the Empire's leash. They control our trade with Earth and with the other colonies, tax us to death, and tell us we can't develop our own technological base . . . 'for our own good.' But then, you're an Earther, aren't you? Core World. So you wouldn't understand how we feel on the Frontier."

"Yeah," Dev said, his own anger rising. Their arguments had followed this pattern before, and he knew the script. "I'm from Earth and I'm proud of it. I'm also proud to be an Imperial officer." He touched the starburst at his throat. "I'm proud of *this*."

"Don't be too proud of that trinket. Remember, I was there too."

Yes, she'd been there. She'd descended into that pitch-black hole after he'd fallen in, overcoming old, old nightmares of the dark to come after him. She'd loved him once. What had happened to them?

"Katya—"

"Good-bye, Dev," she said firmly. "We won't be seeing each other again. Congratulations on your new posting."

"Uh, thanks. But—"

"And if I catch you and your Imperial friends on New America, you're dead meat." She turned sharply at that and walked away. Dev started to go after her, then stopped. It was over. Clearly and definitely, his relationship with Katya was over.

And, like his insisting on seeing her in person, maybe that relationship had been a mistake as well.

Chapter 2

There are those, particularly among the ultra-Green radicals, who hold that Man, as defined by his culture and technology, is no longer entirely human. The focus of their argument, of course, is implant technology.

Consider: nanotechnically grown cephlinks and RAM intracranial implants, palm interfaces and link sockets, have utterly transformed work, entertainment, economics, communication, education, indeed, have revolutionized every aspect of civilization over the past four centuries. The Greens miss a crucial point. Man's tools may well be the foundational basis for his evolution. The crude, chipped-stone implements of Australopithecus, *by improving his diet and encouraging an upright stance, may well have put him solidly on the path to* Homo erectus; *who can today imagine the final destination of the path we have already chosen?*

—Man and His Works
Karl Gunther Fielding
C.E. 2448

Two weeks later, Dev was up-tower at Singapore Orbital, continuing his almost single-handed crusade before the Imperial Staff and the Council of the United Terran Hegemony to implement the plan that had become known as Operation Yunagi. He'd returned to his quarters and downloaded the day's accumulation of messages from his console. Some small, irrational part of him continued to hope that there'd be a message from Katya, even though she must still be en route to New America.

Travel times between the stars being what they were, it would be two months at least before he could expect something from her. New America—26 Draconis IV—was 48.6 light-years from Sol, clear out on the fringe of the Shichiju's Frontier. Typical travel times for the big liners averaged about a light-year per day, a fast courier carrying mail perhaps twice that, and . . . well, the numbers spoke for themselves.

Besides, that last time he'd seen her she'd been pretty flat-out definite about not wanting to see him again, ever. He had the room prepare him a drink, which was delivered in a squeeze bottle. One wall was set to show Earth, a cloud-wreathed, three-quarters' sphere hanging in space. Dev floated in the microgravity of synchorbit, trying to turn his mind from Katya to something productive.

To *Yunagi.*

The Nihongo word was a poetic reference to the calm that falls at evening. Operation Yunagi had been Dev's single-minded pursuit for almost the entire two and a half months since he and Katya had returned from the Alyan expedition. It had been his idea, one he'd first discussed at length with Katya, then later with the Emperor's military staff. He was the acknowledged expert on the Xenophobes for the simple reason that he'd actually brushed minds with one; a small part of that alien presence was still with him, giving him a unique perspective on the Xenos . . . and on humans as well.

What had that ViRsim actress said at Kodama's party? He concentrated for a moment, retrieving the girl's image and words from his RAM: *I understand that, because of what you did down in that* awful *cave, the Empire's won the Xeno war!*

No, they hadn't won yet, but Dev was convinced that Yunagi would make that final victory, that final peace of the evening calm, possible. His thoughts flashed to Katya for a moment, as he wished she could have enjoyed his success . . . then drew back sharply. *Damn!*

Katya's comment about his father had bitten deep. He didn't like to admit, even to himself, that the elder Cameron's unprecedented transfer to the Imperial Navy had had anything to do with his own success. It felt to Dev as though he'd been battling his father's shadow for a long time now. With the award of the *Teikokuno Hoshi* from the Emperor's own hand, he'd finally stepped into the sunshine on his own and even managed to make peace with his father's ghost. Michal Cameron was no longer on the Navy's lists as a traitor.

Hegemony and Empire. The two together straddled the worlds of Man like a colossus. Imperial Nihon ruled directly a relatively small percentage of Earth's surface—the home islands, the Philippines, and a scattering of territorial enclaves ranging from the states of the Indian subcontinent to Kamchatka and Vancouver. By puppet governments and the presence of Imperial Marines, they dominated perhaps half the planet beyond those borders, maintaining the *Teikokuno Heiwa*, the Imperial Peace, in such scattered former war zones as central Asia, South China, and Africa.

Japan's real political presence, however, was expressed through its silent control of the Hegemony, the interstellar government consisting of fifty-two member nations on Earth, plus the seventy-eight colonized worlds in seventy-two star systems that comprised the far-flung Shichiju. Technically autonomous, the extrasolar colonies were overseen—*ruled* was too harsh a word—by governors appointed in Kyoto. Local planetary governments made laws, managed industry, and even maintained armies, the planetary militias, in almost total freedom.

The single restriction lay in the Hegemony's control of trade and travel between the stars and of the technology that made such travel possible. Only Hegemonic and Imperial ships possessed the K-T drives that let them cruise the *Kamisama no Taiyo*, the "Ocean of God" that reduced to days or months voyages that otherwise would have taken decades or centuries.

Katya, Dev knew, saw Japan's monopoly on space-based technology and trade as tyranny, its taxes on colonial industries as crippling, its veto power over Hegemony affairs as nothing less than absolute dictatorship. For Dev, the system had its faults but it possessed one notable advantage: it *worked*. Until the first of the Xenophobe incursions, the Japanese had kept the peace for three centuries, save for a few inevitable isolated uprisings and the odd minor rebellion. By retaining sole control of nuclear weaponry they'd kept a fragmented humanity from destroying itself. And for the past forty years, they'd coordinated the Shichiju's defense against the Xenophobes, succeeding—usually—where the scattered response of dozens of frontier worlds would certainly have failed.

On the other hand, he understood Katya's bitterness toward the Shichiju's masters even if he didn't fully share the feeling himself. Certainly, some individual freedoms were restricted under the Imperial Peace. Citizens of the former United States in particular had long traditions of domestic independence that had been sharply curtailed by the Hegemonic Act of Union three centuries before, and in some areas bitterness against Imperial Japan still ran surprisingly deep. There'd been some ugly incidents; the Vancouver Massacre of '21 and the Metrochicagan Riots were still fresh in most Americans' minds.

Those attitudes had spread to the half dozen or so worlds of the Shichiju where colonists of American descent had tried to resurrect some measure of their imagined past glories. Worlds like New America, Katya's homeworld. She might have been raised in that planet's Ukrainian colony, but she'd obviously been infected by the positively ancient, conservative atmosphere of the place.

All things considered, Dev thought, the Empire was at worst a cumbersome and unwieldy bureaucracy, but at best the instrumentality that had made Man's outreach to the stars, even his very survival, possible. In his firm opinion it was both. For him and his family, the Empire had long been both blessing and curse.

To begin with, Michal Cameron had been forced to divorce his wife when he won his appointment to the Imperial Navy. Command officers, those ranking captain and above, were expected to marry for political advantage and to mingle within circles defined by the Imperial Court, and Mary Jean Pruitt-Cameron—a *gaijin* girl from West Scranton who couldn't even speak Nihongo—simply hadn't been of the proper social class. A new marriage had been arranged for Michal by the Emperor's Council of Protocol.

Even so, Michal had been allowed to retain his former wife as mistress, and he'd been able to provide for his two sons. Dev would never have been able otherwise to acquire his hardware, an NOI Model 10,000 Cephimplant, with left-palm-embedded control interface, twin temporal sockets, and a cervical receiver for direct feedback work.

Without those high-priced C- and T-sockets, Dev Cameron would never have shaken free of Earth or the Hegemony Protectorate Arcology. He would have been just another of the hundred million BosWash citizens plugged into recjack feeds and living on the *Fukushi* dole, the welfare handouts provided by the government to its unemployable citizens.

After his father's disgrace and suicide, Dev had nursed a black bitterness toward the Empire, but he'd not been able to maintain such personal hatred toward so large and impersonal a system for long. From Dev's point of view, it was his father's enemies who had rigged the court-martial's outcome, not the system. The Empire was far, far larger than any individual citizen, larger even than the Emperor himself.

His father's disgrace had very nearly ended his own career as well, and before it was properly started. He'd already received his appointment to the Hegemonic Naval Academy at Singapore when word of the Lung Chi disaster reached Earth, and the appointment had been quietly revoked after the court-martial, "to avoid unfortunate repercussions to the Academy's reputation." Ultimately, Dev had taken working passage aboard the freighter *Mintaka* to the Frontier just to escape the onus of his father's name, but that could hardly be blamed on the Empire, could it?

Nor was it the Empire's fault that, after joining the Hegemony Guard on Loki, he'd been selected, not for ship training as he'd requested, but as a striderjack.

All his life Dev had wanted to be a shipjack, and he'd picked up plenty of experience aboard the *Mintaka*, jacking everything from cargo handlers to second helm. Even now he still found it surprising that, after years of dreaming about cruising the godsea as a starship, he'd ended up jacking warstriders. He'd never wanted anything to do with the lumbering fighting machines, the heavy mobile armor of twenty-sixth-century warfare, and had always looked down on the men and women who ran them. It had taken a hard-fought campaign against the Xenophobes infesting Loki, followed by the four-month voyage to contact the DalRiss symbionts of distant Alya to convince him that it was the *people* who counted in a fight, not the technology, and certainly not the outward form of his cybernetic prosthesis. He was proud now of his skill at handling LaG-42 Ghostriders or ponderous Warlords, and he rarely thought anymore about jacking starships.

Dev had changed a lot in the past couple of years, in his attitude and in his relationships with other people. Once he'd been stiff, suspicious, even hostile with those he didn't know, a loner who insisted on doing things his own way. Now he got on well with everybody . . . nearly everybody, at least. Katya's rejection still burned. He'd loved that fiery Ukrainian company commander—still did, if the turmoil he was feeling now meant anything.

A chimed note interrupted increasingly bleak thoughts, shaking Dev from a gloomy contemplation of the cloud-swathed Earth below. Someone was asking for a ViRcom link. He concentrated on the mental formula that unlocked the communications circuit in his cephlink implant.

The thought materialized his analogue ViRpersona, attired in dress blacks and with the Imperial Star at his throat. In his own mind, he stood, seemingly unmoving and unprotected in open space, Earth beneath his boots, the gleaming thread of the sky-el dwindling with the perspective of distance against the clouds below and the star-dusted night above.

"*Chu-i* Devis Cameron?" The woman's voice seemed to speak from emptiness beside his left ear.

"Yes?"

"Excuse the interruption, sir, but *Taisa* Kukuei Tsuru desires immediate ViRcom linkage. Will you accept?"

"Of course."

The rank of *taisa* was equivalent to a colonel in a planetary militia, but rank was less important here than position. Tsuru, Dev knew, was an Imperial Liaison, one of some tens of thousands of Japanese officers who served as links between the Imperial government and the Hegemony military forces. Their word carried the mass of official orders, even when delivered to ranks nominally superior to their own. Theoretically, a raw *sho-i*, if he were a liaison officer, could give orders to a Hegemony general, though such a situation would never be allowed to occur in practice simply because senior officers could not afford to lose face. The *sho-i* might advise that general, however . . . and the general would be expected to listen carefully. Imperial Liaisons carried considerable political clout.

Their own name for themselves was *Annaisha*, "Guides."

Tsuru's ViRcom analogue, the "public mask" presented through ViRcom linkages, was tall, trim, and fit in Imperial blacks resplendent with gold braid and decorations. Though he'd never met the liaison officer formally, Dev had seen him once in the flesh—at another of Kodama's parties, as a matter of fact. He knew that the real Tsuru was a corpulent slug of a man, only seventy-five centimeters tall and still massing at least 130 kilos.

It was more pleasant to deal with his AI-generated analogue.

"Konichiwa, hajimemashte," Dev said formally, bowing. He was guessing that Tsuru was on Singapore time, which was now mid-afternoon. *Konichiwa* was the appropriate polite greeting for any time between mid-morning and early evening. "Cameron *des.*"

"I know who you are, Devis Cameron," Tsuru's image replied, his Inglic fluent, precise, and curt. "Your orders have just come through."

"Hai, Tsurusama." He used the very polite *-sama* honorific and bowed again. He tried to mask his excitement and his curiosity, both of which could be construed as bad manners. Besides, he could sense a hard edge, an undercurrent of trouble, perhaps, locked behind the bland and emotionless mask of the Liaison's analogue.

"Operation Evening Calm has been approved," the image said bluntly. "You are to take charge of the field phase of the project, effective immediately."

Dev's heart leaped. Wonderful!

"Thank you, *Tsurusama*. But where, please—"

"Eridu." The analogue's dark eyes regarded him without emotion. Information, meanwhile, unfolded in Dev's implanted RAM. Eridu, he noted, was Chi Draconis V, twenty-five light-years from Sol.

"Thirty days ago," Tsuru continued, "several Xenophobes broke through to the surface near Winchester, the capital city. There has been fighting, and casualties. Until that time, the only activity noted on the planet was some minor seismic disturbances and a few cavern traces fifteen thousand kilometers from the nearest human colony. Eridu's governor has requested immediate Imperial support."

Which meant *military* support. Damn! "But if fighting's already started . . ." Dev began, hesitant.

"Your orders will explain everything," Tsuru said. "Stand by for direct RAM feed."

Dev manipulated the necessary codes in his mind. Data flashed across the ViRcom interface, flowing from Tsuru's AI to the random-access memory of Dev's cerebral implant. He saw that it was marked *gokuhi*, "secret," and could be scanned only through the use of his personal authorization code.

"Feed complete," Dev said. "Sir, I wonder if—"

He stopped. The ViRcom interface had been broken from Tsuru's end, a cold and bluntly discourteous ending to the conversation that left Dev uneasy. Was the Imperial Liaison worried about link intercepts? The Imperial Staff and the Court at the *Tenno Kyuden*, the Palace of Heaven, itself had far more than their share of intrigue and politics. Was that what was behind Tsuru's curtness, a need for secrecy? Or something more?

Hesitantly, he unfolded the electronic text orders in his mind.

Yes! Yunagi had been okayed, its funding approved by the Colonial Affairs Council! He was being attached to the office of Eridu's Imperial Governor; he would report to *Chiji* Prem himself, though his immediate military supervisor would be a Hegemony Colonel, Emilio Duarte, of the 4th Terran Rangers. A fast courier, the *Hayai*, was being put at his disposal to get him to Eridu that much faster.

He forgot Tsuru's manner, forgot the pain of Katya's leaving, as he thought about what this would mean for his career. He felt as though everything that had happened to him in these past few years would at last be given meaning.

Man had been at war with the Xenophobes for forty-four years, ever since the first surfacing on the colony world of An Nur II in 2498. Only last year, however, with contact with the alien DalRiss, had he begun to learn just what it was that he faced.

They were called Xenophobes because it was assumed they feared or hated all other life forms, an assumption that Dev had personally learned was not true. In fact, the Xenos were not even aware of other life forms; they reasoned in a curious black-white, yes-no world of Boolean logic and had trouble even perceiving the existence of creatures such as humans. They lived deep within the planetary crust, a kind of group mind, two-kilogram "cells" resembling black gobs of jelly linked together like the neurons of a human brain, but filling underground caverns that spanned hundreds, perhaps thousands, of kilometers.

They absorbed rock—though they seemed to prefer the purer elements and components of human technology—to reproduce, and to hollow vast caverns for themselves in the depths, where they metabolized the heat of the planet's core. Their life cycle spanned worlds and eons. When a planetary crust was riddled with tunnels and enmeshed in the webwork of a single organism that called itself the "One" and that humans called the "World Mind," it hurled cell-colonies into the emptiness of the Great Void, protected in shells that rode the magnetic winds between the stars; after millennia, some few of those seed pods might be drawn to suitable worlds with the magnetic fields and core heat the Xenos found comfortable, there to begin all over. There was no communication between one Xenophobe world and the next.

And perhaps strangest of all, their worldview was inverted from that of humans. They saw the universe as an infinity of rock, with the Great Void a hollow emptiness within.

This much Dev had assimilated on the DalRiss homeworld when he'd encountered a Xenophobe One and touched it with the organic communicator called a comel on his arm. He'd learned that the One was extremely intelligent, though the nature of that intelligence might well be beyond human grasp. He'd learned that it responded to attack—perceived as the loss of some of its scattered parts—by striking back with technologies assimilated from other species on other worlds ages ago, and transferred from World Mind to World Mind through the passages of each generation.

And he'd learned that the Xenophobe World Mind of Alya B-V, say, had nothing to do with the Xenophobes infesting Loki . . . or Eridu. Each was distinct, sundered by light-years of distance and many thousands of years in time. The World Mind, the so-called "contemplative phase" that was no longer struggling to integrate itself throughout the planetary crust, did not even think of the earlier "acquisitive phase" as intelligent, though there was plenty of evidence to the contrary.

All of which meant that Dev had not ended the war simply by talking with one contemplative-phase Xenophobe. For peace to be won, humans would have to seek out the Xenophobes of every world they'd infested and contact them independently.

And that was precisely what Operation Yunagi was all about.

Chapter 3

The Xenophobe War is like no other conflict in Man's bloody history because, for the first time, his opponent is a complete unknown. In past wars, at least, the enemy was human, his science known, his reasons for fighting rational or at least intelligible, his worldview comprehensible. After four decades of war, however, the only motive we can ascribe to the Xenophobes is hatred or fear of other life forms—hence their name. Some researchers go so far as to suggest that their thought processes may be so alien to ours that we may never understand their reasoning.

—*The Xeno Foe*
HEMILCOM Military ViRdocumentary
C.E. 2537

The Imperial courier *Hayai* was waiting for Dev at Bay Three, Berth Seven, a stubby, thirty-meter lump of outsized power tap converters and receptor nacelles capped by a heavily shielded crew module smaller than some lifeboats Dev had seen. Captain Tokuyama, a small, wiry man with a clean-shaven scalp, greeted him at the docking tube.

"*Konichiwa*," Tokuyama said, extending a reader for Dev's palm interface. He wore rather shabby green coveralls bearing, not military insignia, but the patch of the *Sekkodan*, the Imperial Scout Service. He shifted easily to Inglic. "You must be my special cargo."

Dev pressed his hand to the reader, transferring identity data and the relevant part of his orders to *Hayai*'s artificial intelligence. "I guess so. I'm afraid I still don't know why the rush. I thought they would send me out on a starliner, or at least aboard a regular military transport."

Tokuyama grinned mirthlessly. "And when you get to Eridu they'll keep you waiting until the next starliner catches up with you, and you find you could have made the trip in comfort after all. I know the routine well, *O-nimotsusan*."

Dev chuckled and gave the captain a wry bow. *Nimotsu* was Nihongo for "baggage," and even with the polite construction and the suffix meaning "honorable" it was an unflattering but accurate assessment of Dev's status aboard the courier.

Eridu was the fifth world of Chi Draconis, an F7 star twenty-five and a quarter light-years from Sol. Typical passage time for a Tsukai-class fast courier would be anywhere from twelve to sixteen days, depending on the skill of its five-man crew.

Unfortunately, the Artificial Intelligences aboard fast couriers rarely had much in the way of simulated diversions for passengers. Most of their capacity was reserved for navlinks with the ship's helmsmen, and there was little to spare for "honorable baggage." Two weeks for the K-T portion of the voyage, plus time for in-system maneuvering; no matter how he looked at it, Dev was in for an extended period of mind-numbing boredom.

Dev wished he'd had time to pick up some long-run ViRdramas at some Singapore Orbital shop. He did get permission from Tokuyama to access the ship's ephemeris. Memorizing data on Chi Draconis V might not only be useful at his destination, it would help pass the time and let him emerge at the other end still sane.

Four hours after he'd boarded the *Hayai*, Dev was outbound from Earth at a steady three-G boost. Swaddled in a bodysuit and hooked into mechanisms that kept his physical self fed, hydrated, and clean; sealed inside a tank of heavy fluid that helped ease the strain of constant high-G acceleration; Dev began marking the time as best as he was able, immersing himself in research.

He went carefully through his orders again first, of course. From a close reading, it was evident that Yunagi had been approved by a relatively small majority on the staff. He'd expected that, after the trouble he'd had winning some of them over to his side. Many simply didn't believe meaningful communication with the Xenophobes was possible at all. Others were politically motivated. *Gensui* Munimori, he knew, and a number of others, were openly hostile to *gaijin*, preferring only Japanese to work on potentially high-prestige projects like this one.

Operation Yunagi was, of itself, fairly straightforward. A number of DalRiss comels, budded from the comel that he'd used to talk to the Xeno World Mind on Alya B-V, had been prepared in laboratories on Earth. When Xenophobes were discovered on another human-colonized world, the comels would be shipped there.

Ideally, the attempt to communicate should have been tried before humans and Xenophobes clashed on the target world; according to Tsuru, it was too late for that on Eridu, and that aspect of the plan may have been unrealistic to begin with. It was hard to keep colonists from shooting at something that persisted in snacking on city domes, power plants, or warstriders. In fact—Dev's arguments before the Imperial Staff had stressed the point—it might only be possible to approach Xenos on a world where active fighting had already broken out, simply because there was no way to get at the ones that were still kilometers underground.

Perhaps the biggest unanswered question was whether or not he could even get close to an acquisitive-stage Xeno without being killed.

That was a question which could not be answered until he tried.

Dev didn't like looking at that aspect of Yunagi too closely, though he'd watched enough Xenos to be pretty sure he'd be able to at least approach the things, once he found some on the surface. He filed that for later, and tapped into *Hayai*'s ephemeris.

Linkcode accepted. Datafeed commence—
Stellar Data: *Chi Draconis*
Type F7 V, mass 1.25 Sol, luminosity 3.0 Sol, stellar radius 1.13 Sol.
Planetary system: six major bodies, including one Earthlike world (V) located within the star's habitable zone. . . .
Planetary Data: *Chi Draconis V (Eridu)*
Mean orbital radius: 1.78 a.u., eccentricity: .00513, period: 2.124^y; natural satellites: two.
Diameter: 11,244 km, mass: 4.1 x 10^{27}g, density: 5.501 g/cm^3, surface gravity: .879 G; rotational period: 32^h 15^m 24.119^s; axial tilt: 01° 13' 28"; magnetic field: .47 gauss. . . .
Albedo: .58; temperature range (equatorial): 40°C to 50°C; Atmospheric pressure (sea level): .81 bar; composition: N_2 87.1%, O_2 9.5%, Ar 1.2%, H_2O (mean) 2.1%, CO_2 845 ppm, SO_2 2.7 ppm, O_3 0.515 ppm. . . .
Note: Due to low partial pressures of atmospheric oxygen, plus somewhat elevated carbon dioxide and ozone levels, the atmosphere of Chi Draconis V is not breathable by humans without artificial assistance. Plans to modify the planetary atmosphere for human needs have met with surprisingly widespread local resistance. . . .

For hours, Dev walked the ViRsim surface of Eridu, getting a feel for the world and its terrain, his cephlink persona unaffected by the thin and oxygen-starved air.

Hot and *wet* were the words best characterizing Eridu. Popular sims and travelogue feeds described the place as a jungle world, though such a simplistic characterization of any planetary ecology was patent nonsense. The air was humid, and at the equator where temperatures hovered around fifty degrees Celsius, steaming, brackish swamps and continent-wide tangles of exotic native flora reminiscent of Earth's long-lost jungles were the rule.

The climate at Eridu's iceless poles, however, was equivalent to that of northern BosWash, say, or the Pacific Northwest. An almost nonexistent axial tilt eliminated seasonal variations; climate was determined entirely by latitude and altitude, not by winter or summer. North and south of fifty degrees, the gently rolling hills were blanketed in open woodlands or steppelike grasslands. Winchester, near the planet's southern pole, was one of the largest of Eridu's colonial settlements. Unlike on other colony worlds, where an equatorial towerdown had become the planet's principal city, Eridu's towerdown at Babel was little more than a stopover for freight and passengers going up- or down-tower. Transport to the more pleasant climes of the poles was accomplished by rail magflitter or by hydrofoil. Perhaps half of the world's surface area was given over to small landlocked seas; more of Eridu's original allotment of primordial water had escaped to space early in its history than had been the case on Earth, beneath a milder, gentler sun.

There'd been quite a lot of political controversy over Eridu, Dev noted. Universal Life was active there, as were several modern offshoots of the old Green Party political activists. In Winchester, he watched a demonstration by anti-Hegemonists, a chanting mob of dissidents advancing through the city's main dome. A thin line of Authority Police blocked their way with stunners and light laser weapons.

"Troublemakers," Tokuyama's voice said, seemingly at his side. Dev opened a RAM code extending a silent invitation for *Hayai*'s Captain to join him. Tokuyama's ViRpersona, Dev noticed, was identical to his real-world self, right down to the grease-stained and shabby green coveralls. "Hooligans and troublemakers."

"What's the argument all about?" Dev asked. "Whether or not it's ethical to terraform?"

"Eridu'd be easy to T-form," Tokuyama said. "Double the partial pressure of oxygen. Lower the CO_2. You could manage that in fifteen years with a single atmosphere converter. That'd make the air breathable for humans and have the added benefit of reducing the greenhouse effect enough to make the equatorial regions bearable. A cinch compared to some hellhole like Moloch or Loki, *neh*?"

"It would also exterminate the local flora and fauna," Dev noted. With an effort of will, he shifted his vantage point from the city square to a point outside, where a forest of odd, mushroom-shaped things that might have been trees, stained in shades of red, gold, and brown, crowded close together above orange-tinted things that looked like dry-land sea anemones. Something fluttered through the air, all gauze and crimson streamers, but Dev couldn't see it well enough to tell what it was. "Double the oxygen and you'd poison the natives. Their metabolisms are geared for nine percent oxygen and thinner air."

"So? It's our planet now. Hell, some people say we didn't have the right to T-form prebiotics like Loki or Hephaestus, but we do. Better'n letting them go to waste, right?" He shook his head in disgust. "Some people are *baka*. Fools. They don't know when they have it good."

Dev didn't answer, but Tokuyama's curt dismissal bothered him. He was no enviro or greenie, certainly, but the Hegemony had taken a lot of public relations flak over the years for its rape-and-plunder colonial policies. There'd be less talk about rebellion on the Frontier, he thought, if some of those centuries-old policies could be softened.

Besides, according to the entry in *Hayai*'s ephemeris, Eridu's ecology already provided several important trade products. A fungus from the humid equatorial forests, for example, provided a drug useful for biological memory enhancement, while a chemical extract taken from a freshwater weed called grennel was reputed to improve sexual performance.

"Any rebel activity on Eridu?" he asked Tokuyama.

"Oh, the usual who-was," the Captain said. *Who-was*, an Inglic corruption of the Nihongo *uwasa*, was slang for "rumors" or "hearsay." Tokuyama was as earthy and as colloquially direct as most Americans Dev knew.

"Like what?"

"Nothing official. The greenies keep threatening to start an armed rebellion if the Hegemony starts T-forming. Eridu was colonized by Americans, though. Americans and Europeans.

That makes it a breeding ground for weird anti-Imperial notions, *neh*?"

Dev wondered whether Tokuyama was trying to get a rise out of him, or if he'd genuinely forgotten that his passenger was an American. After a moment's thought, he decided that his being an Imperial officer was all that counted for the old scout captain. He would relate to Dev as he would to any other Japanese official.

As for dissident activity at Eridu, well, it wouldn't affect his mission there. The sudden emergence of Xenophobes suggested that even anti-Imperial rebels would be keeping their heads down for the time being. Travis Sinclair and his New Constitutionalists might hate the Hegemony and everything about it, but even they couldn't prefer Xenos to their fellow humans. Humans you could talk to, negotiate with. Eventually you could reach an understanding with them. Xenophobes were so alien it was difficult to know what they were thinking . . . or even whether or not they were capable of thought at all.

As he continued experiencing the sims recorded on Eridu, however, Dev couldn't help wondering about the factions that seemed poised for battle, ready to duel for control of Eridu's destiny. He felt a certain sympathy for the people fighting to preserve the planet's natural order, if for no other reason than that mass extinction within the planetary biosphere would ruin the livelihoods of tens of thousands of colonists. Until an Earth-based ecology could be established, there would be mass dislocation, poverty, even famine if the local government failed to address the colonists' needs.

On the other hand, surely the Hegemony had the best interests of the people at heart. Worlds where men could walk without E-suits and breathe the air unaided, like New Earth or Elysia or Earth herself, were achingly rare. Terraforming created such worlds, given the proper raw materials and a few centuries in which to work.

Most T-formed worlds in the Shichiju had begun as prebiotic planets, worlds of water and ammonia and carbon dioxide that had the potential for evolving life but had never done so. One theory held that they would never do so; the Lunar Hypothesis suggested that only on worlds with large, close, natural satellites could prebiotic chemicals form the complex chains of amino acids, proteins, and ultimately DNA analogues. Tides, the proponents of the Lunar Hypothesis argued, tides such as those on Earth or Elysia, were necessary for the appearance of life. If humans didn't terraform such worlds, they would forever remain lifeless, poison-shrouded wastes.

On Eridu, the situation was a bit more complicated, but different only in degree, not in principle. There, life had formed some hundreds of millions of years ago, but the most advanced phyla were insectlike pollinators of the plant life that girdled the planet from pole to pole. Most animal life remained in Eridu's shallow seas, a recapitulation of Earth some three hundred fifty million years earlier. Intelligence, if it was to evolve at all, could not possibly arise on such worlds for many tens of millions of years yet to come.

The environmentalists, then, were interested in preserving primitive local life forms, creatures of particular interest to the exobiologists, of course, and to the locals who harvested grennel or trekked through the jungle searching for patches of *Dracomycetes mirabila*. But a world open to full habitation and exploitation would benefit everyone.

Surely, Dev thought, new careers could be found for out-of-work grennel harvesters, for example, and modern medical nanotechnology promised that any chemical compound could be perfectly and cheaply synthesized. It wasn't as though Mankind was losing anything by terraforming such a world. He was gaining an entire planet, one with blue skies and breathable air, and the chance for launching new art, new achievements, a whole new expression of the diversity and the inventiveness of Man.

Besides, a scattering of local rebels and malcontents would be no match for the Hegemony Guard. They must see that their cause was hopeless.

Why then did they persist? Dev returned to the ship's simulation of Eridu many times, walking invisibly with the protestors, listening to their shouted curses and slogans. *"Don't poison our world!"* What was *that* supposed to mean? *"Leave us alone!"* and *"Down with the Imperial Hegemony!"* and *"Chiji no! Life yes!"*

Didn't the chanting, angry citizens know that they'd not

survive on a hostile world like Eridu for six weeks without the Hegemony? They might grow food enough for themselves in the orbital hydroponics farms, but machine parts, tools, replacements, AI computers, weapons, all of those came from Earth or the other developed worlds of the Core.

To Dev, it seemed that the whole colony was on the verge of going mad.

Still, the disturbances appeared to be caused by a relative handful of extremists. Simwalking the demonstrations and riots, it was easy to forget that the vast majority of a world's citizens were law-abiding, wanting nothing more than to be left alone. It was those people who would suffer most if civil war broke out . . . or if the Xeno threat wasn't contained.

Dev refused to think about it anymore. The governor and his guard would have to look after the threat of rebellion. Dev's concern was for the Xenos and how he was going to carry out his orders, especially if the fighting between Xenos and humans on Eridu had already begun. That situation was more than enough headache for any one man.

Any rebellion on Eridu could look after itself.

Chapter 4

Travis Ewell Sinclair—soldier, politician, author, statesman, philosopher . . . and principal author of that remarkable document called The Declaration of Reason. *If the Confederation Rebellion doesn't owe its existence to this man, it at least owes him much of its character.*

—Rebellion
ViRsim documentary
Richard Fitzgerald Kent
C.E. 2542

It had been years since Katya had been on New America, and she wasn't entirely sure how she should feel about her homecoming. What she actually felt was . . . numb. She had no family here to speak of any longer, and her memories of growing up on a farm in the Ukrainian colony were not good ones.

The world was as she remembered it, though—wild, rugged, and beautiful. New America was one of the handful of worlds in the Shichiju that had evolved an ecology of its own before men from Earth had come . . . and it was one of the even smaller number of worlds where the organic chemistries were sufficiently like those on Earth— right down to left-handed amino acids and right-handed sugars—that many native foods could be eaten by humans. A garden world, unspoiled and beautiful, at least so far.

Perhaps the world's single disadvantage from a commercial viewpoint was its lack of a space elevator; New America possessed a single large, close moon, Columbia, whose pale and ruggedly cratered face loomed huge in the sky even in daylight, and whose tidal pull was so strong that no sky-el would have stood for long without becoming dangerously unstable.

But for Katya, that had always been one of the place's few charms. No sky-el meant no cheap surface-to-orbit transport, and that meant little Imperial or Hegemony interference on a world where shipping costs were high. It made for a precarious planetary economy, but the Hegemony government stayed more or less off the people's backs.

Inevitably, perhaps, that and the fact that two thirds of its population were descendants of American colonists, had made it notorious as a breeding ground for dissident groups, strange philosophies and religions, and would-be rebels.

Katya's liner, the *Transluxus*, had docked at the New American Orbital, a space station in low planetary orbit. She'd ViRcommed ahead from the station, then transferred to a civilian ascraft shuttle for the descent to Jefferson Spaceport. They were waiting for her when she walked through the arrivals gate.

"Katya! Good to see you!"

"Hey, how was Earth?"

"Where's Dev? Is he coming?"

"Welcome home, by God!"

The Thorhammers had returned to Loki after the Alyan expedition, but with the Xenophobe threat gone from that world, the Hegemony had announced that it would be cutting back on the size of its Lokan garrison, and that veterans of the expedition could take early outs if they wanted.

Many had, including most of the striderjacks of A Company, 1st Battalion, Alessandro's Assassins. Significantly, many of the unit's Lokan warriors had ended their hitches as well, investing their mustering-out pay in passages to New America.

For revolution was brewing.

Vic Hagan hugged Katya and gave her a brother's kiss. Lara Anders took her hand, beaming welcome. Harald Nicholson took her flight bag from her, and there were Lee Chung, Rudi Carlsson, Torolf Bondevik, Erica Jacobsen . . . God, it looked like half the company was present!

Of them all, only Vic Hagan and the small, black-haired Lee Chung were, like Katya, native New Americans, all that were left of the original 2nd New American Minutemen who'd formed up right here in Jefferson just five years ago. Katya sometimes felt like a fugitive from the law of averages, for all of the rest were Lokans, men and women who'd signed on after the unit had been stationed on 36 Ophiuchi C-II and become the 5th Loki Warstriders.

"Hi, people," she said as warmly as she could manage. "Dev's . . . he's not coming."

She saw the disappointment in their faces, and the questions. After the unit had returned to Loki, only she and Dev had gone on to Earth to be honored by the Emperor. They'd expected that both of them would be coming back.

"We've got a room for you at the Hamiltonian," Lara said.

"Good," Katya said. "I'm just about dead."

"Forget about sleep," Erica said. "You've had two months to sleep. Tonight, we've got something special planned."

Katya groaned. Long trips always wore her out, not because they were strenuous but because they were boring.

The flight to New America had taken sixty-three days, with stops at Loki and at P'an Ku along the way. The *Transluxus* was renowned for its extensive ViRsim drama and travel library, but Katya had always preferred the real thing to simulations, and never mind that there was supposed to be no reliable way to tell one from the other. Two months of virtual reality trips to various colony worlds, skin diving in the Great Barrier Reef, ViRdramas both modern and old, and a review of Imperial history since the Tokugawa Shogunate had been too much. The one ViRsex encounter she'd tried had left her unsatisfied and wistful.

Why hadn't she been able to get through to Dev? Why couldn't he see that she *had* to do what she was doing?

She'd not been able to talk freely at that damned orgy at Kodama's island, but she'd discussed it openly with him other times, during their stay on Earth. She'd told him about her contacts in Singapore Orbital with an underground organization that called itself the Network, and how she was convinced that the Empire, the real political power behind the Hegemony, was strangling human effort and creativity on every world of the Shichiju.

In fact, she'd maintained such contacts for years. Only lately, though, since she'd seen Imperial stupidity and heavy-handedness in the Alyan campaign, had she finally begun working for the Network. The organization's goal was nothing less than the eventual overthrow of the Hegemony, and an end to Nihonjin rule of the worlds of the Frontier.

Even on the twelve worlds of the Core, even on and around Earth itself, the Network was surprisingly strong, with a membership never accurately reported but certainly numbering in the hundreds of millions. The Empire was not popular, especially on the outlying worlds of the Frontier like New America, and the only reason it still held power was the fact that it still held the monopoly on interstellar travel.

But when she'd told Dev about it, when she'd tried to explain how she felt about the Empire and its ruinous policies, he'd thought it was a joke, had actually laughed at her.

Only much later did she realize how much Dev *needed* the Empire. She was pretty sure it had to do with his father's political rehabilitation, almost as though Dev thought he owed his father his loyalty to the Imperium.

Not long after that, Katya had noticed that they were drifting apart. Dev had been terribly busy at the time, delivering a long series of lectures to the Hegemony Council on Space Exploration. With his medal and his new Imperial uniform and his endless round of appointments at the Court and with the Emperor's staff, he'd rapidly become inaccessible to her.

She'd stuck it out for six weeks before deciding to give up and return to New America.

They took a public magflitter to the Hamiltonian, where her old friends helped Katya unpack. Then they whisked her up twenty floors to a private suite decorated in dark wood paneling, thick carpets, wood-beamed ceilings, antique books, and a surprisingly realistic illusion of a fire in a great stone fireplace.

A man stood in front of the fireplace, his beard more salt than pepper, his hair long and still mostly dark. He wore a costume typical of the New American Outback— kilt, plaid shoulder cloak, and tan blouse—and a white plastic commpac embracing the back of his head from ear to ear. "Hello, Captain Alessandro," he said, and to Katya's ears his Inglic carried the soft drawl of home. "I'm Travis Sinclair. I imagine you may have heard of me."

Heard of him? Travis Sinclair was arguably New America's most famous citizen, the self-styled philosopher and political writer who'd helped form the New Constitutionalist Party. If any one man could be said to represent the disparate, fragmented, and contentious groups on forty worlds that called themselves the Network, Sinclair was it.

"This . . . is an unexpected honor, sir."

"Please, it's Travis. And you're Katya?"

She nodded, totally at a loss for words as he extended his hand in the old-fashioned manner and she took it.

Katya had seen Sinclair once, years ago, right here in Jefferson. He'd been in the capital to deliver a speech, and his call for resistance to the Imperium's dominion over human government had led to Hegemony-wide warrants for his arrest. She was pretty sure that her own interest in politics dated from that rally.

Sinclair had been in hiding now for over eight years, though the who-was had it that he still managed to travel a lot among the Frontier worlds. How he'd kept from being picked up by the Directorate of Hegemony Security for this long was a mystery known only to the hundreds of loyal supporters who'd helped him stay free so far.

"I apologize for all the secrecy bringing you up here," he said. "And for not telling you ahead of time who you were coming to see. But at last report, there was a reward of fifty thousand *sen-en* on this shaggy head. I have to be careful."

"Fifty million yen?" Erica whistled. "That's a pretty fair chunk of credit."

"Please," he said genially, gesturing toward a bar complete with a spidery-armed servot programmed for mixing drinks. "Grab yourself something wet and get comfortable. I've been looking forward to meeting you for a long time, Katya."

She refused the offer of a drink and took a seat, as the others scattered about the sunken conversation area and made themselves comfortable. "Why me?"

"I've met the others, of course," Sinclair said. "And I appreciate their help. But I was particularly fascinated by the media accounts of you and . . . was it Dev? Dev Cameron. On Alya B-V. I'd like to hear more about that."

"I'm afraid Dev isn't here."

"I heard."

"He's . . . well, I think he has too much of a commitment to the Empire. I'd hoped he would join the Network, but . . ." She shrugged.

"That's too bad. What do you know about Project Yunagi?"

Katya started. Dev had talked about that quite a bit, at least early on, before it became shrouded in secrecy. In fact, the two of them had spent much of the trip from Alya B back to Earth discussing the possibility that humans might one day be able to establish regular communications with the Xenophobes, ending the threat they posed to civilization without further war.

"Some," she said cautiously. "We discussed it a lot. He

had the idea that we could use DalRiss comels . . . uh . . . you know about them?" Sinclair nodded and she went on. "Anyway, that we could use comels to approach Xenos, even acquisitive-phase Xenos, and put a stop to their attacks. They don't think like we do and it might be hard finding some common ground, but something as simple as 'Don't eat our city and we won't wipe you out with nuclear depth charges' might work."

Nuclear depth charges, first used on Loki, were the breakthrough that had ended the Xeno menace there. Kiloton atomic warheads were fitted into devices that used captured Xenophobe technology to sink them kilometers into the ground and detonate them . . . with catastrophic results for the deep-buried Xeno nests.

"Could the Xenos respond to that kind of negotiation?"

"He thinks so," Katya said. "I'm not so sure. They seem so . . . well, *different*. But he says the One he talked to was tremendously intelligent, more intelligent in absolute terms than a man, though the two can't really be compared to one another."

"And what do you think, Katya?"

"It might work. The person who tried it would have to be suicidal, though. To actually climb down a hole and *touch* one of those things . . ."

"Mmm. Indeed." He seemed to be far away for a moment, thinking. "Captain," he said at last, "I must ask something of you. Something unpleasant. I know you've joined our organization on Earth, but frankly I need some proof of your commitment to us."

Her eyes narrowed. "What kind of proof?"

"These folks have all demonstrated their loyalty to the cause already. Each one of them has vouched for you, of course, but now *I* must know, directly. And, perhaps, it would be fair if I had the same pledge from you all."

"I hate the Empire," she said. "I don't know what else I could—"

"Would you submit to a truthprobe on it?"

"A linked truth assessment?" She swallowed. "I guess so. If I had to."

"I don't like the idea any more than do you. You understand, I'm sure, that we can't accept the word of everyone who shows up on our doorstep volunteering to join our organization."

"My oath's not enough, I suppose."

"My dear, if I understand aright, you are still a reserve officer in the Hegemony. You're breaking your oath by not turning me in. Are you not?"

She felt her cheeks burn. "Yes."

"Actually, all I need is some RAM-stored statement of yours, something that might tell me what you feel about the movement. Can you think of something you might have said and stored that would help?"

She thought, then nodded. "I've got something."

He held out his hand, palm up. The threads of silver and gold embedded in his skin glinted in the room's overhead lighting. "Play it for me. Please."

Katya nodded, then closed her eyes, composing herself. She stretched out her hand, touching palm interfaces. Using key alphanumerics, she called up a menu in her mind, ran a quick search, then requested a projection of a particular segment.

Personal RAM file, extract 1213:281/41—

Dev stood before her once again, resplendent in Imperial blacks, the Imperial Star glittering at his throat. Water music plopped and gurgled in the background above the murmured conversations of Kodama's guests.

"Where are you going?" Dev asked. He clutched at a sensphere, squeezing it, knuckles white. "Loki? Or New America?"

"Away from Earth and the Empire." She felt again the pain she'd felt that night. And she felt, too, Sinclair watching, measuring. It was possible for a good AI to determine whether a RAM segment was real or a digital construct, a fantasy, and that commpac he was wearing could serve as a modem, allowing an Artificial Intelligence to look over his shoulder, as it were. She reminded herself that it would be more interested in, say, the texture or the cloth in Dev's uniform than in her emotions.

The thought steadied her somewhat, but she still felt embarrassed at this naked revelation.

"I wish you'd change your mind."

"And I wish you'd open your eyes, Dev. I wish you'd see what the Empire is, what it's doing . . ."

Dev shook his head, eyes narrowing. "Arts and entertainment," he said softly.

"I've said nothing treasonous," she snapped back. "And they don't own my mind. Not yet. And admit it. The fact that you feel you have to shut me up proves just how bad things are getting—here on Earth, anyway."

"Things really aren't so bad."

"Are you saying that for yourself, Dev? Or for your father?"

"Leave him out of it!" He stopped, breathing hard, his face flushed. "You're wrong about the Empire, you know. Except for the odd insurrection or two, they've kept Man at peace for better than three centuries. The Core Worlds are prospering, the Frontier worlds are as free as they can be—"

"Good God, Dev, why don't you link in and switch on? The Frontier has just as much freedom as the length of the Empire's leash. They control our trade with Earth and with the other colonies, tax us to death, and tell us we can't develop our own technological base . . . 'for our own good.' But then, you're an Earther, aren't you? Core World. So you wouldn't understand—"

"That's quite enough, Katya," Sinclair's voice said, breaking in. "More than sufficient. Thank you."

—*Interrupt*—
Cancel. Return.

She was again in the room on New America, blinking back the tears in her eyes.

"That must have been difficult for you, Katya." Sinclair spread his arms. "Again, believe me, I'm terribly sorry to put you through that, but I had to be sure. You see, I have a very special need of your services, and we needed to be certain that we could trust you."

"What services?" Katya demanded. "So far, Mr. Sinclair, we've been giving and you've been taking. Perhaps now you'd like to tell us what you want of us."

"It's 'General Sinclair,' actually," he said a bit stiffly.

"And we are fighting a war. Oh, the real shooting hasn't started, not yet, anyway. I pray God that it never does. But we are fighting for our independence from *Dai Nihon*. More, we are fighting for the chance to be ourselves. This may be the most important struggle our kind has ever faced. At stake is not just the survival of the Constitutionalist movement but the survival of the human species itself."

"I'm not sure I understand," Rudi said.

"*Diversity*," Sinclair said, whispering the word as though it were holy. "Our species thrives on diversity. In human society, as in nature, it's survival of the fittest, with a million failures for every million-and-one experiments. American Independence in 1776. The French Republic. The Bolsheviks and Communism. The Nazis. The American Left Socialists. The Greens. All of them were social experiments of one sort or another. Some succeeded, at least for a time. Others destroyed themselves, top-heavy and slippery with blood. The Hegemony was an experiment too, but for the first time it's an experiment with all of Mankind's eggs in one small basket. If *it* fails . . ." He raised a hand, then let it fall.

"Ancient Greece became the beacon for Western civilization," Sinclair continued. "Why? The separate city-states—Athens, Sparta, Corinth, a hundred others—each evolved on its own, isolated from the others by the mountains that divided their tiny peninsula. When exchanges between the city-states began, new ideas took root, new ways of looking at the world were discovered. Democracy. Atomic theory. Heliocentrism. It was a golden age that touches our lives even today.

"The move into space should have opened the opportunity for social experimentation," Sinclair said. "In a way, it may be unfortunate that we stumbled across the K-T drive so soon. Maybe, if we'd had a few thousand years of developing separate societies in separate, scattered worlds and planetoids, each with its own vision of what makes life worth living . . ." He shrugged. "But it didn't happen that way. And now the Hegemony is directing our cultural evolution, and with a damned heavy hand. Our lords care less for their colonies than they do for the means of exploiting them. We have one approved culture, one approved way of doing things. Our growth is stifled by the taxes Kyoto drops on us to pay for feeding the arcologies on Earth. We need to shake loose, find the stars again, and make room for a thousand destinies instead of only one!"

"Won't all those destinies make for some pretty nasty wars?" Katya wanted to know. "I seem to recall that there was as much fighting between those old Greek city-states as there was cultural exchange."

"Greece was limited in area, and limited in productivity. We face the challenge of expanding into a Galaxy of four hundred billion stars. I think there will be room for us, in all of our diversity, without resorting to war."

It was, Katya thought, an optimist's ViRdrama, a universe of plenty with war obsolete. Somehow, she could not quite believe in it. Man would remain Man, however far he spread.

"In the meantime," Sinclair said, "I need you. All of you."

Katya thought she saw where he was going. "Operation Yunagi," she said. "You're afraid that if Dev communicates with the Xenos, the Hegemony'll find a way to use them against you!"

"That's part of it. My sources tell me that he and at least one DalRiss comel have already been dispatched to Eridu for the attempt.

"So, I have a proposal for you gentlemen and ladies, one that is strictly for volunteers. I and my staff are leaving for Eridu in three days. I would like the eight of you to accompany us. Once there, we'll join up with the local Network. You can be of invaluable help there, by the way, organizing and training our military forces.

"But more important, I want to assemble an assault team to steal a DalRiss comel, get it to a safe place, and use it to communicate with the Xenos for *our* side." He waited, smiling expectantly. "Well? What do you say?"

"You," Katya said quietly and with great deliberation, "are out of your goking mind!"

Chapter 5

Chi Draconis V offers exobiologists special insight into the evolution of life, and special problems as well, for the stellar explosion that transformed the star's binary companion into a white dwarf must have sterilized the system's worlds within the past billion years.

Yet life, of bewildering variety and energy, undeniably exists today on Eridu. Togo and Namura (2465) have suggested that the system's F7 sun, coupled with the world's slow rotation, introduced sufficient cyclical variations in temperature to favor the evolution of complex life from prebiotic compounds that fortuitously survived that early holocaust. Even so, Eridu remains a testimony to the native stubbornness and tenacity of Life, wherever in the universe it may be found.

—*Dawnings: A Survey of Evolutions*
Dr. Ella Grant Walker
C.E. 2488

Dawnings was one of the twelve books in *Hayai*'s tiny shipboard library, and Dev read it through three times during the passage to Chi Draconis. He paid particular attention to Walker's chapter on Eridu.

Nothing he read, however, explained the Eriduan colonists' determination to keep the Hegemony Colonial Authority from redesigning their planet. The Universal Lifers and the greenies were a tiny minority, and the workers whose livelihoods would be affected by terraforming the planet had been promised retraining, even relocation. Perhaps, after all, it was as Tokuyama had said: "Some people are *baka*."

For Dev, the two-week flight had passed with relative ease. There was plenty of technical data on hand, both in *Hayai*'s library and through linkage with the ship's AI. Better still, once Tokuyama had been willing to let Dev look on through the navsim as the courier's helmsman threaded the little ship through the blue-glowing storm of the Quantum Sea. It had been a long time since Dev had ridden the currents of the *Kamisama no Taiyo*, the godsea of quantum space. He wasn't allowed to patch in his C-socket and interface with the ship's drives, of course; he could do no more than watch as the blue-white glory of the K-T plenum exploded past his senses, but it reminded him again of his old dream of being a starpilot, a whitesuit like his father.

Against all reason, there were still times when he felt that old tug of longing, even now. He shook his head at the unwanted thought. He'd had his chance. The Emperor himself had as much as told him he could take any posting he wanted, a pure dreamjack. He'd elected to remain a warstrider, and now . . . what was he?

He felt a bit lost, actually. He couldn't maintain the fiction of being a striderjack when he was no longer a Thorhammer. For almost two years the 5th Loki and Alessandro's Assassins had been both family and home.

Now he had the Empire, a concept too large to provide any sense of belonging. Once he'd made his decision to accept the Emperor's offer and transfer from the Hegemony Guard to the Imperial forces, he'd been enthusiastic enough about the change. The Imperial Navy was by far the most powerful spacefaring force in human space, and the appointment itself a singular honor for any *gaijin* officer.

What then, he wondered, was he supposed to make of his assignment to the 4th Rangers, a Hegemony unit? His orders were for TAD—Temporary Attached Duty—so it wasn't like this was a permanent demotion.

Why did it feel that way?

He watched impassively through his cephlink as the blue light engulfing the *Hayai* flared and vanished, replaced by the black of space. One star, brighter than the rest, detached itself from the sun-strewn backdrop. *Hayai*'s AI picked out worlds against the stars, marking them with brackets and

scrolling columns of data. The fifth world was less than
a hundred million kilometers ahead, already showing the
red-gold tint of vegetation. Two small moons circled at a
distance, reminding Dev of the Lunarian Hypothesis. Could
those tiny twin worlds raise tides enough to explain the presence of life on Eridu? Or did they merely demonstrate that
human exobiologists didn't yet know all there was to know
about life in all its forms and haunts?

Numerous points of colored light crawled slowly across
Dev's vision, each identified by coded data. *Hayai* was
beginning to pick up the radio transponders of ships in-
system and was projecting their locations and IDs on the
cephlink display. Slowly, slowly, as deceleration dragged at
Dev and made him feel ponderously heavy, Eridu swelled
into a mottled disk of oranges, blues, browns, and dazzling
swirls of white. Babylon appeared as a point of silver light
three and a half planetary diameters out.

Linkcode accepted. Datafeed resume—
Synchorbital facilities: Single sky-el link, Babel to
Babylon, height 39,690 km, permanent orbital popu-
lation (2536) 112,219. . . .

Thanks to the planet's thirty-two-hour-plus rotation, Eridu
possessed one of the tallest sky-els in the Shichiju—almost
forty thousand kilometers. The synchorbital facility, though
home to over a hundred thousand people, was a relatively
small and primitive-looking straggle of pressurized habs and
modules and a single docking facility, Shippurport. Several
ships were already docked at the sprawling orbital gantries,
including an Imperial destroyer, the *Tokitukaze*. Dev wondered what had brought her to Eridu, and whether her arrival
had anything to do with his mission.

In keeping with the system's ancient Mideast naming
motif, the spaceport's town was Shippur, the main orbital
city was Babylon, and, inevitably perhaps, the sky-el itself
was the Tower of Babel. The towerdown was called Babel,
little more than a large frontier trading camp located on an
equatorial plateau between jungle and sea. Eridu had little to recommend it as a site for human colonization, mild
polar climate or not, but there would always be a few,

Dev knew, who would tolerate impossible conditions for the chance of striking it rich . . . or simply for a chance to start life over.

The Governor's official residence was in Babylon, not far from the spaceport, inside a rotating carousel that duplicated Eridu's eight-tenths surface gravity. Five hours after the *Hayai* finally docked at Shippurport, Dev, wearing his best dress Imperial blacks and with his *Teikokuno Hoshi* at his throat, was palming his ID into the Residence AI, then being led by bowing courtiers to the Governor's office.

Eridu's *Chiji* was not an ethnic Japanese, though like many Hegemony governors he was of Imperial birth. Prem Thanarat was from Bangkok, one of Japan's Imperial enclaves on Earth, and it was said that he owed his post to his long and personal friendship with the *Fushi* Emperor himself.

"So, Lieutenant Cameron. You are the Emperor's expert on the Xenophobes," Prem said in perfect Inglic as Dev stepped up before the Governor's ornate work desk. He was a small man with nut-brown skin and old-fashioned, thick-rimmed glasses balanced on his nose. He didn't look older than fifty or so, and Dev wondered just when and how he had gotten to be friends with an Emperor who had already ruled for eighty-five years. Possibly Prem, too, was on an anti-aging regimen . . . which just might explain why his dark eyes looked so tired. His voice, though, was light, almost musical in its intonation.

"*Hai, Chijisama.*" Dev bowed formally. "*Hajimem-ashte.*"

"Please, no formalities and no Nihongo," Prem said, carelessly waving a hand. He gestured and an aide produced a comfortably padded chair on a frictionless base. "Sit, sit. How was your trip from Earth?"

"Fine, Your Excellency. A little tedious." His weight in the chair locked the base to the floor, and the back shifted to a more comfortable position. Most of the technology and art in the room, Dev saw, had come from Earth or other Core Worlds.

"I can imagine. Scant room on a courier for civilization. *O-cha?*"

"Yes, thank you, sir."

Prem gestured, and a young woman appeared with cups and a pot of green tea. Dev wondered how much it cost to export that staple of Imperial *shakai* across twenty-five light years.

"I would be gratified, *Chuisan*," Prem said as Dev took his first sip, "if you would tell me more about this Operation Yunagi."

"Of course, sir." Dev began reviewing the plan carefully, wondering as he did so whether Prem was one of those, like Admiral Munimori, who opposed communication with the Xenophobes. Quite a few people on the Imperial Staff felt that the success of the so-called nuclear depth charges on Loki should be exploited on every world the Xenos had infested.

Genocide, in other words . . . a literal xenocide. It was easier to kill the things than to talk to them.

"The most difficult part," Dev concluded, "is actually approaching them. On GhegnuRish . . . uh, that's Alya B-V, the DalRiss homeworld, the Xenos had already progressed from the acquisitive phase to the contemplative phase, a single world mind. I stumbled, literally, into a cavern where I could touch the organism with my comel. We just don't know if we'll be able to approach acquisitive Xenos. They're not all linked together, like the One, and they're not nearly as intelligent. But they do coordinate their actions on the surface. There have been times when small units have been able to get quite close to Xenophobes on the surface without triggering an attack. That's what we hope to do with Yunagi."

"It still sounds dangerous," Prem said. "And there is, shall we say, a small complication. The comels have not yet arrived from Earth."

Dev was taken aback. "But I was told—"

Prem shrugged. "A temporary delay, I am sure. I am surprised they did not ship them aboard the *Hayai*."

"It sounds," Dev said slowly, "like someone screwed up."

Or like deliberate sabotage. Had someone deliberately done this? Munimori, for instance? Or someone in the Court's anti-*gaijin* faction?

"Tell me more about the comel," Prem said. "As I understand it, it allows you to share thoughts with the Xenophobes. Telepathy?"

"With the Xenophobes, not quite. Their thoughts are just too different. You get, well, impressions. Memories. Feelings. Mental images, though those are awfully distorted." He described the DalRiss-engineered creatures to Prem, answering what questions he could and admitting ignorance on the rest. Much about comels, how they worked, how they were programmed, was still a mystery, though biologists on Earth were beginning to learn how DalRiss biotechnics duplicated certain aspects of human technology.

The comel was a living creature, designed by DalRiss bioengineers, that somehow bridged the gap between two mutually alien neural systems, allowing an exchange of sensory impressions. The data transmitted from one species to another was necessarily crude and incomplete, but until Dev had confronted a Xenophobe Self with a comel on his arm, no one had even been able to say for sure whether or not the Xenos *had* feelings.

"I see," Prem said, as Dev finished describing what he knew of DalRiss biotechnics. "And, as I understand it, the Xenophobes form a community mind. Each individual is in constant communication with all of the others."

Dev hesitated on that one. "With the . . . the phase I talked to on Alya B-V, all of the Xenos occupying the planet, trillions of them, were in physical contact with all of the others. Think of the trillion or so cells in your body. They think, *act*, as a single organism."

"But not this, ah, acquisitive phase you mentioned. The dangerous ones. Could one man, with nothing but this comel creature, actually hope to approach a Xenophobe machine without being killed?"

"Well, Your Excellency, we're not going to just walk up to one and try to shake hands. Operation Yunagi calls for someone to try to approach a Xeno cell group that's been isolated—in a damaged Xenophobe combat machine, say, or building the crystal structures we've observed next to some of their exit craters. While he tries to get close, he'll be covered by a squad, preferably a warstrider section armed with flamers."

"And if you can talk to them, you'll give them a message to take back to the rest, is that right?"

"Essentially. At least we'll be able to decide whether or not there's any point in trying to approach one of their underground nests." He shrugged, spreading his hands. "It's the only approach that makes any sense."

An electronic tone sounded from Prem's desk. "Excuse me, Lieutenant. We have guests." He gestured, and an aide manually opened the large, dark wooden doors to the room. Dev stood and bowed as two men, a Hegemony *taisa* and a civilian in an elaborate gold-trimmed cloak and bodysuit, walked in.

The *taisa* was a Westerner, a Hegemony army colonel, his two-toned grays bearing an array of battle honors and ribbons. The civilian was Japanese and wore the red sash of an Imperial *daihyo*.

Prem, too, rose behind his desk. *"Ohayo gozaimashte, Omigatosama,"* he said, bowing. He looked at Dev. "My Lord, this is *Chu-i* Devis Cameron. He arrived moments ago, aboard the *Hayai*, and is the man behind Operation Yunagi." He turned to Dev. "I have the honor, *Chuisan*, of presenting His Majesty's special envoy, the *Daihyo* Yoshi Omigato."

Dev bowed low. *"Hajimemashte, Omigatosama."*

Omigato acknowledged with a grunt and stiff nod. Imperial *daihyos*, or representatives, commanded fantastic authority, speaking for the Emperor and reporting personally to him. This man, Dev realized, was why that Imperial destroyer was docked at Shippurport. It must be Omigato's personal transport.

"And this, Lieutenant," Prem continued, indicating the Guard officer at Omigato's side, "is *Taisa* Emilio Duarte, commander of the 4th Terran Rangers. He will be both your commander and your escort while you are here on Eridu."

Dev glanced at the collar devices and rows of ribbons on the man's uniform as he bowed. The man was strider-trained. Two battle ribbons and a Medal of Valor, eighth *dan*. The scarlet *Shishino Chi*, the Lion's Blood, indicating a serious wound in the line of duty. A blue-and-white Alyan Expeditionary Force ribbon; he'd been to the DalRiss worlds, too.

Duarte seemed to sense Dev's question. "You are right," he said, smiling. "I was at Alya A. Aboard the *Saiwai Maru*.

But we stayed with Yamagata at ShraRish while you were doing your thing with General Howard over at GhegnuRish." He grinned. "Some guys get all the luck, eh?"

Omigato scowled, and Dev had the feeling he disapproved of Duarte's manner . . . or perhaps he didn't like the public airing of the near split in the command of the Imperial Expeditionary Force. Admiral Yamagata, Dev remembered, had very nearly removed Howard from command over the issue of using *gaijin* troops at the DalRiss home systems.

"We should concern ourselves with more immediate problems," the *daihyo* said, speaking Nihongo. "I am concerned with this entire plan to communicate with the Xenophobe enemy. Perhaps we should discuss our strategy should the honorable Cameron's attempt fail."

Now *there* was a cheerful thought. If he failed to communicate with the Xenos, it was quite likely that he would be dead.

"You are speaking of the nuclear option, of course," Prem said.

"A number of ground-penetrating nuclear charges were brought here aboard the *Tokitukaze*," Omigato said. "We will release them for deployment as necessary. The Imperial Marines already on Eridu will take charge of the operation."

"I take it you're not too hot on the idea of talking peace with the Xenos," Duarte said in Inglic.

Omigato appeared to understand him, even though he replied in Nihongo. "The plan is foolhardy and can confer no advantage to us. How could we sense whether or not such alien creatures are lying? Simpler to destroy the threat once and for all."

"If we could talk to them, my Lord, it would make terraforming this world a hell of a lot easier," Dev pointed out. "They could do the job for you."

That idea had been discussed before, once it had been learned that a Xeno world mind could nanotechnically alter the chemistry of a planet's atmosphere. Some day perhaps, Xenos and humans could form a symbiotic partnership, taming worlds together for the benefit of both species. Exchanges with the Alya B World Mind had hinted that such cooperation might well be possible.

Only a few people within Imperial or Hegemony command circles shared that vision so far, however, and Omigato clearly was not one of them. *"Baka mitai!"* The blunt phrase, meaning roughly "That's stupid," was deliberately rude. "They are aliens!"

Dev blinked, startled. Omigato had called the Xenophobes *gaijin*, literally "outsiders," a word that could mean aliens or foreigners. The same word was used to refer to anyone who wasn't Japanese. It was strange, Dev thought, to be verbally lumped with the Xenos.

Did Omigato think of everyone who wasn't Japanese—human and nonhuman alike—as the same, as a foreigner, not to be trusted? An interesting question. It was possible, Dev thought, that language shaped a culture's point of view at least as much as the other way around.

"I return to the *Tokitukaze*," Omigato said abruptly. "You will, of course, keep me informed of Operation Yunagi and of all new developments."

Prem's boot heels clicked as he bowed. *"Hai, Omigatosama."*

"Now there's an iridium-plated, unalloyed bastard," Duarte said to the silent room seconds after the Japanese *daihyo* had left. "Cheerful sort, eh?"

Ignoring Duarte's assessment, Prem turned to Dev. *"Chuisan*, you will be assigned to the 4th Terran Rangers during your stay here. *Taisa* Duarte will show you your quarters and get you settled in."

"Very good, Your Excellency."

"You will have the official position of *koman* with the unit, which gives you a certain measure of authority. Please remember, however, that Colonel Duarte must maintain the respect of his people if he is to maintain discipline. I will brook no interference with his command."

A *koman* was a military advisor, usually answering to an authority outside the normal chain of command. Dev opened his hands. "I'm just a *chu-i*, Your Excellency. I'll stay out of the way."

"I will inform you when your comel arrives." He sighed. "Until then, we will do what we can. Perhaps you can familiarize yourself with this world, and with Colonel Duarte's people and equipment."

"What is the Fourth, Colonel?"

Duarte smiled. "It *was* a mechanized scout regiment. Light stuff, mostly, RLN-90s and Ares-12s. LaG-42 command vehicles. After your experiment with leggers last year, though, we've been experimenting with combined arms tactics, too. Companies of armored troops working in close support with light warstriders. That'll be something you can help us with, maybe."

Dev smiled. Cameron's Commandos had been the name of his legger close-support company. "I'll do my best. You think you can find a strider to fit me?"

"Oh, we'll dig something up, I expect."

"I leave it to you gentlemen, then," Prem said, in obvious dismissal. "I will expect weekly reports."

Dev and Colonel Duarte were ushered from the room by a pair of staff servants, and two hours later they were aboard a delta-winged ascraft descending from Shippurport toward Eridu's atmosphere. The sky-el trip, Duarte explained, took two days, and another two were required for the magrail trip from Babel to the polar zones. With the air-space craft, they would be on the ground in Winchester in a few hours.

Operation Yunagi was off to a bad start. Confusion within the Imperial Staff, his one piece of vital equipment missing . . . and the Emperor's personal representative at Eridu seeming implacably opposed to the entire project . . . almost as though he had some hidden agenda of his own.

At least, Dev thought, he was finally going to get to jack a warstrider again.

Somehow, that seemed a small consolation.

Chapter 6

Simply being part of a crowd affects a person. Each person in a crowd is, to some degree, open to actions different from his usual behavior. Crowds provide a sense of anonymity because they are large and often temporary congregations. Crowd members often feel that their moral responsibility has shifted from themselves to the crowd as a whole. . . .

—Field Manual 19-15
"Civil Disturbances"
Department of the Army, 1985

"According to Intelligence," the briefing officer said, "we can expect another mass demonstration today, beginning at the Assyrian Concourse. We have been directed by HEMILCOM to initiate a period of martial law within Winchester and its environs, and we should anticipate the possibility of a hostile response from an aroused populace. All patrols will operate under Class Five ROEs."

A chorus of low-voiced murmurs echoed through the squad bay. Class Five rules of engagement called for the unit to arm and engage their weapons only if they were fired upon. Still, it was a step up from Class Six, which prohibited any use of weapons or lethal force under any circumstances. And martial law! That had been threatened for months now, but the reality had never materialized.

Things must be getting desperate.

Dev sat with the other striderjacks of A Company, 1st Battalion of the 4th Terran Rangers in an open space in the bay. Each morning briefing for the past month had been more of the same—"Expect mass demonstrations or civil disturbances"—but the pace of events seemed to be picking up. So far, there'd been remarkably few incidents between the local population and the Hegemony peacekeeping units stationed on Eridu, but the change in ROEs was almost a sure-fire guarantee that the situation was also going to change.

The staff briefing officer stepped away from the small wooden podium that had been erected in front of the ranks of folding chairs. Colonel Duarte took his place. "Thank you, Captain Ranescú." He paused for a moment, gripping the sides of the podium as he stared out over the faces of the assembled company.

They were in the capital city of Winchester, not far from Eridu's south pole. Company A currently mustered twenty light warstriders out of a usual complement of twenty-four, organized into two platoons of eight each, plus a command section. Present were the strider crews, along with key maintenance and armorer personnel, plus 115 men and women of Company D, one of the regiment's two close-support leg infantry units. Companies B and C were stationed in a neighboring city, while the 2nd and 3rd Battalions were posted halfway around the planet in Eridu's north boreal region.

"Okay, people," Duarte said. "You've heard the word. There are rumors in the city that there's been a major Xenophobe breakout just a few kilometers from here. The rumor is false, but the dissies are using this to stir up the mobs, convincing them that we're about to use the Imperial solution."

Dev whistled softly to himself. "The Imperial solution" was a military euphemism for ground-penetrating nuclear warheads. By Charter law, only Imperial forces could deploy nuclear warheads. "Dissies" were dissidents, the anti-Hegemony or anti-Imperial factions who had been stirring up trouble on Eridu for nearly a year.

If Dev had learned anything during the two months he'd spent on Eridu, it was that the locals—the vocal minority involved in the demonstrations, at any rate—were fanatically opposed to the use of nuclear weapons of any kind on their world.

How did the majority feel about it? Dev wasn't sure. There were several pro-Hegemony groups on the planet that supported Imperial intervention, but their voices tended to be lost in massed freedom-for-Eridu chants. Most Eriduans, Dev suspected, wanted nothing more than for the noisy people, pros and antis alike, to go away and leave them to get on with their lives. After six months of demonstrations, strikes, and protests, Eridu's economy was in chaos.

"Our mission until now," Duarte continued, "was simply to keep the peace. Today, however, we have been directed by Hegemony Military Command to disperse the mob and declare martial law.

"HEMILCOM does not believe there will be armed resistance to the order. Nevertheless, we have been directed to use every precaution. We will return fire only if fired upon, but we will maintain a highly visible presence within the city until the Governor's office has time to restore calm through political means. Warstriders will at all times avoid the use of unnecessary force. Company C squad commanders, you will see to it that your troops are issued with Iijima-44 sonic stunners in addition to their regular combat gear. Our call sign will be Blue Lancer. Are there questions?"

Dev wanted to ask about events elsewhere on Eridu. The 4th Terran Rangers were one of just two Guard Regiments stationed on Eridu; the other was the 3rd New American Mechanized Cavalry, which, like the Rangers, had units scattered across the planet. What was happening with the two companies of the 4th stationed at Memphis and Chaldee, just a few hundred kilometers from Winchester? Or at the towerdown outpost of Babel, or at the equatorial plantations? Was there rioting out there as well, or was the trouble just here in Winchester? There'd been no news for weeks, ever since Governor Prem had ordered total censorship of all media broadcasts and news linkfeeds.

Damn, Dev thought, you'd think that someone would tell the people tasked with trying to keep a lid on things.

He held his questions. He'd already heard the current who-was on the matter. Dev's most reliable sources insisted that there'd been riots in most of the cities on Eridu where Guard military units were stationed. Tensions had been mounting for two months, ever since a sniper had killed a couple of off-duty Rangers at a sidewalk restaurant in Memphis.

Dev leaned far back in his chair, arms folded. And still the promised comel had not arrived from Earth! He'd decided that Omigato, or someone, had blocked the comel's shipment, or intercepted it, for reasons of his own. He'd queried Earth twice in six weeks, though it was impossible to tell if his courier messages were even getting through until he got a reply; there was nothing more that could be done until the bureaucratic tangle—or sabotage—sorted itself out.

Meanwhile, he was stuck on Eridu, with his TAD to the 4th Rangers dragging relentlessly toward a permanent transfer. The local mincies—the word was derived from *minshu*, a Nihongo word for "civilians"—had long ago replaced the Xenos as Dev's primary concern. He rarely even thought about Operation Yunagi anymore, so caught up had he become with the day-to-day routine of life in a Guard warstrider regiment.

He was still in an uncomfortable, lame-duck position with the Rangers, though, for he was senior to all of the line officers in A Company except for Captain Siegfried Koch . . . and Koch had been reassigned to HEMILCOM headquarters in Babylon three weeks earlier. Duarte himself had taken command of the company until the bronze-bearded Koch returned. Technically, Dev was on Duarte's staff as part of his command section; in fact, he was a third leg who helped with the administrative work when he could, helped with the planning and organization of the battalion's two legger companies, and otherwise tried to stay out of the way.

Dev continued to listen as other members of the unit asked questions about deployment and parts availability. Duarte answered them, asked if there were more, then stepped from behind the podium. "Okay, striderjacks. Mount up and plug in! Let's impress hell out of the mincies!"

With a clatter and scraping of folding chairs, they rose and dispersed, the striderjacks heading across the steel grate floor toward their waiting machines, the leggers queuing up in front of the stores arsenal to be issued their lasers and sonic stunners.

The company's warstriders lined both sides of the vast interior space of the squad bay, silently waiting giants of durasheath armor, steel-gray surfaces, and menacing weapons. Dev broke into a trot, angling across the floor toward his strider, which stood quiescent, partly obscured in the tangled embrace of a maintenance access gantry. It was a single-slotter, an RLN-90 Scoutstrider similar to the machine he'd jacked during the Alya campaign.

Standing three and a half meters tall, the light recon strider massed nearly twenty tons. The Scoutstrider was among the most strikingly anthropomorphic of warstrider designs, most of which tended to look vaguely like aircraft or cannon shells slung between massive, back-angled legs. RLN-90s had a rather stubby, squared-off upper torso section rotating freely above the lower chassis and leg assemblies; the right arm could mount either a 100-megawatt laser or a high-speed autocannon, while the left arm sported a massive four-fingered hand. Kv-48 weapons packs on each armored "shoulder," mounting rockets, grenades, and machine guns completed the strider's primary armament. Almost as an afterthought, an M-90 Chemflamer had been strapped to the left forearm, a field modification made necessary by the chance of combat with Xenos. The strider's hull nanoflage hadn't been charged yet, so the machine's overall color was still a dark and lusterless gray.

Dev's eyes strayed to the Inglic letters picked out in white paint high up on the torso's armored carapace. Some wag in the company's maintenance team had painted the word *Koman-do* there, and Dev had accepted the bilingual pun with good humor. The phrase translated as "the way of the advisor," but it put him in mind of his old Cameron's Commandos. His Scoutstrider's name was a kind of memorial to those men and women who'd fought with him, first on Loki, then on the worlds of a star system over one hundred light-years from home.

He wondered how the Thorhammers were getting on now without him.

One question led smoothly to the next. Where was Katya now, and what was she doing?

"Everything set, Gun?" he asked the squat man with silicarb-blackened hands and arms standing before the strider. *Gunso* Gio Olivetti—his rank corresponded to that of sergeant—was crew chief of Dev's Scoutstrider.

"All set, Lieutenant," he said, wiping his hands with a dirty rag. "Your C-90 tanks are dry, but you shouldn't be needing them. Your '48s are loaded with DY-20s and 30s only. No rockets, no MGs."

"Fine." Facing a civilian mob, there'd be no need for flamer, rockets, or machine guns. DY-20s were tube-launched grenades that detonated with a dazzling flash and an earsplitting noise. DY-30s were gas grenades. Depending on the type, and he would be loaded with a variety, they could blind, stun, or panic a crowd, and were generally used for riot control. With a last look around the cavernous squad bay, Dev started up the gantry ladder, climbing three meters to the accessway.

The narrow, circular pod hatch was already open. Careful not to snag his military bodysuit, Dev squeezed feet-first through the opening, snuggling down into a horizontal tube somewhat more cramped than a coffin.

His VCH—the vehicle cephlinkage helmet—was hanging in a recessed nook above his head. Carefully, he snapped the interior jacks home in all three of his sockets, then pulled the helmet down over his head. Other fittings, tubes and cables, plugged into connectors in his bodysuit. While he was jacking the strider, the machine's AI would watch over his physical body, keeping it clean and healthy while his brain was otherwise engaged. Connections secure, he snapped the couch harness into place, then brought his left palm down on the interface built into the console at his side.

With a dazzling inner flash of light, Dev's claustrophobic surroundings vanished. He was standing again in the open squad bay, the framework of the gantry pressed close about his torso. Olivetti stood below him, his head barely at the level of Dev's hips. Again, Dev felt the surge of power, the thrill of majesty and irresistible strength that accompanied the cephlinkage of Man and Warstrider.

Through that link, Dev was not the combat vehicle's pilot; he *was* the Scoutstrider, and he could feel the texture of the waffle-molded steel deck beneath his flanged feet, could sense the air temperature and noted automatically that it hovered at close to thirty degrees Celsius. Alphanumerics cascaded across his vision, indicating power levels, systems status, and weapons readiness. Below him, Olivetti touched a control and the gantry folded back out of the way. Dev gestured, effortlessly raising the one-ton mass of his left arm in a casual salute. His crew chief returned the gesture, then moved back out of the way as Dev took his first step forward.

"Okay, Blue Lancers," Duarte's voice said over the tactical link, sharp within Dev's mind. "We'll take it in open deployment. No straggling."

Duarte's command strider was twenty meters ahead, just inside the high, trapezoidal opening of the squad bay door. His LaG-42 Ghostrider was more typical of warstrider design, over four meters tall and massing better than twenty-five tons, a blunt, cylindrical fuselage slung between heavy legs with digitigrade articulation, like a bird's. A 100-megawatt laser paired with a chemical flamer jutted from a chin turret beneath the blunt prow. Instead of arms, it mounted Kv-70 weapons packs, larger versions of Dev's Kv-48s, though external waldo manipulators could be plugged in at need. The Ghostrider was a double-slotter, with two jackers lying beneath the long, paired blisters on the hull's dorsal surface. Duarte's number two was an experienced *chu-i* named Charles Muirden.

Duarte's Ghostrider bore one touch unusual for a modern combat vehicle. Rising from its back between the weapons pods was a slender telescoping mast with a crosspiece mounted at the top. Hanging from the crosspiece was a Hegemony banner, the blue-and-white globe of Earth displayed against a gold-bordered field of green. Such banners seemed like an affectation from another age, harking back to some medieval era of military regalia, but at times they could play an important psywar role. It was vital that the citizens in Winchester's streets who saw the advancing warstrider platoon *know* that it was the Hegemony Guard that they faced.

Dev fell into line with the other warstriders, two rows of ten facing the door. To the rear, the legger troops were filing into their waiting hover APCs. Slowly, the huge doors began sliding aside, opening onto the interior of the city of Winchester.

Eridu's capital was not the largest city on the planet, but it was one of the oldest, dating back to the very first colonial outposts in 2312. The city's main dome was over two kilometers across and housed a warren of older structures, pressurized domes and habs, industrial facilities, and warehouses. The Rangers' squad bay was part of a smaller, adjoining dome on the east side of the city called the Armory, which served as barracks and training center for A and D Companies. The Armory opened directly into the main dome, where Tarleton Avenue ran straight to City Center and the Assyrian Concourse at the commercial and government heart of the city.

The Concourse was a broad, open park surrounded by modern buildings, with Government House brooding over the north end, the older Workers' Guild Hall at the south. The dome overhead was transplas. Angling his optics toward the city's roof, Dev could tell it was raining outside. Water was streaming down the dome's curved surface in rippling sheets.

"Keep it tight," Duarte's voice said. "Close it up. Set nanoflage for display. Show the colors!"

In Hegemony practice, the thin layer of programmed nano coating each strider normally was set to reflect surrounding colors, while deleting bright flashes of light or quick movement, creating a kind of camouflage that was extraordinarily effective at ranges of a hundred meters or so. Within the close confines of city streets, such camouflage would be of little use. Besides, the point of this exercise was to be seen. Each warstrider in the column shimmered, then flashed to a deep, brilliant blue, with white trim at each set of joints.

Blue and white—the colors of Earth, and of the Hegemony.

Dev was right behind Duarte's Ghostrider, walking alongside a smaller LaG-17 Fastrider jacked by an Eriduan *sho-i* named Beverly Schneider. The double line moved swiftly through nearly empty streets. Ground transport in Eridu's cities tended to be floaters levitated by magnetic rails embedded in the pavement, and the streets could be crowded at times, but the area seemed almost eerily deserted. The few civilian pedestrians out ducked for cover into the surrounding buildings as the warstrider company trooped by.

"Hey, *Chu-i* Cameron?" a voice said over a private channel. Dev recognized it as a young *sho-i*, new to the unit, Martin Koenig. Like Schneider, he'd been recruited here on Eridu, rather than on Earth where the Rangers had been organized.

"What is it, Koenig?"

"Just wondering if you'd heard the latest who-was, Lieutenant," Koenig said. "They say that all these demonstrations and strikes and stuff are being caused somehow by the Xenophobes, maybe Xenos that're somehow taking people over. They say they're trying to weaken Eridu before they launch their big attack."

"You've been simming too many ViRdrama thrillers, Koenig," Dev replied dryly. "Xenos don't understand human politics. Hell, they don't understand *humans*."

The Xeno World Mind he'd communicated with on Alya B-V had barely been able to comprehend that humans were sentient non-Xenos. To their way of thinking, the terms *sentient* and *not-Self* taken together were an oxymoron, an alien and virtually incomprehensible concept. The Xenos loose inside Eridu's planetary crust almost certainly shared that same bias. The idea of Xenophobes lurking in their deep caverns and tunnels and somehow subverting human groups and organizations on the surface struck Dev as ludicrous.

"I don't know about that, Lieutenant," Koenig replied. "There's this guy I know in Memphis who—"

"Koenig," Dev interrupted, "I've *been* there, okay? We're not facing Xenophobe agents masquerading as humans, and we're not up against a Xeno secret weapon."

"Lieutenant Cameron's right," Duarte's voice cut in. "We're facing scared, misguided humans this time, not monsters, and that's the straight hont. Are you linked on that?"

"Yes, sir," Koenig said. He sounded hurt. "Linked."

"Let's keep the chatter down, then, and stay alert. We've got something happening up ahead."

The demonstration, Dev saw, had already begun. Perhaps the reason the city streets seemed deserted was the fact that most of Winchester's population appeared to be crowded into the park at the Assyrian Concourse. They were facing the Guild Hall, where speakers were addressing the crowd from a broad, open balcony. Dev engaged his telephoto optics, letting his vision zoom in on individuals within the crowd. DOWN WITH THE HEGEMONY and ERIDU IS OURS were two popular banners, though dozens of others hung in the air above the mob, bobbing up and down with the chants that punctuated the speakers' deliveries.

Dev let part of his mind scan the local broadcast frequencies. With a crowd that large, the speakers must be using some sort of radio transmission.

There it was! Dev heard the usual political blather, the same stuff he'd been hearing for weeks until Prem had ordered the media censorship to begin. Something about the New Constitutionalists . . . and taking power back from the tyranny that was grinding them beneath its duralloy boots. . . .

The warstriders entered the Concourse, spreading out in a single line, keeping the mob before them. Behind the strider line, the hover APCs grounded, their opening hatches disgorging ranks of armed and armored Hegemony leg infantry.

A shrill warble sounded in Dev's ear and he switched off his monitor; Duarte had just started jamming the transmission frequency. Seconds later, he heard Duarte's voice booming out over the crowd, relayed through the Ghostrider's external speakers.

"Citizens!" the voice thundered. "This is Colonel Duarte of the Hegemony Guard. This is an official order to disperse! Martial law has been declared in all portions of Winchester and its satellite domes. You are to disperse and return to your homes immediately. . . ."

It began as a low, rumbling sound, interspersed with catcalls and wild yells, but it grew, swelling rapidly to a pounding, chanting roar like the crash of waves on a rocky seacoast: *"No! No! No! No!"*

More soldiers were running into the square, men in red-and-green uniforms with ferriplas cuirasses. They were locals, Dev knew, members of the 1st Eridu Legion, a militia force quartered in a satellite dome on the west side of the city opposite the Armory.

He sensed the increase in tension. The Hegemony troops behind the warstrider line didn't trust the militia, and Dev was sure the feeling was mutual, but for the moment at least they were still following the government's orders, deploying in a thin, colorful line between the mincie crowd and the Hegemony Guard forces.

"No! No! No! No!"

From where his Scoutstrider was standing, Dev had a good view of Duarte's Ghostrider, just ahead of him and a little to the right. Something was happening there, movement up on the strider's dorsal surface. An access hatch popped open, and Duarte himself rose into view astride his machine.

He must be trying to overawe them, Dev thought, like a man on horseback confronting a man on foot.

"I say again," Duarte's voice roared, drowning out the crowd. His link with his strider broken now, he was using a throat mike to transmit his words. The green Hegemony banner hung limply behind his bare head. "Go home! Go home! Governor Prem has declared martial law in Winchester and its satellite communities. . . ."

"No! No! No! No!"

From half a kilometer away, in a window high up in one of the buildings beyond the Assyrian Concourse, *Gunso* Isamu Kimaya, 3rd Imperial Marines, saw that his opportunity had arrived at last. He'd been watching for such a chance for weeks now, but not since those Hegemony soldiers had offered themselves to him in Memphis had his target been so perfectly available.

He raised his weapon, an Ishikawajima Type-83 sniper's rifle, a rugged, heavy weapon that fired explosive 15mm rocket rounds almost as long as his thumb. The interface in his left palm was already resting against the contact plate in the weapon's forward grip. As Kimaya peered through the weapon's optics, targeting data was relayed directly to the marine's cephlink. He zoomed in on the Hegemony *taisa*'s bare head, bracketed it, locking in the chambered round's tracking computer.

Kimaya let out his breath partway, letting his mind focus on a *kokorodo* mantra that focused his concentration on the target: *Shi-da!*

I am death.

The Type-83 had no trigger. Instead, Kimaya's mind gave the order to fire, gently, without the misaligning tug of a trigger pull. The shot, muffled by the weapon's sound-suppressor barrel, was no louder than a harsh cough.

An instant later, in Kimaya's optics, the bracketed head of the Hegemony colonel disintegrated in a spray of blood and fragmented bone, splattering the green banner behind it. . . .

Chapter 7

O judgment, thou art fled to brutish beasts, and men have lost their reason!

—*Julius Caesar*
Act III, scene 2

Sheer, raw chaos had engulfed Winchester's city center. As Duarte died, the mob's roar faded, then resurged, a rolling wave of sound echoing across the plaza.

Dev watched, horrified, as Duarte's bloody, headless body sagged backward, legs still caught in the strider's open dorsal hatch, outstretched arms dangling over the Ghostrider's hull above the primary heat exhaust manifold. Almost automatically, he replayed the instant of Duarte's death in flashing, freeze-frame images fed from his Scoutstrider's AI to his cephlink RAM; a trained portion of his right brain calculated possible vectors for the explosive shell based on the snap of Duarte's head and body as the projectile struck.

The round had come from *that* direction, high and to the right. Dev pivoted his upper body, enhancing the visual scan image, zooming in on row upon row of windows.

Infrared. Overlay.

Smeared colors, warm reds and yellows, cooler greens and blues, blurred his vision. Literally hundreds of shapes were visible in or behind those windows, people watching the mass demonstration below. Only one heat-glowing shape was moving, however, shifting with remarkable speed as it faded back into the cooler depths of the building.

That particular window vanished in a sun-bright dazzle of heat, and Dev's strider AI cut out the thermal visual component to preserve its optics. Lieutenant Muirden, jacking Duarte's command strider, had performed the same trajectory scan-and-track as Dev, spotted the same moving figure, and cut loose with a pulse from the Ghostrider's chin laser.

One hundred megawatts of laser energy discharged in a hundredth of a second was the equivalent of the detonation of perhaps a quarter of a kilo of high explosive, fractionally less than a single stick of old-fashioned dynamite. The window shattered, spraying out from the face of the building in an avalanche of debris.

"Cease fire!" Dev snapped over the tactical link. "All units, hold fire!" Prisoners would be better than charred bodies . . . but in any case, the half-glimpsed heat source had been moving quickly the instant before the laser hit. Had Muirden nailed the sniper? There was no way to tell, at least until someone searched the wreckage of that apartment. Switching to thermal again, Dev saw that the hole in the building's facade was now a white-hot mass of thermal radiation. It was impossible to see anything.

And the Rangers had other, more pressing problems now. The mob was surging forward against the red-and-green line of militia troops, a tide pounding against the shoreline in an attempt to reach the higher ground beyond. The militia line was struggling to hold its position . . . was sagging dangerously in a dozen places. . . .

"All units! This is Cameron, taking command." The decision was effortless, completely automatic. He was now the senior officer present, and it was vital to avoid confusion in the transition of command. "Set weapons pods for DY-30C, wide dispersal, air burst. One from each strider, on my command . . . *Fire!*"

The DY-30C gas grenade contained a binary chemical charge with a white smoke marker. On bursting it released an allophenothiazine derivative—or APT—an incapacitant with a powerful tranquilizing effect.

Unfortunately, tranq gas took time to take effect, sometimes as much as three or four minutes. The other gases in the warstriders' magazines—hallucinatory psychotomimetics, temporary optoinhibitors, phobinducers that caused attacks of acute fear, and irritants like tear and vomit gas—were all faster . . . and in this instance, far more deadly. With a crowd this large, widespread panic would inevitably lead to tens, maybe hundreds of people being trampled to death. Dev could see kids in the crowd: a few infants in parents' arms, many older kids obviously caught up in the excitement of the mob. He didn't want to be responsible for a massacre of innocents.

The gas grenades exploded with deceptively gentle pops above the heads of the demonstrators, eliciting screams and a momentary surge of the very panic Dev wanted to avoid. Clouds of white smoke descended across the plaza.

He switched on his external speakers. "Citizens!" he called, his voice echoing back from the face of the Guild Hall. "The demonstration is over! Go home! You will not be harmed! Go home!"

Like a frayed rope stretched too tight, the red-and-green line dissolved and the crowd surged through. Someone in the vanguard brandished a laser rifle wrenched from the grip of a militiaman, shaking it above his head. Then, horrified, Dev saw that many of the militiamen had actually turned around, joining the front ranks of the mob as they closed with his own forces. "It's the revolution!" someone was screaming over and over again. "It's the revolution!"

"Kill the Impies!" The yells were shrill, mindless, like the bellowing of animals.

"Lieutenant!" It was Koenig's voice, quavering at the edge of panic. "Can we shoot?"

"DY-30As only!" Dev snapped. The 30A was a smoke grenade. If he could create a forbidding-looking wall of smoke between the Guard forces and the mob . . . "Two grenades each! Target the front of the crowd. *Fire!*"

White smoke blossomed, mushroomed, spread . . . and the front ranks of the advancing crowd staggered to a ragged halt, not knowing whether they faced smoke or something more dangerous.

"Company C!" Dev called over the tactical net. "Sonics only! Advance and fire!"

In situations such as this the towering bulk of the warstriders was actually a disadvantage. Almost anything a strider did to defend itself would result in mass death and destruction; the support infantry, however, armored against the mob's weapons and armed with sonic stunners, were better equipped to break the mob's charge.

As the central mass of the crowd kept pressing ahead, the vanguard was catapulted forward, into the smoke. Guard foot soldiers, each in full combat armor, trotted past the line of warstriders, their lasers and heavier weapons slung over their backs, sonic stunners at the ready. As sergeants barked orders over the tac frequencies, each trooper dropped to one knee, aimed into the swirl of smoke, and fired.

Caressed by ultrasonic pulses, dozens of charging civilians faltered, stumbled, and collapsed.

A warning flashed across Dev's vision. Forty megawatts of laser energy had just washed across his left leg, scouring the nano coating of his armor but otherwise causing no damage. Turncoat militiamen, or civilians with captured rifles, were firing at the warstriders towering above the smoke. Another pulse of coherent light smoked from his right shoulder, melting some of the armor and leaving a small, puckered crater.

The leggers of Company C continued firing, gradually wearing away the front ranks of the mob. Why hadn't the warstriders been equipped with sonic stunners? Even a makeshift job, like the strap-on flamers, would have been better than nothing. The unconscious bodies were stacked now three and four deep on the pavement. Behind that wall, the rest of the mob hesitated like some huge, confused beast, unwilling to press forward, unable to turn back. The question was whether they would break before the battery packs in the troopers' stunners started giving out.

There was a swirl of color and motion to Dev's right. Turning, he saw a new threat, an arm of the mob spilling around the Guard unit's right flank, running, turning inward, colliding with the kneeling line of legger troops in a wild hand-to-hand melee.

Then they were everywhere, bearing down the Guard troops. "Company C, fall back!" Dev ordered. Those who could retreated. Others continued to fight, surrounded now by the tide of rioters. Sheer weight of numbers had knocked several troopers to the ground, where they were helplessly pinned and stripped of their weapons. "Warstriders on the right!" Dev called. "Forward!"

Each Scoutstrider and Fastrider was twice as tall as a man. They advanced slowly, sweeping forward with relentless power. Few rioters were able to stand unmoving before the approach of a twenty-ton monster, however determined they might be. Dev glimpsed Bev Schneider's Fastrider alongside Koenig's Scoutstrider, wading into that human sea. The mob's charge was broken, the demonstrators beginning to turn and flee back toward the Guild Hall.

But ten meters away, the crowd had engulfed Duarte's Ghostrider; several men had clambered up on the torso, clinging to the hull fittings, groping past Duarte's corpse for the bloodstained green banner still hanging from its mast. Muirden was trying to pivot the Ghostrider to throw his attackers off, but there were too many of them. Even a warstrider could be overwhelmed by enough sheer mass and determination. Dev saw the LaG-42 shudder, then visibly tip as a hundred rioters hurled themselves against Muirden's legs.

Turning, Dev moved forward, plowing into the mob, parting it before him like a steel-and-duralloy Moses. The noise was deafening, a thunderous roar of chanting voices filling the entire volume of the huge city dome. Targeting the Ghostrider, he fired another smoke grenade. It detonated against the LaG-42's hull, the burst of choking white smoke panicking the climbers, sending them tumbling back to the ground or on top of their fellows. Others crowded back as Dev's machine approached, a towering blue shadow in the thick mist that was beginning to envelop everything at ground level.

One determined young man clung to the top of the Ghostrider, still tugging at the green banner. He wore a gas mask, which let him ignore the smoke, and Dev guessed he might be one of the leaders of this insurrection. Swiftly, delicately, Dev reached out his left hand, opening duralloy fingers. The man, half blinded by the smoke, had not noticed Dev's approach, but he heard something now and spun, eyes wide behind the transparency of his mask. Gently, but irresistibly, Dev closed his fingers around the man's waist, plucking him off the Ghostrider's hull like a grape from the stem. The man shrieked and struggled, arms flailing, legs kicking wildly, but Dev swung him effortlessly above his head, holding him well above the crowd below.

"Thanks, Lieutenant," Muirden's voice said over a private channel. The Ghostrider's upper torso spun, free now, and he took a careful step forward. "I'm clear now."

"Pull back," Dev said. He shifted to the primary tac channel. "All units, pull back slowly! Give them room!"

The noise was dwindling, and so too were the movements of the crowd. It seemed as though the entire mob had somehow had a change of heart. At the perimeters, people were beginning to break away and wander off, straggling clear of the riot.

The tranq gas was beginning to work.

"HEMILCOM," Dev called, switching to the command frequency. "HEMILCOM, this is Blue Lancer Leader."

"Go ahead, Lancer," a voice replied in Dev's mind. "We've been monitoring your situation."

He'd known they would be. "Roger that. The DY-30C is starting to take effect. We're going to need medics in here, and fast."

"Affirmative, Blue Lancer. Medical personnel are on the way."

The effects of tranq gas varied widely, depending on the age, physical condition, and size of the victim. The instant "knock-out gas" popular in adventure sims simply didn't exist; what would render a twenty-year-old male in good condition unconscious would probably kill a man of ninety . . . or an infant. Tranq gas didn't knock people out. Instead, it inhibited dopamine receptors in the brain and central nervous system, blocking emotions, slowing thought and memory, sometimes interfering with the victim's motor response.

As a result, most of the rioters forgot they were angry and began wandering about, dazed, confused, even lost. Some would suffer amnesia. Others lost consciousness and slumped to the pavement, or responded in unexpected ways, panic or hysteria. A few lay on the ground, twitching helplessly or jerking uncontrollably as they were wracked by convulsions.

Dev felt a dark and bitter anguish rising within. There were certain to be casualties; damn it, when hordes of screaming, unarmed civilians charged ranks of armed troops and warstriders, there were going to be casualties! He'd tried to minimize them, but . . .

"Company C," he ordered. He scanned the dissolving crowd, looking for the infants he'd spotted earlier. They might need help, too. There was an antidote for tranq gas, but it had to be given quickly. *Where* were the medics? "I want one man in three to holster weapons and go try to help those people." The ones going into convulsions might swallow their tongues or injure their heads; some of the unconscious rioters at the bottom of that human wall felled by the leggers' stunners might be suffocating. Glancing up, Dev saw that he was still holding the body of the rioter he'd plucked from the LaG-42, now as limp as a rag doll. The guy had fainted.

Gently, Dev lowered him to the ground. "Sergeant Brunner," he called.

A squad *gunso* trotted up in front of Dev, saluting. "Yes, sir!"

"Take charge of this man. I think he was one of the mob leaders. Intelligence will want to question him."

"Yes, *sir*!"

Dev was tired, the inevitable aftermath of combat.

Of all the battles Dev had fought in his life, this was one of the hardest, facing men and women, civilians, most of them unarmed, all of them determined to get him and his people, with him not wanting to hurt them in return. Warstriders were marvelously flexible war machines, but they simply were not designed for this type of action.

Suddenly, Dev wanted to unplug, to immobilize his strider and climb out, to join the leggers moving now among the hundreds of victims lying on the pavement of the plaza. He could not, however. By assuming command of the unit, he'd assumed the responsibility to stay where he could monitor communications, tune in on orders from HEMILCOM, or assess developing threats.

Where were the medics?

Three days later, Dev stood again in Governor Prem's office, describing the events of the clash in the Assyrian

Concourse. Prem had conducted the interview, but a third figure, Omigato, stood silent in crimson robes in a far corner of the room.

"The final count was twelve dead," Dev was saying, "and perhaps fifty who required hospitalization." He glanced once at Omigato, then fixed his eyes steadily on Prem. "The medical assistance never did arrive from HEMILCOM, Your Excellency. I patched a call through to a hospital in Winchester, however. They dispatched trauma techs and ambulance flyers to the Concourse."

"Hmm. A mix-up in communications, I expect. And casualties among your troops?"

"One, Excellency. Colonel Duarte."

"Yes, of course. A good man." Prem sighed. "He will be difficult to replace."

"Major Barton is an experienced officer, Excellency." Barton, currently the CO of the Rangers' 1st Battalion, had been stationed with B Company at Eridu's towerdown. "He should prove to be an excellent regimental commander."

"Mmm, I daresay. To tell the truth, it was a replacement for CO of A Company I was thinking of. *Taisa* Duarte has been doing double duty and covering that post since *Tai-i* Koch has been stationed up here."

"But . . . surely Captain Koch will be coming back—"

Prem exchanged glances with Omigato. "*Tai-i* Koch has important duties here. Actually, *Chu-i*, I was thinking of you."

The Governor's words caught Dev completely by surprise. "M-me!" He shook his head. "Excellency, I'm flattered, but—"

"Flattery has nothing to do with it. You acted with skill and precision in Winchester, taking command of two companies at a moment of great danger, when Duarte's assassination could have shattered both units' cohesion. You held the line against that mob when a single mistake would have led to your being overwhelmed. You also showed keen judgment in assessing precisely the right level of force to use . . ."

"I killed twelve people, Excellency." Would it have been better if he'd tried panicking that mob with tear gas? He still didn't know.

"Most of them were suffocated after being hit by stunners and then being covered over by other bodies, or they were trampled. *Chu-i*, HEMILCOM Intelligence estimates that there were three thousand people in that plaza. Almost anything you tried would have resulted in some deaths. If you'd used panic gas or tear gas . . ." He shrugged. "Hundreds could have died in the stampede. More important, your skill at handling both the warstriders and the foot soldiers in the battle may well have saved both companies."

"Your action also won us a prisoner," Omigato said suddenly in Nihongo. It was the first time he'd spoken at all since Dev had entered that room nearly an hour before. "He has been broken. His confederates are being rounded up as we speak."

Something about the way Omigato said the word *broken* sent a chill down Dev's spine. He did not want to hear more about what had happened to the young man he'd captured.

"*Cameronsan,*" Prem continued, "the *Daihyo* has recommended, and I concur, that you be given brevet promotion to *tai-i* and put in command of both A and C companies of the 1st Battalion."

Dev was stunned. There were other *tai-i* in the battalion, other *chu-i* with more experience and time in service than he. Bumping him over their heads could cause some bad feeling among the other officers.

Besides, did this mean he was back in the Hegemony Guard for good?

"It has been decided," Omigato said, again in Nihongo. "The experience will do you good."

"*Hai, Omigatosama,*" Dev said, bowing. "*Domo arigato gozaimashte.*" There was nothing else to be said.

Chapter 8

The Emperor shall be the symbol of the state and of the unity of the people, deriving his position from the will of the people with whom resides sovereign power.

—The Constitution of Japan,
Article I
C.E. 1946

Yoshi Omigato sat cross-legged on emptiness, unsupported, unprotected against the vacuum of space. Beneath him, filling the AI-generated universe of this, his private ViRsim, the splendor of the Galaxy stretched across one hundred thousand light-years, the nucleus a red-gold furnace, the spiral arms an entwining mist of blue-white gossamer streaked and smeared by vast rivers of dust and gas.

Omigato's physical body floated weightless within his quarters aboard the *Tokitukaze*, but here his spirit moved unfettered across the galactic sea. It was sobering to realize that at this scale, from this simulated distance, the entire one-hundred-light-year reach of the Shichiju was invisible, a microscopic clumping of dust motes lost among so much glory.

"My Lord . . ."

The voice was that of his analogue and was identical to his own. "Speak."

"The marine has returned from Eridu. He wishes to make his report."

Briefly, Omigato considered having his analogue handle the debriefing. That, after all, was a primary function of such computer-generated alter egos, to serve as buffers against the outside universe.

Not everyone could afford full-range analogues, computer programs that could flawlessly duplicate the thinking of their human counterparts, but those who could often used them as personal secretaries and chiefs-of-staff. They could double for their owners over a ViRcom link, where it was impossible to tell whether you were talking to a software construct or the person behind it.

He rarely used it that way, however. Yoshi Omigato was a traditionalist who believed that personal contact—and personal supervision—were necessities for anyone who wished to exercise true leadership.

"I will see him here."

Gunso Isamu Kimaya's persona materialized before Omigato. The black of his uniform so perfectly matched the velvet black of space that his head and hands and the white and blood-scarlet flash of the 3rd Imperial Marines on his shoulder appeared disembodied, pale shapes against the night. In this, Omigato's virtual reality, Kimaya was a tiny figure, a toy before the looming, planetary bulk of the brooding Imperial *daihyo*.

"*Ohayo gozaimashte, Omigatosama,*" the figure said, bowing. "So sorry, I am unworthy. Thank you so much."

"Not at all. I rejoice that you survived your mission."

Kimaya made a dismissive gesture. "My survival was unimportant, my Lord. However, the disciplines of *kokorodo* served me well. By the time the warstriders returned fire, I was out of the room, shielded from the blast by a sturdy interior fire wall. I would have remained, of course, had that been your will."

"Of course. But it was important that your body not be found in the wreckage." He did not add that others in his employ had been within the building at the same time, waiting to remove or destroy Kimaya's corpse if his escape had not gone as planned. "Your report."

"Of course, my Lord. As you predicted, the demonstration became a riot when the Hegemony officer died. The Guard forces were nearly overwhelmed. Also, as you predicted, the warstriders managed to restore order and disperse the mob. I'm sure my Lord has already seen the casualty figures and damage reports." At Omigato's nod, the marine pressed ahead. "The atmosphere within the city is now one of intense frustration and deep-seated anger. The casualty reports are being deliberately inflated to feed that anger. In the three days since the Winchester demonstration, dozens of minor incidents have occurred. Yesterday, an off-duty Guardsman was assaulted and killed by a local patriot with a knife. There is open talk in the streets of revolt against the Hegemony."

"Very good," Omigato said. "You have done well, Isa-musan."

The marine visibly preened under Omigato's praise. *"Arigato, Omigatosama."* He bowed deeply. *"Domo arigato gozaimashte.* What are your orders?"

"For now, you will wait and watch. Be certain that you and your men are not involved with events on the planet. No Imperial must be connected with these events. Is that understood?"

"Perfectly, my Lord."

"Within a week, two at the most, the balance of your unit will be transferred to Eridu's surface. At that time, you will take your place again with your war-brothers."

"I live only to do your will, my Lord, and the Emperor's."

"The two, *Gunso*, are one and the same. You are dismissed."

Kimaya's image winked out, and Omigato was alone again in the emptiness of intergalactic space.

Gaman, he thought. Patience. That was the key to everything.

A very ancient folk tale contrasted the three great heroes of sixteenth-century Japan by picturing them sitting together, waiting to hear the first cuckoo's song in the spring. Nobunaga, who attempted to unite the fragmented provinces of the Empire by force, who at sixteen years of age had proven himself to be a man of inflexible will and purpose, was supposed to have expressed his mind by the haiku:

> The cuckoo—
> If it does not sing
> I'll put an end to it.

Hideyoshi, the peasant's son who succeeded Nobunaga, who in ten whirlwind years extended his power over all of Japan, organized the country's central government, and attempted the conquest of Korea and China, Hideyoshi, known as the *Taiko*, or "Great Lord," was supposed to have said:

> *The cuckoo—*
> *If it does not sing*
> *I'll show it how.*

And finally, there was Tokugawa Iyeyasu, victor of Sekigahara, the shogun who ultimately and completely united the nation's warring factions and warlords under one rule, who established the Tokugawa Shogunate that eclipsed even the power of the divine Emperor for 265 years. Iyeyasu's approach was characterized by the haiku:

> *The cuckoo—*
> *If it does not sing*
> *I'll wait until it does.*

Yoshi Omigato had always thought of himself as Iyeyasu reborn. He did not believe in literal reincarnation, of course, for privately he was both agnostic and realist, but he nurtured within himself the spirit of the crafty shogun whose patience and understanding of men had won an empire and founded a dynasty.

And perhaps he bore with him some measure of Iyeyasu's karma as well. The shogun had confirmed in his rule the greatness of Japan, founded in the excellence of *Bushido*, the Warrior's Code. In Omigato, that greatness would blossom again, in time to reverse the Empire's decline.

There was within the *Tenno Kyuden*, even within the Imperial Staff itself, a powerful group of officers and aristocrats who called themselves *Kansei no Otoko*, "the Men of Completion." The Kansei Faction feared and detested the blurring of the traditional boundaries that separated the historic purity of the *Nihonjin* from the *gaijin*, the outsiders who had followed *Dai Nihon* to greatness, and the stars. Nowhere was that blurring more apparent than in the humiliation of the Emperor.

Once, the Emperor had been divine, the Son of Heaven, the most perfect of men. After the national disgrace of 1945, he had been demoted to the ranks of ordinary men, the country's leader, nothing more. Within the terms of the foreign-dictated constitution, he'd been relegated to little more than a figurehead, "a symbol of the state and of the unity of the people." His power, the glory that had defined Japan and its people, had been stripped from him.

In nearly six hundred years, that nakedness of spirit and character had never been corrected. The Japanese constitution had been revised several times in those centuries to keep pace with the changes and shifting balances of power on Earth and across Earth's domain among the stars, but still the Emperor remained a man like any other.

Omigato's facial expression betrayed no emotion, but the very thought was like the steady drip of some implacable acid within his heart, searing and destructive. *Tenno-heika*, the Son of Heaven, the divine Lord of the Stars, actually stooped to presiding at conferences, awards ceremonies, and ViRnews interviews with an earthy familiarity that appalled Omigato and the others of the Kansei Faction. He had ordered that *gaijin* like that fool Prem, like Cameron, and like Cameron's accursed father be appointed to high positions within Imperial service that traditionally had been held by Japanese alone. He had actually *encouraged* foreigners to approach him, to think of him as a mortal, and by so doing he had lessened the power that the very idea of *Dai Nihon* and the *Tenno* held over the hearts and minds of men.

Omigato was dedicated to changing all of that, and to erasing this last trace of the Empire's ancient disgrace.

The irony gave Omigato a small, grim pleasure; that he, an agnostic, should be dedicated to restoring the cult of the divine Emperor! He saw no hypocrisy there, however. If he did not believe in the gods, he believed implicitly in the divine purity, worthiness, and destiny of *Yamato*, the spiritual heart of ancient Japan. The Emperor's disgrace must be cleansed, and to do that he would use men like Kimaya and Prem, and even foreigners like Devis Cameron, when they could be molded like potter's clay into the workings of his plan.

Besides, though the fact was not well known, Omigato himself hailed from the Imperial line. The current Emperor was his cousin, as well as a childhood friend and confidant. It was not unthinkable that Omigato himself might one day aspire to the Sun Throne, if such was indeed his karma. . . .

In the meantime, Yoshi Omigato, like Tokugawa Iyeyasu, was willing to wait with an almost superhuman patience as his masterful spinnings rewove the tapestry of history.

Chapter 9

The less government we have the better—the fewer laws, and the less confided power. The antidote to this abuse of formal government is the influence of private character, the growth of the individual. . . .

—*Politics*
Ralph Waldo Emerson
C.E. 1844

The straight-line distance from 26 Draconis to Chi Draconis is 36.11 light-years, and even with no stops along the way the voyage took over a month. Katya and the other former Thorhammers, Sinclair, and his staff had all taken passage as civilians, traveling under false IDs imprinted on their cephlink RAMs provided by the New Constitutionalist underground on New America. Their ship was a freighter, though the passenger accommodations were comfortable enough. Despite her name, the *Saiko Maru*, her captain and crew were all members of the New Constitutionalist Network.

Or the Confederation, as Sinclair had begun calling it. A committee of rebel leaders on New America, he told them, had appointed him to lead the drafting of a document—one very like the Declaration of Independence that had presented American sovereignty to an astonished world 766 years earlier. He had needed a name, something less cumbersome than the New Constitutionalists and less obvious than the Rebellion, that would describe the framework of virtual nongovernment that was holding the movement together.

"There was once," Sinclair explained to them in the *Saiko Maru*'s passenger lounge, one shipboard evening while they were still in K-T space, "a political party in the old United States of America called the Libertarians. Their fundamental philosophies could be summed up, more or less, in two statements: the less government, the better; and what is immoral for the individual or an organization ought to be immoral for the state."

"Sounds like your New Constitutionalists, General," Bondevik said.

"A lot of the NC platform was patterned on the Libertarians, Torolf. Coincidentally rather than deliberately, I should add, since not too many people today have heard of them. But if seven centuries of progressively larger and more powerful governments have taught us anything at all, it's that the bigger the government, the greater the chance for the abuse of power. People are not free when the state taxes their productivity for programs that they don't have a say in. People aren't free when the state that rules them is too big to respond to their needs, or when there's no way to keep the state out of private life."

Katya had thought about her conversation with Dev at Kodama's party, and shivered. Nothing had happened, no one had been listening, but the Hegemony's DHS could easily have picked her up for questioning that night if they'd happened to overhear her. Modern technology, with AIs that could listen in on whispers at thirty meters, optical scanners the size of fingernails, and Virtual Reality communications monitored and enhanced by computer together all created an opportunity for eavesdropping and supervisory government unequaled in any other period of history.

"So what happened to the Libertarians, General?" Anders wanted to know.

"Something else they espoused was the need for people to be responsible for their own actions. Sounds good in principle, but in fact, life is simpler when you can download the fault to parents or poverty or society. The Libertarians were reviled, ridiculed, even accused of sedition simply because they proposed that people should think for themselves. And at the time—late twentieth, early twenty-first-century America, by the way—the clear trend was toward bigger and more powerful government, even though socialist superstates were crashing left and right at the time. The United States government crashed not long after its rivals, of course. Government micromanagement of the economy." He shook his head. "When ordinary mortals have trouble keeping track of their own credit balance, even with RAM implants and AI-assisted transactions, you can't expect a committee, or a bureaucracy, to do better. And that's when *Dai Nihon* stepped in and picked up the pieces.

"Anyway, what we're proposing for the worlds of the Shichiju that want to shake free of the Hegemony is not another interstellar superstate, but something more like a loose alliance. A confederation of equals, rather than a centrist federal state. Something like what the framers of that first Declaration of Independence had in mind."

"Are we going to get a look at this declaration you're writing?" Hagan wanted to know.

Sinclair had smiled. "Not yet. The draft is complete and agreed on, but I'm still cleaning it up. Maybe later."

The *Saiko Maru* docked at Eridu's Babylon synchorbital a week after the events at Winchester, to find the underground buzzing with rumor of open revolt. Despite martial law, enormous demonstrations had continued to erupt in all of the major domed cities. Public assemblies of more than three people were forbidden, but there seemed to be no way of enforcing the rule without lining up a company of warstriders and opening fire. People would meet in twos or threes in a dome's central plaza or park, the threes would mingle . . . grow . . .

And then the plaza would be filled, often with thousands of citizens. Apparently, these were less opportunities for public dissent than they were chances to communicate within the Network. Packets of RAM data were downloaded from person to person at these rallies as part of a kind of welcoming ceremony at the beginning, when everyone present would be asked to join hands for a moment in a display of public solidarity. Those packets could be letters or essays from Network leaders; lists of people arrested by the government; reports of rebel activity censored by the media; organizational directives; stories of government mismanagement, force, or stupidity; even copies of government documents lifted from secure files by Network hackers or by secret members still on the Hegemony payrolls. "Freedom of information," Sinclair had noted, "has always been the foundation stone of individual liberty."

Travis Sinclair used his commpac to make contact with the Eriduan Network from synchorbit, and then the party boarded a sky-el shuttle for the two-day descent to Babel.

Sinclair was in disguise, his appearance completely altered by the application of some specially programmed medical nano. He'd only trimmed the beard and changed its color to brown, claiming that no amount of technology could mask a weak chin, but the infiltration of submicroscopic devices into the skin of his face had puffed out his hollow cheeks, changed the look of his eyes, raised his hairline, altered his nose, and made him look at least fifteen kilos heavier. In gravity, he walked now with a slouch, and Katya suspected that he'd put something in one of his boots to alter his gait. The actual change in his appearance was slight, but the overall effect had been stunning. Wearing a fungus prospector's synthleather bodysuit, which added to the illusion of greater mass, he was unrecognizable.

On the surface, Katya could see most of the city through the Towerdown dome transparency as she stood with the others on a rumbling slidewalk that carried them from the sky-el shuttle complex toward the heart of Babel proper. The city domes hugged the top of a bare rock plateau atop white cliffs plunging one hundred meters to the blue-violet sea. The city had a population of about thirty thousand, most of them employed either by the sky-el, the monorail service, or by a local company called Dahlstrom that provided local flora for several major Imperial pharmaceutical firms. A second, smaller town, called Gulfport, had sprung up along the coastline at the base of the plateau, some one hundred meters below, connected to the towerdown proper by funiculars and enclosed people-mover tracks.

From her vantage point at the top of the plateau, Katya could look east across the Dawnthunder Sea and see the crisp, **V**-shaped tracks of hydrofoils and hovercraft. Closer at hand, monorail tracks snaked their way above the red-and-gold jungle to the north and to the south; Eridu's major cities were in the more temperate zones closer to the poles.

Dev, she'd learned, was almost certainly at Winchester, the planetary capital, some eighty-five hundred kilometers south of Babel.

They were met at the entrance to the Babel dome by a big, rangy, fair-haired man in a military jacket who introduced himself as Lieutenant Vince Creighton. On his left shoulder was a patch bearing a design in white and light blue, a horse's head and lightning bolt above the numeral three. Katya recognized the device at once. It was the insignia of the 3rd New American Mechanized Cavalry, one of the Hegemony units stationed on Eridu, but Sinclair embraced the man like a long-lost comrade. "Not to fear," he told the others. "Vince is on our side even if he hasn't quit his job yet, right?"

"Any time now," the soldier said, grinning. He wore the collar pin of a strider vet. "Just tell me where to park my strider."

"Equipment is still something of a problem in the Network," Sinclair explained to the others. "It's not easy finding safe facilities large enough to store heavy stuff like warstriders, or to repair and maintain them."

"We've got a new lead on that, General," Creighton said. Talking animatedly of rebel logistical problems, he led the way to a skimmer.

The rebels' secret base at Babel—*under* Babel, rather—was a complete surprise.

There were two main city domes resting side by side: Towerdown, surrounding the base of the sky-el and including both the elevator machinery and the shuttle access and debarkation concourses; and Babel itself, a kilometer-wide dome directly adjoining the first. A third city lay below these first two, under ten meters of rock.

Space elevators are not towers built up from the surface of a world. They are bridges hanging down, suspended from synchronous orbit and positioned above the equator so that they never move from the same spot. For engineering reasons, however, they are anchored in place, usually by pylons driven deep into a convenient mountain.

The first colony on Eridu had actually been built underground, as part of the sky-el anchor during its construction. The workers had used nanominers to excavate tunnels radiating out from the elevator base, sealed and pressurized them, and used them as living quarters until the RoPro molds for the first city domes were in place. Later the tunnels were used as storage space for equipment used in the construction of the secondary domes scattered about Babel, and as reservoirs for cool air for the enclosed city's climate control. Though most were still used for storage and all served as cool air reservoirs, the Network had appropriated some of these tunnels, creating a literal underground for the rebels.

Access to the lower levels was through any of dozens of elevators leading to the city's sublevels from either dome; Katya and the others were escorted through the accessway into Babel, then into an apparently empty warehouse, Number 1103, one of dozens in the main dome's warehouse district. Creighton led them down a ramp hidden beneath a meticulously faked shipping crate that slid back into place to conceal the entrance. Other secret routes, he explained, led elsewhere in the city, even winding down through solid rock to the docks of Gulfport at the base of Babel's plateau.

The tunnels were cramped but dry and well ventilated, lined with RoPro sheeting, plastic storage containers, vacuformed triphylene sheets, and durite, the ultradense rockform created by nanomining. A number of interconnecting chambers had been eaten from the solid rock and made as livable as the crowded circumstances permitted. She saw dozens of people as they passed in those corridors, many of them women and children.

Creighton was walking just ahead of Katya, so tall he had to stoop each time they came to a frame opening at a tunnel intersection. "Three of us are New Americans too," she ventured.

"Always good to see a fellow Newamie," Creighton replied. His casual use of the southern New American slang for an inhabitant of 26 Draconis V startled and pleased her. It had been a long time since she'd heard it used.

"So where're you from, *Chu-i?*"

"Please," he said, wincing. "We don't use Impie ranks down here."

Imperial forces, naturally, used Nihongo ranks, while local militias used their equivalents in the local language. Hegemony forces officially used Nihongo rank, but more often and informally used the Inglic form, *lieutenant*, for instance, instead of *chu-i*. Evidently, the rebel forces were shedding every vestige of the Imperial structure.

"Sorry," she said.

"Hey, no static. Anyway, I'm from Faraday," he said, naming a large town on New America's largest south-hemisphere continent. "Been ages, though."

"Are you all Newamies in the 3rd Mech Cav?" she asked.

Creighton tossed a smile back over his shoulder as they walked. "Hardly. I guess it's about half and half now, the old hands from back home and the new kids from here."

It was standard Hegemony practice to station Guard units on some other world of the Shichiju than the world where they were raised. It was difficult for nationalistic or revolutionary fervor to take root in a military unit stationed among strangers in a foreign country. Homeland and family were the two major rallying cries of any war, *especially* a revolution, and it was always better for the state if its military personnel didn't form too close an attachment to the people they were protecting.

That, at least, was the theory, but it didn't take into account the fact that the Guard units continued to recruit at their new posts. They had to, to replace the old hands who retired or transferred or died, and the newbies taking their place were mostly kids drawn from the world where the unit was stationed. Men like Devis Cameron—an Earther who'd traveled all the way to Loki to enlist in the Guard—were the exception rather than the rule.

It gave Katya an eerie, almost superstitious feeling, realizing how a unit could melt away like that. There were damned few Thorhammers like her left who'd been recruited on New America. So many people she'd known from her homeworld were dead now. Raul Guiterrez, Mitch Dawson, Chris Kingfield; they'd all been fellow Newamies, and all had died fighting Xenos on Loki. She missed them; sometimes, when she hooked into a strider's circuit, she could still feel them, as though the linkages they'd shared with her in combat lingered still, electronic ghosts adrift somewhere within her RAM implants.

She still had nightmares about Dawson and Kingfield, sometimes, and RAM dumps and therapy didn't seem to help. They'd died while linked with her aboard her warstrider.

"So what happened?" she asked, her voice sharper than she'd intended. The bad memories had upset her. "Did your whole unit desert? Or just you?"

"Oh, I haven't deserted, ma'am. Not yet, anyway. Some have, but I'm still puttin' in my watches at a base south of here called Nimrod." He grinned at her. "I'm just a rebel in my spare time, you might say."

"Doing what?"

"Oh, weapons training. Strider maintenance. We help people get away, mostly. Like those folks we passed back there. The government's been cracking down pretty heavily on violators lately . . . the people who don't like what the Hegemony's doing and are dumb enough to say so."

"Dissidents," Hagan said.

"Free people," Sinclair corrected him, "who simply want to stay that way."

"I'm still having some trouble pulling all of this together, General Sinclair," Katya said. They came to a door in the passageway, and Creighton stopped, ushering them through. "I'd heard there was a rebel underground, of course, but I've never heard of anything like *this*! What do you do down here, anyway? Build bombs?"

They entered a large room, well lit and with a conference table that made the place look more like a planning center in a HEMILCOM headquarters than something in an underground, illegal city.

Sinclair smiled. "For obvious reasons we don't advertise our presence. However, we run what we are pleased to call our 'liberty-el.' A few centuries ago, the term would have been 'underground railway.' "

"Railway?" Rudi asked. "Is that like a monorail?"

"A monorail with two maglev floater tracks instead of one," Hagan explained. "Old technology."

"We try to help get people out from under the authorities' heels," Sinclair went on. "We let them hide in places like this, or we smuggle them to places where they're not likely to attract official notice. Some we even move off-planet. Most we resettle in Outback towns where the officials don't look or don't care."

Even that, Katya thought, would be difficult on a world of enclosed bubble-cities. Someone who got in trouble with the local authorities couldn't simply leave. There would be ID checks at each airlock door, passes for travel aboard monorails or hydrofoils, bodyscans for weapons, internal passports. . . .

"We have our own printing presses down here," Creighton said. "And facilities for generating new cephlink IDs and records."

"How'd you get into all of this, Lieutenant?" Hagan asked Creighton. "If you don't mind me asking."

Creighton looked away. "A year ago I married a local girl," he said. "She was a Lifer. Didn't care for the Hegemony idea of wiping out the local flora and fauna in favor of ours." He shrugged. "Me, I didn't care much one way or the other, but she got arrested in a demonstration in Karnak. They let her go after a couple of weeks, but, well, the rebriefings were pretty rough for her. She . . . wasn't the same after that."

Katya had heard stories about DHS interrogation techniques . . . and about "rebriefings." There were ways of using a person's own RAM and link implants against them. . . .

"She was terrified of getting picked up again," Creighton went on. "Some buddies of mine in my unit told me about the liberty-el, and that's how I got mixed up in it. They helped her dump the garbage the DHS fed her, got her a new cephlink ID, and got her away to . . . well, to a small town, a plantation, really, a few kilometers up the coast. The Hegemony Authority doesn't have more'n three people in the whole dome up there, and the Impies never bother with little places off in the Outback."

"And now you're here helping other people . . . escape."

He looked at her, his eyes hard. "Something like that."

Sinclair was sitting at the conference table, an odd, blank look on his face. Katya had seen analogues look like that, when they paused in the middle of a conversation to refer back to their human control. It was, she realized, his commpac. He must be in communication with someone else, or with a computer net AI. The color had drained from his face, and for a moment she thought he might fall.

"General? Are you okay?"

He held up a warning finger and continued to stare into empty space, listening intently. The others around the table waited, the silence unbearable.

Then something inside Sinclair seemed to let go and he sagged a bit. He closed his eyes. "Oh my God."

"What's wrong, General?" Lee Chung asked.

His eyes opened, and he looked first at Chung, then at the others. "It's the Imperials," he said. "They've just used what they like to refer to as 'the nuclear option.' "

Chapter 10

Experience should teach us to be most on our guard to protect liberty when the government's purposes are beneficent. Men born to freedom are naturally alert to repel invasion of their liberty by evil-minded rulers. The greatest dangers to liberty lurk in insidious encroachment by men of zeal, well-meaning but without understanding.

—Louis D. Brandeis
U.S. Supreme Court Justice
C.E. 1928

"Who is he?" Katya asked. The lights in the conference room had dimmed, and holographic ghosts shimmered and glowed above the center of the table. At the center was a corpulent, swarthy man in expensive-looking garments, addressing a city crowd from the depths of a public holo-screen.

"Jamis Mattingly," Sinclair replied. "Fusion power plant executive. He also happens to be the Network leader on Eridu."

Several other people had joined the group in the conference room. A thin, redheaded girl named Simone Dagousset had been introduced as one of the rebels' sharpest AI system hackers. Another was an Eriduan *oberstleutnant*, a lieuten-ant colonel with the Babel militia named Alin Schneider. Silver-haired, spare-framed, surgically precise in his speech and manner, Schneider was the coordinator of all Network cells in Babel.

"He and his followers had their headquarters in Winches-ter until the riot last week," Schneider added. "We have had reports that the dissident organization in Winchester was completely destroyed when they sent in the Hegemo-ny warstriders."

"Affirmative on that," Creighton said. "Since then, Mattingly and his top people have been hiding out in Tanis. That's a mining community in the Euphrates Valley, about a hundred klicks northwest of Win-chester."

"Mattingly himself sent this report," Sinclair said. The images they were watching were being downloaded from Sinclair's RAM through his commpac to the room's projection system. The scene shifted from Mattingly's speechmaking to a line of black Imperial warstriders stilting across a plain foot-deep in yellow vegetation. Katya could read the Imperial designations on their hulls.

"We've been staying out of the public eye for the past week," Mattingly's voice said from a hidden speaker. "But things have started moving damned fast down here, and we're going to have to act. This morning, Impie Marine striders planted two nuke penetrators not ten klicks from Karnak. They claim they've picked up sign of Xenophobe movement underground, and that they were delivering a preemptive strike. Listen to this."

The scene shifted again, this time to a Japanese man wearing the red sash of an Imperial *daihyo*. "The Emperor recognizes your discontent and your concerns for your own well-being," the man was saying. His words were in the artificial and slightly stilted Inglic of a translator program, and didn't match the movements of his lips. "It is my solemn promise to you, the people of Eridu, that your questions, your concerns, yes, your demands for greater autonomy in your own affairs be addressed at the earliest possible time.

"I must tell you now, however, that a grave danger to our mutual well-being on this world has forced upon us the need for drastic and far-reaching action. The Xenophobes, which have begun surfacing at diverse points on Eridu, threaten to destroy the Hegemony colonies on this world and render moot such relatively minor questions as how to administer an autonomous republic within the Hegemony, or whether or not it would be wise to terraform the planet. . . ."

"*Kuso*," Creighton said. "Old Oh-my-gosh's been dangling that 'autonomous republic' carrot in front of our noses for a couple of months now."

"Quiet, please," Sinclair said. "Listen. . . ."

"Now is the time to drop our differences," Omigato continued. "We are faced with an alien plague, a danger that threatens dissident and loyalist, Imperial and Hegemony colonist alike. Acting in my capacity as representative for His Majesty the Emperor himself, I have this date directed that nuclear weapons be released for use against deep concentrations of Xenophobes identified underground in the area near Karnak. The operation has already been carried out and has been judged a complete success.

"However, for the common safety of the citizens of the Euphrates Valley, I am directing that an evacuation program be started, effective seven days from now. Special refugee centers are being constructed now at sites closer to Winchester, where Hegemony and Imperial forces can offer full and complete protection from these enemies of Humankind. . . ."

"My God," Simone said, her eyes very wide. "They're actually going to do it."

"That's always been our biggest worry here," Sinclair explained to Katya and the other Thorhammers. "That the Imperials might use the Xenos as an excuse to exert more control over the populace. Since the first Xeno surfaced here a few months ago, there's been talk about bringing in depth charges, and the need to relocate large parts of the population for their own protection."

"They didn't do that on Loki," Katya pointed out.

"Loki's population isn't as dispersed as Eridu's," Schneider said. His face looked gray, and his voice was weak, as though he was having trouble getting the words out. "And here . . . here those weapons are aimed at the people as much as at the Xenophobes. Excuse me." Abruptly, he rose and left the room.

"You have to understand," Simone said quietly after he'd gone. "His daughter is stationed in Winchester. With a Hegemony strider unit. This . . . this latest declaration almost certainly means war, and he's wondering if he's going to be meeting his own daughter in combat."

"I still don't understand," Katya said. "Nukes worked against the Xenos on Loki. What's the problem here?"

"The Imperials' biggest worry on Eridu isn't the cities so much as it is the little outlying communities, the places where the Heggers can't maintain control." Sinclair's eyes flicked to Creighton, who was sitting at the table with his hands folded before him. "Places like where Vince's wife is hiding. The nuclear option gives them the excuse they need to eliminate that problem. They'll call for all the outlying plantations and towns to be shut down . . . 'for the duration of the emergency.' The populations will be transferred to camps 'for their own safety' and interned in some sort of protective area."

"How do you know this?" Hagan asked.

"We've seen the plans," Simone said.

"And Simone should know," Creighton added. "This is the lady who hacked them from HEMILCOM's Babylon AI files." He shook his head slowly. "If they pull this off, we'll never be free of 'em. It'll be rules and regulations, 'Where's your internal passport?' and 'Let me see your link ID.' "

"Do any of you know what it's like in the big metroplexes on Earth?" Sinclair asked.

Katya nodded. "Dev—Lieutenant Cameron—was from BosWash," she said. "He told me about them."

"Then you know about the system that feeds and houses the majority of Terra's population." He sighed. "Sometimes I think that the government wants nothing more than to reduce the entire human race to *fukushi*. Put every man, woman, and child on social welfare. Take care of all their needs. Give them free implants so they can work and pay taxes and stay happily linked to their sims. Feed them, educate them, entertain them. Number them, watch them, tax them, *control* them."

"I guess the control part follows, huh?" Bondevik asked. "If the population depends on you for everything—for food, security, whatever—then you've got them right where you want them."

"Government thrives by growing at the individual's expense," Sinclair said. "Unless it's pruned back from time to time, the state's power only grows. That's what the New Constitutionalists are all about. We're gardeners."

"Unfortunately, many people prefer the security offered by the state," Lee Chung said. "They don't want . . . pruning."

"We have no argument with those billions on Earth happily vegetating in their metroplex towers," Sinclair said. He was speaking quickly now, the anger sharp in his words. "We *do* object to the Hegemony telling us how to run our lives, harassing our citizens, demanding ever bigger bites of our lives, of our *souls*. No government as ponderous as the Hegemony can speak on behalf of all of the citizens living in one small nation or colony. To try to force one government on every citizen on seventy-eight worlds is absurd, a monstrous exercise in applied megalomania. What does some bureaucrat in Singapore Orbital know about me living out on New America, about how I live, about what I think of ViRdrama sex or the Imperial cult or how I want my kids educated? Damn it, he *can't* know, and he has no business putting his nose in my affairs."

His vehemence surprised Katya. Sinclair's reputation was that of a philosopher—quiet, studied, rational, perhaps a little on the eccentric side. But he was visibly furious now.

"You're still going to have a hell of a time getting most

people to understand that," Lee said. "Or getting them to care."

"Fortunately," Sinclair said, "revolutions don't involve *most people*. At least, not at the beginning. . . ."

Later, Katya and the others were taken on a tour of the underground facilities, and they met some of the people living there. Katya was frankly astonished at the range of people joined together under the rather all-inclusive banner of the Eriduan Network.

On Eridu, the environmentalist movement had been the catalyst for rebellion, but there were as many different approaches and agendas to what they perceived as Eridu's problems as there were groups advocating them. Over a year before, the Hegemony had first announced the plan to terraform Eridu, promising a world of abundance where breathing masks wouldn't be needed for out-of-doors, where homesteaders could live where they wanted without being forced to huddle together in transplas domes. The plan had generated a bewildering melee of envie and dissie factions.

One group, the Scientific Rationalists, suggested that studies be undertaken to find a means of helping the Eriduan ecology adapt to changing conditions, genetic nangineering on a planetary scale. Several offshoots of the old Green Party held that Man had no moral right to interfere with an alien ecology simply because it was different. Universal Life held that view and added that even tampering with prebiotic worlds like Loki was robbing whole worlds of their evolutionary destinies. They suggested that Man should restrict himself to totally dead worlds with the heat, gravity, and water appropriate to human settlement—rare—or to planets like New America that were more or less compatible to Terran biochemistry—rarer still. Perhaps most extreme were the Weberites, named for their founder, who advocated a wholesale return to Earth, with the Imperium footing the bill. Man had never been meant, they insisted, to spread beyond the boundaries of the perfect blue world created by God for Man.

The environmentalists might have started the dissident movement on Eridu, but the issue had grown far beyond environmentalist concerns. Fungus prospectors and grennel harvesters feared that there would be no more work with the wholesale extinction of Eriduan life. Antimonopolist activists pointed out that terraforming Eridu would grant more power to Japanese space-based industries, which disliked competition from nonsynthesized raw materials imported from worlds like Eridu and New America. Anti-Hegemonists feared greater control over private lives, while every Eriduan colonist feared the higher taxes that would be levied to pay for planetary engineering. Large segments of the populations at Eridu's north and south poles pointed out that a reduction of planetary temperatures might well bring on extensive glaciation, even an ice age, and force the migration of most of the population to warmer, ice-free zones. A few doomsayers pointed out that glaciation would lock up all of Eridu's limited surface water and divide the planet between ice caps and barren desert.

"It's amazing that so many different factions have found a home with you," Katya told Sinclair. They were walking along one of the Babel Underground's tunnels. "You can't possibly keep all of them happy."

"We're not in the business of making people 'happy' with us, Katya. It just happens that, no matter what their background, all of these groups see the same problem—the government. The Confederation doesn't promise to make things better, but it does promise to let them have a crack at fixing what they think is broke. Ah! Listen!"

They stopped in the passageway, and Katya could hear music. Sinclair gestured toward an open door farther along the passageway and she stepped through, entering a large circular room that had been made over into a lounge.

Perhaps thirty men and women were gathered there, most of them young. They sat in a circle around a woman with somewhat Amerind features, straight black hair, blue eyes, and a red headband. She was sitting cross-legged on the floor and she was playing a mentar, its curved sounding board resting in her lap as her hand caressed the slick black glossiness of an implant 'face. Music danced and wavered in the air, weaving chords and rhythms called from the woman's mind through her link with the instrument.

Those in the room seemed linked as well, though not physically. Their voices blended with the mentar's as they sang along. Katya recognized the tune at once, an old, old folk song she'd known on New America and not heard for years.

> Worlds grow old and suns grow cold
> And death we never can doubt.
> Time's cold wind, wailing down the pass,
> Reminds us that all flesh is grass
> And history's lamps blow out.
> > But the Eagle has landed. Tell your children when.
> > Time won't drive us down to dust again.

"It's called 'Hope Eyrie,'" Sinclair murmured during the bridge between verses. "Know it?"

Katya nodded, listening.

> Cycles turn while the far stars burn,
> And people and planets age.
> Life's crown passes to younger lands,
> Time brushes dust of hope from his hands
> And turns another page.
> > But the Eagle has landed. Tell your children when.
> > Time won't drive us down to dust again.

> But we who feel the weight of the wheel
> When winter falls over our world
> Can hope for tomorrow and raise our eyes
> To a silver moon in the opened skies
> And a single flag unfurled.
> > For the Eagle has landed. Tell your children when.
> > Time won't drive us down to dust again.

The people in the room singing along or listening seemed totally caught up in the music. Katya saw several faces, men's and women's alike, with wet eyes. Chung was in the group, she noticed, nodding with the beat, and Hagan too, a far-off smile on his lips.

One of the handful of popular folk classics surviving since the earliest days of space exploration, "Hope Eyrie" was popular on New America, where something like sixty percent of the population was descended from American colonists. In haunting, minor chords it recalled both the glory of Apollo and the bitterness of lost opportunity.

Irrationally, the song tugged at old memories, making her almost homesick. Her Ukrainian mother, years before, had told her a story about "Hope Eyrie," how translated first into Russian, then into Polish, it had become an underground song for *Solidarnosc*, a revolutionary underground in late twentieth-century Europe very much like the Network. The Eagle, she gathered, had been a totem of powerful nationalistic imagery for the Poles.

We know well what life can tell:
If you would not perish, then grow.
And today our fragile flesh and steel
Have laid their hands on a vaster wheel
With all of the stars to know
    That the Eagle has landed. Tell your children when.
    Time won't drive us down to dust again.

From all who tried out of history's tide,
Salute for the team that won.
And the old Earth smiles at her children's reach,
The wave that carried us up the beach
To reach for the shining sun.
    For the Eagle has landed. Tell your children when.
    Time won't drive us down to dust again.

There was no applause when the last chord sparkled into silence, only a long, collective sigh. "That piece has a very special meaning for Americans," Sinclair told Katya in a low voice. "I suppose it reminds us that *we* were first, before the Japanese, before the Terran Hegemony. We were great once. We will be again."

"My ancestors came from Kiev and Athens, General. We remember that those first pioneers came in peace for *all* Mankind."

"I guess you can look at it either way. The triumph of a nation. The triumph of the species. Either way, it should have been the beginning of a whole new era. An explosion of human diversity and culture and social experiment that filled Earth's Solar System.

"But the next men to set foot on Earth's moon were Japanese. They created a monopoly on space-based industries and never let go. We're living with the results of that to this day."

Katya studied the faces in the circle as they started another song. Most of them were so young . . . the student body of a school rather than an army. "Who are all these people anyway?" she asked Sinclair. "Refugees? They don't look like revolutionaries."

"Oh, they're refugees, I suppose. Most of them. But they're also the Confederation army." He pointed to a boy sitting across from the mentarist. "That guy was a Lifer activist. The Authority arrested him, forced him to download his entire RAM, and tried to rebrief him. It didn't take and he came here.

"The girl next to him, in the red skinsuit? That's Natalia. She couldn't afford anything better than the government's level one implant, but she had a friend who could get her the nano for a Model 200 and some unlicensed T-sockets. She got the implant, but the ID imprint was faulty. It gave her away the first time she tried to get a job. She managed to get away, though, and her friend brought her here.

"Now the guy in green, with the mustache . . . he's dangerous, a deserter. From Creighton's company, in fact. Name's Darcy, and he'd be shot if the bastards caught him. Next to him is Simone. You've met her. She's an absolute wonder with computers. Maybe too much so, because she was arrested for hacking the Heg Authority's tax offices.

"And that," he said, pointing at the mentarist, "is Lorita Fischer. She's in trouble because of her music."

Katya's eyebrows arched. "Her music?"

Creighton was sitting close enough to hear. He turned, grinning. "Hey, stuff like what she sings is seditious, didn't you know? Makes Newamies like us proud to be what we are, proud to be independent sons of bitches . . . instead of following the party line."

Katya listened to the next song and applauded softly with the others when it was done. But some deep reservations had taken hold of her, and she was having trouble shaking them.

The Rebel army consisted of kids and a ragtag mob

of people representing a dozen different factions, political movements, and even criminal elements—a deserter, an illegal hacker, and maybe worse. None of them could be expected to have the same agenda or even the same way of going about the deadly serious business of revolution as their comrades. It was a recipe for chaos at best, for disaster at worst.

She might believe in the revolution now and subscribe to its ideals, but she had a terrible presentiment that the movement was doomed to failure. How long could such a disjointed and fragile alliance last against *Dai Nihon*?

In her own mind, she gave them perhaps one chance in ten.

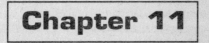

Chapter 11

> *Weapons are an important factor in war, but not the decisive one; it is man and not materials that count.*

—Mao Tse-tung
C.E. 1938

The Confederation army needed three things desperately: equipment of all kinds, professional training, and seasoning. The Thorhammers couldn't help with the first, and only combat, God help them, would help the last, but Katya could set up a training schedule in an attempt to pass on to the newbies some of what she and the others had learned in years of Warstrider service.

Since Katya had arrived on Eridu, the notion of hijacking a comel and using it to run a Confederation version of Operation Yunagi had nearly faded away, not so much forgotten as moot. Network Intelligence had not even been able to learn if there were comels on Eridu yet, or where they might be stored. The Imperial use of nuclear weapons proved that the Imperials weren't interested in peaceful communications with the Xenos, and that meant that Katya and the others might never get their chance.

Almost in compensation, then, Katya threw herself into working with the newbies. She'd run military training programs both on New America and on Loki, and she was able to help now with the selection and indoctrination of warstrider recruits. Only those with both T- and C-sockets could jack warstriders, of course, since temporal sockets were needed for data input, while the cervical socket was necessary for direct neural feedback to the cybernetic actuators. Few of the recruits had direct experience with anything more complex than constructors or the various all-terrain striders used in the rugged Outback.

That was enough to get started with, however, for the principles of cybernetic jacking were the same whether the machine was a warstrider, a starship, a four-legged cargo hauler, or a fifty-ton constructor. In fact, many of the handful of warstriders in the rebel inventory were actually converted civilian machines. Those newbies without the proper hardware were slated for the legger infantry, learning how to maneuver in full combat armor and how to operate, clean, and assemble laser weaponry, assault rifles, and stunners. With seemingly endless drill, and with simulators rigged from ViRcom units smuggled into the Babel Underground, the recruits began shaping up.

They'd already chosen a name for themselves: the Eridu Freestriders.

The Freestriders' few available combat machines were kept at a jungle base, a collection of domes and underground storage facilities called Emden on the maps, located about fifty kilometers southwest of Babel. A fungus prospectors' trading and outfitting center for the past forty years, it had a permanent population of about fifty settlers, with perhaps half that number of transients at any given time . . . precisely the sort of place that Omigato would want to shut down. Already a Network member, the *husmeister* of the place had invited the rebels to use Emden for field training, for maintenance and storage of their heavy equipment, and as a staging area for operations in the jungle.

In Katya's opinion, the Freestriders were a warstrider unit in name only. It possessed one LaG-42 Ghostrider, two RLN-90 Scoutstriders, an Ares-12 Swiftstrider and a LaG-17 Fastrider, all of them compscammed from various Hegemony stores depots on the planet. Simone Dagousset, Katya learned, fully deserved her reputation as a genius when it came to any kind of computer hacking, and there were a handful of others like her in the rebel organization. By hacking false repair, replacement, or breakage write-off orders through various HEMILCOM stores facilities, they'd had those striders shipped to cargo depots at Babel, where rebel jackers had faked authorizing 'face IDs and simply walked them away.

By similar methods, four lumbering construction striders had been appropriated from some city dome or other and fitted out with bolted-on sheets of duralloy and jury-rigged lasers. Ammo, spare parts, and maintenance gear were almost nonexistent, however, and the strider squad bay was an empty equipment shed in the jungle.

Someday—come the revolution, as Sinclair liked to say—Creighton and other part-time rebels in the 3rd Mech Cav would add their own striders to the Confederation inventory, but that couldn't be allowed to happen until the rebels were strong enough to take on the Hegemony openly. In the meantime, the part-timers' positions with the government's forces were too valuable to jeopardize. Until covert insurrection became outright war, the rebels would have to make do with what they had: nine warstriders—four of them totally undeserving of the name—with almost nothing in the way of service or maintenance support if they broke down.

"This," she told the assembled group of recruits, "is a warstrider. It is bigger than you, faster than you, one hell of a lot stronger than you, and it's heavily armed enough to take on an army all by itself. Nonetheless, any one of you can take one of these things down solo, *if* you know how to go about it."

They were gathered in a clearing outside of Emden's main dome, in front of the hulking, unmoving statue of a LaG-42 Ghostrider. Nanoflage netting, designed to screen them from the prying eyes of HEMILCOM almost directly overhead, cast a pool of welcome shade, but it was still stiflingly hot.

They all wore breathing masks and life support packs, of course, but most, men and women both, had stripped down to briefs and boots in the steamy, early morning heat. Part of the training was getting these kids used to living and working outside, whatever the climate, and working with machines too big to demonstrate inside was a good excuse. But as the long morning wore on, they would be forced to move indoors. Eridu's sun, which the locals called Marduk, was too intense to take unprotected for long.

As she stood in the clearing lecturing her class on the weaknesses of warstriders, her T-shirt already plastered unpleasantly against her skin, it occurred to Katya that a little terraforming on this hothouse might not be such a bad idea. Eridu, baked by a hotter sun in its early history, had less water overall than Earth, with shallow and land-locked seas, but the humidity still hovered around ninety percent in the equatorial zone. The vegetation surrounding them was a riot of red and orange; the molecule that served as chlorophyll on this world, transforming sunlight to energy, was a sulfur compound that stained the vegetation with its characteristic golden hues. It was a strange world, and a hostile one; humans could not walk abroad without respirators and masks. Chi Draconis—Marduk—provided energy enough to create an amazingly active local flora, including species that moved fast enough to be considered hunters in their own right.

But Katya knew that of all the life forms encountered in Eridu's jungles, the deadliest was certain to be Man.

"We've had warstriders now since the twenty-second century," she lectured. "There've been God knows how many designs since they first saw service, but their basic appearance and function haven't changed much in three hundred fifty years."

She knew the history of combat machines cold, the way any good craftsman knows his tools. She did not have it loaded into her RAM, however, which was why she had to pass the data on through lectures rather than palm-to-palm 'facing. Besides, Katya was old-fashioned enough to feel that knowledge acquired by more traditional means—through Mark I eyes and ears, especially—was somehow more a part of a person than data downloaded through nano-grown circuitry into personal RAM.

It just might be the difference between artificial and natural memory that saved a trooper's life someday, especially if he was on foot and facing a twenty-ton, two-legged behemoth.

Tanks—those lumbering, treaded, steel monsters of the twentieth century—had been rendered obsolete early in the twenty-first century by the worldwide proliferation of shoulder-launched AP rounds and smart missiles that could penetrate any armor. It had been another century and a half before materials science had produced lightweight armor that could survive the modern battlefield, leading to the revival of armored combat machines.

The first warstriders had been bipedal construction and freight vehicles that could traverse nearly any terrain. Jury-rigged with armor plate and light laser weaponry, the warstriders of the 1st Dai Nihon Mechanized Cavalry Division had been irresistible at Seoul and Shenyang, during the Manchurio-Japanese War of 2207.

Even after three centuries, though, warstriders were still controversial. Their critics liked to observe that, like the tanks of an earlier era, they were slow and cumbersome compared to aircraft or airspace vehicles; their advocates insisted that basic infantry combat still required ground forces capable of crossing a battlefield, taking the high ground, and holding it, tactical doctrine unchanged since the armies of Sumer and Egypt. And warstriders were infinitely more survivable on the modern battlefield than armored infantry, as well as being more mobile in varied terrain, better armed, and more terrifying to any nonstrider adversary. During the past three centuries they'd done far more than survive the modern battlefield. They had transformed it.

Yet throughout those centuries, warstriders had only rarely faced one another in combat.

That was one aspect of the Rebellion that had been troubling Katya since before her arrival on Eridu. Save for the simulated reality of training exercises, striderjacks rarely had to think about strider-to-strider tactics. Not many planetary militias could afford even one warstrider regiment, though most had a few old-model clunkers for show. More modern designs were restricted to Hegemony units, while Imperial forces were equipped with the very best—the fastest, smartest, and deadliest war machines in human space. In theory, at least, the distribution meant that planetary militias could never challenge Hegemony forces militarily, while Hegemony units would not be able to win against *Dai Nihon* Imperials. Long ago, the threat of striders fighting striders had become as improbable as . . .

. . . as improbable as the collapse of the Hegemony. That, she realized with a start, was a large part of what had been troubling her these past few weeks. If the gathering anti-Imperial movement triggered war, it would be a *civil* war, rending the Shichiju and setting former Hegemony strider units against loyalist and Imperial forces together. The thought terrified her, but it took her a moment to recognize why.

It wasn't the fact of armored combat alone, certainly. Katya had faced warstriders of a sort in battle before; Xeno Betas were human combat machines captured and nanotechnically reworked by the Xenophobes into parodies of their former selves, shattered, half-melted hulks known with biting black humor as "Xenozombies." But in a civil war things would be terribly, gut-twistingly different. Colonel Schneider might find himself up against his own daughter on the battlefield.

She might find herself jacking a rebel strider in combat against an identical machine jacked by Dev.

The thought, when she let herself examine it, carried with it an almost paralyzing depression. Could she fight Dev, if she had to, in the dirty, thunderous, close-ranged exchange of an armored clash? She honestly didn't know. Hell, could she face *any* warstrider in combat, knowing that the pilot might be an old friend, a fellow New American maybe, someone who'd trained with her or maybe once jacked a Ghostrider in her platoon?

She didn't know, and that shook her worse than anything she'd ever had to face.

Since arriving at Emden, she'd learned more about where Dev was and what he was doing. Network Intelligence had confirmed that he was a company commander now, stationed with the 4th Terran Rangers in Winchester, further that he had been the one responsible for shutting down Network operations in the capital by breaking up a mass demonstration and personally capturing a rioter who, unfortunately, had known most of the Winchester Network's organization.

Dev Cameron, damn him, was still taking his loyalty to Hegemony and Empire seriously.

"So the weak points in any strider under twenty tons," she was telling her class, "are the leg joints—ankles, knees, and hips. No matter how the armor shields are arranged, those spots are going to be vulnerable to satchel charges or point-blank energy discharge."

A faceted, mag-levitated sphere drifted toward Katya from the direction of Emden's main dome, and she interrupted her lesson. "Captain Alessandro," it said with Sinclair's voice. "Sorry to intrude, but I need to see you in my office, ASAP."

Damn. "Right away, sir," she said, and the teleoperated speaker bobbed once and departed. She turned back to the class. "Okay, people. It's getting too hot to work out here anyway. Lieutenant Chung is waiting inside to go over combat field nanotechnics. Dismissed."

Five minutes later she was in Sinclair's office, a small, spare compartment that had once been a Dahlstrom purchasing agent's cubby.

"You weren't wearing your compatch," Sinclair said as she walked in. His face was back to normal now, and his beard was slowly reverting to its original color.

"Sorry, sir," she said. Katya's cephlink equipment didn't include a radio, something for which she'd always been grateful. Soldiers and officers alike usually wore compatches, small adhesion disks that either stuck to the skin behind the ear and jacked into a T-socket, or plugged in directly. In Eridu's climate, though, the adhesion patches made her skin itch and she didn't like wearing them.

Which meant that Sinclair had had to send a speaker hunting for her.

"Our position out here is precarious," Sinclair told her. "Suppose a Hegemony attack had gone down? I would've needed to be in immediate communication with all my officers, instantly."

"Yes, sir," she said, feeling her face burning. Damn, but that had been stupid. "It won't happen again."

He raised a hand. "Easy, Katya, no static. I didn't really call you in here to dress you down. I've got some news for you. We may have a comel spotted."

Katya shivered, but put that down to her sweat-soaked T-shirt cooling in Sinclair's office. A comel! "It's on Eridu? With Dev?"

Sinclair scratched at his beard. "Not quite. The situation is complicated . . . and we suspect that there are some strange political maneuverings going on behind the scenes. The word we've been given is that at least one comel was aboard the *Tokitukaze* all along, and that it's now coming down the sky-el. It'll be in Babel in another thirty hours. After that, it will be loaded aboard a monorail and shipped to *Taisa* Ichiro Ozaka at Karnak. Ozaka is the commanding officer of the Imperial Marines on-planet."

Katya's brow furrowed. "It sounds like they're cutting Dev out of the circuit."

"Could be. There's a power struggle going on behind the scenes right now on Earth. The Kansei Faction—that's a group of very powerful military and civilian traditionalists, including Omigato and Chuichi Munimori himself—is moving to block the appointment of *gaijin* like your friend Cameron from high-ranking posts in the government or in the military. Cameron could be heading for a big fall."

"But why comels? I thought the Impies were nuking the Xenos, not trying to talk to them."

Sinclair's mouth twisted unpleasantly. "Um. Everyone's been damned excited about how comels improve communication between human and alien, with the DalRiss or the 'Phobes. Have you ever thought what they might mean to communication between human and human? Especially, ah, involuntary communication?"

"Interrogation."

"That's what we believe."

She let a hiss of air whistle tunelessly through her teeth. DalRiss comels probably wouldn't allow true telepathy between people, but they would certainly pick up memories, emotions, and impressions. The things would be unparalleled as lie detectors, and they might help an interrogator determine what his subject was most afraid of. There were other possible uses—screening large numbers of people being herded into an internment camp, for example, searching out Network activists or fugitives. All a comel-wearing guard would need to do was touch each person as he or she filed by.

"So our original operation here is on again," Sinclair said. "I want to grab that comel, not only because we can still use it to talk to the Xenophobes, but because of what the Imperials could do with the thing if they get it. Interested?"

She considered. It wouldn't be easy, and her original question remained: Would it even be possible to find an isolated Xenophobe and approach it closely enough to touch the thing without getting killed in the process? Now that the Impies had started nuking them, would humans be able to approach the Xenos at all? If her work with the rebel recruits these past few days had taught her anything, though, it was that they needed help, *allies*, and fast, and maybe the Imperial attacks could be used to convince the Xenos to join the rebel cause.

Maybe. Did she want to try? "Yes, *sir!*"

Chapter 12

Strike where you are strong and the enemy is weak, says the Master, Sun Tzu. Warstrider combat is exquisitely tailored to this basic law of war. The keys to warstrider combat are surprise, firepower, and mobility.

—*Kokorodo: Discipline of Warriors*
Ieyasu Sutsumi
C.E. 2529

Katya pressed forward through almost impenetrable brush, her Ghostrider's outer hull reflecting the warm golds and reds of the surrounding vegetation. Her machine's nanoflage was spotty and imperfect; the molecule-thin layer of reflective nanotechnic units—"nanits" was the popular term—needed to be replaced frequently, for normal wear and tear on a combat strider quickly abraded the surface and weakened the camo effect. The jungle was thick enough, however, that camouflage was only marginally effective anyway. This operation would depend far more on speed, timing, and sheer luck than on technological flourishes like nanoflage.

It did feel good to be back in harness again. Katya had been given the Freestrider's lone LaG-42, which, until then, had been operated by a pool of five or six young jackers, none of whom had been in combat before. "It's not the machine, it's the man," ran the old military maxim, but, by God, it would help if the men knew how to use their machines in the first place! This op would give a few of them a bit of that seasoning they needed.

They were in the jungle southwest of Babel—the Outback, as New Americans thought of the wilderness beyond the tamed and civilized reaches of a world. Her Ghostrider was the only two-slotter in the rebel arsenal; jacked in with her was one of the rebel recruits, a pale-faced kid from Eridu's Euphrates Valley region named Georg Lipinski.

Three warstriders followed closely: Lee Chung in one of the Scoutstriders, Rudi Carlsson in the Swiftstrider, plus Roger Darcy, the Hegemony *sho-i* deserter she'd met her first day in Babel, manning the Fastrider. Bringing up the rear was one of the jury-rigged constructors, a slow, four-legged beast with Karl Braun jacking and Simone Dagousset riding as cargo.

Vic Hagan had been furious when Katya had pulled rank and ordered him to stay behind, but he was the second most experienced member of their team, and if this op went wrong, she wanted him to survive, to carry on with the Thorhammers' training program. The memory made Katya chuckle to herself. *Could* she still pull rank, on Vic or anyone, now that they were no longer working under the Hegemony chain of command? Vic had backed down without raising that point; she would have to talk to Sinclair later about ranks and command authority within the fledgling Eridu Freestriders.

"Did you say something, ma'am?" Lipinski's voice came through her internal link, nervous and quick.

"Negative, Georg," she said. "Stay alert on that laser."

"Y-yes, ma'am."

Warstrider control circuitry could be divied up between the commander, the second slot, and the strider AI. Katya didn't yet fully trust the LaG-42's rebel-maintained AI, though it had functioned fine so far, so she'd reserved both weapons and maneuvering functions to herself. The exception was the Ghostrider's chin turret with its 100-megawatt laser. That she had assigned to Lipinski, though she retained control of the weapon's arming circuits. The laser, in serious need of routine maintenance, had a nasty tendency to overheat when powered up, and she'd ordered Lipinski to monitor the temperature closely and to engage the coolant flow each time the core jacket temp crept above two hundred.

"Temperature's at one-eighty-five," he said—needlessly, since Katya had put the temp readout on her visual display so that she could keep an eye on it as well. "It looks stable."

"When we get back, we're going to have to rebuild that heat transfer system," she said. "It's leaking. I think it needs new coolant seals."

"Yes, ma'am." She could sense the relief in his thoughts, the unspoken echo: *when* we get back!

The jungle was starkly beautiful, a blaze of gold-and-crimson fronds, tangles of slow but visibly moving vines the locals called kriecherweed, and impenetrable masses of orange anemone plants. Gauze-winged flyers flitted among the scarlet branches of towering rotfarns, and larger, unseen somethings crashed about in the thicker masses of brush. The harsh, almost actinic glare of Chi Draconis filtered down through the canopy in rippling flashes and dapples of glorious light, turned golden by the foliage. It was gorgeous— and deadly. The oxygen content outside would keep a human alive for perhaps eight or ten painful, gasping minutes, until either anoxia or CO_2 poisoning finally killed him.

The outside temperature, at least, wasn't too bad today— only forty degrees Celsius, but then it was still early morning in the long Eridian day.

The jungle opened up so suddenly Katya nearly took a

misstep and stumbled. Catching herself, she swung her visual scanners up and down the long, wide slash burned through the forest.

Most places along the monorail line, the maglev rail ran well above the forest canopy, supported on the smooth, angled struts of duralloy pylons, but here, where the land rose sharply toward the foothills of Eridu's Transequatorial Mountains, it had been easier to burn out the jungle and let the track run a meter or so above bare rock. The ground was rubble and bedrock, still showing black, flamer scorch marks. The rail itself was bathed in harsh sunlight, a gleaming silver rail the thickness of a man's leg, held above the ground by stubby pylons positioned along every fifty meters or so of track. Katya was pleased to see that her navigation through the jungle—and the navdata she'd been programmed with—had been accurate. Their goal, a power relay station and switch house, rose above the trees some thirty meters beyond the rail.

Katya's scan verified that they were alone. Power was flowing through the rail, of course, and within the dome-shaped switch house, but there was no sign of life or movement here, save for the restless background motions of the jungle itself. She took three swift strides into the clearing. "Rudi! Lee!" she called. "Perimeter defense! And check that building. Darcy! You're with me."

"Yes, sir." Darcy's voice sounded sullen over the tactical link. Katya was trying not to form judgments of the Freestriders' personnel until she'd had a chance to see them in action, but she'd definitely detected a measure of resentment in the Mech Cav deserter. Darcy was the dark, mustached man she'd first seen at the sing-along in Babel's Underground, and she still didn't fully trust him. According to Creighton, he'd been accused of theft and had elected to take his chances with the rebels instead of facing a HEMILCOM tribunal.

Was it even possible to trust someone who'd broken his oath of allegiance?

As Katya had.

She shook the nagging thought off. "Where's Braun?"

Darcy's LaG-17 Fastrider, a meter shorter than the heavier Ghostrider, turned on spidery, lightly armored legs. The two

50-megawatt lasers, extending like mandibles from either side of the bullet-shaped fuselage, contributed to the ugly, insectlike appearance of the machine. Perhaps unintentionally, those lasers were pointed right at her.

"Fifty meters back, last I saw of him, Captain."

Damn. She should have ridden closer herd on Braun, instead of trusting Darcy to keep an eye on the kid. She shifted frequencies. "Braun? This is Alessandro. Are you okay?"

"Affirmative, Captain," Braun's voice came back. "Just slow going, is all."

"We're at the rail cut. Snap it up. We need your passenger."

"On our way."

She turned, pointedly ignoring Darcy as she surveyed her surroundings again. The sky was clear and green and filled with the hard white light of Marduk. At dusk, she knew, to the north against the pale-shifting glow of Eridu's aurorae, the sky-el could just barely be made out, a silken thread stretched taut between heaven and earth, but it was lost now in the day-glare.

She checked her internal clock. Their movement through the jungle had taken longer than expected . . . but she'd allowed plenty of leeway. Twenty minutes to go. No problem. Chung reported that the switch house was empty, as expected. It housed the automatic circuitry for controlling a siding switch, visible a hundred meters up the line as a prominent Y in the rail.

Beyond that, higher up against the purple mass of the Equatorials, was a saddle-shaped notch through the mountains called Grimalkin Pass. It was a narrow valley with sheer slopes; the siding spur was designed to route southbound monorails off the main line as northbound monos were coming through the pass. The switch house contained the automated circuitry for reading the relative positions and speeds of the monorails, and for controlling the switches.

Sinclair had insisted that their raid take place at this particular siding spur. The rebels didn't want to totally disrupt the only monorail link between Eridu's south polar zone and Babel, for that would be both political and economic suicide. If they could divert the monorail onto the siding, they could restrict any damage to the spur rail and keep the main line open.

The constructor stepped with cumbersome daintiness from the wall of trees and onto the rail cut. With four dish-footed, elephantine legs, broader and squatter than it was long, it had once been a Kawasaki KC-212 heavy cargo transporter, an eighty-ton monster commonly called a Rhino. Now its belly lift and gripper arms had been removed, armor plate had been bolted to the body, and a pair of 50-megawatt lasers in crude ball-and-socket turrets had been mounted on either side of the body.

"We're here," Braun called. "Where do you want us?"

"Drop Simone anywhere. Move it! There's not much time."

"Rog."

The four-legged beast settled back on its haunches, then jerkily lowered itself to within a couple of meters of the ground. A hatch in the belly split open and Simone Dagousset dropped to the rock. She wore dark brown skintights and boots, with a helmet over her red hair, protecting her head against the glare of Marduk. Her lower face was covered by a breathing mask, connected by hoses to the life support pack she wore strapped to her chest.

"The building's clear, Simone," Katya said. She used her internal taccom channel. Simone had a radio transceiver implanted in her skull. "Hit it! We have fifteen minutes."

Simone replied with a wave and dashed across the clearing, vaulting the maglev rail and disappearing toward the domed building.

"Okay," Katya said. "Lee, you cover Simone. Everybody else, take your positions."

Fifteen minutes . . .

They'd rehearsed this a dozen times in the past couple of days in virtual reality simulators. As Chung stood watch by the small domed building, the other four striders took up positions in the jungle, two to either side of the siding switch.

"Captain?"

Eight minutes. *God, don't let something go wrong now!*

"What is it, Simone?"

"I'm into the program, no static."

"And?"

"I'm reading the target, ten kilometers north and coming fast."

"Get ready to throw the switch."

"Uh, I thought I should tell you. From the data I'm reading here, there are two cars on the train."

That rocked Katya back for a moment. *Two* cars! Sinclair's intelligence had predicted that the comel was to be transported to Luxor aboard a single monorail car—a ten-meter-long self-powered vehicle that might carry thirty or forty troops as guards, if HEMILCOM was expecting trouble, which, please God, they weren't. But if a second car had been attached . . .

"Might be extra troops riding shotgun," Chung said. "The comel could be important enough to them."

If that was *all* that was on the second car. But it was up to Katya to decide, and right now. She didn't like the unexpected twist in the plans, especially this close to zero. Her instincts were telling her to abort the op. That second car could be carrying heavier backup than her tiny command could take on.

But then again, this was their only shot at a comel. What would she do, go back and tell Sinclair, "Sorry, Travis, but I was afraid there was something nasty in that second car, so I aborted"? Sinclair would understand completely and tell her it was okay . . .

. . . which made her that much more determined to carry out the mission.

"Go ahead with the program," she told Simone, deciding. "The rest of you, keep sharp. If that second car is armed, I want it disabled with the first shot."

The others acknowledged. What else could be done? Not a damned thing.

"Simone here. I'm ready to cut in."

Three minutes. "Wait one . . ."

A minute thirty, and her sensors were detecting a shiver in the air. "Okay, Simone. Throw the switch."

There was a click and a high-pitched whining sound. A portion of the rail ten meters in front of Katya's position separated, then slid to the right, linking up with the dead-end spur. Scant seconds later, she picked up the bulk of the oncoming monorail, a dull-gray, ultrasleek shape, a flattened cylinder with a low-riding, jet aircraft's nose. The hull spilled over well to either side of the slender maglev rail, hugging it in a cocoon of electromagnetic fields that supported the vehicle, frictionless, above the rail, and hurled it forward at speeds approaching four hundred kph.

It was not going nearly that fast now, however. As soon as Simone had thrown the switch, the fact would have been sensed by the monorail's computer and the drive fields reversed to slow the big machine to a stop. It still took a considerable distance to slow such mass, however, and the train was rushing toward the warstrider ambush with seemingly unstoppable momentum. Katya wanted to say something, "Get ready" or "Stand by" or something inspiring, but she knew there was nothing to be said. With a buffeting wind that lashed the vegetation around her, the monorail rushed past her hiding place, smoothly gliding off the main line and onto the spur. Its speed was now no more than fifty kilometers per hour, and Katya could easily see details of markings and external fittings on that streamlined hull. She saw the second car, almost seamlessly joined to the first, and with heart-pounding relief saw that it was not, as she'd feared, a military design with armor or gun turrets, but a simple cargo car, windowless, with a wide loading door along the side.

When the end of the second car cleared the switch, she gave the order. "Fire!"

Rudi struck first from his hiding place on the far side of the track, his Swiftstrider's Cyclan Arms high-velocity autocannon opening up with a steady *thud-thud-thud* followed almost instantly by the far louder *slam-wham!* of detonating 18mm shells. Braun, hidden to Rudi's left, opened fire a second later, his twin lasers slicing through the lead car's ceramiplas hull like a hot wire through butter. The monorail shuddered, lurched to the side, then came down on the rail with an ear-piercing scream.

"Captain! The laser safety! Captain!" Lipinski's shrill mental shout reached her at last and she remembered to arm the Ghostrider's laser. A second later, a bolt from the LaG-42's chin turret struck the monorail close to the joining of the two cars, opening up a jagged hole a meter wide.

Lightning played across the lead car's skirt and arced along the rail, and then the vehicle's power failed while it was still drifting forward. The streamlined nose came down on the spur rail, hard enough to buckle it, and there was a piercing shriek of ripping metal. The second car's momentum kept it moving forward, crumpling the stricken lead car with a crash like thunder.

Katya understood now Sinclair's insistence on diverting the monorail first onto the siding. The lead car was twisting the maglev rail out of shape as it rode it to the ground. Scraping along bedrock, the car began spilling over, toppling away from Katya's position. To her left, Darcy's LaG-17 was already out of the jungle and advancing toward the crumpling wreck, its twin fifties alternately loosing pulses of coherent light into the hull, which was splitting now, from front to back. With a final, grating shriek of tortured metal and ceramics, the monorail came to a rest, its nose buried in rubble and the lead car lying all the way over on its side. The second car was still powered. Katya could hear the protesting whine of its gyros trying to keep its mass upright.

"Hold your fire, Darcy!" Katya called. "Everybody, hold your fire!" The comel would be well protected within some kind of transport container, but it still wouldn't do to destroy the prize they were trying to capture in fire or explosion.

The second car, teetering half on the rail and half off, was opening up, its cargo loading door sliding back. She saw movement inside. . . .

"Scatter!" Katya yelled suddenly. "Take cover!"

Troops were spilling from the second car, men in the black armor of elite Imperial Marines. Worse, though, was the black, nightmare shape heaving itself out of the vehicle, a knife-lean shape bristling with weapons, supported between powerful legs that held it five and a half meters above the ground.

It was a Kawasaki design, a KY-1001. The common name was Katana, after the traditional Japanese great sword. Massing thirty tons and armed with multiple lasers, autocannon, and missiles, it was one of the deadliest of the Empire's top-line, two-slotter warstriders.

And it was sprinting straight toward Katya's position.

Chapter 13

The soldier is the army. No army is better than its soldiers. In fact, the highest obligation and privilege of citizenship is that of bearing arms for one's country.

—War As I Knew It
General George S. Patton, Jr.
C.E. 1947

At a range of twenty meters, Katya triggered her left-side Kv-70 weapons pack, unleashing a hissing barrage of grenades and M-21 rockets. She knew the grenades would be useless against the Katana's armor, but they might distract the thing for a moment, and they would certainly give the Impie Marines boiling around the monster's feet something to think about. As for the rockets, they were crude, unguided packets of high-explosive, but at practically point-blank range they could hardly miss. Explosions flashed and snapped across the Katana's left leg and torso, stopping its headlong charge, then forcing it back a step to keep its balance. On the ground, the phalanx of armored troops was shredded as grenade blasts tore through its ranks. Some men folded and collapsed like string-cut puppets; most scattered, seeking cover.

Lipinski fired the LaG-42's chin turret laser a moment later, the beam sharply delineated by the boiling cloud of smoke and dust raised by the rapid-fire blasts. Durasheath armor glowed white-hot beneath the laser's caress, then exploded in liquid splatters, leaving a fist-sized hole in the armor covering the left leg actuator assembly.

Katya saw the telltale shift of the Katana's main gun, a 150-MW laser jutting from beneath the hull in savage, priapic mockery. In strider close combat, maneuver was the key to survival. Operating more on instinct than thought,

114

she threw herself to the right; the LaG-42's shocks and parahydraulics shrieked protest as the top-heavy machine nearly overbalanced. The Katana's laser fired in the same instant, the beam slicing past the left side of her hull and striking flame from her left weapons pod.

Darcy's Fastrider was in the fight now, standing fifteen meters to Katya's left, legs flexed sharply to lower the hull almost to the ground. The LaG-17 was pitifully outclassed by the nightmare power of the Katana, but he was loosing bolt after bolt of coherent light into the monster, concentrating on the relatively thin armor covering its right leg. The Katana sidestepped as two solid hits gouged into durasheath close to the back-angled knee, then unloosed a flurry of shots from the paired 88-MW lasers turret-mounted on either side of its hull. Explosions cracked and hissed about Darcy's Fastrider, but he was already in motion, charging *toward* the monster in a desperate bid to get beneath its arc of fire.

Scant seconds had passed since the Katana had first appeared. Rudi Carlsson's Ares-12 Swiftstrider was only now circling past the front end of the monorail's wreckage, trying to get a clear shot at the Katana, while the elephantine bulk of Braun's Rhino came around the back. With odds of four to one, it might be possible to—

The clumsy Rhino staggered as two bolts lanced from the open interior of the monorail car in quick succession, striking the constructor in its belly. Katya groaned. A second black-armored nightmare was rising out of the wreck. Smaller and leaner than the Katana, massing only twenty-two tons, but faster and nearly as deadly as its larger consort, the KY-1180 Tachi mounted a twin 88-MW laser in a flat dorsal turret and carried Mark III weapons packs mounted at either hip joint.

Darcy's Fastrider collided with the Katana, the shock sending both of them crashing to the ground. The Tachi fired again as it stepped clear of the monorail car, and a slab of makeshift duralloy armor dropped from the quad-legged constructor's ventral side as mounting bolts exploded. Braun swung the Rhino to face this new threat, its side-mounted lasers tracking and firing in a deadly one-two, but the Tachi's reply was a shrieking barrage of rockets with armor-piercing warheads, slamming in full-auto fury into the clumsy, four-legged behemoth. Internal explosions rippled through the Rhino's hull; its right-side laser turret shattered in a dazzling eruption of flame and spinning fragments trailing smoke.

Damn! Katya triggered a burst of M-21 rockets from her right weapons pack at this new threat. Rhino conversions might be effective enough against legger infantry, but they'd never been meant to stand up in combat against top-of-the-line Imperial warstriders. A lucky burst smashed the Tachi's right hip joint. Rudi's Ares-12 opened up with its Cyclan autocannon a second later. High-explosive shells slashed into the KY-1180, toppling it against the monorail with a splintering crash.

Rudi's light machine was hit in the same instant; a rapid-fire burst of eye-searing white flame whiplashed into the Swiftstrider with a savage chain of explosions that blasted away the leg actuator assembly in hurtling, smoking fragments, then ripped its right leg from its torso.

The shot, Katya saw, had come from a plasma gun, a massive, two-meter-long squad-support weapon only marginally man-portable. "Rudi!" she yelled over the tac channel. The Ares-12 was toppling slowly to its right, smoke pouring from the gaping hole where its hip assembly had been. "Punch out! Eject!"

There was no reply as the eight-ton machine slammed into rock. She opened up with both of her Ghostrider's machine guns, hammering off 15mm explosive rounds from the guns mounted in each Kv-70 pack. MG fire was almost useless against heavily armored warstriders, but it could be devastating against combat-suited infantry. Twinkling detonations smashed solid rock to gravel, sliced the plasma gunner's cuirass open from shoulder to leg, and nearly tore him in half.

Turning slowly, she walked that twin stream of stuttering, full-auto death across the line of Imperial Marines, cutting them down like a scythe slashing down wheat. Her external mikes picked their screams, masked by the roar of heavy weapons fire. A rocket-propelled grenade streaked low across the field, slammed into her left leg, and glanced off without exploding. She flicked left and chopped down the gunner, almost regretting it; the guy's antiarmor round hadn't had time to arm itself, so close was his target. His mistake cost him his life.

But she couldn't concentrate on the marines, not now. The Katana was already struggling back to its feet. Bringing a fallen warstrider upright after it had been knocked down was always tricky, requiring the pilot's full concentration. Katya pivoted hard, then sent the last of her rockets screaming into the rising machine. Explosions flashed across the KY-1001's hull. The concussion popped an access hatch in a puff of smoke, exposing the colorful bundles of circuit wiring and parahydraulic tubing stuffed beneath the stricken machine's skin. Broken wiring sparked and smoked.

Lipinski still had control of the Ghostrider's main gun, but Katya could show him where she wanted him to shoot.

"Targeting!" she yelled, and in her mind's eye a bright red set of brackets closed on the gaping, sparking wound, which slashed across the Katana's dorsal hull centimeters from the blister housing one of its two pilots. "Hit him, Georg!"

The laser fired, the hundredth-second pulse flashing into the open panel with a sputtering eruption of molten insulation and circuitry. Warnings flashed across her visual display. "We're gonna lose the laser!" Lipinski yelled.

Then the laser circuit went dead as the core overheated and the cooling jacket ruptured. Steam clouds enveloped the Ghostrider in white mist as coolant gushed past melted seals and boiled into the open air.

She shut down the circuit and kept advancing. On the stricken Katana, lightning arced and snapped between the smoking crater in its hull and the ground, and then Katya was hurling the yammering fury of her machine guns at that pried-open chink in the bigger machine's armor. She was so close now to the fallen hulk that shrapnel pinged and ricocheted off her own hull. The enemy strider started to rise once more, and then an internal explosion savaged the Katana, slamming it down, tearing a twin-88 from the side of the fuselage and peeling back a meter-wide strip of duralloy like cardboard.

Shifting, she turned back to face the Tachi, which was hurt but not yet out of the fight. Her rocket volley and Rudi's full-auto cannon barrage had knocked the Tachi back against the side of the monorail and disabled its right leg, but it was still pumping laser fire into Braun's Rhino from an unsteady, leg-bent crouch. The four-legged constructor was standing motionless now, unable to burn in the oxygen-poor air, but with black smoke pouring from its gashed-open hull.

Katya advanced, pounding at the Tachi. She had no weapons left now save for her machine guns, and the ammo loads on those were rapidly dwindling toward zero as she kept hammering round after stuttering round into the chaos of fallen striders and struggling men before her. Dust and smoke gouted from her exploding rounds, and bits of wreckage were flung into the sky from strikes against the monorail's hull. The surviving marines were pulling back now, snapping off shots from their laser rifles that flashed ineffectually from Katya's armor, scattering back into the forest, twisting and dying and falling as Katya's heavy machine guns swept through their ranks. Smoke from the smoldering striders hung like a blanket across the battlefield.

Unstoppable, Katya strode forward, driven now by battle lust. She was a giant on the battlefield, a steel-and-duralloy Valkyrie striding forward in wreathed smoke and flame, death hammering from her weaponry pods. The Tachi's damaged laser turret whined through ninety degrees, taking aim . . .

Then a thundering pulse of explosions shredded the Tachi's armor, smashed aside the laser turret in a tangled ruin, then nearly tore the Tachi's body in half. Lee Chung had arrived from the switch house, his curiously anthropoid RLN-90 Scoutstrider hammering away at the Tachi with a stream of high-explosive shells.

The battle ended with stark abruptness; according to Katya's internal clock, eighteen point two seconds had elapsed from first shot to last.

"Lee!" she called. "Where's Simone?"

"Still in the switch house, Captain."

"Stay with her. I don't want those marines circling back and finding her alone. Darcy! Are you okay?"

"Still here, Captain," Darcy's voice replied. "Power's down thirty percent but I'm still moving."

"You've got overwatch," she told him. "Watch that those Impie leggers don't try a counterattack."

"Yes, sir." There was no resentment, no hesitation in his voice now.

"Lipinski, unbutton and come with me."

She coded the shutdown sequence for the Ghostrider, then pulled her hand from the palm interface. She woke up inside her link pod, a close, dark, chokingly hot tube in a claustrophobic darkness relieved only by a small, wan lighting strip. Removing her cephlink helmet and the connections to her bodysuit, she pulled on a breather mask and life support pack, then donned a pair of gloves that sealed themselves against her cuffs. She slapped a release and the Ghostrider's dorsal hatch whined open. Releasing an access ladder, she climbed to the smoke-clotted rail cut. Lipinski, breathing hard behind his mask, joined her a moment later.

She unholstered her sidearm, a ProTech M-263 rocket pistol, and touched Lipinski's shoulder. "Stay with me," she told him. "We'll check Rudi's strider first."

The Lokan striderjack hadn't had a chance. His light machine was gutted, his link pod torn open by the deadly kiss of a plasma bolt. The pod's interior was splashed with blood and shredded, meaty fragments, very little of it recognizable as human.

Behind her, she heard Lipinski's gasp of recognition, followed by the fumbled sounds of him removing his mask before he vomited explosively. Katya struggled to contain her own rising gore. She'd seen death as violent and as bloody, but it was always a thousand times worse when the broken wreckage was what remained of someone you'd known.

Ghosts, Chris Kingfield and Mitch Dawson and other men and women she'd known through too many years, moaned and whimpered in her ears.

"C'mon," she said roughly. "Get that mask back on."

Lipinski, already pale, tried to draw a shuddering, gasping breath and nearly strangled on the thin, CO_2-heavy air. His eyes bulged in his face.

"Now!" Katya barked, and with trembling hands he pulled the mask back on. She reached over and pressed the feed rate control on his chest pack, giving him an extra kick of oxygen to purge his lungs. CO_2 poisoning could be an insidious thing, unfelt and unsuspected until the victim keeled over unconscious.

He took several deep, shuddering breaths, then nodded, eyes blinking at her against the harsh light.

"Your gun," she reminded him. "We have to check the train."

She led him across the rocky clearing, ducking under one maglev rail and approaching the second, where the two monorail cars lay silent behind the scattered heaps of dead Imperials and the smoking ruin of two warstriders. The Katana, she saw, had been wrecked as badly as the Swiftstrider, with both linkage pods slashed open. The headless and armless torso of one of the pilots hung upside down from a jagged finger of hull metal, still draining into the dust. The black, scorch-streaked fuselage was splashed with blood.

With difficulty, Katya and Lipinski picked their way past the debris and heaped bodies. Some of those men, she noticed with sick horror, were still alive, moving legs and arms in nightmare slow motion.

She wanted to help, but there was nothing to be done for them now. Her unit was too small, their numbers too few, to even think about stopping to render first aid. The suits of most of the wounded had been breached; anoxia and the carbon dioxide in the air would claim them in minutes.

Scrambling up crumpled metal, Katya peered into the second car's interior, ready to duck back if some surviving marines were waiting for her approach. The monorail car was empty. It was dark inside, though sunlight spilled through the open loading door and painted the sharply canted floor with a dazzling slash of white. By the reflected glare, Katya could see the large horizontal braces that had been used to transport the two warstriders. Judging by the speed of their reaction, though, the striders must have been powered up and battle-ready, their pilots already sealed in and linked. Seats lined the car's walls, all empty now. There were weapons lockers tumbled in a pile on the floor, open and empty, and several crates of ammo and weapon power packs. Two armored bodies, marines who'd tumbled back into the open car after being hit, sprawled unmoving at the angle of floor and wall.

There was nothing that might be the prize they sought.

"Forward," she said, gesturing with her pistol. The second car was joined to the first by sliding doors. The first door opened smoothly; the second ratcheted halfway open and then hung up in its twisted frame, but Katya was able to turn sideways and squeeze through. The forward car was smoke-filled and dark, dark enough that she had to switch on the light mounted on her belt. There were more dead marines here—unarmored men who'd died when cannon fire and lasers had slashed open the vehicle—and the hull-crumpling wreck had slammed men, seats, and cargo into a tangled pile at the forward end of the compartment.

Lipinski found what they were looking for after nearly five minutes of desperate searching, a large safe with a palm 'face reader to open it.

The owner of the interface that would have opened that safe was dead. Katya opened it the hard way, burning through the locking mechanism cover with her hand laser, then twisting together a pair of wires inside. A circuit completed and the door hissed open.

Inside was a metal box, as long as her forearm and twenty centimeters deep. A simple touch-lock opened to her thumb.

Within the box was a comel.

She stared at the prize, heart quickening. It was still alive, a rippling, translucent slug perhaps the size of a basketball. She hoped it would stay alive in Eridu's atmosphere . . . but she knew from experience that the bioengineered creatures were uncannily tough, able to survive in a broad range of atmospheres and conditions. Lipinski produced an empty knapsack of heavy plastic-weave cloth, and she sealed the box and packed it away.

"Company coming, Captain." It was Simone's voice, speaking over the radio compatch behind her left ear. "Aircraft, from Babel."

The marines would have radioed for help when the first shots had been fired. Reinforcements would have been dispatched at once.

"On our way out," she replied. "Darcy! Start setting the charges!"

"Already done, Captain. Just give the word."

"Let us get clear first."

Katya and Lipinski scrambled clear of the wreckage and back into Marduk's burning daylight. Crossing to the waiting Ghostrider, they swarmed up the access ladder, wiggled back into their pods, and sealed themselves in. Moments later, Katya was linked in again, the daylight outside now dimmed to human levels by the strider's AI. Data cascading across her visual display identified three incoming aircraft as probable Hachi fliers.

Hachis—the name was Nihongo for "Wasp"—were swift and deadly air-to-ground killers, ascraft designed to provide close air support for infantry. They were coming in low and fast, with an ETA of less than three minutes.

"Into the jungle," Katya ordered. "Simone, you climb in with Chung. It'll be a tight fit, I'm afraid."

They waited while Dagousset climbed aboard the Scout-strider and wriggled legs-first into the open hatch. Katya knew what it was like riding that way, squeezed body-against-body in near-total blackness, and she sympathized. Simone would have an uncomfortable ride back to base.

Hatches sealed again, the three warstriders turned from the wreckage and with swiftly scissoring strides plunged back into the jungle. It was urgent that they get well clear of the battlefield fast. The surviving Imperial Marines might still have strider-busting shoulder weapons; worse still, those Hachis had IR sensors that would be able to pick up a warstrider's heat through the forest canopy. It wouldn't take long, however, for the vastness of the jungle to swallow them up. The enemy fliers would have their figurative hands full tracking the scattered marines.

Behind them, a thunderous blast echoed off the mountains to the south, followed swiftly by a second, a third, a fourth. Charges placed by Darcy one by one disintegrated the wrecked striders. If the rebels couldn't use them for spares, then neither would the Imperials.

Katya regretted not being able to take the time to give the wreckage a more thorough search. They'd hoped to be able to load Braun's Rhino with captured weapons, but the four-legged walker was still smoking furiously, its hull utterly charred and gutted. As they left, Lee had stooped and retrieved one squad support plasma gun from among the Impie bodies, and he carried it now like a handgun in his strider's massive, armored fist; that SSPG and the comel would be their only prizes this day.

That sharp skirmish, less than twenty seconds in duration, had been a victory . . . but it was a victory with a high price. Two of the Freestriders' nine striders had been destroyed—twenty-two percent of its entire mechanized strength. Two men had died . . . one of them Rudi Carlsson, whom Katya had known since their campaign on Loki. In exchange, they'd destroyed two of the Empire's inexhaustible supply of warstriders, killed perhaps twenty marines, and scattered another ten or fifteen into the jungle.

The rebellion could not afford to trade the Empire and the Hegemony strider for strider, not even if the exchange was Rhinos for Katanas. Katya thought about the comel, tucked away beside her inside the pod, and wondered if the damned thing was going to be worth it.

Chapter 14

Is a Xenophobe intelligent? Or a Barnard's sky island? Or a comel? What about dolphins, gorillas, elephants, or the other fabulous beasts of Terra's recent past that pique our curiosity with largely anecdotal records of their use of language, memory, or tools? I think the question we must set for ourselves is not whether a given life form is intelligent, but whether or not that intelligence takes a form that we conceited and self-centered humans can comprehend.

—*Intelligence in the Universe*
Dr. Paul Hernandez
C.E. 2532

There was Self, and the myriad extensions of Self that inter-twined through the sheltering warmth of Mother Rock like the lacy twistings of veins of metal ore. As always, Self dreaded the parting, the tiny death of separation of Self from Self that was necessary as an extension of Self into the surrounding unconsciousness of not-Self. It was pre-cisely like the amputation of a limb as several hundred of the component cells of one slim pseudopod of Self nestled within the Self-manufactured prosthesis of a rock threader and, cell by pain-wracked cell, severed each link with the main body.

White agony . . . and loss . . .

For both of the two sundered aspects of Self there was diminution. For the main body, resting within the cav-ernous, interconnected voids of not-Rock deep within the depths of Mother Rock, the loss was slight. The Self-mass was continually fissioning off bits of itself and sending them off like exploratory probes, independent bearers of tiny, micro-Selves that wormed out through the surround-ing rock as messengers of intelligence and self-awareness. Usually they returned. Sometimes they did not.

For those slivers of awareness, however, amoebic, organic-inorganic composites of awareness, the loss was catastrophic. Perhaps half of those micro-Selves could not endure the transition, the shattering loss of identity, of memory, of ego that was part of the golden warmth of Unity. Sealed within the sleek, artificial body of the rock threader, the fragment of diminished Self struggled to come to grips with its truncated scope and being, ››self‹‹ now, instead of Self.

Shrunken, isolated, ››self‹‹ could remember snatches of its former life as Self, but dimly, as splintered dream-memories. Awareness once had been the shifting and blended thoughts and perceptions of trillions of tightly organized, interconnected units; now its awareness encompassed the being of a few thousand units only. So much had been lost! For long moments, the Self within the artificial body of the rock threader shuddered, writhed, and very nearly went mad.

It was a madness of loss and of something that might translate roughly as grief.

Of what remained of ››self's‹‹ *awareness, strongest was the need to quest out from the parent body, a drive hardwired both into the complex molecular rings analogous to chromosomes within each unit's organic material, and within the molecule-sized computers adrift within its inner, cytoplasmic seas. That need granted* ››self‹‹ *a measure of control, gave it purpose and a means of filling the yawning chasm of loss and need howling behind* ››self's‹‹ *brutally amputated mind.*

Gradually, madness subsided, though it remained as a churning subset of rigidly controlled need, boiling constantly just beneath the highest levels of ››self's‹‹ *thoughts. The rock threader, a slender and inorganic extrusion grown from Self's body, became a kind of mobile exoskeleton for the oozing mass of* ››self's‹‹ *gelatinous units. Magnetic fields flicked on, shifted, and grew in power. As* ››self's‹‹ *perceptions reached out in the surrounding Rock, the threader began moving.*

There was Rock, and there was ››self‹‹, *the former parting for the latter in the powerful magnetic flux that turned it plastic. The rock threader followed the track of another* ››self‹‹ *that had passed this way before, a* ››self‹‹ *that for reasons unknown had never returned to Self for reabsorption and a sharing of new perceptions and memories.* ››Self‹‹ *followed the old track partly because the rock, once deformed by another threader's passage, was softer and more yielding there; it followed, too, in a dimly perceived quest for that lost fragment of the vaster Self.*

Threats, both to ››self‹‹ *and to Self, had to be found and absorbed if Self was to continue its age-old expansion through the comforting warmth of Mother Rock.*

The old track led upward, away from the sustaining heat of Mother Rock. Ahead, dimly sensed now, ››self‹‹ *could taste the magnetic savor of pure metals and other less-identifiable substances in seemingly boundless concentrations. Closer at hand, in every direction, in fact, it could sense the energy flux and movement of other* ››selves‹‹, *all climbing through the yielding Rock away from the comfort of Self, closing on a treasure trove promising boundless raw materials, growth, and survival.*

››Self's‹‹ *pace through the rock increased.*

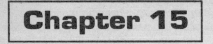

Chapter 15

Everything we know about Xenophobe psychology comes from the testimony of those few of us who actually made physical contact with them. Unfortunately, it's difficult to tell how much of the story has been filtered by our human prejudices and opinions.

—from a report given before the
Hegemony Council on Space Exploration
Devis Cameron
C.E. 2542

Twenty-eight kilometers west of Babel, a kilometer-wide crater marked the site of the last Xenophobe breakthrough. There, the jungle pressed close around the scar of that last battle, overlooked by a modest, thick-forested slope called Henson's Rise. The crater itself had been tagged Site Red One.

Hegemony Military Command, with the experience won on twelve other worlds infested by the Xenophobe invaders, had erected defensive barriers against the possibility of a second breakthrough at this place. Shortly after that first encounter, walls more massive than those of any Terran castle had been grown in place; earth and dead vegetation had been poured into hastily erected plastic molds, then seeded with self-replicating nanits that had transformed rubble into solid rock, a treatment known as the Rogan Process.

The improvised fortifications overlooked the crater rim, ringing it in completely with ten-meter RoPro walls and brooding gray towers, each capped by a robot gun emplacement. The automatic defenses were backed up by troops, both Hegemony warstriders from the 3rd New American Mech Cav and leggers of the Eridu 1st Home Guard Militia.

Less than an hour after sunrise, the assault was heralded first by an earthquake that caused the nearest trees to shiver. Mud fountained into the air as the ground split wide. Seconds later, a dense, milk-white fog began issuing from the gaping fissures, spreading across the crater floor to create a white, circular lake almost a kilometer across, a pool of heavier-than-air gas far thicker than any morning mist but too thin to be properly called a liquid. As it pressed relentlessly against the crater's inside rim, sampling robots planted there tasted the gas and transmitted their findings seconds before they died; the fog consisted of trillions of molecule-sized machines, nanodisassemblers, each carrying a few atoms of what once had been solid rock.

Then a sudden magnetic flux at the crater's center hurled shattered stone and gravel into the sky, and the thread-slender, questing tip of the lead Xenophobe slithered into view, weaving above the surface of the white fog sea.

Xenophobes, when they traveled underground, usually followed the Subsurface Deformation Tracks of other Xenos that had passed that way before, as though the SDTs were underground highways running through solid rock. That preference was one of the few ways in which the alien machine/creatures were predictable, and it had given the Red One defenders some warning. They'd been listening to the growing subsurface sounds—the creaks, snaps, and groans of bending rock—for days now, and were already at full alert. When the actual breakthrough began, they'd been prepared—or at least, so they'd thought.

It was the sheer savagery of the attack that caught them by surprise, as one Xeno after another boiled from the tortured ground, streaming white fog, turning the area deadly with the disintegrating touch of drifting nano-D clouds. Turret-mounted plasma guns and lasers had crisscrossed the crater's bowl with searing flame, shells laden with anti-nano-D countermeasures had been pumped into the fog by rapid-firing autocannons, but the Xenophobe Alphas had smashed clear of the geysering earth and snaked their way toward the crater rim like twenty-meter serpents, breasting the white fog like eldritch sea serpents with writhing whips for heads.

Several of the monsters died in the crater, sliced to bits by the withering, AI-directed fire or the bolts of light from warstriders posted along the defensive wall. Others, however, began transforming, their snakelike forms blurring and melting, their quicksilver bodies collapsing into new, more compact shapes. Most common were things like terrestrial sea urchins, flattened spheres two meters across with slender spines reaching five meters beyond that. Embedded in crackling auras of electromagnetic force, they floated on Eridu's magnetic field. The maglev effect did not render them weightless, quite, but they drifted along lightly enough that their rippling spines snapping against the ground or the wind itself could waft them toward the nearest human defenses more quickly than any warstrider's pace.

Two of the drifting monsters died in the high-energy crossfire from the surrounding towers, but eight more serpents surfaced in the meantime, and the fog sea was rising now, spilling across the crater rim and lapping against the inner base of the RoPro fortifications themselves. Counters recorded dizzying concentrations of nano-D in the atmosphere; the walls were softening under the assault of submicroscopic weapons that pulled them apart in the same way that they'd been assembled, a molecule at a time. Foundations weakened and walls cracked; a gun tower settled slightly, tilting ominously inward toward the white sea as foot soldiers manning its ramparts scrambled for safety.

Five minutes after the breakthrough had begun, reinforcements arrived at the scene, a dozen circling ascraft with ground support weapons, and a pair of VK-141 Stormwinds, each carrying four Mech Cav warstriders in external hull slots. With shrieking jets, the Stormwinds set down in a jungle clearing east of the crater amid swirling clouds of dust and uprooted vegetation. The striders had unhooked and swung into action, loping toward the Red One fortifications just as the first tower crumbled into the pit in an explosion of RoPro fragments and debris.

The nano-fog spilled through the gap in the wall like a flood gushing through a broken dam. Monsters followed, black or silver or dull pearl-gray nightmares of lashing spines and twisting, medusoid tentacles, Xenophobe Alphas that fought by using powerful magnetic fields to hurl BB-sized fragments of themselves at hypersonic speeds, or killed with the deadly embrace of a tentacle laden with nanodisassemblers. A Mech Cav RS-64 Warlord opened fire with thundering, left-right-left blasts from its charged particle guns; forked lightnings played across the leading Xeno horror, then shattered it into fragments.

Horribly, those fragments kept moving, as though the Xeno machines were themselves alive and *continued* to live even when they'd been smashed into smoking pieces. The fragments, dubbed Gammas by the humans who fought them, some no more than a meter across, hunched and wriggled themselves across the battlefield, each steaming with the release of trillions of deadly nano-D units from their writhing surfaces that steadily ate away at whatever they touched. The nano count hit point four-eight and climbed steadily. The circling ascraft accounted for two more Alphas, but the rising nano count soon forced them back, their air surfaces and intake fans already corroding in the deadly, invisible cloud of nano-D drifting above the battleground.

Tensions were still high between the local militia troopers and the Hegemony forces, but politics were forgotten as combat was joined at point-blank range. Legger militiamen fought in the shadows of Hegemony warstriders, turning hand flamers and lasers on the carpet of crawling fragments. AND rounds burst overhead, bathing the area in anti-nano-D clouds to combat the disintegrating effect of the Xeno fog. For six long minutes, the issue was in doubt, as warstriders smashed down the Xeno Alphas and foot soldiers mopped up the Gammas with blasts of flame and radiation.

Then a fresh wave of Xenos emerged from the tunnel entrance, smashing down a fifty-meter stretch of RoPro wall and spilling onto the seared battleground east of the crater. The nano-D count reached point six-five, high enough to gnaw through the armor of the legger infantry in ten minutes or less. At a command, the troops fell back, covered by their huge, cephlinked comrades-at-arms. The warstriders fought on until Gammas began clinging to their legs and foot assemblies, eating through durasheath armor like acid through paper. For a time, the strider warriors cleansed one another in brief, hissing blasts of flame, but soon there were just too many of the creeping horrors, armor panels were failing, internal mechanisms corroding. Unable to battle so many at once, the striders began to retreat. A second line of defensive fortifications was being erected five kilometers to the east, between Red One and Babel.

The fight to save Babel and Eridu's space elevator would continue there.

   ››Self‹‹ had emerged from the rock suddenly, to find itself in the midst of a searing storm of energies unlike anything it had ever before encountered. The environment was bizarrely alien, a near-vacuum of not-Rock, a gulf that ››self's‹‹ senses strained to bridge and measure . . . and failed. Other ››selves‹‹ were nearby; ››self‹‹ could hear their calls across the low-energy end of the electromagnetic spectrum and sense that they'd been attacked by some unseen, terribly destructive threat.

   Without conscious volition, threat triggered response, a shifting of body surface from rock threader to defender.

   The transformation to the defender form was not an ability native to the original evolution of Self, but something adopted in the distant past from contact with another species, a not-Self intelligence that had manipulated matter in much the same way that Self manipulated Rock. The trait was now part of ››self's‹‹ gene-analogues, an inborn conditioning transmitted through each reproductive cycle, the response virtually automatic each time a ››self‹‹ emerged from the protection of Mother Rock into the Void at the heart of the universe.

   Theoretically, with each combat encounter, Self—the massive, growing Self still safely hidden within the womblike embrace of Mother Rock—would learn, acquiring skills, reflexes, even weapons from the not-Self opponents the individual ››selves‹‹ met and defeated. Those skills and memories had to be returned to Self first, however, before they could be reproduced and disseminated throughout all future, budding ››selves‹‹, and so far in this cycle, no ››self‹‹ had survived the encounter to return to Self with its prize of knowledge. ››Self‹‹ was thrown into combat, completely unprepared. Seconds after reaching the Void, a searing blast of coherent radiation had slashed along the still-unformed side of the defender-form. Half of ››self's‹‹ organic units had died, shriveling in white heat unlike anything it had ever before sensed.

It was quiet now, the battle swirling to other parts of the Void. ››Self‹‹ clung to the wall of the Void, fearful that at any moment it might be flung from the Rock and into that disconcerting emptiness that gaped above and around it. It understood gravity as direction rather than as a force; to its senses, ››self‹‹ seemed to be hanging, suspended at the edge of a precipice, in immediate danger of dropping into the Void.

The feeling passed, but slowly. The direction leading toward Mother Rock, toward warmth, security, and the yearned-for reunion with the fully sentient glory of Self, seemed somehow to be holding ››self‹‹, leechlike, to the surface of Rock. Eventually, ››self‹‹ dared to move, inching back toward the not-Rock crevasse through which it had emerged into this terrible, disconcerting space.

To ››self's‹‹ perceptions, the Void was not empty; true vacuum would have been incomprehensible. Void was a sea of energy, of magnetic lines of force and of electromagnetic radiations, most of which seemed to originate with a diffuse mass of heat and radio noise suspended within the not-Rock gulf. Trembling, ››self‹‹ tasted its strange surroundings, detecting familiar elements but in unfamiliar guises—oxygen as a gas, for instance, instead of as part of solid chemical compounds. Most common of all was molecular nitrogen—rare in the depths of Mother Rock, but present here as fully four-fifths of the Void's chemical composition. When Self ate new cavities for itself within the deep Rock, the not-Rock that remained usually consisted of carbon dioxide and various other carbon- and sulfur-compound gases, the products of Self's metabolism.

Movement was difficult, hampered by the damage. Part of ››self‹‹ had not completed the transition from rock threader to defender, and the machine-life shell was trapped now between the two, unable to return to the Rock, unable to defend. It would have to heal itself before it could move far. Worst was the loss of its own organic body mass. That would have to be replaced, and quickly. Fortunately, pods bearing more amputated fragments of Self were nearby, rising from Rock, dispersing into Void on magnetic winds.

››Self‹‹ recognized ››self‹‹ and called out to it. . . .

Xenophobe psychology is patterned on their physiology, with a kind of hierarchy of organization. At the bottom are individual units—football-sized blobs of jelly made of an intriguing mix of organic cells and inorganic . . . call them machines, cell-sized structures representing an organically based nanotechnology that gives the Xenophobes an adaptability that we can only guess at. So, too, is the Xeno concept of "Self" organized into layers, the combined experiences and perceptions of many separate Nodes capable of joining together as a self-aware whole.

—from a report given before the
Hegemony Council on Space Exploration
Devis Cameron
C.E. 2542

The VK-141 Stormwind descended toward the clearing on screeching, ducted jets, lashing the surrounding trees into a hurricane frenzy. The ascraft shuttle, registered with the Babel militia, was one of a handful of transports used by the rebel forces. Katya, cocooned inside the Ghostrider clamped to one of the craft's external rider slots, waited until they were two meters from the ground, then gave the mental command that broke the connections between ascraft and strider. She dropped free, landing with a heavy thud. Vic Hagan's RLN-90 Scoutstrider dropped seconds later, a few meters away.

Most ascraft possessed external cargo bays, called riderslots because they could be adapted to carry striders in magnetic grapples, tucked away beneath the vehicle's delta wings. Stormwinds had four, two to either side, but only two were filled on this run.

If this crazy idea didn't work, Katya had argued, then four striders would be no advantage over two . . . and the rebels would lose only two of their precious combat machines.

"Okay, Lara," she called over the general frequency. "We're down, all green."

"Copy that, and I'm out of here," the ascraft pilot shot back. "Call when you need your dust-off. Good luck, you two." With a gathering roar, the Stormwind lifted above the clearing, pivoted until it was facing southeast, then accelerated, streaking away just above the treetops.

It was a calculated risk, of course, conducting an ascraft strider drop less than thirty kilometers from Babel, where their activities might be noticed by the always-present watching eyes at synchorbit, directly overhead. It was unlikely that they'd be noticed, however. Right now, all HEMILCOM eyes would be focused on Site Red One, where the Xenophobes had broken through the surface scant hours before, overwhelmed the defensive line, and begun chewing their way east through the jungle, arrowing straight for the Babel towerdown.

"We'd better start moving, Vic," she called. She rotated her optics slowly, studying their surroundings. The clearing was an old storm blowdown, and the footing was treacherous even for warstriders. "I make it three-one-three. Looks like I'd better break trail."

"Roger that, Captain. After you."

Their steps were slowed by the tangle of vegetation underneath. There was supposed to be a path here, the remnants of a seventy-year-old logging road, but Eriduan flora, beneath the high-energy light of an F7 sun, proliferated, grew, and even moved with a most unplantlike haste. Numerous Nomad trees had migrated from the higher slopes in search of moister ground, and the ubiquitous anemone plants had sprouted everywhere. The trail, its topography downloaded into her RAM by Creighton back at Emden base, was no longer there.

Its loss would slow them, but there was no danger of becoming lost. Site Red One had been carefully mapped and plotted, its coordinates downloaded to their cephlinks. Katya could check the navdata displayed across one corner of her visual field and see that Red One was now some twelve kilometers away . . . *that* way.

They'd heard the news at the rebels' Emden base last night: early-warning sound detectors at Red One had detected a large number of Xenophobe tunnelers a scant few hundred meters beneath the ground, pinpointing their probable breakout point. A military alert had been sounded, and both the organic and robotic defenders of the crater itself brought to peak readiness. From the ground recordings tracking the rumbling DSA, this would be no isolated breakthrough but an all-out assault, probably aimed at Babel and the space elevator.

That added a note of deadly urgency to the op. For the moment, at least, the Rebellion was on hold, as the Network rebels joined Babel's defenders. Armed revolution might be necessary for Sinclair's "explosion of diversity," but for human diversity to have any chance at all the humans had to survive, whether they were Hegemony colonists, placard-waving demonstrators, or Imperial Marines.

The Eriduan Network was continuing its covert activities, of course, but the overtly military units—and the men and women like Creighton who remained with the Hegemony's garrison forces—all reacted as they'd been trained, deploying to meet the suddenly emerging threat in the jungle west of Babel.

There was, of course, some question as to whether rebel military forces could join in Babel's defense without attracting Imperial notice. The easiest means of handling the problem was for them to pass themselves off as loyal militia units. Every city on Eridu had at least one small, locally raised self-defense force, and since the exact number of operational warstriders fluctuated daily with breakdowns, repairs, and conversions, not even the vast HEMILCOM AI systems at Eridu Synchorbital could list or track them all with any degree of accuracy.

Katya, however, had suggested an alternative.

The appearance of Xenophobes near Babel gave the Network the opportunity it had been looking for, the chance to find an isolated Xenophobe machine, possibly one damaged in battle, and use the comel to try to establish contact with its operators. If the Xenophobes could be reached, could be made to understand what was at stake, a kind of alliance might be struck, something along the lines of *Help us fight our war, and if we win, we'll find a way to share this world with you in peace...*

Katya had argued that her experience made her the logical choice to go. She still wasn't sure why she'd insisted on that point with such fire. Partly, she realized as she guided her LaG-42 across the sharply sloping ground through the patterns of golden light spilling through the forest canopy, it had to do with Dev, almost as though her success in contacting the Xenos for the Confederation would atone for Dev's working for the Hegemony, for the damage he'd done to the Winchester Network.

Too, there were still so many unknowns, right down to the question of whether or not acquisitive-phase Xenos could even be reasoned with. Katya had virtually appropriated the idea of trying direct contact for herself, and she damn well wasn't going to send others out to shake hands with Xenos while she stayed behind.

She concentrated on her footing, her heavier LaG-42 in the lead, pressing through the undergrowth and trampling it down for the lighter Scoutstrider behind her. The ground sloped sharply skyward to her left. The putative trail worked its way crabwise along the flanks of the Pipe Mountains, a thickly wooded spur of the Equatorials that circled west of Babel like a protective wall eight hundred meters high. The jungle was thick, almost impenetrable in places, and heavily shadowed in the lower layers. Eriduan trees were mushroom-shaped, though with caps made of thousands of slender, interlacing fibers instead of a solid mass. Many had three or four levels, the better to trap every scrap of the energetic radiation from Marduk. Beneath them, in the shadows, saprophytic sponge brush and tentacled anemone plants made footing treacherous, even for a warstrider.

She wondered just what they would find waiting for them at Red One.

Vince Creighton had encountered a Xenophobe outside of Winchester several months before, and he'd been able to feed the rebels all of his own briefings on the threat. The Xenos on Eridu appeared to be identical to those she'd encountered on Loki and on the DalRiss homeworlds, shapeshifting Alphas that fragmented into amoebic Gammas when destroyed. So far on Eridu, no human machines had been captured by the Xenos, so none had yet been transformed into the Beta or "Xenozombie" form that utilized a disturbing parody of human technology.

A month after that first Xeno surfacing just outside the capital's domes, a second had occurred twenty-eight kilometers west of the sky-el and had been destroyed by Babel militia striders rushed to the spot. The 3rd New American Mech Cav had been hurriedly shifted back to Babel to defend against the expected next attack. RoPro walls had been grown, and the robotic defenses put in place. Xenophobes tended to use the same exits from their subterranean highways repeatedly.

That next attack had not materialized, however, until now. For several days, every military unit on Eridu had been on full alert as HEMILCOM tracked the SDTs of Xenophobe Alphas far underground. By the previous evening, it had been a fair certainty that the Xenos would be emerging, and soon, at Red One. Imperial Marines were already being routed to the Babel towerdown, both from other Eriduan cities and from orbit; Xenophobes seemed to be attracted to large masses of metal or artificial composites, and by far the largest such mass on the planet was the towering silver needle of the Babel sky-el. A successful Xeno attack on the space elevator would spell disaster on a cataclysmic scale. Unfortunately, from Babel's point of view, nukes could not be employed this time. No one wanted to even think about the results if subsurface nukes severed the space elevator's underground anchors.

As they'd skimmed above the Eriduan Outback toward their drop zone, Katya had listened in on fragments of communication between the ground forces and HEMILCOM. She'd heard the announcement that eight Hegemony striders had landed and were engaging the enemy; minutes later she'd heard the order to fall back. From the sound of things, the Xenos had been left holding the field around Red One. There'd been a call sent out for warships to bombard the crater from orbit; many worlds had large laser batteries mounted in their synchorbital installations, but the only heavy weapons in Eridu orbit at the moment were those of the Imperial destroyer *Tokitukaze*, and those would be employed only as a tactic of last resort. Reportedly, Omigato had already requested both additional warships and more warstrider units to bolster Eridu's defenses, but it might be weeks before those reinforcements arrived.

According to Katya's topo download, Henson's Rise passed the Red One crater less than a kilometer to the west. The human defenses would have concentrated on the crater's east side, and the retreat would have been toward the east, toward Babel. It was Katya's plan to move along the crest of the ridge to a point where she could observe the crater itself from above and from the west. No decision about actually attempting to approach the Xenos would be made until she had a clear view of the battlefield.

"Watch it, boss," Hagan called to her over the tactical link. "I think the trees are thinning up ahead. We're almost there."

"Roger that." Her Ghostrider was in the lead, weapons already armed and ready. "I'm starting to get a background nano count. Point oh-two and rising."

"Affirmative. There's some fog up ahead."

It looked like a harmless mist, and the nano count was still low enough that it might be harmless in fact. The viscous white gas that accompanied nano breakthroughs was actually a waste product, nano-D already rendered harmless by their submicroscopic mouthfuls of disassembled matter. The real danger, live nano-D, was visible only through the electronic senses of warstriders and battlefield scanners.

Some of the nearest mushroom trees, Katya noticed, were brown and straggly looking, with long shreds of bark hanging from cancerous-looking patches on their trunks. The forest here was already dying, brushed by the Xenos' nanotechnic touch. Katya pressed forward.

"Captain?" Lipinski called from the Ghostrider's second slot. The decision had finally been made that she would keep her Hegemony rank, at least for now. "We're picking up something weird on UHF."

"Let's hear it."

Static crashed in her mind, overlaying a reedy, almost plaintive warble of harmonics. It was a familiar tune, one she'd heard plenty of times on Loki. Xenophobes gathered powerful electromagnetic fields about themselves, using them to hurl bits of matter or disintegrating nano-D as weapons, to deflect bolts fired from strider charged-particle guns, possibly as a means of communication among themselves. The code, if that's what it was, had never been broken. The only meaning it bore for Katya was that Xenophobes were nearby.

But we knew that going into this. God, what am I doing here?

The jungle ended with heart-stopping abruptness, opening onto a hideous, gray-black scar that had devoured trees and rock alike. The fortifications that had surrounded the crater were still visible, like the slumping walls of a sand castle laved by the incoming tide. There were no sharp angles left, no hard edges; every surface had been *softened*, half melted and smoothed over by the passage of the Xenos' nano-D cloud.

Tatters of white fog drifted above the ruin, though most had dispersed back into the ground. A coal-black, tarry ooze had appeared where the Xenos had surfaced, and *things*, pearl-gray bubbles adrift on magnetic fields, were rising from the tunnel opening and floating across that hell-blasted wasteland.

"Travel spheres," Katya said. She'd seen them before, with Dev on Loki and on Alya A-VI. Researchers still weren't sure what purpose they served, but they knew that each was filled with the flaccid, jellylike lumps of mingled organic and inorganic substances that were known to be the real Xenophobes, the puppet masters of the larger, snake-named combat machines.

"Can we try contacting one of them?" Hagan asked. His voice was broken, the words distorted by the hiss and wail of static.

"Vic, you're breaking up. Switching to laser com," Katya said, and an invisible beam of light connected the two striders. "How do you read?"

"Solid L-LOS lock," Hagan replied, his voice clear now.

"Okay. As for contacting travel spheres, I don't know. If we can get close enough, maybe." The travel spheres had been seen at other Xeno breakthrough sites, but no one knew what they were for sure, or why they appeared.

Fear twisted in her mind. This was where she decided, once and for all, if she really believed in this scheme to contact the Xenophobes for the Confederation. How could she approach them? How could she make them understand? Open warfare had already broken out between the Xenos and humans here. It must, surely, be too late now for attempts at communication.

Or was it? Movement caught her eye, a thrashing within the white fog that still clung to the inner rim of the crater. Katya focused her optics on the movement and engaged her telephoto zoom. Enlarged, the sinuous object could be resolved as a Cobra, one of the dozens of different Xeno Alpha types, all named for Terran snakes. The flattened spreading of the anterior end that had given it its name was clearly visible. Fog clung to its body like a viscous fluid, streaming from its black flanks with each movement. Enlarging the image again, she saw that the Cobra's posterior end seemed to be entangled with a Xeno combat mode. There were the spines and the tentacles, weaving about weakly now, and she thought she could make out battle damage, a slash that had nearly cut the Alpha combat module in half.

Enhance . . .

She wasn't looking at two Xenophobes, but at one. She could see how the Cobra's body swelled into the distended black mass that had been a combat sphere. Had the thing been damaged while in the middle of shapeshifting from one form to another? It seemed possible. Several of the travel spheres hovered above it. Were they helping the Xeno somehow? Repairing it? On guard?

Or merely curious?

One thing struck Katya about the scene, however. The Xeno machines, whatever they were, were *not* warlike. At least, they weren't at the moment. Strangely, they didn't even appear to be aware of the two warstriders standing on the barren slope above them. If she was to have a chance at approaching a living Xeno machine, this was it.

"Okay, Vic," she said, deciding. "I'm going out."

"Yeah." His voice was hard, brittle. She could detect traces of his earlier anger. Earlier that morning, as they'd readied to leave the Emden base, Vic had argued with her about which of them should approach the Xenos. She'd had to pull rank on him—the second time she'd been forced to do so—to win even a grudging acceptance. "It's your show. But I'll have the bastard in my sights, Katya. If that damned thing even twitches wrong, I'm burning it."

It was the plan already worked out with Sinclair back in Babel. From what Dev had told her, she was pretty sure this was the substance of Operation Yunagi as well. Isolate a damaged Xeno machine, approach it with a comel . . . but with backup support ready to fry the monster if it looked like it would rather fight than talk.

The problem was, she would have to make the approach with at least her arm bared; the DalRiss comel functioned only when in direct contact with a living wearer's skin.

She glanced at the data on her visual display. The external nano count was at point zero five, low enough for prolonged exposure even without full armor . . . but the count was certain to be higher closer to the crater. How much higher? She couldn't guess, and she wasn't about to go tramping toward the damaged Xeno and its strange companions in her Ghostrider, not and risk having her approach mistaken for an attack.

Sighing inwardly, she transferred control of the Ghostrider to Lipinski, then broke her linkage. She awoke within her own body, lying inside the strider's cramped interior.

If she hesitated, she knew she would never be able to carry this off. Quickly, she removed her helmet and began readying her gear.

Chapter 17

We still don't understand precisely how comels work. Somehow, the DalRiss have genengineered a creature—intelligent, yet not self-aware—that can create a kind of neural bridge between one thinking species and another. What comes across that bridge aren't thoughts, exactly, but perceptions, awareness, empathy, patterns that our brains interpret as memory. It's not unpleasant, but it can be disconcerting.

—from a report given before the
Hegemony Council on Space Exploration
Devis Cameron
C.E. 2542

Katya had used comels before. At least, she'd used them in ViRsimulation with the DalRiss, though she'd never actually communicated with a Xenophobe before. She'd been present when Dev had done so, however, and the memory of that encounter was still seared into her brain with the vividness of a particularly gruesome and paralyzing nightmare.

Stepping off the access rungs of her strider and onto softly yielding ground, she turned to face the Cobra. It took an effort of will to take a step away from the comfort and perceived safety of her Ghostrider . . . then another . . . and another. She was wearing her bodysuit, which, when sealed, doubled as a full environmental suit; a chestpack with regulator and two hours' worth of air; and a breathing mask that included a visor designed to screen out Marduk's ultraviolet. She'd opened the sleeve on her left arm and rolled it back to her shoulder. Clinging to the bare skin of her arm was a translucent, gray-black mass—the comel taken from the maglev train a week before. Wet and glistening, it coated her hand

and forearm like a heavy rubber glove. It felt cold where it touched her skin, almost bitterly so compared to the forty-degree temperature of the air around her. A thermovore, it was feeding on the heat generated by her body.

She wondered again if this scheme of hers could possibly, possibly work.

The Xenophobe hadn't reacted to her presence yet, and that, at least, was comforting. It suggested, as Dev had reported after his contact with the Xeno World Mind on Alya B-V, that the Xenos didn't simply blindly attack humans, but that, possibly, they were quite unaware of them.

If that was true, she might be able to get within touching distance of the things before they sensed her. *Maybe . . .* She fought the trembling weakness in her knees and stomach that threatened to stop her in her tracks each time she took another step.

Her old, old dread of confinement threatened to shake free from the mental boundaries and restraints that she'd so carefully built up around it. She could remember the acrid stink of her own fear as she'd lowered herself into that vertical pit on Alya B-V, within a dead city on what once had been the DalRiss homeworld. At the bottom, with the amorphous walls of that cavern closing in about her, she'd first found Dev's Scoutstrider, its hatch open and its headlights angled toward an uneven, slime-coated patch of wall.

Then she'd seen Dev, his form nearly engulfed in a living cocoon of glistening black shapes, each the size of a man's head. Minutes earlier, Dev had emerged from the shelter of his warstrider in order to touch the Xenophobe cell mass directly; lost in the monster's eldritch, siren's song he'd not even been aware of how comel and Xenophobe together had drawn him into that oozing mass.

It didn't hurt him, she told herself. *It didn't hurt him. At the end, he stepped out of the slime and talked to me. The thing didn't hurt him.*

The surface beneath her feet was not muddy, as she'd expected from its smooth and uniform texture, but was coated in a talcum-fine dust that puffed about her boots and hung, weightlessly suspended, in the still air. An analytical part of her mind noted the phenomenon and explained it. *Molecular rock. The Xeno nano-D carried rock molecules out of the ground and off the RoPro walls and deposited them across several square kilometers. . . .*

Around her, the land looked blasted and barren, and she fought the desire to turn and flee for the treeline of the jungle at her back. The heat was stifling and wet, only barely held at bay by the intricate layering of her close-fitting bodysuit. The crippled Xeno Cobra and its strange attendants were some forty meters below her, not far from the base of the hill.

From here, she could see that the Cobra had indeed been caught halfway through its protean transformation between one incarnation and another. Part retained the slender, almost filamentary reach of a Cobra, the flattened hood that had given the monster its name limp on the ground but easily recognizable. The other end seemed grotesquely bloated, expanded into a partially deflated sphere trailing dozens of black spines and tentacles, the typical shape of a Xeno-phobe Alpha combat form. The sphere, kissed by the passing of some warstrider's weapons, had been ripped open; the interior, black and glistening, was alive with an oozing, deliberate movement. It looked like hot tar, within which floated half-dissolved lumps of some organic matter. Several of the pearly spheres, she saw, lay close by, half their surfaces melted away to reveal more of the black slime-things.

Reinforcements, she thought, applying the obvious military interpretation to what she was seeing, trying to understand. *Part of the crew was killed, and reinforcements are climbing aboard. Or is it an engineering team, arriving to make repairs?*

It was difficult to make sense of any of what she was seeing. Blocky, sharp-edged crystalline shapes, like faceted blocks of cut glass, had grown from the dust and the fog, a jackstraw tangle of fantastic shapes that Katya had seen before, in Xeno-occupied regions of the far-distant DalRiss worlds. Less definable shapes grew from the Cobra's broken body, almost as though it were somehow slowly growing, healing itself as she watched.

Twenty-five meters now. It still hadn't seen her.

Seen her? Those tar-slimed lumps had nothing like eyes, nothing even recognizable as sense organs. She remembered that Dev had reported the Xenophobes possessed senses unlike those of humans, but she couldn't imagine what their view of the world must be like. Xenophobes, Katya decided, must be deaf and blind; perhaps they only perceived the outside world dimly through the artificial senses of their organic machines.

"Katya?" Hagan's voice sounded ragged and on edge, a whispered rasp from her compatch. Static blasted the words, but at this range they were intelligible . . . barely. "You okay?"

"I'm fine, Vic." She'd plugged the compatch into the T-socket behind her ear, so she could think her answer and transmit it through her cephlink. It was good only for close-range communications, but it meant her speaking voice wouldn't be muffled by her mask . . . or betray the dry-mouthed terror she felt. Unfortunately, it functioned on radio frequencies rather than through her strider's laser com, and the Xeno static roared in her ear like the crash of a heavy surf. "No response yet."

"We're—*sssssst*—you hit the dir—*sssss*—you hit—*ss-sss*—the overkill."

"Sorry, Vic . . . didn't quite catch that. Boost your gain and say again."

She heard the hum as Hagan increased his signal power. "I said we're locked onto that thing. If I yell 'Down,' you hit the dirt. I'd hate to singe you with the overkill."

"I hear you. But . . . iceworld, okay?" The military slang meant to stay cool, unemotional. "Let's give things a chance."

She couldn't tell if he'd heard her or not.

From fifteen meters, it was clear that the Xeno Cobra, which she had always thought of as a combat machine akin in spirit, if not form, to a human warstrider, shared some of the traits of living creatures. Its surface had the luster-less sheen of a metal-plastic or metal-ceramic composite; its interior was wet and pulsing, like the body cavity of something alive.

Where, Katya wondered, was the dividing line between creator and created, between tool-user and tool? The Xeno-phobes obviously possessed a technology similar in some respects to the bioengineering of the DalRiss. Rather than manufacturing tools, the Xenos grew them within their own bodies, building them molecule by molecule through some means of inward-turned perception and manipulation incomprehensible to humans.

A shudder as icy as the touch of the comel on her arm shivered down the length of Katya's spine. She was afraid, and what she feared was not the Xenophobe strangeness or ugliness of outward form; the things were so unlike anything recognizable that there was nothing to trigger Katya's own xenophobic instincts, instincts that might have left her screaming had the creature before her in some way resembled, say, a spider, a reptile, or some other, more familiar, stranger.

Instead, it was the Xeno's unknown and perhaps unknowable qualities that terrified. Did it see her as a threat? As lunch? Did it even see her at all? And when it finally reacted to her presence, as it soon must, what would it do? Her right hand brushed against the holster riding low on her hip. She hesitated, then flipped open the catch, freeing the Toshiba Type 07 laser pistol resting there. Not that it would hurt a Xenophobe Alpha any more than a flashlight might . . . but its weight against her thigh was strangely, irrationally reassuring.

Eight meters, now. Had it seen her yet? She felt an unpleasant tingling against the bare skin of her upper arm, her right hand, her face and neck exposed by the mask. What was the nano count here, she wondered? She could imagine the dead layers of her epidermis beginning to dissolve under the unseen assault of Xeno nano-D. Or was the tingling psychosomatic only? She couldn't tell.

She was afraid.

Under the direction of its organic components, the rock threader was repairing itself. »Self« did not, could not, differentiate between those parts of its body that were organic and those smaller, internal fragments that were complex, self-replicating machines, for that symbiosis between organism and living machine was old, old . . . billions of years old, perhaps. Even the far vaster and more able memories of Self had long since lost all but hazy impressions of its own evolutionary genesis within the caverns of some cooling, far-distant world, and those impressions

*were not part of the group-mind memories retained by
>>self<<.*

*It did retain memories of Self, of course, memories of a
vast and dazzling intelligence from which >>self<< had been
agonizingly torn at some vaguely recognized period of time
in the past. Alone, here on the thin and alien shores of the
great Void at the heart of the universe, it knew that its one
chance of completion was to repair the damage it had suffered so that the threader could return to the warmth and
wholeness of Self. The damage was not severe; worst was
the loss of nearly half of the individual fragments of >>self<<
that directed the threader; these were being replaced from
the pods still rising on the magnetic sea from the not-Rock
passage nearby.*

*Since it experienced its surroundings as blendings of
separate sensations from separate parts of its being, the
group organism did not think in terms of linear time, but
it knew that it would return to Self in the not-distant future.
Stored within its inorganic memory were millions of bits of
data acquired during its short stay here at the edge of the
Void. Self would especially savor the taste of data about the
mysterious opponents here, the not-Selves that, impossibly,
moved and fought and destroyed almost as though they were
somehow alive. Self would welcome that data, replicating it
and distributing it throughout the body for future buddings
of >>selves<<.*

*And >>self<< would again be part of Self, merging >>con-
sciousness<< with Consciousness, >>mind<< with Mind. The
pain, the loss, the utter diminishment would at last be
gone.*

*The emotion-analogue shivering through its separate units
at that group thought might have been recognizable to
humans as joy.*

*>>Self<< possessed eighteen separate external senses. None
of these quite corresponded to sight, though three perceived
and measured electromagnetic energy falling upon the surfaces of its bodies. Most were distantly analogous to human
senses of taste or smell, enabling >>self<< to sample its chemical and electrical environment. Only one, sensitive to nearby
heat sources at frequencies of between 10^{12} and 10^{14} hertz,
created something within the group mind that could be*

thought of as a visual image. Another, sensitive to vibrations through the surrounding rock, was something like hearing.

Still, ››self‹‹ was only dimly aware of the approaching not-Self, a pattern of greater heat against lesser heat, a shambling but regular tremor of vibrations through the rock, a thing almost invisible. In its Boolean framework of is and is-not, ››self‹‹ could perceive the heat-shape and recognize it as not-Self.

Neither was it Rock, for it was moving, though it did taste, rocklike, of chemical salts and hydrocarbon compounds, of water and incredibly pure traces of metal and less-identifiable but apparently artificial substances. If it moved, was it alive the way ››self‹‹ was alive? That was difficult to say, though the thing jittered and flickered with the electrochemical currents that mimicked, distantly, the more powerful ebb and flow of life within ››self's‹‹ group being.

The tastes of chemical salts and water were very strong now, and ››self‹‹ recoiled. It could absorb most substances, using its internal chemical control to disassemble and rearrange their chemical structures in order to grow inorganic machine components or to reproduce itself. Some substances, however, posed special difficulties, and liquid electrolytic compounds—such as salt water—could be deadly, for they could disrupt the electrical conductivity within ››self's‹‹ tissues and inorganic components, a disruption equivalent to intense pain that was potentially fatal. Self, ››self‹‹ remembered, had more than once sensed vast reservoirs of salt water within the universe of Rock and drawn back from them, unable to approach.

And a glowing column massing nearly sixty kilos that was at least seventy percent salt water was now moving steadily toward ››self‹‹ with something that might be interpreted as grim purpose.

Though it wasn't aware of the fact, ››self‹‹ possessed one emotion fully in common with humans, a reflexive and primitive urge toward fight or flight basic to any species' survival.

››Self‹‹ was afraid.

The wounded Xenophobe machine/creature was only a handful of meters away now, a limp, black tube thicker than

Katya was tall. The entire mass was faintly pulsing with some inner life, like the steady thud of some monstrous heart.

One of the broken travel spheres lay at her feet. Inside its meter-wide bowl-shaped hollow, three Xenophobes floated on greasy slime trails, black slug-things like lumps of grease that were somehow managing to slide up the walls of their prisons, defying gravity. Their movements did not appear to be due to muscular contractions, or any other mode of organic locomotion Katya was familiar with. Individual Xenophobe cells, apparently, could also somehow use or manipulate the ambient magnetic field.

Within the opening in the Cobra's flank, dozens of Xeno bodies appeared to be meshed together in a network of thread-thin, translucent filaments. It reminded her, somewhat, of a crude model of a human brain, with neurons joined to neurons in a complex web of cell bodies, axons, and dendrites, multiple paths whose traceries determined the shape of human thoughts.

That, Katya knew, was a simplistic interpretation colored by her own prejudices of what was and was not life. Each individual Xenophobe cell, a slug shape the size of her head, was an incredibly complex mix of living and inorganic parts. Was it intelligent apart from the main body? No one knew, not even Dev, for his communication had been with a network of some trillions of the things spanning the crust of an entire planet. Most researchers assumed that a single Xeno unit was unintelligent .... no brighter than a single neuron in a human brain.

But was that true? Impulsively, Katya stooped above a Xenophobe sliding slowly across the ground between the broken sphere and the Cobra, thrusting her comel-clad hand down and touching its glistening surface, feeling its black, soft-skinned slickness through the cold and cushioning layers of the living DalRiss translator.

. . . move . . . move . . . move . . .

. . . and a desperate, soul-wrenching need to be joined to others . . . emptiness . . . loneliness . . .

Katya screamed, a despairing wail reflecting the emptiness coursing through her soul.

"Kat!" Hagan's shrill cry cut through the static. "Kat! Are you—"

"I'm fine!" She hoped he could hear her. Her compatch didn't pack much power. Dazed, she stood, her knees threatening to give way entirely and pitch her back to the ground. Lone Xeno organisms were not intelligent. That was clear enough now, though they burned with a kind of programmed lust for some particular action. The comel, she realized with a kind of detached wonder, had somehow translated that programming, the blind instinct to join with others of its kind, into something recognizable as emotion.

An empty wanting, a hunger that had nearly overwhelmed her.

"*Sssss*—in the way, Katya! Move aside—*ssst!*"

"Negative! Negative! Nothing's wrong!"

Nothing *was* wrong . . . for the Xenophobe horror a few meters before her remained unmoving. From here, she could see the intricate weave of its repair work around the edges of the hole in its side, as fibers grew from tar-dripping edges according to some master program whose workings she could appreciate but only dimly perceive. The Xeno organism she'd touched was flowing up the side of the Cobra now, and into the embrace of outflung, living fibers. Almost, she imagined, she could sense a kind of relief in the way it slithered in close against a hundred identical, glistening bodies.

Something reached for her from the interior of the Xeno combat machine, a tar-black pseudopod that was part molasses-thick liquid, part living units.

How do they do that? she wondered. The creatures possessed nothing like skeletons, internal or external, but working together they seemed able to exercise considerable strength. Perhaps the micromachines inside their bodies somehow interlocked, creating temporary skeletal support.

The arm swayed closer, an extension of self like the hungry embrace of an amoeba. Dazed, Katya took a half step back, then stopped. Was this an attack, or . . .

Damn it, we're here to try to communicate with these things! She thrust her comel-covered arm forward, touching the swaying, dripping extension of self growing from the Xeno machine's wounded side.

She touched the mind of ››self‹‹ and nearly fainted.

The pseudopod spilled down over her arm . . . her chest . . . her head, engulfing her in blackness.

Chapter 18

*At the bottom of the Xenophobe hierarchy is what
we call the cell, because it seems to resemble a single,
gigantic neuron within a complex nervous system. Like
a plant or animal cell, it is composed of smaller units
and is quite complex, a living organism that can survive for a time isolated from the parent body. This cell
is constructed from something like cytoplasm, microscopic subcells that are analogous to the cells in our
own bodies, and nanomachines. It measures perhaps
twenty-five centimeters across and masses about a
kilogram. As far as we can tell, it can carry memory,
perhaps a kind of organic programming, but is not, of
itself, intelligent.*

*A number of cells networked together, however, can
display a definite intelligence, even though that intelligence appears to be quite different from anything we
are familiar with.*

—from a report given before the
Hegemony Council on Space Exploration
Devis Cameron
C.E. 2542

From his vantage point halfway up the barren slope of
Henson's Rise, Vic Hagan watched with dumbstruck horror as something like molten asphalt extruded itself from
the wrecked Cobra and spilled over Katya's body, engulfing her. Lipinski was screaming at him over the comlink to
fire, *fire*, but he couldn't shoot without hitting Katya, who
might still be alive.

He kicked his RLN-90 into motion, lumbering down the
slope toward the Xenophobe machine. He needed to do

something, but he could only watch helplessly as the black, tarry mass withdrew back into the opening in the Cobra's side, leaving nothing behind at all.

"My God, it *swallowed* her!"

And now, the Cobra was in motion, gliding with a serpent's undulations toward a black-pit fissure at the center of the crater. Hagan had seen similar craters on Loki and elsewhere. They were called tunnel entrances, though there was no actual tunnel as such, and they appeared to be gateways of a sort to the network of SDTs that formed the Xenos' underground highway net. Xenophobe machines had been seen leaving and entering those fissures, which consisted of rock somehow turned plastic and yielding by intense magnetic fields.

"Lieutenant, you gotta help her!"

Hagan bit back a curse. Lipinski's shrill commentary was doing little to help the situation, even if the kid was right. Experimentally, he raised his Scoutstrider's right arm, engaging the targeting system for his autocannon.

The agonizing part of the situation was not knowing whether Katya was alive or dead. He'd just watched the thing gulp her down whole . . . but he'd seen ViRrecordings of the first contact on Alya B-V, where Dev Cameron had been nearly completely engulfed by a mass of Xenophobe cells lining the walls of a subterranean cavern. This *could* be the same thing and Katya might still be alive inside that monster, but if so she was being kidnapped. Once the damaged Cobra reached the tunnel entrance, there'd be nothing anyone could do for her.

Grimly, he targeted the ground in front of that writhing, misshapen serpent and triggered a long burst of high-explosive shells. The Cyclan autocannon slammed off three rounds, the heavy *thud-thud-thud* rocking Hagan's strider back with the recoil. The detonations walked across the Cobra's path, a triple burst of man-sized explosions that tore up the ground and splattered the crawling horror with stinging shrapnel and rock.

The Xeno machine ignored him, writhing over the cratered ground with an almost comical haste. Hagan took aim again, this time targeting the machine-creature's flattened hood. Katya had vanished into the thing's swollen midsection and must be there still. Perhaps he could kill the monster by cutting off its head, then free Katya before the thing crushed or smothered her.

He fired again, a second chain of autocannon fire barking and snapping across a range of nearly one hundred meters. With enhanced, telescopic vision, he could see the shells slamming into the Xeno's neck just behind the raised and quivering cobra's hood, saw the explosions savage that black-gray hide from the inside, blowing out great, gaping holes with each impact.

Lipinski, controlling the Ghostrider's 100-MW laser now, added his machine's high-tech violence to the attack. The Cobra's hooded head seemed to deflate suddenly, then dropped away, literally blasted from the Xeno's body.

But the Xenophobe machine kept moving, crawling now, if anything, faster than before. Hagan could see the body reshaping itself as it moved. The swollen rear portion was smoothing over now, the spines and tentacles reabsorbing into the rest of the body mass. The stump behind where the head had been rounded itself off, the ragged end smoothed over, and Hagan felt a sick, jabbing anguish at the realization that this, this *creature* did not keep its brains in the same place that terrestrial animals did. *He*'d known that, of course, but he'd had to try. The "head" lay discarded on the barren crater floor, already fragmenting into deadly Xeno Gammas; the rest of the Cobra continued to slither toward the tunnel entrance, half a kilometer away.

Lipinski loosed another laser bolt, searing the Cobra's side.

"Hold fire, damn it!" Hagan barked.

"But . . . but . . ."

"Look, kid," Hagan said, rage and terror and hope all draining from his thoughts at the same moment, leaving him terribly tired. "If she's dead, there's not a damned thing we can do for her. If she's alive, we could kill her. Either way . . ."

He didn't add that maybe, horribly, Katya was still alive and *wishing* she were dead, because trapped inside the Xeno she didn't have a chance. Her life support pack and mask would give her a couple hours of air; she might live that long, if the thing didn't . . . *digest* her before that.

Hagan's strider AI recognized the symptoms of a profound psychological shock building within Hagan's brain and body; had the man been in his body, that body would have been violently sick. Skillfully, the AI interceded, interrupting a series of C-socket impulses that could have thrown the Scoutstrider on its side, all coordination and control gone. As it was, the RLN-90 stumbled to a halt, autocannon arm tracking back and forth helplessly, almost as though it was trying to make up its mind.

The Cobra reached the tunnel entrance, nosed into it, and vanished as slickly as a snake slithering down a hole.

Katya was sure that she was going mad. When the Xenophobe's mass engulfed her, cocooning her in suffocating blackness, her old claustrophobia had risen from nightmare corners of her mind, a haunting horror thought dead, now demonically alive and hungry and wildly raging through the fragmenting shards of her awareness.

She couldn't move, she couldn't see, she couldn't hear. With her eyes wide open, she was surrounded by a dark more profound than anything she'd ever experienced, worse by far than that time, years before, when equipment failure had awakened her, isolated and alone, within the linkage capsule of a starship and nearly driven her insane. She could feel her captor's body—bodies?—pressing around her. Where it touched clothing or survival pack or comel she felt only pressure; where it touched bare skin she felt a wet, faintly cool clinginess that reminded her of thick mud. It was like drowning, like being buried alive, her worst, worst nightmares given substance and form and texture.

Her throat was raw; she thought she must have screamed, even though she had no memory of it. For a horrible several moments, she felt she was going to be sick in her breathing mask, but by clenching eyes shut and fists closed and jaw tight she battled back, fighting the choking, gagging raw terror that threatened to consume her, and pushed it back, holding it, by main force of will, at a metaphorical arm's length.

Strangely, when she was able to think again at all, she was steadied by the presence of . . . something that seemed to be with her inside her skull, an awareness not her own that manifested itself, not in words, but as impressions.

. . . curiosity . . .

. . . fear—pain—need-flee-Unity . . .

. . . wonder . . .

Most powerful of all was the realization that she was alive, that the Xeno had not killed her. She could not move; the interlaced cells were pressed roundabout her, covering every square centimeter of her body. If it hadn't been for her mask, she would certainly have suffocated . . . or drowned. It felt as though she'd been stuffed into a barrel filled with some heavy, viscous liquid. She could feel the Xeno's movements as a rippling, almost peristaltic surging, but her cocoon muffled the sensations and protected her from injury.

I'm aboard a Xenophobe combat machine, she thought . . . and she was scared by the hysterical edge that grated around the borders of that thought. *It's . . . taking me for a ride. . . .*

Where?

Though she'd lost all orientation when she'd been swallowed, the blood pounding in her temples, the congested feeling behind her mask felt like the sensations of being upside down. Desperately, she tried to organize the limited data reaching her panic-shocked brain. Yes . . . it definitely felt like she was upside down, or nearly so, moving in a generally downward direction. It was a little like sliding headfirst through a dark and cramped tube, like, she imagined, dropping down a garbage chute while trapped in a wet and clinging mass of garbage.

That imagery did her no good. Again, she very nearly vomited, and claustrophobia gibbered insanely somewhere behind her disorientation and fear.

Katya concentrated on what she knew. It seemed the only way to hold madness at bay.

She was moving downward, and that meant the Cobra had gulped her down and bolted for its tunnel. What, she wondered, had Vic and Georg made of that? Though the cell-body of the thing holding her had completely engulfed her, it hadn't hurt her, at least not yet. Its grip was paralyzingly strong. She couldn't move, couldn't even free her right hand enough to reach her holstered pistol. She had the impression that, had the Xeno chosen to do so, it could have exerted a tiny fraction of its potential strength, and she would have been pulped into a homogeneous mass of blood, tissue, and splintered bone.

But it *hadn't*, it *hadn't*. What did that mean?

That it was taking her somewhere.

Where?

Underground, obviously. Back to . . . wherever it was that Xenophobes came from when they emerged from their lightless deeps.

So little was known about them.

What? Review the data, girl! Work it out! Your life depends on knowing the answers!

But damn it, what's the question?

Dev's brief contact with the World Mind of Alya B-V had revealed the Xenophobe's racial cycle. That Xeno—it had called itself the One—had been a single mind embracing some trillions of Xeno "cells" networked throughout the planet's crust. That was the so-called "contemplative" phase of the Xenophobe, when it could expand no more and had settled down to a lifetime that might well be measured in geological ages, absorbing heat from the planet's core and . . . *thinking*, thinking about whatever it was that such minds thought about.

The Xenophobes of Eridu, and of every other human-colonized world where they'd been encountered, had not yet reached that stage. They were still in the "acquisitive" phase, active, growing, and scattered as hundreds or thousands of separate organisms, each consisting of millions or billions of head-sized cells. Until this moment, no one had even been certain that the acquisitive Xeno stage was intelligent. Rational thought, it was suggested, might arise only after the One had ejected planet-seeding bits of itself on the magnetic winds of the "great void" which they thought lay at the center of their universe of rock. Only then, perhaps, did they settle down to become a peaceful, nonaggressive, and intelligent world mind.

That, Katya realized, was not entirely true. She had felt . . . *something* when her comel had first touched that black pseudopod, and she felt something now. The impressions were vague, more instinct and blind hunger than anything else, but there were flashes of something else.

. . . expectation . . .
. . . urgency . . .
. . . Unity . . .

That last tugged at Katya's awareness, and at her curiosity. There were—were they truly memories?—yes, distance-dimmed memories of . . . of completion. Of wholeness. Of something called "Self."

What would a finger feel, given a mind of its own, when it was sliced from its hand? This was like that, an urgent need to reunite with something far larger, far more power-ful than the mind Katya felt in the black, rippling mass around her. She sensed intelligence there, a curiosity . . . and, weirdly, a fear of *her* that was at once both reassuring and disquieting.

If it was afraid of her, what might it do to her to pro-tect itself?

Other impressions were clearer, but at the same time more jumbled, confused, and fragmentary. There was a memory-picture of the battle, shapes that might have been thermal images that were almost unrecognizable; they *would* have been unrecognizable had it not been for the landscape that gave her a sense of up and down, of moving across terrain. The—call it the sky—was black and cold and empty save for a vague white flare of warmth and radio noise that must be Marduk. It carried with it a sense of horror and dread: *lonely-deep-Void-emptiness-not-Rock.* Opposite was Rock: *warm-solid-shelter-food-safe.* She sensed ››self‹‹ clinging to Rock, drawing security from it. She sensed . . . *others*, things not-Self and not-Rock and bewildering in their contradic-tions—and those others were *threat*, pillars of intense heat, moving across rock, hurling death and pain.

Is that how Xenos see us? She shuddered. It was a won-der it hadn't just crushed her and fled.

Then she realized that, though it was hard to judge scale in those alien memories, the pillar-things she was "seeing" were the heat images of warstriders. Individual humans were little more than shimmering patches of warmth and—taste?—chemicals, nearly invisible, indistinguishable from unmoving pillars of warmth that might be Eriduan vegeta-tion, easily overlooked.

Why did the Xeno fear her? She was sure that she

detected that emotion in that confused bundle of comel-relayed impressions. Indeed, it felt as though *fear* might be the one emotion she had with a clear counterpart in the Xeno's thoughts. No amount of questioning or concentration or inward listening revealed the answer, however. She did get the impression that her captor was trying its best to be gentle with her, to protect her from harm.

Nice of it, she thought. *Maybe it's saving me as a snack for later*. But she dismissed that, an undisciplined thrust of black, gallows humor.

One thing's for damned sure, Katya told herself. *When this is over, girl, you're either going to be cured forever of claustrophobia or you're going to be drooling on the carpet*.

When this is over? She had no way of telling how long she'd been trapped in this black shroud, but she did know that she'd started out with two hours' worth of air in her life support pack . . . and that was two hours based on a slow and regular breathing rate. In the past few minutes, she'd been panting and gasping like a beached fish, driven by panic to gulp down air at a far higher than normal rate. If her support pack hadn't been automatically monitoring the CO_2 in her breathing and constantly adjusting the gas mix accordingly, she'd have swiftly hyperventilated herself into unconsciousness.

It's got to want to talk to me, she thought, thrusting away unpleasant specters of suffocation, alone in the depths of cold, crushing rock. *I came here to communicate with one of these things, and by God, I'm going to communicate!*

I just hope I don't run out of air first.

The thought images that had reached ››self‹‹ *from the not-Self thing it had captured were disturbingly like the impressions exchanged between two* ››selves‹‹ *in momentary direct contact, except that they were . . . strange, so distorted as to be almost unintelligible. There were no impressions at all relating to such primary senses as magnetic field or electrical flux or chemical composition or even direction.*

Of the thoughts that did come across, strongest, perhaps, was the feeling of being enclosed and trapped and surrounded, of being buried beneath a vast and crushing

mass of rock. What was puzzling about that image was that
the feelings of security and warmth and life and union that
were normally associated with the sense of being closed in
were missing, replaced instead by a gnawing, scrabbling,
frantic urgency that tasted like raw fear.

Fear of being closed in? For ››self‹‹, that was an oxymoron, a statement as paradoxical as, say, enjoyment of the
aching, yawning emptiness of the central Void.

Self might be able to comprehend. ››Self‹‹ could not understand the images that seemed to arise through direct contact
with the not-Self thing, but perhaps the far greater mental
powers of Self would assimilate and interpret them. ››Self‹‹
was all too aware of its own limitations.

Besides, it was necessary to transmit to Self an account
of what had happened in the Void, so that it could refine its
strategies, its weapons, and its purpose so that it could deal
with the strange not-Self opponents that had been encountered there. ››Self‹‹ felt the growing hunger for Unity and
increased the pace of its descent.

The rock grew warmer with depth.

Chapter 19

We can imagine hierarchies of Xenophobe awareness, then, with thousands of separate cells networked
together like so many unintelligent computers into a
low-level kind of consciousness. We know that vast
Xeno communities exist far below the surfaces of worlds
they've infested. Perhaps these, with millions or hundreds of millions of interconnected cells, have more
powerful, more intelligent minds, minds of human or
even superhuman scope and power. Finally, when all of
the Xenophobe communities of a world join together in
the contemplative stage, we can imagine that they enter

*a new and higher state of consciousness, the "One,"
the World Mind we encountered within the depths of
Alya B-V.*

What, I wonder, do such minds dream of?

—from a report given before the
Hegemony Council on Space Exploration
Devis Cameron
C.E. 2542

Katya tumbled from her prison in a wet gush of tarry liquid. The darkness surrounding her was still absolute, a primal night unrelieved by the slightest trace of illumination. She could sense the space surrounding her, though, a hot and steaming void. She could hear things—drippings, rustlings, unnameable slitherings and squishing sounds—that sounded close and helped describe the unseen emptiness around her.

There was atmosphere here, at least. She'd wondered about that during the descent, since the Xenophobes' underground highways weren't literal tunnels, and their deep caverns didn't necessarily open to the outside air. Her mask wouldn't have been able to handle vacuum. She'd imagined, though, that the air underground would be the same mix as on the surface, or else it might be the gaseous product of some Xeno-related chemical reaction. Either way, she wouldn't be able to breathe it. She pressed her fingertips against her mask, checking the pressure seal.

Secure. Next, she tried exploring this new prison by touch. Her outstretched right hand met soft and yielding surfaces in one direction, empty space in another. The floor was soft too, as though she stood on small and somewhat lumpy cushions beneath a few centimeters of some liquid with the consistency of thick syrup. Reaching above her head she could not feel a ceiling, but there was an impression—possibly psychosomatic, perhaps the workings of some latent human sense beyond the normal five—of a vast and crushing weight balanced precariously above her head.

This was worse, far worse than the Alyan vault where Dev had encountered the Xeno World Mind, for there'd been other people there, the troops of Cameron's Commandos who'd followed Dev into the bowls of the planet, and there'd been light from Dev's Scoutstrider and there'd been Dev himself, emerging from the wet cocoon of Xeno cells that had pinned him temporarily against the living wall of the cavern. She knew she was in a similar cavern far below Eridu's surface.

Grimly, she wrestled again with her claustrophobia. It had receded for a time during her descent, but it reemerged now, plucking at her tautly strung nerves, a devil's music of heart-thumping terror throbbing at the ragged edge of sanity itself.

The heat made it infinitely worse. Where it touched bare skin, the air was stiflingly hot, hotter by far than the equatorial jungle west of Babel. A fragment of geological data from her cephlink RAM reminded her that, in general, the temperature increased by twenty-five degrees celsius for every kilometer of depth beneath an Earthlike world's surface. Eridu's surface temperature was something over forty degrees, and though she didn't know the temperature here, she guessed that she must be between five hundred and a thousand meters down, with a mountain range of solid rock pressing down above her head.

Until now, she'd been afraid that her air supply might give out; now the question was which would get her first, running out of air or collapsing from heat stroke. Her bodysuit's multiple layers and microcircuitry were designed to cool or warm as needed, but she was quickly reaching the point where the suit would fail her. Her face and neck were slick with sweat, and it felt as though she was standing inside an oven.

She drew a deep, shuddering breath. She was going to die. There was no way around that now, if only because the monster that had dragged her down here would never be able to get her back to the surface before her air supply ran out.

Strangely, that didn't seem to matter.

Katya felt preternaturally calm. Had she, in fact, gone insane? Was this clarity of thought and of every sense save vision some kind of madness-engendered hallucination?

Shock, she told herself shakily. *You're still dizzy from the shock.*

All she could do now was try to make the best of the situation. She'd approached the Xeno Cobra to communicate, and communicate with the Xenos was what she would try to do. She doubted that her kidnapper had brought her all the way down here just to terrify her. It was intelligent, even if that intelligence was different from hers. There had to be, *had* to be, reasons for the things it did.

Once again, she stretched out her arm, probing this time with her left hand, the one still encased in the cool slickness of the DalRiss comel. The soft shapes she'd felt on the wall, on the floor beneath her feet must be Xenophobe cells; like the cavern on Alya B-V, the cave walls around her must be covered with hundreds, with thousands of the things. If she could touch them . . .

Self had reunited with ››self‹‹, receiving the flow of data from its scout with an emotion that combined feelings of happiness and completion with the succoring warmth of success. As the ››self‹‹ fragment of Self merged back into the whole, stored memories of the great Void flooded through Self's tens of millions of networked cells, a self-aware mass that spread like a vast, gelatinous web through nearly a hundred cubic kilometers of not-Rock.

As expected, the edge of the great, not-Rock Void was colder than the depths of Mother Rock, poorer in life-sustaining warmth. The blaze of heat hanging in the Void, however—a phenomenon remembered still from the time ages before when the first of Self's cells had crossed the Void and penetrated this part of the universe—was still there. It would provide heat enough to sustain life along the precarious interface between Rock and Void.

And there was more than reason enough for Self to extend itself in that direction, for ››self's‹‹ samplings of that interface confirmed the vague hints and traces Self had detected from within the rock; there were concentrations of pure metals there, of undreamed-of alloys and materials unlike anything tasted within Mother Rock. The chemist within Self's being quivered with anticipation at what could be grown from such a treasure trove.

Within those memories, too, were stranger things, moving things that might be rocks on the interface between Rock

*and Void that demonstrated volition, yet were patently not
››selves‹‹ spawned from Self. Selves that were not of Self?*

Incomprehensible.

*Selves-that-were-not-Self, they had attacked, destroying
many of the ››selves‹‹ as they emerged from the rock.
Threat . . . These things would have to be neutralized if the
treasures of the Rock-Void interface were to be exploited.*

*And finally, there was a particular mystery, the sample
››self‹‹ had brought within its damaged rock threader.*

*Self's thoughts, relayed through nanotechnic switches
and organically grown microcircuitry, moved with lightning speed and precision, but its physical reactions were
ponderously, laboriously slow. The . . . thing lay within a
hollow formed by the encircling cells of Self's own mass,
a not-Self tasting of salts and carbon, of oxygen and water.
As yet, it had made no threatening move. Indeed, ››self's‹‹
memories, merging now through Self's entire mass, recorded its tentative attempt at communication.*

*The thing, apparently, was as terrified of ››self‹‹ as ››self‹‹
had been terrified of it. It stood now, a trembling pillar of
radiant heat somewhat cooler than its surroundings, a dimly sensed, almost invisible specter unlike anything in Self's
long, long memory.*

*No . . . that was not quite true. Before Self had crossed
the great Void, eons past, there had been memories of other parts of the universe of Rock, of other confrontations
with volitional selves-that-were-not-Self. The forms of rock
threaders and defenders both had been copied from such
entities, though the forms of the entities themselves were
long forgotten and lost.*

*Curiosity . . . mingled with fear. Did this entity think;
was it self-aware, as Self was Self-aware; or was it a
natural and mindless phenomenon of the Rock-Void interface?*

*It seemed to be reaching out, and Self extended a subunit
of its own cells to meet it. . . .*

Images, memories flooded through Katya's awareness,
cascading thoughts, ideas, *strangeness.*

She saw heat . . . and tasted the warm comfort of Self, a
node of life and thought and awareness within an infinite

universe of rock. She struggled to retain her human perspective in a swirl of alien concepts.

A universe inside out . . . infinite Rock with a central core of emptiness, a vast, vast bubble of nothingness. Was there a center to infinity? There must be, for Rock extended endlessly in every direction from the Void at the center of All, growing hotter and hotter with distance.

Need . . . not for food, but for the raw materials necessary for propagation . . . and the need to spread through Mother Rock, opening not-Rock bubbles within the warm encompassment nurturing thought and being.

There was only Rock and not-Rock and Self.

Confusion . . . Self was by definition the knowing of Self. Could there be . . . an outside *awareness like the fragmented points of view called ››self‹‹, another Self?*

Memories, stronger now, of not-Self units that once, eons past, attempted to destroy Self. The defenders once were manifestations of those not-Self units, now long vanished. Their knowledge had become part of Self, their molecules utilized in the endless propagation of Self.

Katya struggled to remain standing. *This is what Dev saw, what he felt.* Two mutually alien worldviews, hers and the Xeno's, were colliding, and the shock very nearly overwhelmed her.

Somehow, she hung on, calling in her mind to the alien awareness surrounding her. *This . . . this war between your kind and mine is an accident!* Was any of this making sense to the monster she sensed beneath her hand and clinging to the night-hidden walls around her? *We thought you were an enemy when you attacked our cities and vehicles and space elevators but now I don't even think you knew we were there. We're human and we make mistakes and you are not human at all but you make mistakes too and . . .*

She knew her thoughts were babbling on, almost beyond her control. Somehow, somehow, she had to establish meaningful communication with the Xenophobe. . . .

No! Not "Xenophobe." It thought of itself as "Self," or as "the One," or, in some twisted sense just barely within Katya's comprehension, as the means by which Rock knew itself. She caught another image: *Child of the Night.* Did it understand night? She doubted that. Perhaps that was her own interpretation of something not expressible in words, a sense that it perceives itself as having been spawned by the night-black gulf of the Void.

"There are humans—things like me—that want to destroy you."

Denial. Not possible. Rock protects. The Child of the Night survives.

"It is possible. There is a weapon that . . . that changes rock into energy. Radiation. Great heat. They will do this to reach you even in the rock. To destroy you. They've already tried it, not long ago, at a place south of here."

Understanding. Not "weapon" or "place" or "south," concepts that Self could not easily assimilate. But Self remembered pressure waves rippling through Rock, remembered Rock boiling, remembered the sharp pain of separation as a portion of Self, a far-outlying portion of Self, had been lost.

Still, that incident had been no more important to Self than the frequent loss of bits of itself in the ››self‹‹ probes it continuously sent into its surroundings.

Far more keenly felt was something else, an astonishing emotion that threatened to overwhelm Self as it communicated with this dazzlingly not-Self point of view. The not-Self thought, reasoned, felt as Self did.

Wonder!

Katya had expected an argument. Self seemed to accept her statement about the nukes, however, without question. Did it read her urgency as an indication of truth? Or might this strange organism not understand the difference between the truth and a lie?

There are humans called Imperials, she tried to explain. *Humans who want to destroy you. There are other humans, humans like me, who don't want to do this. They want to communicate with you instead.*

Confusion. Paradox. How can not Self-thinking-thing both want and not want destruction of Self?

"There are . . . fragments of yourself. They leave you, travel to the surface—"

What is "surface"?

"To the, uh, interface, then. The interface between Void and Rock. Those fragments—"

›› *selves* ‹‹

"—*fight enemies, gather information. They think for them-selves*—"

—*think for Self*—

"—*but they have different points of view*—"

—*until they reunite with Self*—

"*Okay! Think of humans as many, many* ››*selves*‹‹ *that haven't reunited yet! They have different points of view! Some want to destroy Self. They are bad. Some want to talk. They are good. We need you to help the good humans fight the bad. . . .*"

Strangeness . . .

What is "good"?

What is "bad?"

If "good" and "bad" are opposites, how can humans be both good and bad?

Katya could feel just how thin her argument was. She'd glimpsed how Self perceived her—as a wisp of alien salts and pale heat. How could such a being possibly, possibly perceive the differences between Hegemony and Rebellion, between an Imperial Japanese and a rebel? Even she didn't believe her simplistic explanation of good against bad, and she was afraid that Self might perceive it as a lie . . . or as stark impossibility.

God in heaven, Katya thought with sudden, new agony, Self was incapable of sensing the difference between male and female! It might well have trouble realizing that a human and, say, an oak tree were members of different species!

Damn it, how much did the monstrous being around her understand?

A warning note chimed in her ear, and with a sudden-ness that caught her totally unprepared, a dazzling flare of ruby light exploded in the darkness a hand's breadth beneath her chin.

Laser . . .

No. It was the darkness that had enveloped her for so long that had tricked her eyes. The dazzling red light was nothing more than a tiny LED indicator on the life support pack strapped over her breasts.

It was warning her that she was almost out of air.

Oh, God, don't let me die until I get through to this thing! I've got to talk to it, got to make it understand, but it doesn't understand you've got to understand please understand . . .

There was much in what the not-Self was saying that Self could not grasp, much that tasted incomprehensible, like moving rock or a ››self‹‹ that was somehow not a part of Self.

Could there be a . . . a kind of Self, independent of Self and composed of many ››selves‹‹ that could actually be divided against one another?

Strange . . . though the idea might explain some of the not-Self things that had struggled with Self in the distant past, in other parts of the Universe of Rock. The not-Selves that had possessed the original patterns of the defenders, for instance.

Within Self's own life cycle, the cells of its body multiplied until it inhabited a vast area of rock between the region where there was too much heat to sustain life and the great Void itself. When Self inhabited an area of Rock limited in some difficult-to-define way that restricted further growth, it cast pods filled with ››selves‹‹ into the Void, pods that would navigate the magnetic currents of the Void until they reached some other, far, far distant part of the Rock-Void interface. Each, when it reached its destination, would grow into another Self.

Another *Self.*

Self rarely examined that curiously disorienting concept, but it knew the general idea to be fact, for its own inborn memories, replicated with each replication of its own cells, extended back . . . back . . . back across countless such crossings of the Void. From Self's point of view, its current awareness was simply a continuation of an earlier existence, but it knew, rationally, that there was at least a chance that others of the seed cast into the Void had reached Rock, burrowed into the depths, sought warmth, lived, replicated. . . .

What would it be like to meet another Self, one with its own point of view, with its own chain of memories, related *to but distinct from Self's own? What if, in the course of its endless expansion through the Universe of Rock, it were to encounter the outlying tendrils of such a separate Self?*

Could that be what was happening here?

Not that this thing tasting of salt water and oxygen glowing in the sheltering hollow of Self's body was literally another Self or even a ››self‹‹ . . . but . . . could it possibly be like Self, with its own mind, its own thoughts and memories, its own existence within infinite Rock?

The thoughts and images flowing across the bridge between the human and Self were almost painfully thin and sluggish. The thing, apparently, could move and react far more quickly than could Self, but its thoughts were laboriously slow. Self had time to taste and savor each in turn. The self-that-was-not-Self seemed to be in some distress. Somehow, in a way that Self did not entirely understand, its environment was degrading, threatening its survival.

Why, then, did it not simply change its environment?

Perhaps it was unlike Self after all.

The red light was flashing now, the tone in her ear tolling her death. Her air was almost gone. Funny. She still didn't know what the air in this cavern was like. When her tanks were exhausted . . . would she strangle slowly in Eriduan air, with only nine percent oxygen at eight tenths of an atmosphere, or would she start breathing carbon dioxide or some other poison that would smother her in a few seconds? Almost, she wanted to tear the mask from her face, to take a breath and find out and get it over with all at once. She felt dizzy . . . and a little giddy. Maybe her reserves were already gone and she was slipping into the mental ramblings of oxygen starvation.

Dev . . . why couldn't you have come with us? Perhaps it was part of the delirium. She thought that Dev was there, as she'd seen him at Kodama's party, and she knew with a hot, inner rush of feeling that she still loved him and wanted him even while she hated him for so completely embracing the Empire and all it stood for.

If she just could have talked to him one more time, maybe she could have convinced him. . . .

She wished she could leave him a message, but of course,

no one would ever find her body or download her RAM, not when it was trapped here so very far beneath the surface in this living, literal hell of heat and darkness.

There are humans like me up on the surface who can talk to you, she told the darkness. *You can work with them to stop the enemy from destroying you or . . . or . . .*

Katya felt a dull shock in her arms and legs. She'd fallen to her knees, breaking contact with the Xenophobe. She couldn't get up. . . .

There was no more air. Suffocation loosed Katya's rigidly bound claustrophobia, a nightmare storm of rising dread and horror. Convulsively, her fists clenched and she tried to scream, but no sound escaped the mask. For a moment, she stared at the winking red light as though it were her last link to light and life and sanity . . .

. . . and then the blackness swallowed even that tiny flicker of illumination, as, consciousness fading, she sank facedown into the warm, unseen ooze.

Chapter 20

Xenos are natural-born chemists, real magicians when it comes to taking things apart or putting stuff together, atom by atom. If we ever learn how to get along with them, we may find them rendering our notions of nanotechnology obsolete.

—from a report given before the
Hegemony Council on Space Exploration
Devis Cameron
C.E. 2542

Tendrils explored, probing the not-Self, sliding across alien surfaces, tasting chemistries strange to Self's experience. The . . . human, it had called itself . . . the human appeared to be a single integrated unit, like a single one of Self's cells, but massed perhaps sixty times more. Self withdrew as it tasted moisture . . . and the electrolytic bite of salt water.

The human was organized in layers. Outermost was an intricate shell or partial covering of some sort, multilayered and woven through with myriad threads of silver, copper, and other metals. The next layer below that was clearly organic, of far finer and more labyrinthine detail than the outer skin, a tough but flexible membrane of dazzling complexity. . . .

Threads of Self penetrated this deeper layer, still probing, expanding, tasting. Carbon, nitrogen, oxygen, sulfur, water, phosphates . . .

Astonishing. Alien as this human-thing was, its body chemistry was similar in many respects to Self's own. Not identical, certainly. Self's body employed somewhat different percentages of the same elements, and some others, such as nickel and germanium, were not present in the human at all in measurable quantities. Self's body tissues were particularly rich in silicon, iron, and copper, elements which formed much of its electrically based internal communications network, as well as the complex of nanotechnic machines within its cells.

The nature of the metabolism was different as well. Where Self converted heat to energy and assembled tissue from elements drawn from Rock, the human broke down sugars and other ingested, specialized compounds using oxygen drawn from its not-Rock surroundings. An iron-chelated protein in cells carried by an electrolytic circulatory fluid distributed oxygen through the organism and sequestered wastes for elimination.

Strange . . .

But at the level of basic chemistry the similarities between human and Self were far more numerous than the differences.

One lateral extrusion or appendage on the human was coated with a specialized skin that showed yet another form of chemistry. It, too, consisted primarily of carbon, nitrogen, oxygen, and hydrogen. Self recognized it as distinct from the human. Might this be a "bad" human? Or was this something else entirely? Like Self, it was a thermovore, drawing *heat from the not-Self it clung to and converting it to energy. Tendrils infiltrated the mass, recognizing its translation program, adapting it. It called itself a* comel . . . *and clearly was an artificial construct, an organic symbiont artificially designed to facilitate direct neural transfer between Self and human.*

Wonder!

And intense curiosity. Self had never imagined such diversity in a universe that until now had consisted of nothing but that which was Rock and that which was not. The comel *provided the key to the images now flooding through Self's awareness.*

Self explored deeper, nanotechnic threads each a molecule or two wide extruding from the mass of cells cradling the human now, an almost invisible fuzz sinking through protective layers, sliding unnoticed between the molecules they sampled, growing rapidly, penetrating tissue, tasting, relaying data.

Cells . . . not like the huge, detachable, and malleable units that made up Self's far-flung body, but minute, packaged miracles of chemistry. Cytoplasm and nucleus. Ribosomes, mitochondria, nucleotides, DNA, RNA . . . Self did not know the terminology but it analyzed the chemistry. This was quite different from Self's experience, but it understood most of the workings and could anticipate others. Some aspects of human physiology Self missed entirely. Sex, for example, was totally outside its experience, and the human's reproductive organs and processes were mysteries, completely unfathomable.

Of particular interest were the artificial implants within the organ the human called a brain, though Self did not think of them as technological additions but as highly specialized and organized regions of silicon, cadmium, and other elements not found in other parts of the body. These areas had been nanotechnically grown in place and obviously served as data storage and transmission devices of some kind. Since its own intelligence required nanotechnic prostheses, Self took for granted the fact that the human used them as well.

It took Self fifty-seven seconds to learn enough to realize that the human was dying. The notion of death was itself something of a revelation, since, though individual cells could be destroyed, Self as a whole could not die unless all of its cells ceased to function, and that was unthinkable . . . or had been until the human had suggested that Rock could be transformed into energy by "bad" humans. Self struggled to understand, to overcome prejudices determined by Self's own nature. The way the human organism was designed conferred upon it serious disadvantages. Why had it not adjusted its operation to a more convenient format?

It took another thirty-two seconds for Self to determine why the human was dying. Part of its body covering, apparently, provided a gas mix, a self-contained atmosphere different from that within the not-Rock occupied by Self. That gas supply was nearly exhausted, though enough remained for Self to analyze. Evidently, the human required more oxygen than was available . . . while at the same time carbon dioxide was beginning to poison its metabolism.

That was simple enough to correct. Self did so . . . and at the same time, adjusted the surface area of its cells in that area to begin altering the gas mix surrounding the human.

But the human posed a critical problem. It was at once so similar to Self on a chemical level . . . and yet it could not alter the simplest aspect of its environment or of its own chemistry. For the first time, Self considered the possibility that the human was, indeed, a not-Self organism separate from Self, but a relatively unintelligent one, an organism more like Rock than Self.

Self monitored the shifting balances of gasses dissolved within the human's unpleasantly electrolytic circulatory fluid and decided it would have to think about this further.

"Lieutenant!" Lipinski was growing desperate. "We gotta get out of here! I tell you she ain't comin' back!"

"Go on then, if you have to!" Hagan barked. "I'm staying!"

"But the Hegleggers are going to be here any minute!"

The two rebel warstriders stood side by side at the center of the crater, a few tens of meters from the black flow of the tunnel entrance. The brutalized landscape around them was barren, and at the moment completely deserted save for the two isolated warstriders. There was no other sign of life or movement; the last of the Xeno travel spheres had vanished on the winds hours before. The only movement at all was overhead, where Lara Anders's VK-141 Stormwind circled Red One. The stub-winged ascraft had reappeared moments earlier, bearing word that the last of the Xenos had been stopped at the second defensive line, and that government troops and warstriders were on the way.

"Let 'em come," Hagan replied. He gestured with his strider's autocannon, raising it as though in demonstration. "We're just more local militia, right?"

"You guys might not want to hang around for too many hard questions though," Anders said over the comlink. "They might wonder where you were in the fighting."

Her voice sounded terse, hard. Hagan remembered that Anders and Katya had always been close, ever since the ascraft jacker had started piloting strider drops for the Thorhammers back on Loki. She'd been shaken by the news that Katya had been missing now for almost three hours, but she was also a realist.

"Vic," she called. "We've got to unplug and odie!"

Odie . . . Inglic military slang from the Nihongo word for "dance," *odori*. It meant to leave in a hurry.

But Hagan didn't want to leave. "Lara, you pick up Ski and head back to Emden. I'll stay . . . and mingle with the militia when they show up. Things're bound to be pretty confused after that fight. They won't notice me."

"Lieutenant!" Lipinski sounded panicky. "She's been gone three goking hours!"

"Face it, Vic." Lara's Stormwind was dropping now, angling toward the crater floor, her engines kicking up a small tornado of dust. "Katya's been dead for at least an hour!"

"We don't know that." He tried to sound logical . . . rational. He knew he failed. "If she was able to make contact, they might have been able to take care of her life support needs. We know from Alya that they're wizards at analysis. Cameron talked about using a global-stage 'Phobe to terraform a whole planetary atmosphere! If she made her needs known, maybe—"

He broke off as Lara's Stormwind touched down, her squat and ugly ascraft momentarily obscured by the blizzard of whirling dust. The keening whine of the engines spooled down the scale until he could hear her voice again.

"We got Imperial Marines in the van, fellas, and not just crunchies, either. I saw at least five of the big Katana jobs, and a couple of big monsters that might have been Daimyos. Vic, when those bastards show up, you might not get the chance to explain anything. They'll shoot you and claim they nailed a Xenozombie Beta!"

She was right, damn it. But he couldn't just leave, not when there was even the faintest chance . . .

"*Watch it!*" Lipinski yelled over the tactical circuit. "Something's coming through!"

Hagan whirled his Scoutstrider to face the puckered, soft black dimple at the crater's center, where something was rising like a bubble from hot, liquid tar. Sunlight gleamed from an opalescent surface; it was a bubble . . . one of the travel spheres, but it was larger than any of the strange constructs that Hagan had ever seen before, over two meters across. Breaking free of the embrace of the ground with a dull, watery plop, it moved toward the striders, dragging in the dust.

Lipinski twisted, his chin turret laser swinging to center on the approaching Xeno pod. The turret on the belly of the Stormwind swiveled about with a whine, bringing Lara's high-velocity Gatling cannon to bear, as Hagan snapped to targeting mode and raised his Cyclan 5000. Travel spheres had never been known to attack, but still . . .

As though melting under a blast of intense heat, the upper half of the globe shriveled away, exposing a human figure slumped inside. Hagan's breath caught in his throat, choking him as he tried to blurt out the name.

"Katya!"

There was no response as the sphere dissolved away almost completely, leaving Katya limp on the ground. She was alive—the Scoutstrider's sensors proved that much almost at once—but she seemed dazed. She was wearing her mask and life support pack and, impossibly, she was breathing, though it was possible that she'd been hurt in some other way. Hagan froze the RLN-90 and broke his link with it, fumbling with in-the-dark clumsiness to remove his VCH and pull on his own mask and chest pack. Katya was standing by the time he'd cracked his hatch and vaulted the Scoutstrider's ladder to the ground, but she responded to his touch like someone walking in her sleep.

"Katya!" he yelled again, his voice muffled by his mask. He placed his palm on her life support pack interface, then read the cascade of data flowing into his cephlink. The air tanks were almost full, the regulator functioning perfectly. *Somehow* she'd recharged her tanks, and Hagan felt a cold chill prickle at the base of his neck as he realized what must have happened.

His first thought, a twisting, sick memory, was of Xeno-zombies he'd fought on Loki, human machines absorbed by Xeno nanotechnics and converted into . . . something else. A weapon. On Alya A-VI, he'd seen living DalRiss "machines" taken over the same way.

Was it possible that the same thing had happened to Katya, that she'd been killed, then reanimated by those amorphous horrors?

Some cold and hard, rational part of him was shouting that since Katya couldn't be alive, she *wasn't* alive, that she must be something else. *Kill it! Kill it!*

But instinct told him she was still human, and the data coming through the datalink confirmed that. Katya's bodysuit was disheveled but intact, save for her left sleeve, which was still rolled up above her elbow. The comel was still in place. He touched it. . . .

It's inside me oh God it's inside me, reading me reading me and it's dark so dark and it doesn't understand what it sees oh please don't let me go mad don't let me die here in the dark—

The shock of touching Katya's mind through the comel rocked Hagan so hard he nearly fell. Somehow, he hung on, detecting levels of emotion and impression and memory flowing through the comel, knowing that it was Katya and terrified of that raw, naked emotion bridging the gap between them.

"I'm here, Katya! I'm here!" *God, I love you* . . . had she heard that? He'd never so much as admitted it, even to himself.

Her eyes snapped open behind her tinted UV goggles. "Vic?"

"Right here, Captain. You okay?"

"I'm . . . fine. A little shook." The eyes closed and she shook her head. "Oh, Vic! Tell me you're real!"

"I'm here, Katya, and I'm real. It's all over now. You're safe."

"Safe . . ." The eyes closed. "I . . . talked to them. It . . . I mean, there's only one." A shudder passed through her body and Hagan held her close. "It . . . it *read* me. . . ."

Lipinski arrived at Hagan's side.

"Help me get her into her slot," he said, and the two of them supported Katya as they guided her back to the Ghostrider, which was crouching, legs folded beneath it, a dozen meters away. Together, with some difficulty, they got her up the ladder to the dorsal hull, then helped her clamber through her hatch.

"I've got Impie striders in sight," Lara warned. Her Stormwind was grounded now, but she'd released a small, high-flying remote that was still circling the battlefield, scanning the surrounding area and transmitting the results to Lara's link. "They're coming through the jungle from the east, range, three klicks. I'm also picking up ascraft now, forming up over Babel. You guys've got five minutes, max."

"Almost set." Hagan completed hooking up the strider connections to Katya's bodysuit, as Lipinski scrambled over the top of the Ghostrider's fuselage and reentered his own slot. The LaG-42's AI would assess her injuries and physical condition far more quickly and completely than Hagan could, and stabilize her until they could get her to a med center and a staff of somatic engineers. He didn't remove her mask—he couldn't seal the Ghostrider's hatch and recycle the pod's atmosphere while he was still leaning in through the access—but he got her helmet on and jacked in, then switched on the AI-governed link enabler. He pulled back out of the hatch and closed it; he could hear the hiss of pressurization as he slid down off the machine's hull.

Linking in once more aboard his own warstrider, he heard Lara on the tac channel with word that the Imperial striders were approaching the edge of devastation several hundred meters to the east of the crater. Engaging his strider's maneuver systems, he lurched toward the waiting Stormwind, which crouched on the crater floor like a great, ugly bird of prey. The Ghostrider, jacked by Lipinski, was there ahead of him.

Huge, padded grippers within the VK-141's riderslots secured the warstrider about its midsection, drawing it partway back into the slot's recess. It took less than thirty seconds for Hagan's Scoutstrider to be secured. The jets shrilled to full power, stirring again a swirling dust storm that cloaked the slow-rising ascraft, and then they were soaring into the sky, with the crater and the battle-seared scar in the jungle looking like an angry, gray slash against the red-and-orange foliage. Just visible now as a line of black specks, the first Imperial warstriders stepped from the jungle, deploying across the plain in open battle formation. Behind them, a quintet of black specks above the horizon marked a flight of swift Imperial Marine Hachis approaching at just below the speed of sound.

"Are we gonna outrun those ascraft?" Lipinski wanted to know.

"Outrun 'em?" Lara replied, voice tight. "Not if they chase us, no way. Whether or not we get away depends on whether or not they're interested in us."

Apparently, they weren't. The Imperial flight began circling above Red One, providing air support for the approaching striders. The Stormwind dropped until it was skimming the jungle top, then slid smoothly across the crest of Henson's Rise to block itself from marine scanners and radar.

"Vic?"

Hagan was surprised to hear Katya's voice, relayed through her strider's link with the Stormwind. He'd thought she'd be unconscious by now. "Yeah, Kat? You okay?"

"I'm fine." There was still a faraway gentleness to her voice, but she did, in fact, sound all right. "Listen . . . we've got to find Dev, get to him."

"Cameron?" Hagan gave a mental scowl. He had no use for the man. "Why?"

"I think I understand now what happened to him, back on Alya B. I need to . . . to talk to him."

She didn't hear me, after all. Maybe that's a good thing. "That might be a bit difficult, just now." Hagan wondered if she'd slipped into delirium. He checked her health readouts and saw that they were approaching normal, though there were clear signs of psychological shock. What had happened to her down there?

The Stormwind shrieked low across red-and-orange jungle toward the rebel base.

Chapter 21

I do wonder what the Xenos think of us. Two sexes, a bewildering variety of races, myriad ideologies, cultures, languages, religions, worldviews. It's not enough to say we're as alien to it as it is to us. It could be that humans, who are already used to diversity in a diverse universe, are better prepared to understand the Xenophobes than they could ever possibly be prepared to understand us. I suspect the Xenophobes are more intelligent than we are in absolute terms . . . but less adaptable.

—from a report given before the
Hegemony Council on Space Exploration
Devis Cameron
C.E. 2542

Yoshi Omigato contemplated the virtues of *gaman*—of patience. The ViRsimulation surrounding him was the creation of Masaru Ubukata, the twenty-third-century Buddhist artist who'd used the themes of cherry blossoms floating on the surfaces of still ponds to communicate the perfect peace that comes with recognizing one's place in space and time. Omigato floated, silent and invisible, one with the blossoms, one with the pool. . . .

The inner alarm broke his reflection and he scowled his displeasure. His analogue had been instructed to handle all communications from the outer world. What event warranted an interruption of his meditations?

"Forgive this intrusion, my Lord," his analogue's voice whispered in his ear.

"I very much hope this is important." He wondered if analogues were self-aware enough to appreciate pain.

"It falls within the parameters you set for me, my Lord. The demonstration has begun at Tanis."

"So!" Omigato's anger vanished. He'd been expecting this news, of course, but not this quickly. His mind leaped to the one incident that might upset his carefully prepared timetable. "And the Xenophobes at Babel?"

"Decisively beaten, my Lord. All were destroyed at the second barricade a few hours ago. There was no damage to the space elevator, and casualties were light."

"Excellent!" He'd been less interested in the Xeno attack than in the news from Tanis. It helped, however, that the threat to Babel had been eliminated before his plan went into its final phase. More of Eridu's population would be grateful to the Imperial forces for coming to their aid. "What is HEMILCOM's assessment of the Xenophobe situation?"

"HEMILCOM estimates that it will be some time before there is another assault. The Xenophobes, when beaten, appear to require considerable periods of time before they renew their attempts to surface. We may have as much as two to four months before another incident occurs."

"It is time, then, to execute our move against the *gaijin*."

"Yes, my Lord."

"Alert Nagai. We may need his marines."

"And the *gaijin*, Cameron?"

"I will compose his orders myself."

"As you will, my Lord."

The analogue vanished from Omigato's mind, leaving him alone. With a thought, the cherry blossoms and pond vanished, leaving a gray, inner emptiness. Kanji characters began appearing in the air, brush stroke by graceful stroke, as Omigato started composing his message. It would be translated later, of course, and cast as official orders from the Governor himself, but Omigato thought more clearly in Nihongo.

There could be no chance that Devis Cameron, hero of the Empire, would misunderstand them. . . .

Chapter 22

Those who won our independence by revolution were not cowards. They did not fear political change. They did not exalt order at the cost of liberty.

—Louis D. Brandeis
U.S. Supreme Court Justice
C.E. 1927

Spread apart at twenty-meter intervals, the warstriders of the 4th Terran Rangers moved through the forest single-file, their hulls repeating the reds and oranges of the surrounding vegetation. On point was Bev Schneider's Fastrider *Nothung*, following the track of one of the old construction trails that crisscrossed between the Eriduan cities. Eleven more striders followed, LaG-17s, Ares-12s, and RLN-90s. It was an impressive force, fast-moving and hard-hitting.

Dev's machine was Duarte's command Ghostrider. His maintenance crew had transferred the name *Koman-do* from his old strider to the new when he'd returned to the Armory from orbit with his promotion and new orders. Officially, he was still listed as an advisor, but for all practical purposes he was no longer a *koman*, but a full-fledged member of the 4th Terran Rangers.

He was trying not to think of it as a kind of demotion, as getting broken from Imperial staff officer back to Hegemony striderjack. His position on the staff had always been predicated on his expertise on Xenos, and when that expertise no longer applied, it was only natural that his superiors slot him in someplace where he could be useful.

But the reassignment rankled nonetheless, his brevet promotion to *tai-i* not withstanding.

He'd feared morale problems with his takeover of the unit, but so far there'd been no complaints and few problems—none, at any rate, that hadn't been handled by a quiet talk in the privacy of his office. There'd been some of the usual soldiers' grumblings, of course, but Dev's prestige—the striderjack who'd once talked face-to-face with the Xenos and lived to tell about it—had proved to be both ID and authorization. It had become a special mark of distinction for the men and women of A Company: "Yeah, but our skipper knows the creep-crawlies personal, on a first-name basis!" More than that, Dev knew each of his men personally, and they liked and respected him for it.

For several days, he'd immersed himself in A Company's records, familiarizing himself with the myriad details of supply, maintenance, and logistics vital to the functioning of any military unit. It had been a colossal and thankless task, and he'd used his cephlink to bypass sleep for four nights running. The effects were starting to catch up with him now. He was going to have to let himself get some sleep soon.

"Hey, *Tai-i*," a voice called to him over the tac channel. It was *Sho-i* Gunnar Kleinst, a kid from Eridu's Euphrates Valley who'd enlisted with the Rangers shortly after they'd arrived on-planet. The kid barely spoke any Inglic at all, but over the AI-coordinated tactical com link, his German was translated as smoothly as if Dev had taken a Deutsch RAM implant. "Think we can stop off for some R&R? My mother lives in a little farm outpost just over that hill."

"Not this time, Gunnar," Dev replied.

"Aw, let the kid go see his momma, *Tai-i*," another voice suggested. It was *Chu-i* Giscard Barre, from the state of Gascony in Terra's European Federation. "We'll cover for him."

The Rangers, Dev had found, were unusually close, surprisingly so given that they'd been drawn from a dozen Terran nations, including both Europe and the American states. Old national rivalries died hard sometimes. Half of the states of the European Federation hated the other half, and animosities were still close to the surface in some parts of the continent despite the *Teikokuno Heiwa*, but those nationalistic divisions vanished, for the most part, within a tight-knit group of men and women stationed light-years from their homes.

That closeness was rarely extended to the locals, even though the colonists were also mostly from north-central Europe and from eastern North America. The Terran-born troops didn't like the mincies—hated them after Duarte's death, in fact, because Duarte had been popular with his men—but after a suitable probationary period they tended to think of recruits like Kleinst as fellow jackers, not as mincies or locals. It was an odd twist of human psychology, Dev thought, that European-born troops could hate European-descended locals, yet accept one of those locals as a fellow comrade-in-arms to the point that they even thought of members of his family as "people" instead of mincies.

"Sorry, guys," Dev said, replying to Barre's suggestion. "We have our orders and we're on a short leash. No time . . . and somehow I don't think HEMILCOM would approve of consorting with the enemy."

He meant it lightly, as a joke, but it fell flat. "My mother is not an enemy," Kleinst said.

"Aw, gok HEMILCOM," an unidentified voice added. Dev thought it might be the big Dutch *chu-i*, DeVreis.

"Yeah, the dissies are all back in the city," another voice said. "Out here, it's just folks."

"Quiet, people," Dev ordered. "Open circuit."

He hoped HEMILCOM hadn't been listening in. He doubted that the Hegemony brass would understand, and Imperials like Omigato would be downright peeved at any hint of fraternization between the troops and the locals. So far as his troops were concerned, *the enemy* was any outsider, whether he was a local, an Imperial, or some fat Hegemony *gensui* in his comfortable office up in Eridu synchorbit.

They were moving down a gentle hill into the district known as the Euphrates Valley. The region was nothing like its Terran namesake. The land was lush and fertile, the forest open and airy, the sky showing through the canopy alive with sparkling light. This close to the south pole, Marduk barely rose or set at all. The land was in perpetual twilight, with the sun always either just above the horizon, reddened by the atmosphere, or just below, with aurorae filling the sky with eerie, pearl-luminous shafts and curtains and sprays of light. The trees around them were the characteristic, multitiered mushroom shapes of Eridu's trees, some reaching fifty meters in height, but the ground was more open, less choked with saprophytes and walkers than in the equatorial regions. Eriduan flora was not as active at the poles as it was near the equator; the low angle of the sun eliminated most of the harsh ultraviolet, making both temperatures and UV levels pleasantly temperate.

The Euphrates was one of the largest rivers on Eridu, sinuously winding across some three thousand kilometers from one side of the south pole to the other, before emptying into the Clarke Sea. The names of cities, towns, and outposts in and around the river delta region echoed the placenames of Terra's ancient Near East: Ur and Lagash; Assyria and Sidon; Karnak, Tanis, and Valley-of-Kings.

Named for a city that had once existed in the Niłe Delta rather than the fertile crescent, Tanis was a domed community—a village, really—of about eighteen hundred inhabitants. Most settlements in the Euphrates Valley were agricultural combines of one sort or another; denigrass, a local plant that provided an easily dyed and woven fabric as soft and as pliable as synsilk, was the foundation of the valley's thriving textile industry. Tanis, however, was a mining community. A largely automated thoridite mine had been tunneled into the rocky slopes of the Sinai Heights. Most of the people in Tanis worked in the processing plant just outside of the village dome.

Tanis lay just ahead, on A Company's line of march. Their exact mission still hadn't been transmitted to them yet, but the who-was had it that there were Xenophobes in the area. DSAs—the deep seismic anomalies that meant Xenophobe tunnelers were working below ground—had been tracked in the area for almost three months now. Ever since those two nuke depth charges had been used near Karnak, there'd been intense speculation about where the next ones might go down. This area was a good bet, and some were speculating that Tanis would soon be evacuated so the Impie marines could trot out their nukes.

In any case, he'd been ordered to deploy his company into the Euphrates Valley east of Tanis, then stand by for further orders. Their warloads included anti-nano countermeasures and rockets with high-explosive warheads, so it didn't look like they would be gassing mincies this time around. Everyone in the regiment was convinced that another Xeno breakout was imminent and that they'd been positioned to make the first intercept.

Dev had heard about the recent Xeno attack near Babel, of course, first as a furious round of who-was spreading through the regiment's maintenance personnel and enlisted troops, then as a terse announcement from HEMILCOM. He'd felt a sharp, mounting frustration at the news; if there'd just been a comel available . . . but HEMILCOM still insisted that the long-awaited comels from Earth had not yet arrived.

At least, that was the *official* story. The who-was going around the Rangers' barracks carried a different tale, and Dev wasn't sure yet how to take it. Rumor had it that bandit raiders had intercepted a government monorail earlier that week somewhere in the Equatorial Mountains, killed several Imperial Marines, and made off with a classified piece of DalRiss bioengineering.

The only DalRiss artifact Dev could think of that might be on Eridu was a comel, *his* comel. If the story was true—and Dev had the typical soldier's faith in any juicy who-was—then he'd been lied to.

Just as mystifying was the question of what bandits wanted with a comel. From all of the reports he'd heard so far, the various bandit groups operating in some of Eridu's wilderness regions were a bloody, undisciplined lot, and it was unlikely that they'd know what to do with the thing once they had it. Possibly they intended to hold it for ransom.

Well, none of that was Dev's concern now. He was back to fighting Xenos, and if his superiors saw fit to keep secret the comel's arrival, that was their affair. Still, the situation had left Dev depressed and disillusioned. The Hegemony's military bureaucracy was so vast it made him feel lost, vulnerable, and helpless all at once. It was hard to tell what to think, what to believe. Sometimes it was all he could do to just keep pushing ahead, following orders and taking each day as it came.

The strider company reached the edge of the woods, where the trees and brush thinned away to nothing and an orange-yellow sward dropped away beneath them. A kilometer ahead, a cluster of domes nestled about the base of a low, rock-rugged hill. The broad gleam of the Euphrates shone in the sunlight beyond that. The twelve warstriders moved slowly into the open, straggling into an uneven line along the crest of the hill.

Tanis. The nearest, largest dome was the town proper. The farther domes housed mineheads, separators, and processing plants. The silver thread of a monorail wove in from the northwest; the refined thoridite was loaded aboard freight monorails for shipment to Babel and loading aboard sky-el shuttles and transport to orbit.

Time to check in.

"HEMILCOM, HEMILCOM, this is Ranger Blue One. We have reached our objective. Awaiting orders."

There was a long pause. "Ranger Blue One, Hegemony Military Command copies. Wait one."

They stood there, the striders casting long, long shadows in the light of the horizon-skimming sun. Dev could sense movement visible through the transplas surface of the largest dome. He engaged his telescopic vision, zooming in for a closer look and enhancing the image.

He could see color . . . and a throbbing, rippling movement. At first, he thought he might be looking at some sort of panic, and he felt a slick, hot flutter of fear. Xenophobes were able to sense large concentrations of metal from far beneath the surface, especially the ultrapure concentrations of cities and other high-tech assets. Had a Xeno surfaced inside Tanis?

"Enhance again," he told his Ghostrider's AI. The image shimmered, then steadied. He could see . . . faces, yes, a sea of angry, chanting faces, clenched fists, signs, and banners. He could almost imagine he heard the mob's roar. A holoscreen four stories tall projected a vast and angry face above the crowd, silently mouthing passionate phrases.

"God, *Tai-i*," his number two said. "It looks like another riot." *Sho-i* Wolef Helmann had replaced Charles Muirden in the Ghostrider's second slot.

"See if you can pick up an audio channel that'll let us listen in," Dev told him. "I want to hear what they're saying."

"Yes, sir."

"Say, *Tai-i*?" That was Martin Koenig's voice. "You don't think HEMILCOM's going to use us for mob-busting again, do you? We're not rigged for it!"

"Don't anticipate them, Koenig. Iceworld until we get the word."

But Koenig was right. They had rockets with HE and AP warheads, heavy machine guns with explosive rounds, and a deadly antipersonnel weapon called CM—canister monofilament—that promised to be effective against Xeno machines as well. They did not have gas or dispersal grenades—or sonic stunners either, for that matter. And this time they did not have infantry support.

Had they been sent here to quell another riot? Or was the appearance of that mob down there pure coincidence?

"I've got a broadcast channel, sir," Helmann said. "I think it's their speaker system from that big screen."

"Let me hear."

" *. . . the foul poison of the Hegemony and its Imperial masters! I say, citizens of Eridu, that we must fight! Yes, fight to reclaim our world, our rights, our lives, our souls from this—*"

"Who the hell is that?" Schneider wanted to know.

"Jamis Mattingly," Kleinst replied. "Local troublemaker."

"An agitator?" Helmann wanted to know. "Who with, the NCs?"

"They say he has Network connections."

"Kill it," Dev said. He didn't know if that rally was being staged by Green dissies, New Constitutionalists, or old-fashioned anti-Imperial agitators, but he'd heard enough.

"Ranger Blue One, this is HEMILCOM. Stand by for special direct feed. Unit CORAM only."

If Dev had been in his human body, his eyebrows would have arced up high on his forehead. A special direct feed? That was reserved for extraordinarily secret orders, a transmission directly to the unit commander's personal RAM—

CORAM, in military parlance—that bypassed normal communications systems.

Dev pulled up the appropriate mental code. "Okay, HEMILCOM. This is *Tai-i* Cameron, CO of Company A. Standing by for direct feed."

"Authenticate."

Dev transmitted his personal code, in effect confirming that he was who he said he was.

"Roger," the HEMILCOM voice said a moment later. "Authentication received and confirmed. Here it comes."

Data flowed through Dev's cephlink, a short, hard cascade of data already packaged in a private RAM file. "Transmission complete," the voice of HEMILCOM said. "Execute immediate."

"Affirmative."

He broke the mental seal on his orders, and words spilled across his visual overlay.

SECRET
TO: COMMANDING OFFICER, COMPANY A, 1ST BATTALION, 4TH TERRAN RANGERS
FROM: HEMILCOM, ERIDU STATION, ERIDU SYNCHORBIT
RE: OPERATIONAL ORDERS
1. DANGEROUS REVOLUTIONARY FORCES HAVE SEIZED THE MAIN CITY DOME OF THE TOWN OF TANIS [MAPREF 243-LAT 87°15'32"S/LON 02E]. THEY ARE ARMED WITH MINING LASERS AND WEAPONS STOLEN FROM LOCAL ARMORY, AND ARE BELIEVED TO HAVE A LARGE STOCKPILE OF ARMS HIDDEN IN THE CITY.
2. IT IS IMPERATIVE THAT THIS INSURRECTION BE PUT DOWN IMMEDIATELY AND WITH THE UTMOST VIGOR, AS A DEMONSTRATION OF HEGEMONIC WILL AGAINST REVOLUTIONARY ELEMENTS.
3. UPON RECEIPT OF THIS ORDER, YOU WILL DEPLOY YOUR COMPANY IN OPEN ORDER AGAINST THE TANIS TOWN DOME. YOU WILL USE ALL AVAILABLE MEANS TO BREACH SAID DOME, DISPERSE THE MOB, AND END THE INSURRECTION. YOU ARE AUTHORIZED TO USE MAXIMUM FORCE.
4. A SEARCH IS TO BE CONDUCTED FOR WEAPONS

STOCKPILES. THESE SHOULD BE INVENTORIED AND PLACED UNDER GUARD FOR SURRENDER TO IMPERIAL FORCES.

5. MINING AND ORE PROCESSING FACILITIES ARE TO BE PRESERVED IF POSSIBLE. THE MAIN HABITAT AREAS, HOWEVER, ARE TO BE DEMOLISHED. A HARSH DISPLAY WILL IMPRESS THE REBELLIOUS ELEMENTS AND CONVINCE THEM OF THE HEGEMONY'S DETERMINATION TO MAINTAIN CONTROL.

6. THREE COMPANIES 1ST BATT, 3RD IMPERIAL MARINES HAVE BEEN DEPLOYED FROM LUXOR [MAPREF 243-LAT 86°11'02"S/LON 01E] AS BACKUP, AND WILL BE AVAILABLE AS ACTIVE RESERVES AND CLOSE SUPPORT. COORDINATE ACTION AND CLOSE SUPPORT LOGISTICS WITH TAI-I NAGAI [VIRCOMCHAN 39874].

                                                    —PREM

Dev stared with his mind's eye at the orders, aghast. It couldn't be . . .

Unexpectedly, the image of his father rose from somewhere in the back of his mind. At Lung Chi, Michal Cameron had been faced with a split-second, life-or-death decision, one that had him weighing the lives of some millions of civilians and military personnel already in synchorbit against the lives of half a million people still trapped on the surface of the planet with a surfacing horde of Xenophobes. The horror of that decision, Dev knew, had had more to do with his suicide than had the court-martial or the official disgrace.

He thought of almost two thousand people as the air pressure relentlessly dropped, as their oxygen bled away until there was simply not enough left to sustain life. And it wasn't just the order to breach the dome, either, though that part of things demonstrated that HEMILCOM was determined that there would be no survivors. Turn lasers, monofilament rounds, and rockets on a crowd of civilians? Gods of humanity, there were *children* in there!

Someone, cool and remote and with the analytical detachment that high-level command brings, had decided that the village of Tanis should be eliminated as a lesson to the rebels. Such Olympian detachment rarely took into account the *human* aspects of a situation. Dev didn't believe for a moment that the order had actually originated with Governor Prem.

For all of his relatively brief military career, Dev had tried to be the good soldier, the faithful warrior, following each order given without question. He was realizing now that, sometimes, there were orders that could not be obeyed, not if he was to live with himself afterward. *These* were such orders. . . .

And Dev refused to obey them.

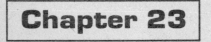

Chapter 23

> *The Imperium, through the Hegemony, has block-*
> *aded our worlds, raped our industry, deprived our*
> *people of life and liberty, and denied us redress. Where*
> *then is justice? Where equality under law? The Imperial*
> *Peace is not our peace!*

> —from a speech given on New America
> Travis Sinclair
> C.E. 2537

Dev reread the RAM document, disbelieving, feeling like he'd somehow gotten caught up in an unusually realistic ViRdrama and needed only to break contact with a palm interface to lift the spell. The alphanumerics suspended in his mind remained stubbornly unchanged, reality, not virtual reality.

A mistake? The name at the end suggested otherwise, though Dev wasn't sure he believed it. Prem was not HEMILCOM, though he technically commanded the Hegemony military forces on and over Eridu. Dev guessed that Omigato was a more likely source of those orders; if that was true, if the Emperor's representative was making the decisions now, Hegemony Military Command might even be out of the command loop entirely.

What would *Chusa* Barton think about this? Apparently he didn't even know, since there was no copies-to tag line. The regiment's commander was at Babel, sorting things out after the battle with the Xenos. Possibly that was deliberate as well; Dev had the cold, ice-slick feeling that he personally had been maneuvered into this.

Were the orders Omigato's? Or Prem's? It didn't matter. The orders themselves were . . . monstrous. Unthinkable. There *had* to be a mistake.

"HEMILCOM, this is Ranger Blue One. Come in."

"We read you. Go ahead, Blue One."

"There's been a transmission error of some kind. You people can't mean this."

"Ah, Ranger Blue One, please clarify. What are you talking about?"

"These orders you just fed me! What the hell is going on up there?"

He felt the feather-light touch of an ID check probing the upper layers of his RAM, checking once again his authentication codes. "I don't know the precise nature of your orders, *Tai-i*," the voice came back. "But I can tell you that they came through proper channels from a very high source and they have been verified. I suggest that you carry them out, immediately and without question."

"Who am I talking to?"

"This is *Shosa* Hector Sandoval, and I have just received confirmation of your orders from the transmitting authority. You are directed to carry out your orders."

A *shosa*—the equivalent of an army major, and relatively low on the hierarchy of the HEMILCOM staff.

"*Shosa*, these orders require us to breach the dome of an Eriduan town and attack the civilians inside. That is nothing less than murder! Anyone who survives the attack will die when their dome depressurizes!"

"I suggest, *Tai-i*, that you not discuss these orders over communications channels. They are classified secret, which is why they were fed to you as coded RAM data. I also suggest that a company commander is not qualified to assess the nature or the military necessity of the orders he is—"

"*Gok* military necessity, we're not carrying out these orders!"

"*Kuso, Tai-i!*" Koenig's voice interrupted. "What's going on?"

The rest of the company hadn't been told the content of the orders yet, but they must have picked up at least part of his exchange with HEMILCOM. Dev decided to bring them in at once, since his disobeying a direct order would certainly involve them as well.

"We've been ordered to breach the Tanis dome and attack that demonstration," he said curtly. "They're telling us to kill everyone."

The responses chorused through Dev's head. "My God!" "They can't do that!" "What?" "Someone's screwed up, right?"

Dev was already considering alternatives . . . seizing the town's main airlock, say, and deploying into the city. But the orders *specified* that the hab areas be destroyed. Someone up in synchorbit wanted eighteen hundred civilians to die.

Horror choked him; had he been in his body instead of linked to the Ghostrider he might have been physically ill, but the cephlinkage itself was damping down the most savage of his emotions. Anger flooded through his brain like a dark red tide, leaving him temporarily paralyzed, unable to activate a single circuit in the strider.

There'd been a long moment's delay, but now another voice sounded in Dev's mind. "This is Omigato. There has been no error. Attack the town."

He was speaking Inglic. Dev wondered if he was really speaking the language or if the AI was translating for him. The words were flat and without expression, but there was no way to tell one way or the other.

This, at least, confirmed that Omigato was the source of the orders, and not Prem. Why was the Imperial representative hiding behind Prem's authorization? The answer seemed obvious. If records were checked later, Prem's codes would be on the transmission authorization. The monsters who'd destroyed a small town would be Prem and Cameron, not Yoshi Omigato.

Was there a way to prove it? Dev checked his communications circuits, verifying that all transmissions were being recorded, but at the same time he knew that the precaution was meaningless. Recordings could be rewritten as easily as ViRsimulations could be edited.

"No, sir," Dev said. He found he could move again, think again, though horror lingered. "With respect . . . no. We won't do it."

He'd cut the rest of his company in on the channel. "You tell 'em, Captain!" someone called in the background. Was that Barre? *Shut up, you idiot, do you want to get court-martialed too?*

"Tanis is occupied by hostile rebel forces," Omigato said, the voice cold and implacable. "You are directed to attack the town."

"No, sir! *Iyeh!*" His resolve was stiffening. "There are women and kids in that town. My men are not murderers. We will not indiscriminately slaughter civilians!"

"If it is atmosphere loss you are concerned about, you may rest assured that we have that covered. You can't possibly put a hole in that dome large enough to depressurize the entire dome in anything less than six hours. A marine unit has been detailed to follow up your assault. Their engineers will effect immediate repairs on the dome. There will also be medical units standing by to assist with civilian casualties. Now, will you carry out your orders?"

Dev thought of the demonstration in Winchester. *Where are the medics?*

"No, sir."

The silence that followed was deadly.

"You are relieved of command. *Chu-i* Paul DeVreis!"

"Y-yes, sir."

Dev held his mental breath. Was he going to order DeVreis to continue the mission, to wipe out the town? What would happen?

"You are now in command of A Company. You will return your unit to base. *Tai-i* Cameron is to be placed under close arrest."

"Uh . . . yes, sir." Dev heard the confusion, the pain in DeVreis's voice. "Captain . . ."

"You'd better do it, Paul," he said gently. "Before they order you to do something worse."

"*Damn* the bastards!"

"Open circuit," Dev warned. "Lieutenant DeVreis, carry out your orders."

"Yes, sir. Let's get the gok out of here."

Dev heard the men muttering among themselves as the striders turned and pushed back into the woods.

Who, he wondered, were the Xenophobes? The shape-shifting monsters tunneling away kilometers below his feet? The anti-Hegemony mobs that urged dissolution of a government that had kept the peace for centuries?

Or the Imperials like Omigato, who called alien and human alike *gaijin*, and who issued such monstrous directives?

"Uh . . . *Tai-i*?" It was Gunnar Kleinst.

Dev shifted his optic feed to a rear scanner. Kleinst's Swiftstrider was still at the edge of the woods, shifting its weight back and forth between its slender, birdlike legs. "DeVreis is in command now," he said.

"I don't care who's in command," Kleinst shot back. "Look, I can't . . . I can't go back. Do you understand? My family lives near here. Those are my *people* down there!"

"Captain?" DeVreis said.

"You're in command now," Dev said. "Not me."

But it was not the sort of decision that could be casually tossed off to someone else. The entire company was still in a kind of shock, unable to decide which way to move, or how to react.

Dev knew what he had to do.

Swinging his Ghostrider about, he broke away from the others, smashing through the underbrush toward the lone Swiftstrider standing at the forest's tree line. "Open for a direct feed!" he snapped, and he felt Kleinst's RAM open for direct access. In less than a second, Dev copied the orders he'd just received into Kleinst's files. "Get going!" he said, his voice urgent. "Fast! Tell the people in Tanis what's going on, and show them the orders for proof! Tell 'em Imperial Marines are going to show up any time, and they'd better be ready for them."

Dev wasn't sure what the civilian population of Tanis could do if the Impies launched an all-out assault on the dome. At the very least they would have time to get breathing masks and oxygen ready, or even to begin evacuating the dome. At best, they might manage to get the word out to other cities on Eridu, to the shadowy forces of the Rebellion, perhaps. The government could try to wipe out one small village with secret orders to an isolated unit, but there was no way to carry out such orders against the aroused population of an entire planet.

"Sir?" Kleinst sounded desperate. "Come with me!"

"Go!" Dev roared over the link. "Now!"

The Swiftstrider pivoted on spindly legs, then broke and ran from cover, long, scissoring strides carrying the recon vehicle rapidly down the slope toward Tanis.

Dev found he wanted desperately to follow, but he still wasn't sure just where his real duty lay—to himself or to his unit. If he deserted now, the fury of HEMILCOM might well descend on the entire company.

Besides, he wanted the kid to make it and he didn't know yet how the others were going to react.

"Hey! He's deserting!" Barre called.

Turning, Dev faced them. Barre was crashing his Scoutstrider through the brush toward the edge of the woods, the bulky 100-MW laser comprising his machine's right forearm coming up into firing position.

Smoothly, Dev stepped between the laser and the fleeing Swiftstrider. "Do you want to shoot me?" he said calmly, "or carry out your orders and arrest me?"

"Ranger Blue Two!" Sandoval's voice snarled over the voice circuit. They would have observers monitoring the company's communications links, which meant that they'd seen and heard everything. "This is HEMILCOM. Stop that deserter!"

Koenig was moving his Swiftstrider forward, well to Dev's left, where Dev couldn't block him and Barre as well. Dev swung sharply, tracking with his chin laser.

"*Tai-i!*" Helmann's voice sounded frightened. "You can't—"

Dev ignored him, concentrating on the targeting brackets closing now on the Swift's chin turret with its bulky 18mm autocannon. He was terribly conscious of the Ares-12's vulnerability; the eight-and-a-half-ton machine had almost no armor at all, and the slightest error in targeting could pierce Koenig's life support pod and kill him.

Locked ... *fire!* The muzzle of Koenig's main gun glowed white-hot for an instant, then puffed away in a sparkle of vaporized metal.

"*Damn* it, Cameron!" That was Barre's voice, anguished and shocked.

All of the warstriders were in motion now, some toward the treeline, others toward Dev. Dev could also sense some outside party working at the encoded locks guarding access to the Ghostrider's artificial intelligence. He was running out of time.

Schneider's LaG-17 moved between Dev's Ghostrider and Barre's Scoutstrider, blocking the bigger machine's line of fire. In one blazing instant, the company could dissolve in the bloody chaos of strider-to-strider close combat.

"Everybody relax!" Dev yelled over the command circuit. "Iceworld, *iceworld*, right—"

... and then he felt his power going, the drain totally outside his control. He groped with his mind toward an override and found nothing there, no way to switch control back to his cephlink. Vision, speech, all control functions were gone. With a shock, he realized that he was no longer linked to the LaG-42's AI. He'd been bumped off the circuit. His VCH was still connected, his hand still on the interface plate, but no feeds were coming through and he was wide awake, inside his body, harnessed within his life support pod.

HEMILCOM must have inserted a command override and shifted control of the Ghostrider to Helmann. Dev was now deaf, blind, and helpless inside his coffin-sized pod. Tentatively, he laid his palm against the hatch release ... but that, too, was denied him. The access locking system, and no doubt the capsule eject as well, had been sealed off or disabled. He was a prisoner.

As he lay there, sensing the ponderous swayings of the strider as it moved through the woods, he wondered what was happening outside. Had his men been ordered to run Kleinst down? Were they tracking the kid now, or sniping at him with missile or laser fire?

Or had the entire column given up and moved back into the woods? The motions of the LaG-42 suggested steady movement, not battle or a chase. The Ghostrider, at least, was heading back to base.

And Dev was carried along helplessly in its belly, a prisoner.

Chapter 24

> *It is impossible to live in a society and to be free of that society.*
>
> —Vladimir Illych Lenin
> early twentieth century

Aegir Strang did not understand his current orders, but he felt no compunctions about carrying them out. He hated the agitators and speech makers and Constitutionalist rabble-rousers who seemed to have sprouted up like weeds in a dozen south Eriduan cities, and if HEMILCOM wanted continuous reports and updates on the demonstrations breaking out among the cities of the Euphrates Valley, he was delighted to oblige.

For several weeks now, he'd been traveling among several of the cities in the valley—Lagash, Memphis, Tanis, and Sidon in particular—a circuit of south-polar towns and cities where discontent was breeding rebellion, where even the news that Xenophobes had surfaced outside of Babel failed to stop the litanies of sedition and treason.

Strang was not from Eridu, though he spoke perfect Deutsch—as well as his native Inglic and Norsk-Lokan. He'd been born and raised on Loki, but a winning thesis in school on the *Teikokuno Heiwa* had won him the chance at a scholarship to the prestigious Tokyo University. For the young Strang, that had been a literal chance of a lifetime. He hated Loki, its bitter half-T-formed climate, its cheerless people, its crowded domes, and when his one opportunity to get off the frigid Frontier world came, he'd taken it.

Gaijin students in most Japanese schools were still unusual in a country that distrusted foreigners, but Tokyo University was an exception, a showcase institution in the most cosmopolitan of Japan's metroplex cities that ostentatiously solicited the brightest non-Japanese students throughout the Shichiju. After passing the school's grueling, hellish exams, Strang had quickly distinguished himself, majoring in political science and revolutionary theory. He'd been recruited by the DHS three months before his final graduation. For ten years he'd served the Directorate, first at Singapore Orbital, then at Eridu. He'd never returned to Loki.

On the Frontier, the Directorate of Hegemony Security had the reputation of being a kind of political secret police, keeping tabs on the hundreds of dissident groups that flourished throughout human space. In fact, the largest part by far of the DHS's charter involved the so-called "technic crimes" such as unlicensed starship jacking, computer hacking, and file smuggling. The Shichiju required order for efficiency, but there were always elements within society that tried to shortcut or break the regulations for personal gain. The DHS was tasked with running down the criminals who threatened the economic and technical order of things, and Strang had long since decided that he loved his work.

Lately, though, much of that work had centered on the dissident movements on Eridu. There were dissies on every Shichiju world, of course, but Eridu was a breederbed of revolutionary movements, illegal jack tampering, and sedition. Worst were the holdout greenies still fighting the Hegemony's plan to transform their world into a paradise. The battle over terraforming Eridu appeared to have sharpened the political confrontation that was evident across the Shichiju and could easily lead to full-fledged rebellion.

And yes, the DHS was also tasked with suppressing rebellion.

Special Agent Aegir Strang, then, had been assigned to his circuit of towns and cities in Eridu's Euphrates Valley, where he'd assumed the identity of Rudolph Heinz, a Bavarian importer negotiating a deal to import Terran beer to Eridu. The cover let him talk to lots of people, especially the managers of bars, beer halls, and restaurants, places where people tended to gather to vent their frustrations. He'd been following the growing surge of popular discontent and had even spoken to some of the dissie leaders who were planning a series of demonstrations in half the cities of south-polar Eridu. Omigato's announcement that outposts and towns were to be evacuated had generated a tidal wave of protest. Revolution, he was convinced, could break out at any time. All it needed was a push.

Dutifully, Strang had recorded everything he'd seen and heard in his implanted RAM, and, dutifully, every other day or so he'd downloaded the recordings into a millisecond-burst transmission and beamed it to Eridu Synchorbital. He wasn't privy to any important secrets—cephlink technology, after all, made *any* stranger a potential spy—but he was able to keep HEMILCOM apprised of plans to launch the biggest anti-Imperial demonstrations yet. He'd picked up the who-was about hidden weapons and armor and passed those on as well, and when the big rally began in Tanis he'd been on hand to record the speeches for later assessment by the DHS intelligence teams. J. L. Mattingly, one of the most outspoken of the so-called Eridu patriots, was the featured speaker. The man had been arrested twice already for anti-Imperial agitation, and it looked like he was about to make a stab at third-time's-the-charm.

Events in Tanis had rushed ahead at a breakneck pace. A thousand people were gathered in the town square, where a four-story holoscreen had been erected to project the speaker's voice and image. Mattingly had appeared in the screen, a giant delivering a two-hour sermon on the evils of the Empire and its Hegemony puppets. After that, there'd been a succession of lesser speakers, including the administrator of Tanis herself, a woman who'd been appointed by the Governor but had recently and publicly sided with the dissidents.

After her, Sinclair's image had boomed down at them for thirty minutes, a message from "fellow patriots, fighting injustice and tyranny on neighbor worlds." An analogue, obviously, sent from New America, since it was unlikely that Sinclair was here. Strang wished he could have a chance at the real Sinclair. The man, Strang thought, should be shot for his anarchist's attacks on the most just and stable government Mankind had yet managed to devise in a very long and bloody history. Well, who could tell? Once the troublemakers on Eridu were rounded up, perhaps he could swing a reassignment to New America. *That* rats' nest had needed cleaning for a long time now, and the biggest rat of all ought to be easy enough to track down. Someone on New America, surely, could be found who would be willing to trade Sinclair for blood money.

Then Mattingly was back.

Throughout it all, Strang had recorded every word, every gesture, and he'd circulated through the crowd too, filing faces in his implanted RAM for analysis later at Eridu Synchorbital.

He was pretty sure that HEMILCOM was preparing something special. During his last transmission to synchorbit, he'd been warned to keep a mask and life support pack handy and had been given a password in case he needed to identify himself to occupying Imperial troops. He was to lie low until he could approach an officer with an Imperial Marine garrison unit.

It wasn't until the warstrider appeared in the city's main airlock that he realized that something was wrong.

They'd been playing canned folk music over the giant holoscreen, some woman in a red headband singing something in Inglic about eagles and time and dust, meaningless stuff as far as Strang could tell. Mattingly himself had interrupted the show, though, with the warning that Hegemony forces were outside the city and that an attack could be imminent.

Panic had gripped Tanis with the announcement, and Strang had recorded it all. *This* was what he'd been sent to find, he was certain . . . the townspeople's frightened gatherings in tight little knots on the streets, the grim-faced militia troopers appearing, carrying a motley assortment of weapons obviously just unpacked from hidden stores. The Tanis town militia commander himself, a black-bearded former police chief named Duchamp, appeared on the screen, urging the citizens to stay calm and the troopers of the 200-member Tanis Militia to assemble by the main lock and wait for further orders. After a while, a wild-eyed kid, a Hegemony warstrider by the look of the patches on his bodysuit, came on the screen, explaining in a high-pitched, fear-ragged voice that his unit had received orders to attack the town, but that he'd managed to break away and come warn them.

Strang didn't believe the kid at first, though the level of panic in the town went up like a sky-el shuttle as he talked. A Hegemony attack on Tanis? What HEMILCOM officer in his right mind would order such a thing, knowing that such a heavy-handed move would inflame every city on Eridu?

Then someone gave the kid on the big screen an implant jack. He'd plugged it in, closed his eyes . . . and then his image had vanished, replaced instead by words scrolling up the building-sized screen.

SECRET
TO: COMMANDING OFFICER, COMPANY A, 1ST BATTALION, 4TH TERRAN RANGERS
FROM: HEMILCOM, ERIDU STATION, ERIDU SYNCHORBIT
RE: OPERATIONAL ORDERS
1. DANGEROUS REVOLUTIONARY FORCES HAVE SEIZED THE MAIN CITY DOME OF THE TOWN OF TANIS . . . .

By the time the message had reached "A harsh display will impress the rebellious elements," the panic had begun to metamorphose into something else. Strang heard it clearly in the voices of the people around him in the Tanis square, a growing, bubbling anger that swept over the earlier fear like the incoming tide, submerging it in a sea of chanting, hate-darkened faces.

Maybe HEMILCOM had known what it was doing after all. If this kind of emotion had been lurking just beneath the surface, maybe the only way to deal with it was with military force.

Unfortunately, the attack appeared to have been broken off. The warstrider, a kid named Gunnar Kleinst, claimed that his company's commander, Devis Cameron, had refused the orders and given him his chance to escape.

Strang watched the screen, gnawing at his lower lip in an uncertainty born of the knowledge that the operation of which he was a part was collapsing before his eyes. What should he do? The Hegemony, surely, had contingency plans, a backup unit for just this kind of situation, and the DHS no doubt had SWAT forces ready to move in and scoop up Mattingly and the other high-profile traitors.

He would have to make another transmission.

Strang's lasercom link with HEMILCOM was hidden among the rocks on the Sinai Heights above the town, a unit hidden inside a hollowed-out chunk of rock, with only the carefully aligned transmission and receiver arrays showing. All he had to do was compose and encode a cephlink message and zip-squeal it to the laser transmitter through a fist-sized radio relay hidden just outside the dome wall. He had to be within ten meters or so of the relay, but there was a convenient spot, a park close beside the dome that he'd used before. He began pushing his way through the angry crowd, heading toward the south side of the town.

Omigato had taken command of the HEMILCOM communications center at Eridu Synchorbital. The plan, Omigato's carefully crafted and precisely balanced plan, was in danger of being smashed, and it was all the fault of that cursed *gaijin*, Cameron.

It had mattered little to Omigato whether the town was destroyed or not, since his target was not Tanis but Devis Cameron. The American, Omigato had been certain, would do one of two things. Either he would carry out the orders and attack the town, or he would refuse the order and set himself up for a court-martial. What Omigato had not foreseen was the possibility that Cameron would actually warn the rebel populace of the town, dispatching one of his own men to do so!

Damn the man! Some of the men on Omigato's staff, including his own analogue, had guessed that Cameron would carry out his orders and attack Tanis. The orders telling him to do so, of course, could be easily accessed and rewritten before the public trial, and the revised version of them—directing him simply to observe the situation and report to HEMILCOM—was already on file with Eridu Synchorbital's communications AI. Cameron would be tried, convicted, and disgraced for his part in killing hundreds of unarmed civilians.

Omigato himself had expected Cameron to refuse to carry out those orders. True, the man had been diligent and conscientious in the attack on the rioting mob in Winchester, but Omigato had been watching Cameron closely during the interview with Prem. The fool had agonized over a handful of civilian casualties, convincing Omigato that he would never have the stomach to breach a colony dome. Given that some of his men were native Eriduans who would protest such orders, it wasn't likely, in Omigato's opinion, that an attack would take place. Cameron appeared to be one of those *popular* commanders who listened to his men instead of demanding instant and unquestioning obedience. Discipline among the Hegemony troops was not what it was in the Imperial armed forces.

But a point-blank refusal to follow a direct order could be worked into a court-martial as well. By the time the record had been rewritten, it would look as though Cameron and his whole mutinous company had been conspiring with the enemies of His Majesty.

Either way, Omigato would be able to report that the *gaijin* hero had disgraced himself—as had his father before him. The practice of allowing non-Japanese to rise to high positions in government and the military would cease, the advisors closest to the Emperor would be discredited, and members of Omigato's own Kansei Faction, the Men of Completion, would stand at the Emperor's side, advising him, guiding the Imperial hand through the difficult times that lay ahead.

It would be a first step toward erasing the disgrace still born by *Dai Nihon*'s Emperor. It would be the first step toward direct Imperial control of every world in the Shichiju.

And, almost as an afterthought, it might also open the way to allowing direct Imperial control of Eridu. Obviously, if the local Hegemony troops couldn't handle the situation properly . . .

But Cameron had warned the city; worse, the traitor had arranged for a copy of his CORAM-secret orders to be broadcast to every person in Tanis. The rebels there would see to it that every populated dome on Eridu would hear about those orders. It would mean open rebellion.

Why had Cameron done it? Had the man already secretly joined the rebels? Omigato didn't think that could be the case, not when Cameron surely knew that his father's rehabilitation depended on his good behavior. He should have either followed orders . . . or ordered his men back to base, hoping to argue or plead his way out of the inevitable courtmartial. Quietly accepting the trial might preserve his career and it would not affect his father's rehabilitation. Treason would end both.

It didn't make sense.

Briefly, Omigato allowed himself to consider the possibility that he had made a mistake. Westerners, Americans in particular, did not share the Japanese reverence for their parents, but Omigato had studied Cameron's case closely; he'd been certain that the young man would do anything to save his father's name!

What could have been more important in his life than that?

Gaijin. Omigato shook his head bitterly. Animals! There was no understanding them.

"Sandoval!"

The *shosa* in charge of the HEMILCOM communications center turned in his seat, eyes wide. "Sir!"

"Open a secure channel to Captain Nagai."

There was still one chance of salvaging the situation. Nagai and his marines were standing by at Luxor, waiting for orders to move in and support the 4th Terran Rangers in their raid on Tanis.

If Omigato played it right, it might yet look as though Cameron and his *gaijin* warstrider unit had run amuck and sacked the town.

Chapter 25

*How much longer must we suffer the yoke of Japan
and her Hegemony puppets? How much longer must
we slave for others, sending the product of our toils to
Earth for* Dai Nihon's *social welfare programs while
our own children go hungry?*

—from a speech given at a public rally in
the Tanis dome, just before the battle
Jamis Luther Mattingly
C.E. 2542

Nearly two full hours after Tanis had been warned by Gunnar
Kleinst's arrival, the first Imperials began touching down
on the orange-yellow sward outside the main dome. The
air cover arrived first, a flight of four Taka, or "Falcon,"
ground support tilt-jet aircraft. The Falcons were closely
followed by a dozen lumbering magflitter APCs, bulbous,
black-hulled machines that settled to the ground, their gull-
wing access doors already rising.

The attacking warstriders appeared with devastating swift-
ness, emerging from the black interiors of the APCs with
long-legged steps, accompanied by almost three hundred
legger troops.

They were late. Though one company had been standing by in case the Hegemony unit assaulting Tanis needed
backup, the orders for a full battalion deployment had come
as a surprise, and their transports had not yet been prepped
or moved out of their maintenance bay hangars.

As it was, by the time their magflitter APCs were landing
beside the Tanis dome complex, a sizable number of locals
were already outside, protected by stolen military armor or

the heavy E-suits used in the mines and armed with weapons taken from the local armory. Five monorail ore cars had been hauled from the processing yards to the open fields north and west of the town, and there tipped onto their sides, forming a chain of crude but effective redoubts.

The two hundred men and women of René Duchamp's Tanis militia had taken cover behind the ore cars and among the crags and rocks of the Sinai Heights. Despite the reports of hidden arms caches in Tanis, the militia had little in the way of modern weapons. Most of the legger troops carried laser pistols or carbines; squad support weapons had been jury-rigged from 200-MW Mogura mining lasers.

Tanis also possessed six warstriders: an RLN-90 Scout-strider, three constructors with makeshift weapons, and two ancient LaG-3 Devastators. The Devastators were both almost two centuries old and had been purchased stripped, without their original armament. They clanked into flanking positions on the Tanis defensive line now, massing fifty tons each but mounting only machine guns and light lasers. There was one new addition to the defending strider force, an Ares-12 Swiftstrider still wearing the blue-and-white markings of the 4th Terran Rangers.

Facing them were thirty-four Imperial warstriders, three full companies of the 2nd Battalion, 3rd Imperial Marines, better known as the Obake, or "Black Goblin," Regiment, under the command of *Shosa* Nobosuke Nagai. Half of the marine striders were Tachi and Tanto recon striders similar in speed, armor, and weaponry to Hegemony LaG-17s. Of the rest, ten were Nak-232 Wakizashis and six were Mitsubishi Katanas, while Nagai's command strider was a lumbering three-slotter Daimyo. They were accompanied by two companies of foot soldiers in full *do* combat armor.

Though Imperial warstriders were of distinctive design, it was not immediately clear that these were, in fact, Imperial machines. Marine warstriders usually went into combat with their nano surfaces set to a gleaming jet black, and unless stealth was specifically required for the mission deployment, each strider often flew its own *sashimono*, a small vertical banner displaying the *mon*, or family badge, of the unit's commander.

Nagai's striders deployed outside of Tanis, however, without banners and with their nano surfaces set to reflect their surroundings. This was less a serious effort at camouflage—hiding a five-meter-tall warstrider on an open field in daylight is simply not possible—than it was a simple misdirection. Tanis was a civilian city; few civilians knew the technical differences between the various classes and models of warstriders or would think to record their images as they stormed the city, and those who did would probably not live to download them to anybody else. *If* there were survivors—and Nagai's orders were explicit that there were to be none—their impressions would be of varicolored combat machines, big, deadly; and wearing shifting, reflective nanoflage patterns in golds and oranges.

That would be enough like the description of typical Hegemony striders to confuse the issue, especially since HEMILCOM already controlled Eridu's news and communications networks.

The Battle of Tanis began even before the Imperial forces had deployed from their transports. Taka ground support aircraft and Hachi assault ascraft shrieked overhead, circling, threatening, and the Devastators opened fire with machine gun fire, their cumbersome upper torsos pivoting as they tracked the incoming aircraft, sweeping them with stuttering bursts of 12mm Armor-Piercing Explosive-Core rounds. A Hachi ascraft staggered, multiple APEC rounds punching through the relatively light armor on delta wing and stabilizer surfaces, then exploding inside with the force of small antipersonnel grenades. There was a flash and a shower of flaming debris from the ship's port side as a hydrogen fuel storage tank detonated. Somehow, the pilot killed the fire, brought the Hachi around, and nursed it off toward the north, still trailing smoke.

Seconds later, two surface-to-air missiles hissed skyward from shoulder launch tubes. One was decoyed by a flare, but the other locked onto the heat plume of one of the Falcon tilt-jets and slammed home with a flash and a puff of white smoke. The Taka began losing altitude, managed to level off, then suddenly stalled and plunged into the forest, its impact marked by a rising mushroom of flame and black smoke.

The other aircraft, too lightly armored to tangle with warstriders or heavy weapons, pulled back out of range just as the Imperial forces hit the first redoubt.

The outcome of that first clash was never in doubt.

Tightly coordinated and disciplined, the Imperial warstriders moved and fired as a unit, combining their fire on the biggest rebel machines first. The Devastators were heavily armored; when they'd first been introduced in 2332 they'd been the most powerful combat machines ever seen, fifty-ton monsters equipped with heavy plasma guns and 250-MW lasers that had made them undisputed monarchs of the battlefield for almost sixty years. But their weapons now, mining lasers and machine guns, were all but useless against the advancing ranks of Katanas and Wakizashis.

One LaG-3 struck a Tanto with a lucky burst of explosive shells that sheared off its left weapons pack, but the concentrated laser and plasma gun fire of seven Imperial striders caught it an instant later, searing through its slab composite armor in seconds, gutting the big machine with multiple blasts that splattered huge globbets of molten steel for meters across the ground and spilled internal wiring and circuitry in great, smoking, half-melted tangles. For an instant, steel and ceramic burned with a white-hot blaze fueled by the stricken machine's O_2 life support reserves; then its high-explosive ammo stores ignited, and the rippling internal blasts completed the destruction the Imperial fire had begun, ripping arms from body and shattering the squat, massive torso in a cascade of smoking debris.

The second Devastator scored three direct hits on a Katana with its pair of 50-MW popgun lasers, none of which slowed the target. Then a volley of M-490 rockets slammed into its legs and torso, savaging armor, weapons, and hull fittings, filling the air with whining shrapnel. Stricken, the LaG-3 took a hesitant step forward, faltered, then crumpled as its right leg actuator failed. Fifty tons of dead steel-ceramic composite hit the ground with an earthquaking thud, abruptly silencing the shrieks of the militia troops unlucky enough to be sheltering beneath the huge machine.

With machine precision, the advancing Imperial striders shifted their aim. One of the constructors, damaged an hour earlier while dragging ore cars into defensive positions, exploded before it could fire. The other two were cut to pieces by rapier-swift bolts from three directions at once. The RLN-90 Scoutstrider stood its ground, its Cyclan-2000 autocannon hammering away at the advancing Imperials until a Starhawk link-homed missile slammed into its torso and detonated its micronuke warhead.

Kleinst's Ares-12 scored the only rebel warstrider kill, blasting away at a Tanto with a stuttering volley of 18mm HE rounds that shattered its right leg and left it smoking on its side. Then a proton bolt from a Wakizashi's charged particle cannon tore through Kleinst's machine, turning its Y-51D fusorpak to slag and sending jagged, blue-white lightnings arcing between the Swiftstrider's ruptured electronic entrails and the ground.

Gunnar Kleinst died screaming as the Ares-12's short-circuiting AI downloaded 1,200 volts directly through his cephlink's feeds into his corpus callosum.

The Tanis Militia's leggers held their ground for perhaps ten seconds more. Antiarmor missiles and mining lasers fired at point-blank range damaged four of the attacking warstriders, killing the pilot of one of the Katanas. Then, as laser and high-explosive rounds began to sweep through their ranks, they broke and ran. Plasma bolts scratched white fire across the sky as the more delicate traceries of laser ionization flicked from target to target, rending them in sprays of blood and steam-blasted tissue. René Duchamp died trying to rally his men behind one of the ore cart redoubts, burned in half by an 88-MW pulse; his second-in-command was crushed beneath the foot pad of a Wakizashi as she fought to reload a shoulder-fired missile launcher.

Leaderless, the militia forces lost all coordination. Some fled for the Sinai Heights beyond the town, where snipers were keeping up a steady fire on the advancing legger marines. Others bolted for the wide-open cargo locks in the city dome, and were still struggling to crowd in when laser fire began slashing through them from behind. A pair of Starhawk missiles, teleoperated from the Katanas that had launched them, struck the side of the Tanis city dome and detonated with twin, savage thunderclaps. The city's air began shrieking out into the thinner Eriduan atmosphere, raising a howling vortex of swirling sand and dust. The air pressure in Tanis began dropping, though it would be hours yet before outer and inner pressures matched and the windstorm stopped.

Legger marines, supported by Tanto and Tachi warstriders, broke into small strike groups, deploying swiftly across open ground to targets already mapped and loaded into tactical operations memory. One team seized the monorail head and the pressurized station lock, where civilians were still crowding aboard a three-car train. Striker missiles breached the station walls, while flamers took care of the screaming, frantic *minshu*.

Other teams secured the mining facilities and the domes housing the separator and processing plants, although, because of the demonstration in the Tanis town square, there were only a handful of workers present, and none of them were armed. All were rounded up without incident and herded into an airlock "for safekeeping." Opening the outer lock door eliminated the need for keeping them under guard, as marines proceeded to secure the plants and their equipment.

But the real slaughter occurred inside Tanis proper.

Gunso Isamu Kimaya was not proud of what he was doing, but he was determined to carry out his orders with a true samurai's devotion to duty because to do less would dishonor him and the Imperial *daihyo* who had issued them. He was glad, though, that he and his *sensono kyodai*, his war-brothers, had been ordered to drop the black-hulled livery of the Obake Regiment, that they were not displaying the regiment's white-on-black *sashimono*.

He'd guided his KY-1180 Tachi through the gaping rent in the town dome, formed up with the rest of his section, then advanced into the town square. His dorsal turret with its twin Toshiba 88-MW lasers panned back and forth, killing lone targets and using them to set buildings on fire. For the dense crowds of people stampeding ahead of his advance, he used a different weapon, the *sempu*.

The word meant "whirlwind," though that hardly described the thing in action. Heavy-caliber shells fired from his Tachi's Mark III weapons packs exploded as they cleared the stubby muzzles, hurling a cluster of lead balls at the targets with a shotgun's dispersal pattern. Unlike shotgun pellets, however, these balls were strung together by several meters of monofilament, molecule-thin wire that sliced through light armor, cloth, breather packs, flesh, and bone alike with appallingly bloody ease.

In places the dead—and the neatly sectioned body parts of the dead—were piled up four and five deep, especially in the killing fields around airlocks and building entrances, and blood was ankle-deep on the legger marines moving across some of the sunken walkways. Flamers designed to incinerate Xenophobe Gammas worked equally well on flesh. Long before the air thinned to the point where humans could not have breathed it, the dome's atmosphere was choked by foul, low-hanging clouds of greasy smoke.

Kimaya used his machine guns to cut down a man and a woman fleeing together, then waded forward through a wall of bodies. Rigidly, employing every *kokorodo* discipline at his command, he held his emotions in check. In a way, the high-tech linkage of the individual marine striders helped. Under infrared imaging, with computer targeting interlock, the fleeing *minshu* were reduced to rapidly scattering patterns of colored light, faceless save for gaping holes that might be screaming mouths, nonhuman targets no more meaningful than the robotic *ningyo* used in training exercises. Calls over the tactical frequency heightened the practice-exercise feel of the situation.

"*Red Three, Red Three! Come left ten meters. Maintain your spacing.*"

"*Green Five, targeting at three-one-five, range two hundred meters.*"

"*Orange Two, stand clear. I am employing whirlwind.*"

"*I think some targets have moved behind the building on the left.*"

"*Nagumo! Sato! Neutralize that threat!*"

"*I have a lock. Stand by. Target neutralized.*"

Still, he did not feel good. The slaughter seemed to take forever, as Imperial warstriders dispersed through the city. Building after building was set ablaze. Honored ancestors! He'd not given thought to the possibility that there were women and children in here!

"Red Leader, this is Red Two. Objective secured."

"Affirmative, Red Two. Proceed to objective Blossom Four."

"Yoshitomi! Take your squad and check those buildings on the left!"

He had his Tachi's recorders on, of course, and was able to let the strider's AI capture the images he'd been told to get. Why were his superiors so interested in the details of this butchery, he wondered?

Movement captured his attention and he swung to the left. A civilian was approaching the Tachi, a breather mask over his face, a white rag waving in his right hand. He was shouting something, and Kimaya cut in his strider's external mikes to hear what he was saying.

"Hanashi-o tsuzuke-yo!" the man called. *"Hanashi-o tsuzuke-yo!"*

The words made no sense. "Let us continue to talk"? The man was repeating the phrase over and over, and it occurred to Kimaya that it sounded like a code phrase, maybe a password of some sort.

But the man was *gaijin* and Kimaya had been given no passwords or special authorizations beyond the call signs of the assault group. His orders were to take no prisoners. With a twitch of what, in his physical body, would have been his left hand, he depressed his left-side Mark III weapons pack and triggered a single *sempu* blast. The *gaijin* fragmented into a dozen neatly sliced pieces, the face on the severed head still showing shocked surprise as it wetly plopped to the ground.

Gods, there was so much blood. . . .

"My God, what are they doing?"

"The bastards! The filthy, goking *bastards*!"

"Shut up, people! Stay low!"

Jamis Mattingly was huddled beneath a dun-colored thermal blanket with a dozen other people, peering miserably through his mask's dust-coated visor at the scene below. He and most of his staff had escaped through the mining tunnels and access shafts scant minutes after the Imperial Marines had grounded. Now he was hidden among the rocks high up in the rugged Sinai, using the thermal blankets to mask their body heat signatures from aircraft. Grim-faced militiamen crouched among the rocks nearby, watching with stony, emotionless eyes as the Imperial Marines completed the destruction of Tanis.

There was no question whatsoever about the identity of the attackers. Mattingly was a former warstrider; he'd jacked Ghostriders with the Scots Greys on Caledon before emigrating to Eridu and becoming a fusion plant manager, and he knew all of the Imperial designs. This had been a marine op, a show of raw terror and naked force designed to . . . to what? He didn't think the marines were taking prisoners. Damn it, he wasn't conceited enough to think that the Impies were so eager for his head that they'd zero an entire town to get it. They must have a reason . . . but what was it?

There were scattered reports of other survivors, some in the forest, others in the tunnels below. A number of people had fled in magflitters as soon as young Kleinst had arrived with his terrifying news. With luck, they might reach some of the neighboring Euphrates Valley towns and spread the alarm.

A dull thud sounded from the town dome . . . followed by another. They were blowing things up in there, it sounded like. Many of the warstriders were already pulling out, clambering back aboard the waiting transports.

Overhead, the ground support craft circled like vultures.

"Why are they doing this!" a man screamed, his voice muffled by his breather mask but shrill and far too loud. "Why can't they leave us alone?"

"Quiet, Franz," a woman replied harshly. "Quiet or I'll shut you up myself."

On the whole, discipline was good, their chances of survival fair . . . unless those Imperial troops decided to comb the Sinai Heights boulder by boulder.

No . . . the ground troops were also withdrawing, moving back to the transports at a trot. Their ammunition and armored suit power must be running low. Tanis lay silent, the interior of its transparent transplas dome obscured by a thick and oily haze.

The biggest question was whether help would come. Their life support packs had air for two hours or so . . . less after the rugged climb through the tunnels. If no one got here from Sidon or Memphis, they would all be as dead as if they'd stayed in Tanis.

No! They *had* to live, so that the other Eriduan communities could know what had happened here! If he had to compose a RAM message, download it to a volunteer, then give up his own life support pack to guarantee the messenger's survival, he would do it.

With a black-humored stab of irony, Mattingly realized that he and the other survivors were witnessing history in the making. Once word began spreading among the other dome communities on Eridu, the Tanis Massacre would become immortalized, the first armed clash of the Hegemony Civil War.

And with a passionate, fierce-driven conviction, he knew it would not be the last.

Chapter 26

Mankind will possess incalculable advantages and extraordinary control over human behavior when the scientific investigator will be able to subject his fellow men to the same external analysis he would employ for any natural object, and when the human mind will contemplate itself not from within but from without.

—*Scientific Study of So-called Psychical Processes in the Higher Animals*
Ivan Petrovich Pavlov
C.E. 1906

Dev was linked to his warstrider, moving through streets awash in blood. There were bodies everywhere, bodies twisted like rags, bodies soaked with blood, pieces of bodies that looked like they'd been cleanly diced on some butcher giant's cutting board, others torn and shredded and burned, their glistening entrails spilled on the ground.

God, there was so much blood. . . .

He tried to turn his optics away, tried to focus on the burning buildings, on the pall of smoke filling the ruptured dome, but couldn't. He was searching for survivors, hunting them down as if they were scrabbling, scurrying vermin and executing them with clean and methodical bursts from his weapons.

Movement to his left. He turned, and red targeting brackets closed on the lone human figure stumbling toward him, a white handkerchief clutched in blood-smeared fingers. The man was mouthing something. Dev had shut down his external mikes earlier because the screams of the children had hurt so. He switched them back on now.

"Please! Help me!" the man was calling. *"Please, help me!"*

But Dev's orders said . . .

He stopped, trying to recall. His orders had been . . . had been . . . to patrol the area around the Tanis mining complex, to watch for Xenophobe activity, to protect the Tanis civilians if the Xenos attacked. . . .

This, this massacre had been *his* idea.

"Please help me!"

Dev twitched his left arm, and the man fell to pieces, arms and legs, head and slices of torso slipping apart from one another in an explosion of startling scarlet.

Satisfaction. The *sempu* was a devastating antipersonnel weapon. In his report to HEMILCOM he would have to tell them that it was truly . . . truly . . .

Dev tried to move, tried to shake his head in outraged denial, but his brain no longer controlled his body. Dimly, he knew that someone else had taken over that task, as data continued to trickle in through his sockets, filling his cephlink with images of sheer, bloody horror.

"Why did you do it, Cameron? We saw you do it, and we have the recorder memories from your strider. What made you do it?"

"I . . . I didn't . . . what you said . . . I couldn't—"

"You ordered your company to destroy Tanis. Eighteen hundred helpless civilians massacred, the town dome

*cracked wide open. Do you know what happens to people
forced to breathe Eridu's atmosphere? We'll show you. . . ."*

The pictures in Dev's mind were the stuff of nightmares,
but sharpened to a hard, crisp focus that had none of a
dream's sense of unreality, none of the distance or perspective experienced as it faded from memory.

Instead, he experienced the reality of *now* in crisp, viv-
id detail.

A dozen men and women were on the rubbery, yellow-
orange stuff that passed for grass on Eridu, some on their
hands and knees, others sprawled with legs and arms twisted,
fingers clawing trenches in the earth. Mouths gaping, chests
heaving with convulsive shudders, they struggled to breathe
the oxygen-poor air, their lips turning blue, their eyes starting
from their heads in their frenzied battle against suffocation.

"My orders . . . my orders . . ."

*"You're telling us you were just following orders? You
killed all those people and you were just following orders?"*

"Yes! I mean, no. . . ."

"What is the real story, Cameron? What is the truth?"

"I don't know. . . ."

He didn't know. He remembered approaching Tanis with
his company. He remembered receiving his orders: *Patrol
the area around the Tanis mining complex, watch for
Xenophobe activity, protect the Tanis civilians if the Xenos
attack. . . .*

No! No! No! His orders had been something else entirely, but he couldn't remember . . . couldn't remember. . . .

Omigato's holographic image floated centimeters off the
lab floor amid gleaming, white-surfaced sterility. Cameron,
still in his striderjack's bodysuit, lay strapped to the tilt-top
table, his head encased in a cephlink helmet. Tubes and
cables snaked from the ceiling, power and data feeds for
the helmet, medical life support tubes and medical sensor
array cables for the suit. Several medical technicians and
a DHS interrogator named Haas stood about the wired,
motionless body.

"How does the rebriefing proceed?" To Omigato's eye,
it looked as though the subject was dead. He could detect
no movement in the chest.

"Slowly, my Lord," the interrogator replied. "The subject has a comparatively strong grasp of reality."

"How much longer? We will have to make an announcement soon."

"Two more sessions should do it, my Lord," Haas said. "Three at the most. If we proceed too quickly, attempt to batter down his defenses with too much force, he could withdraw, become permanently catatonic. We would have to start from scratch then, with a brainclear and complete reprogramming." Haas shook his head. "The results would not be optimal."

"You have another twenty hours." Omigato broke the connection and he floated once again in the zero-G privacy of his quarters.

Twenty hours. The local authorities should be able to keep things under control that much longer, at least. There'd been the inevitable wave of alarm in the wake of the Tanis Massacre. The governor's office had been besieged with calls, a storm of questions, pleas, threats, and demands for clarification, for news, for some kind of official announcement. There were reports of militias in eighteen towns and cities mustering or on alert, though whether that was to maintain the peace in their own regions or to attack Hegemony forces was still unclear.

That announcement, of course, already composed and ready for transmission, said that the *gaijin koman* assigned to a Hegemony strider unit had gone berserk, ordering his unit to attack Tanis, but that he and those of his men who'd followed him were all in custody. The download from *Tai-i* Devis Cameron's personal RAM, bearing his own access codes and IDs, would prove that he had given the orders, that he and a few of his men had slaughtered the population of a helpless town.

The Tanis Massacre had occurred nearly forty hours earlier, and there were unfortunate, disturbing indications that things had not gone entirely to plan in one respect at least. The Tanis population, apparently, had had warning enough that many had escaped, despite the marine net thrown about the area to catch fleeing refugees. Jamis Mattingly, one of the most important rebel leaders, had turned up alive in Sidon, a city some thirty kilometers downriver from Tanis.

According to observers at the scene, Mattingly and others were passing around direct memories of the attack, memories showing Imperial warstriders and troops slaughtering helpless civilians.

It would have been better—a smoother, cleaner operation—if there'd been no survivors at all from Tanis, but Omigato was already adapting to the situation. Once Cameron's memories of the incident were publicly displayed, it would be one set of claims against another, the radicals against the government, the nuts against those who knew that such things *couldn't* happen here. Opinion on Eridu would be polarized, and the division might even lead to fighting between rebel groups and the government. There would be many, a majority perhaps, who felt that an Imperial attack on Tanis was unthinkable, that such talk was obviously greenie or lifer propaganda.

All of which would provide the necessary excuse for direct Imperial intervention.

And no matter what happened on Eridu, the *real* battle would already be won simply because the Empire controlled the ships—and hence, the communication—between star systems. The news that reached Earth and the Imperial Palace would be that Devis Cameron, the *gaijin* trusted with communicating with the Xenophobes, had gone mad . . . possibly from the strain of his contact with the aliens on the Alyan expedition, possibly because the Xenos themselves had somehow twisted or controlled his mind.

That alone would be the victory Omigato sought. The pro-*gaijin* elements of His Majesty's government and personal staff would be discredited once and for all. The Emperor—dare he hope such a thing?—the Emperor himself might decide to take *personal* responsibility for what had happened. Next in line in the Imperial succession was a protégé of *Gensui* Munimori, like Omigato, a Man of Completion.

As for Eridu, Omigato decided that in the long run it didn't much matter whether the locals knew about the Imperial involvement at Tanis or not. One way or the other, the excuse he needed to turn the full weight of the Hegemony and Imperial armed forces against the planet's rebellious populace was already there. He need only wait for Earth and His Majesty to recognize the situation and grant him the authority to deal with it.

And deal with it he would.

Dev awoke once again on the cot inside his narrow cell. Such dark, disturbing dreams. . . .

Not dreams. Or rather . . . dreams, but not his. Nightmares created by computer, or channeled through his cephlink from someone else.

Shakily, he sat up, swinging his legs off the cot and feeling the cold roughness of the floor beneath his bare feet. Now, in the interlude between sessions, he knew what they were trying to do. Like anyone with a RAM implant, Dev possessed two broad types of memory, one biological, the other artificial. The biological memory could be fooled, or it could be blurred or erased by drugs or neural feeds, but the only way to deliberately implant false memories was through hypnosis—notoriously unreliable—or by feeding falsified data through the cephlink.

He'd heard of this sort of thing, though always as a kind of darkly whispered rumor, as tales without proof or substance. "Rebriefing" it was called, the word coined from RAM-edited briefing. Once it had been a military briefing tool allowing updates in published data to be written directly into their RAMs. His intracranial RAM was not as discriminating as his organic brain and would accept anything fed to it. The treatment he was getting here was designed to distort his personal reality, to smash down his barriers between truth and lie.

If they kept at it long enough, he would either end up forgetting what was real and accepting their memories as truth, or he would be driven hopelessly, mindlessly mad.

Already, his memories were disjointed. He remembered being brought to this place, a military dome on the outskirts of Babel, he thought. As soon as they'd pulled him from his strider down in Winchester they'd snapped a horseshoe device around the back of his head, something like a commpac with plugs that snapped into all three sockets.

After that, things were fuzzy and remote. They called the devilish thing a *Kanrinin*, a controller, and it was just that, operating through his cephlink to cut out his will and leave him pliable and content, willing to do anything his captors told him to do, unable to speak or act or even think on his own. He could remember only fragments of what came next—of boarding a monorail in Winchester and of being switched off, of waking again sometime later and being led here, to this cell.

Then the interrogation had begun.

That, too, was fragmentary—fortunately. He only recalled bits and pieces of his "softening up," as the interrogator had so cheerfully called it. He didn't know whether that was deliberate on the part of his captors, another means of twisting his sense of time and reality, or evidence of some sort of natural cutout in his mind, a way for his brain to protect itself.

The fragments he retained, though, were still painfully fresh and raw. He remembered being strapped naked to a kind of open framework that had allowed them access to every part of his body. He remembered the razor gleam of scalpels turning in the light, the terrifying *pop-hiss* as a blowtorch was lit, his fascination with the flame's glow as it descended toward unprotected flesh. He remembered screaming and screaming and screaming until his throat had gone raw, leaving him unable to voice more than a rasping croak. He kept trying to pass out, willing himself into oblivion, but the trickle of energy feeding through his sockets and into his brain would not let him be anything but hideously, shockingly awake.

But eventually, they'd let him faint, to awaken once more back in his cell, shaking and sweat-soaked, the memory of pain very nearly as sharp as the pain itself. With an unexpectedly strong reluctance, terrified of what he might see, he'd looked down at himself, minutely checking feet, fingers, hands, genitals. He'd brought a trembling but blessedly intact hand to his face, touching ears, nose, tongue, and lips, checking, cataloging . . .

Everything's still there. The trembling stopped, but he still felt kitten-weak. *It was all a dream.*

But it seemed so real!

It *had* been real. Had those images been manufactured, in the same way that an AI could manipulate artificial memories in a ViRdrama? Or had they been the genuine memories of some poor soul tortured to provide his interrogators with a handy instant replay, a tool for breaking the minds of other prisoners without breaking their bodies?

During one session, he'd actually found himself hovering above that hellish rack, watching as the interrogators carved away at his writhing body, and he'd been certain that he'd gone completely mad at last. Again, he'd awakened later, still, impossibly, whole and intact, but with a dimming grasp of who he was and what he'd been doing . . . *before.*

There'd been three initial "softening" sessions, he thought . . . or maybe four. After that, the images had turned to memories of his assault on Tanis.

He remembered, and the shaking began again. He thought he was going to be sick. Had those memories been manufactured? Or were they real? Some of the control discretes and data overlays he'd seen were unfamiliar, and he suspected from the feel of the thing that the warstrider was an Imperial model, a Tanto, possibly, or a Tachi. He'd never jacked an Imperial strider, so those disturbingly real memories had to be from a Japanese unit.

Or had they been memories downloaded from a Ghostrider? It was so hard to remember. They'd been interspersed with questions and harsh interjections from his tormentors.

"You are a traitor, Cameron. Just like your father."

"My father was a hero!"

"Your father turned a Starhawk missile on the Lung Chi space elevator during the evacuation. He was responsible for the deaths of half a million Manchurian civilians."

"The Xenophobes were coming up the sky-el. There were millions of people already at synchorbit. They all would have died if he hadn't acted—"

"There was no danger to them or to anyone else. He destroyed the elevator, allowing the Xenophobes to slaughter the people still on the surface. Just like you slaughtered those poor people in Tanis."

"No!"

He no longer knew what to believe. He did know that the bastards were winning, *winning,* and that, somehow, was the most wrenching torture of all.

They hadn't told him what they wanted of him, hadn't even asked any questions save for those designed to keep him off balance, to make him question his own actions, even his own thoughts.

"Why did you do it?"

"But I didn't! It's a lie!"

"You are lying. We know you did it. This is you killing those people. Why are you lying to us?"

He checked his internal RAM. It had been twenty-six hours since they'd begun interrogating him. He knew that they would keep at him and at him until he broke, until he told them what they wanted him to tell them, or said what they wanted him to say. He'd already decided to make them work for it, though. He would not cooperate with them of his own free will.

The Hegemony had reinforced its Eridu garrison. The soldiers who guarded him in this RoPro-walled fortress were Chiron Centurians, a crack unit raised and trained on Alpha Centauri. Dev thought they must have arrived in the last few days, because he'd heard nothing of their arrival while he'd been at Winchester.

The Hegemony must be nervous about the Eriduan response to Tanis. Dev didn't much blame them, and he could understand why they wanted to pin the blame on him. He wondered if enough people had survived the Tanis Massacre that the truth would get out.

He didn't want to be thought of as the murderer of eighteen hundred people. . . .

Dev felt a tremor in the floor, a grinding vibration somewhere far beneath his feet. Wearily, he closed his eyes. It was possible that *this* was a created dream, a virtual reality being pumped into his brain to further distort the boundaries of what was real and what was not. He might only think he was sitting here in his bare-walled cell, when in fact he was . . .

The trembling in his body began again and he wanted to scream: *Stop it stop it stop it!* Eyes closed, he took a deep breath, then opened them again. Nothing in the room appeared to have changed. His cell was three meters high, four long, two wide, with rough-textured RoPro walls and a wire grating over the single small fluoro light source in the ceiling. There were no other fixtures save a drain in the floor and an iris door in one narrow wall. His cot was a simple affair of tubing and wire, with a bare mattress that stank of ammonia and other stale, less definable odors.

Concentrating, he realized he could hear sounds . . . someone screaming, he thought. And the thud of running footsteps.

What was real, and what a lie? The thumping sound was louder now, and he realized that by the fluorostrip's light he could see tiny, individual dust motes dancing off the far wall. He blinked, then rubbed his eyes. An earthquake?

The building lurched, and Dev found himself lying on his back on the hard floor. The wall opposite his bunk split from floor to ceiling, opening in a ragged crack that spilled dirt and loose gravel into his cell. He felt the tug of a violent wind lashing at his bodysuit and his hair and he knew that the dome must have been breached because he could hear the pale shriek of escaping air. Reflexively, he held his breath, then let it go, knowing that it was useless.

Memory surfaced, of the civilians he'd seen outside of Tanis, bug-eyed, mouths working like beached fish, and Dev, already strung to the very edge of mental endurance, screamed, a shrill and wavering cry of sheer terror. He was up and standing on his cot, both fists hammering against the unyielding wall behind it. "Let me out! Let me out! Let me out!" One dark corner of his mind realized that this, too, must be another illusion, a manufactured nightmare designed to unhinge him, and he no longer cared. He simply had to escape that narrow cell, which had suddenly taken on all of the aspects of a sealed and buried coffin.

Then another explosion knocked him down again, and he lay on the floor as the thinning air howled around him.

The door was irising open. . . .

Chapter 27

Knowledge will forever govern ignorance; and a people who mean to be their own governors must arm themselves with the power which knowledge gives.

—James Madison
Eighteenth century

He didn't recognize the woman who stepped through the open door, a bundle of breath masks clutched in one hand and a businesslike 10mm Steyr-Hitachi subgun in the other. Her features were hidden by a visor and breath mask, and she wore a ceramiplas armor cuirass that left her legs and arms free. No helmet; her long black hair was pulled back from her face with a red headband.

"Who . . . are you?" The air wasn't too bad yet, but it tasted different. Thinner, and there was a rubbery smell to it, like something burning.

"Never mind." Her eyes narrowed as she stared into his face. "You're Cameron."

It was not a question. He decided she must have a RAMed image of him, and she'd just compared the download with what she saw sitting on the floor of the cell.

Shakily, he rose to his feet. "At the moment, I'm not real sure who I am. What the hell's going on?"

"Hey, not a thing. We're just here to rescue you, is all." She held out one of the masks and he took it, pressing it to his face. Instead of a two-hour life support pack, it was fed from small gas bottles extending from either side of its blunt snout. He touched the control and drew a breath of rubbery-smelling air.

As he donned the mask, she reached up behind her left ear and touched the compatch plugged into her T-socket.

"Sierra One, Sierra One-five," she said. "I've got Cameron."
She listened a moment. "Right. We're moving!"

"What's going on?"

She gestured impatiently. "Bad guys coming. Let's odie!"

She ducked back through the door and, his bare feet
crunching on gravel blasted from the walls, Dev followed.
In the passageway just outside, a Hegemony guard in brown
fatigues lay sprawled on his back, a brilliant red hole mar-
ring his cheek just below his left eye.

Dev stared at the body a moment, trying to force his brain
to work. A rescue? Pushing back the fog that still clouded
his mind, he stooped and retrieved the guard's rifle, a PCR-
28 high-velocity rifle. He checked the counter on the stock
magazine: two hundred 4mm caseless rounds, safety on. He
flicked the safety off and followed his rescuer over piles of
debris partly blocking the narrow passageways.

"Captain!"

He turned at the familiar voice. *Chu-i* Paul DeVreis was
moving down the passageway, following a young, sandy-
haired man in partial armor much like the girl's.

"Paul!" How many of the rest of A Company had been
brought here? He had dim memories of seeing others while
he was being taken aboard the monorail in Winchester, but
he'd not seen anyone from his unit since arriving here.

He wanted to ask if DeVreis had seen the others, but the
woman called to them from up ahead. "Hurry, hurry! We're
on a schedule!" She ducked through a gap low in the corridor wall. He followed on hands and knees . . .

. . . and emerged in a blaze of heat and light. Dev blinked
at the sky through his visor; until that moment, he'd not
known whether it was day or night, and he was feeling
disoriented, lost in time as well as in place.

They were standing in a jagged gap in the curving transplas
wall of a fifty-meter dome situated in a circular jungle clearing. The air still escaping from the hab was whipped past
him in a minor windstorm of swirling dust, and the jungle
trees at the edge of the clearing thirty meters distant were
rippling with the gust. The air outside was a furnace after
the relative coolness inside. Dev took three steps, and the
sweat bathing his body plastered his bodysuit to his skin.
Turning, he saw the slender, laser-straight column of Eridu's

space elevator vanishing into a blue-green zenith. So he *was* near Babel . . . only a few kilometers from the main dome, it looked like.

An explosion behind him and to his right made Dev flinch and duck. There was a battle going on. Half a dozen troops held a perimeter about the gap in the dome. Lasers flicked and skittered overhead, made briefly visible by the streaks they scratched through the rising dust and smoke. At the jungle's edge, the nanoflage-blurred shape of a Ghostrider crouched on bent, splay-footed legs, snapping off bolt after flaring bolt from its chin turret laser. Dev saw other bodies, some in the uniforms of Hegemony leggers, others in the mismatched armor and civilian clothing of the attackers.

Bandits, he thought. *These are the hill bandits they told us about.* But it was impossible to think of them as mere bandits. They moved with a quickness and a coordination that suggested they'd had at least some training. One of the men, who looked like he was in charge of the ground troops, was wearing full combat armor displaying the shoulder emblem of the 3rd New American Mechanized Cavalry, and Dev guessed that it was his, not stolen. A strip of red cloth had been tied around his right arm just below the shoulder pauldron, and when Dev looked, he saw that all of the rebels wore similar rags, or had daubed their armor with identifying stripes of red paint.

That's how they knew where we were, Dev thought. *Traitors . . .*

Traitors? He arrested the thought as he stumbled barefoot across the hot ground. *Traitors* had just in all probability saved his life. And who was the real traitor, the soldier who refused to obey a direct order, or the government that issued immoral orders?

He could tell that he was going to have to redefine some of his terminology.

Another combat machine, a LaG-17 Fastrider, lurched from the woods, its torso swiveling back and forth atop its squat actuator assembly like the questing head of a beast of prey. It seemed to track on whatever the Ghostrider was firing at, then joined in with a barrage of laser fire from its hornlike laser mandibles. A rocket streaked in from somewhere, trailing a white contrail, bursting against the

Fastrider's hull with a flash and a bang that scattered tiny chunks of armor, but the machine kept firing with a steady, uninterrupted rhythm, walking its bolts slowly across the upper levels of the dome.

Dev's feet were in agony, already blistering along the soles, though they still didn't hurt as much as what they'd done to him earlier, in his mind. He stumbled and fell to his knees.

"Dev!"

The voice, a woman's voice, boomed from the Ghostrider towering at the jungle's edge. Dev gaped up at the duralloy monster, not daring to believe what he'd just heard.

It occurred to him that this was all some kind of elaborate ViRdrama. It couldn't be Katya in that LaG-42, not *here*!

"Help him," the woman's voice said from the LaG-42's external speaker. "His feet are burned!"

"Katya?" He still couldn't believe it. *It's real! It's real! Please let it be real!* "Katya, is that you?"

"It's a long story, Dev," Katya replied. "I'll explain later."

The big New American trooper scooped an armored gauntlet under his arm and helped him up. A rebel in partial armor took his other arm and helped him limp toward one of ten magflitters resting on the ground twenty meters away.

Katya, here! She'd been heading for New America! How had she gotten to Chi Draconis?

And what was she doing with the hill ban—

—with the *rebels*?

A deadly, squat delta-shape screeched low over the jungle, and the Ghostrider and Fastrider in perfect unison swiveled, elevated, and loosed a pounding laser barrage. Dev saw a flash from the low-flying aircraft but couldn't tell if the hit had done any damage. He heard a shout and saw some rebels nearby drop to their bellies and begin shooting. Hegemony troops were spilling from an airlock in the dome nearby. Dev wanted to snatch up his rifle and join in the firing, but he'd lost his weapon along the way—back where he'd fallen, he thought—and his two escorts were in no mood to let him linger. At a dead run, they hurried him along, his feet barely touching the oven-hot ground. Reaching the magflitter, they handed him up the open cargo ramp to another pair of rebels waiting inside.

Bev Schneider, Martin Koenig, and Wolef Helmann were already there, crouched in the dimly lit, windowless interior. The rest of A Company came limping up the ramp moments later. The harsh rattle of gunfire, the hiss and snap of lasers and plasma guns, intensified outside. A woman harnessed into the pilot's seat up forward, her VCH already jacked in, yelled back at them. "All secure?"

"Go! Go!" a rebel with a smoke-stained face yelled back. The pilot slapped her palm onto her armrest interface and instantly sagged back in her seat, apparently unconscious. Around him, Dev heard the gathering whine of the flyer's mags spooling to full power, the clatter of something hard and metallic striking the outside hull, and then they were moving, lurching from side to side with hissing crashes as the windowless craft bashed its way through the trees.

Katya watched the flitter rise on howling mags, wobble as gunfire struck sparks from its armor, then careen forward into the trees. She still wasn't certain she trusted her own feelings. Dev, a rebel!

The news from the south that Tanis had been destroyed had been closely followed by whisperings that a *gaijin* working for the Imperials had been responsible. Hard on the heels of that rumor had come the news that the *gaijin* had actually been a hero, had defied direct Imperial orders to attack Tanis and even sent one of his people to warn the town.

In both stories, the *gaijin* had been identified as Devis Cameron, winner of the Imperial Star, the man who'd dared attempt communication with the Xenophobes at Alya B.

Long before, Katya had convinced herself that, if she didn't actually *hate* Dev now, she certainly disliked him, that their political views were diametrically opposed, that their relationship over the past several years had been a mistake. How could she possibly *love* a man who so completely embraced the philosophies, the elitist social theories, of *Dai Nihon*? Impossible!

Unexpectedly, her feelings had started to change after her encounter with the Xenophobe Self. She still wasn't sure she understood what had happened to her, but *something* had changed inside her mind, her thoughts. At first, she'd wondered if the Xeno had physically changed her somehow; that had been a nightmare, as she wrestled with a purely human dread of the unknown.

Then, as med and psych tests demonstrated that she'd had a shock but that she'd not been altered in any measurable way, she began to realize that the change lay purely in her perceptions.

Until she'd confronted the Xeno, she'd seen only the differences between herself and Dev, the areas where they disagreed . . . or where they reacted to the world in different ways. Dev was more cautious, she more impulsive; he liked to reason things out, while she tended to act on feeling; he saw the advantages of the Empire's order and security, while she saw the thinly veneered chaos of arbitrary power and a stratified society; he thought of the Empire protecting humankind from itself, and she mourned the loss of individual liberty and personal rights.

Differences . . . as mutually alien, she'd thought, as human and Xeno.

But somehow, ever since her mind had momentarily blended with a Xenophobe's thought processes, differences in merely human points of view no longer seemed so vast . . . or so hard-chiseled in black-and-white absolutes.

"Katya!" Chung's voice called, jerking her back to reality. He was jacking the long-range sensor gear in one of the transports. "We got transports incoming, range five klicks!"

"Okay, people!" she snapped over the general frequency. "Company's on the way! Grab what you can and odie!"

Rebel leggers were trotting from the now-smoking shell of the Hegemony dome, carrying or dragging bundles of weapons, cases of ammo or powerpacks, suits of combat armor. Several of the open magflitters had already been crammed full of military gear looted from the base armory. The haul included four light striders and a pair of DR-80 orbital warflyers, big, black, ugly shapes loaded aboard individual maglev transport sleds.

A successful raid, no matter how you looked at it.

But they'd only had a small garrison to contend with, and now reinforcements were on the way in, big time. It was time to withdraw.

"Creighton! Are your people clear?"

"Everybody's clear, Captain! We're out of here!"

"Right! All units, fall back to the jungle and disperse! Execute E&E pattern Beta, with rendezvous at Green-Five! Move!"

Explosions blossomed from the jungle, mushrooming above the forest canopy and into the crystalline sky above.

They moved.

From a rendezvous site in the jungle south of Babel, they'd returned to the city separately or in small groups after hiding vehicles and equipment in an underground bunker that had once been a prospector's maintenance shed. Dev and most of the other Terran Rangers entered the Towerdown dome aboard a convoy of eight flitters that had been coming up the coast road from the south, from Lagash and Flynnsport. There were plenty of Hegemony patrols on foot around Babel, he noted, but they weren't stopped at the Babel city dome for ID checks as he'd expected.

He found out later that the Hegemony officers tasked with taking downloaded IDs from people entering and leaving Babel were in fact members of the Network, the whispered underground organization that was rapidly transforming Eridu into a center of resistance against the Hegemony government.

That resistance was taking many and varied shapes. DIVERSITY IS LIFE! had been spray-painted across the Towerdown dome above the main airlock entrance. Lorita Fischer, the black-haired woman who'd freed Dev from his cell, was with him in the caravan truck, and she explained that the phrase was one of several Network slogans that had become popular lately. "Law for seventy is not liberty for one" was another. The idea that one government could embrace the needs, goals, morals, and outlooks of hundreds of separate human cultures on seventy-eight different worlds, she explained, was nonsense. By its nature, government was either small and personal, something on the level of a town hall meeting, or it was tyranny, with the few ruling the many for their own benefit, no matter how representational that government might be in theory.

Dev found some of her views to rest little short of anarchist, but he had a hard time answering her charge that the Hegemony was a tyranny supported by military might.

That evening, they assembled in an underground complex that Katya explained was hidden beneath a deserted building in Babel's Towerdown warehousing district. All of the rescued 4th Rangers were there, along with a number of the rebels. Dev had found himself surrounded by familiar faces. Chung was present, and Hagan and Nicholson, Torolf Bondevik, Erica Jacobsen, and Lara Anders. He didn't see Rudi Carlsson, though, and wondered if he'd stayed back on Loki.

And Katya. He found it hard to take his eyes from her. For her part, she seemed . . . tired. A bit washed out, like she'd been working herself too hard. It seemed like a small eternity since he'd seen her last, that evening at Kodama's party on Earth.

There were lots of strangers, too, a small army of men and women—kids, most of them—from Eridu and New America, members of the Network's combat arm.

Dev's first question, of course, had been how they'd known he was being held in that jungle bunker outside of Babel.

"Sinclair had spies in the armory at Winchester," Katya explained. "And Nagai didn't try to hide you when he transferred you from Winchester to Babel. You were seen boarding a monorail, with three of Nagai's bully-boys as escorts." She made a face. "You were wearing a *kanrinin*."

"I remember a little of that," Dev said. "But they put me out for the trip."

"Well, the monorail's an eighteen-hour trip from Winchester to Babel," Katya went on. "By the time they were frogmarching you off at this end, we had people watching the stations. You were seen, and followed . . . to one of Babel's outlying domes."

"They call it Nimrod," Lorita said. "It's the barracks and headquarters for the main Hegemony garrison at Babel, and it's located about ten kilometers south of the Towerdown dome. We figured they'd be keeping you there for a while rather than take you up-tower to synchorbit, because the word was you were going to be used for some kind of propaganda here on the surface."

"Affirmative," Dev said. He tried to smile, and failed. "They wanted me to admit that I was the one who ordered the attack on Tanis. They . . . they damn near made me think I did it."

"We decided the time to try a rescue," Katya said, "was while you were still on the planet."

"Yeah, but how? The place was a fortress!"

A red-headed girl the others called Simone giggled. "That was me," she said. "I hacked into HEMILCOM's alert net and told it the Xenophobes were coming through again at Site Red One. They were falling all over themselves trying to scramble for their magflitters."

"Which explains the tight timetable," Dev said. He glanced at Katya. "You waited until they off-loaded at Red One, then hit the place and were gone in the time it took for them to load up and fly back."

"We had it timed real close," Lee Chung said, nodding. "Eight minutes, thirty seconds max. We did it in seven twenty-five."

"There was still a fair-sized garrison manning the fort," Hagan said. "Only two light recon warstriders, thank God, but a fair number of leggers and some nasty remote laser defenses. There wasn't time to be fancy. We knocked out the Fastriders with a missile barrage, blasted through the dome wall, and sent people on foot running through the complex, looking for prisoners. Meanwhile, the rest of us loaded up on loot. We got away with some pretty good stuff."

Dev's left eyebrow arced. "You've also started yourself a nice little war," he said. "Against the Terran Hegemony. You're going to need more than guns to fight it, I'm afraid."

"Maybe," the big New American, Creighton, said. "What'd you have in mind?"

"An army, for one thing. And allies. Oh, don't get me wrong. You people were magnificent out there today, and I'm certainly in no position to criticize your technique! But you're still outnumbered a hundred to one, and when the Empire gets into it—"

"*We'll* handle the Empire," Torolf Bondevik said. He put his arm around the redheaded girl's shoulders and she snuggled closer. Evidently, members of his old unit were settling in quite happily to life on Eridu.

"We all will," Katya said, looking pointedly at Dev. "You're in this thing too now, aren't you?"

The question startled Dev. He'd not really thought about it before this. "I . . . I guess we are." He glanced at Bev Schneider, across the room. She was sitting in the circle of an older man's arms. She looked radiantly happy. "I was going to say it's a bit sudden to find ourselves on the other side. Some of us seem to be adapting quite well."

Creighton followed his gaze. "That's Alin Schneider," he explained. "Her father."

"God. No wonder they're glad to see each other."

Across the room, Lorita Fischer was caressing a mentar, and the instrument's harmonies, haunting minors, shivered in the air. He listened a moment, trying to place the tune. "What is that?"

"Hope Eyrie," Katya said. "It's become sort of an anthem for the Confederation."

"Anthems are usually more martial than that."

"This one fits. It reminds us that we're reclaiming a heritage, something we squandered a long time ago. 'Time won't drive us down to dust again.' "

"It's . . . beautiful." He'd never heard the piece, but it still sounded familiar somehow. Captivating.

"What happens to you now, Dev?"

He looked at her, surprised. "I guess that's up to you, isn't it? I mean, damn it, you rescued me. I can't go back. I'd like to stay . . . with you."

Her eyes were unreadable. "I can't promise it'll be the same between us. A lot's happened."

He winced. "Me and the Empire. I was an idiot. They *lied* to me—"

"That wasn't what I meant. Dev, we have the Yunagi comel."

Dev's jaw dropped. "You do!"

"There's more. I've already used it. I've talked to Self, to the Xenophobe. I'm not sure, but I think I've arranged an alliance." When Dev couldn't respond for several seconds, she added, "Well, you said we needed allies!"

It took Dev a moment for the thought to work its way past several layers of preconceptions. Then it hit him like a thunderbolt. "The Xenos! You've . . . you've made an alliance with the Xenos? Gods, how?"

"Nothing's certain yet." She closed her eyes, and Dev saw the stress there. "Oh Dev, they're so *different*!"

"They are that."

"No, I mean . . . I had no idea what you must have gone through, out there on the DalRiss homeworld. It . . . I think it all but took me apart and put me together again. It was . . . inside me, trying to understand me. And I'm not sure it succeeded."

Dev felt a nagging worry. "Did it hurt you? Are you—"

"I'm fine, Dev. The medicos checked me when I got back. They said it analyzed my breathing mixture and manufactured a fresh reserve of air for me, right on the spot. Probably treated me for carbon dioxide poisoning too. Those things would be grade-A medics if they could be integrated into our society."

"I'm not sure society's ready for that," Dev said dryly.

"But I did try to explain our need. And their danger. When I woke up back in Emden, I found out they'd left me a . . . a message."

"What . . . in your RAM?"

"No. I'm not sure they understood what that was. No, they . . . they changed my comel."

Dev started at that. "What . . . a Xenozombie?" He was thinking of other DalRiss creatures, taken over by the Xenos and used as weapons.

"No," she said. "Not like that. But there was a kind of impression in it. A memory. I felt it when I touched the comel back at the rebel base. They told me how to contact them again, if we need them."

"What was it?"

She told him.

Dev threw back his head and laughed.

Chapter 28

The chief advantage of space elevators is that they can transport large cargos to and from synchorbit at extremely low cost. Their disadvantage is time. Typically, a sky-el shuttle requires twenty hours for the one-way trip between towertop and towerdown, and in some cases the trip takes considerably longer than that.

When speed is required for ground-to-orbit transfers, air-space shuttles remain the travel mode of choice.

—*Elevator to the Stars*
Jiro Shimamura
C.E. 2412

Triumphantly, the red-haired girl on the couch broke contact with the terminal. "We're in!"

Dev leaned partway into the opening of the gleaming gold tube, one of eight angled cylinders dominating the ViRcommunications center at the Babel spaceport, and stared at the monitor above her head. "What did you do?"

"Bypassed the regular security through a trapdoor I happen to know." Simone Dagousset plucked the jacks from her T-sockets, then slid from the public ViRcom booth. Dev took her hand and helped her up. "I've got a tame subanalogue download persona that thinks it's General Nakamura of the Imperial Staff. You'd be surprised how the military types snap to with heel clicks and salutes when *he* barks an order!"

"Don't you still need access codes?"

She laughed. "Sometimes. I can usually get what I need from the comm system AI though. Their problem is they're too smart."

"How do you mean?"

"You can *reason* with an Artificial Intelligence," she said with a proud toss of her head. "Or fool it into thinking *Shosho* Nakamura wants his ship and he wants it *now*, no questions and no red tape foolishness or he'll know the reason!"

"Great," he said, looking about the concourse. The urgent bustle of Babel's Towerdown spaceport surrounded them with an anonymous blanket of rumbling sound. "So, where do we go, and how long to lift-off?"

"It's a private flight. Discretionary launch." She giggled. "I *think* it's Nakamura's personal launch. At least it's registered under his ID. Gate three, Bay Alpha."

"A personal launch? Is that going to be big enough for all of us?"

"It should be. One-hundred fifty tons. It'll be crowded, I imagine."

"Yeah, well, it's a short flight, three hours max. We can sit in each others' laps for that long. Did you alert the others?"

"Sure did." She dropped her voice to a conspiratorial whisper. "Operation Hope Eyrie has commenced!"

Dev shook his head. Simone seemed to live for intrigue and risk taking, and he wondered if she didn't see the whole conflict as some sort of enormous, elaborate, and challenging electronic game. She was never happier than when she was tweaking the system, looking for new ways to outwit or get past the computer networks that permeated every aspect of modern life.

As they walked, he let his gaze traverse the concourse, then shifted to the railed balconies overhead. There were hundreds of people in sight, most of them businessmen or trader types, travelers arriving at or departing from Eridu's groundside sky-el terminus. He also noticed an unusual number of Hegemony soldiers patrolling the gleaming floor, or standing at intervals along the balconies, and there were no local militia troopers in evidence at all. They wore heavy partial armor and lugged military rifles or lasers rather than the less conspicuous stunners or carbines security troops normally carried, and they stood or paced restlessly at their posts with the air of men warned to expect trouble.

And trouble was definitely in the air, a tension that could very nearly be tasted like the acrid reek of fear. Things were quiet in the Babelport dome, but the larger, adjoining dome of Babel had been the scene of yet another demonstration. Dev had not been there, but he'd seen views of the Babel town square on repeater monitors around the spaceport concourse. Thousands of people had gathered there early that morning. He could hear them now, a faint, far-off, rhythmic chant: "*Tanis! Tanis! Tanis!*"

God, no wonder the security guards were nervous.

Most of them, Dev could tell from their shoulder patches and uniform emblems, were members of the Chiron Centurians. No Terran Rangers that he could see, and only a few New Americans. Maybe the Rangers weren't trusted any longer, after A Company's defection at Tanis. Network Intelligence had reported that downloaded accounts of what had happened at Tanis were circulating among both Ranger and New American units, and morale was reported to be low. There'd been a lot of desertions lately, with whole companies joining the rebels, bringing warstriders and weapons with them. The entire planet was charged, ready to explode; almost anything could touch it off. Sinclair's propagandists had tapped the anti-Imperial resentment and turned it into a monstrous, living thing.

Dev wondered if Sinclair and his people would be able to control it.

They stopped at a transplas window in a lounge overlooking Bay Alpha. Nakamura's shuttle was a large, delta-winged, twin-engine ascraft, an Ishikawajima A5M1 Moketuki with a hull that gleamed like burnished gold in the light of Marduk. The Nakamura *mon*, or family emblem, adorned both wings. It rested on its ventral landing skids, surrounded by the snaking coils of power conduits and feeder tubes and guarded by several armored men on foot. Its belly cargo hatch was open, and Dev could see a line of robot loaders already wheeling up the ramp, each carrying maglev sleds piled high with two-meter canisters of the kind used to transport fragile or perishable goods up to orbit. A human cargo officer checked tags on their sides and made entries on his compad. Good. As long as he didn't decide to spot-check those canisters . . .

Forward, the chunky, organic shapes of a pair of DR-80 Tenrai warflyers were being eased into the Moketuki's external hull rider slots. A pressurized boarding arm connected the port facility to its starboard airlock, and the steam boiling from the craft's cryo-hydrogen slush tanks curled up around its flanks.

It looked like the plan was proceeding smoothly, but Dev's heart was hammering inside his chest. So much could go wrong. . . .

"Loading's almost complete," he said. "We'd better get aboard."

A Hegemony guard stood by the terminal entrance to the Bay Alpha boarding arm. "Sorry, sir, ma'am. This is a restricted area."

"We have orders for that ship." He kept his voice even, commanding.

The man looked them up and down, his right hand resting in casual display on the butt of a holstered laser pistol. "I hardly think—"

Dev extended his left hand, palm out. The man hesitated, shrugged, then picked up a compad resting on the shelf beside him and extended it. Dev placed his interface on the screen and felt the tingle of transferred data.

The man looked at the screen readout, eyes widening with respect. "Sorry, sir! I didn't know . . ."

"Now me," Simone said, grinning.

The guard read her forged ID and nearly turned white. "Please, you can both go aboard immediately."

As they stepped aboard the shuttle, Dev gave Simone a sidelong glance. "What did you tell the damned computer that we were doing here, anyway?"

"Oh, I put you down as Nakamura's personal secretary, his *human* secretary, that is, on your way up to synchorbit for a conference with Omigato himself."

"I see. And you?"

She giggled. "I'm listed as Nakamura's mistress."

Dev wondered if that guard had thought it odd that someone as high-ranking as Nakamura had a *gaijin* secretary . . . or a *gaijin* mistress, for that matter, then decided that it didn't matter. No enlisted man would dare question the fact, if the computer network claimed it was so.

They made their way up to the flight deck, where other members of the Network combat team were assembling.

Each silvery canister had held two cramped rebels, or a pair of combat suits and several weapons. Lara Anders, listed as the ascraft's pilot, arrived a few moments later.

"Places, everybody," Anders said. "I want to light off before someone decides to double-check those orders."

The shuttle was a true ascraft, an air-space interface vehicle that saved fuel mass in atmosphere by gulping down huge quantities of air and converting it to sun-hot plasma in twin fusion furnaces. In space, the tanked cryo-H served as reaction mass, though it could also use water or any other liquid. Smaller ground-to-orbit craft could use the magnetic repulsion effect of magflitters or similar vehicles, but large shuttles like this one still relied on old-fashioned nuclear engines, a design relatively unchanged for three centuries at least. Though the spacecraft could hover, land, and take off like a conventional tilt-jet aircraft, launch to orbit was usually assisted by a hotbox booster that would take the vehicle to scramjet speeds. It had pilot jacking slots for three, though a single person could fly it, and acceleration couches for twelve more on the flight deck. By utilizing every available seat, plus jury-rigging additional acceleration couches with foam pads laid out on the aft cargo bulkhead, Dev had managed to squeeze thirty rebel troops aboard the tiny craft, along with their combat armor and weapons.

After donning a suit of combat armor, save for helmet and gloves, Dev took his place in the co-pilot's jacking slot forward. With his background, he could fly the ship if necessary, but mostly he wanted to be jacked into the ascraft's sensors for the final approach to their target. As soon as he came on-line, he sensed Lara at his side, completing the final elements of her prelaunch rundown. His visual field was a feed through optic scanners in the ascraft's prow, showing the encircling gray wall of Bay Alpha's blast pit, and the domes and hab structures of the spaceport.

"Cryo-H tanks at pressure," he heard Anders saying. "Hotbox fuel feed at three-seven, nominal. Gantry clear and power on internal. Babel Towerdown, flight *Ko-tori* Five-niner is requesting immediate launch."

A window opened in the upper left of his visual field. A bearded face, a traffic controller's ViRpersona, stared at Dev from the depths of the blue-green sky. "India Hotel

Kilo Five-niner, please hold for authorization check."

Dev felt something go cold inside. So much could go wrong with this plan, not the least of which was the danger that some human or AI would become suspicious at the urgency of this shuttle launch, or the large number of cargo containers that had been so hurriedly loaded aboard. If someone decided to hold the shuttle's launch, there wasn't a lot the rebels could do about it, and there was for damned sure no way they could hide the twenty-some commandos packed into the craft's flight and cargo decks. The alternative—initiating an emergency launch and boosting off from Babelport without authorization—would be worse than useless. Transit time from launch to synchorbital docking was pegged at three hours, fifteen minutes; no ascraft that had blasted out of Babelport against orders would be permitted anywhere near the synchorbit facility.

Were the spaceport control people merely double-checking the shuttle's orders? Or were they sending someone out to inspect the craft personally? Dev found himself holding his mental breath.

"You want me to try to head them off?" That was Simone's voice. The young hacker, jacked into the third shuttle control slot, was offering to intercede electronically, through the computer network linking the waiting shuttle and Babelport's space traffic control.

"Negative," Dev replied, a little sharply. "If they felt you in their system they'd know something was wrong. As it is, they might—"

"India Hotel Kilo Five-niner, this is Babelport Control. You are clear for immediate launch."

It *had* been a routine cross-check of their orders, nothing more. And Simone had already taken care of that aspect of things. "See?" he said simply.

"Babelport, India Hotel Kilo Five-niner," Anders said. "Acknowledged. See you again soon."

The melodrama of a prelaunch countdown had long ago been superseded by the silent and ultrafast musings of a ship's AI. Lara Anders gave the mental command, and the ducted jets whined to full throttle, lifting the ascraft out of the blast pit. The Moketuki's flat, squared-off nose came up, and a second later the hotbox ignited.

They rose skyward, balanced on a thundering tower of white flame.

In an observation lounge in the Babelport terminal, Katya watched the delta-winged ascraft climbing on its waterfall of fire and smoke and felt a small, inward shudder of relief. Casually, she reached up and touched the compatch behind her ear. "Sword, this is Watcher. The Eagle is aloft. Initiate Hope Eyrie."

"Copy that," Hagan's voice said, speaking in her mind. "Hope Eyrie is go."

It was time.

Aboard the *Tokitukaze*, Yoshi Omigato was indeed in a conference with senior Hegemony officers, but it was an electronic meeting rather than face-to-face, and those attending were linked from places as far apart as Babel, Winchester, and Boreal, in Eridu's north polar zone. Twelve uniformed men floated in a dimensionless space, observing a five-meter holographic projection of the Eriduan globe. The colors were accurately portrayed as seen from space—clotted masses of reds, oranges, and golds separated by violet seas—but the planet's cloud cover had been stripped away, and important installations, cities, and outposts were represented by color-coded symbols. The space elevator was a thin silver streak extending from Eridu's equator far out into the surrounding night.

Also displayed were numerous flashing points of light—green, blue, and white—each accompanied by a hovering data tag identifying it. Green marked Hegemony forces and blue Imperial; white lights represented probable concentrations of rebel troops.

To one side, beyond the globe, a three-D image presented a realtime view of the Babel town square, where nearly five thousand people were crowded together in a living sea, and more were joining them every minute. It was as though the dome had become a kind of magnet for every malcontent and troublemaker on the planet. Their chanting was muted to a rhythmic, lingering echo: "*T*anis! *T*anis! *T*anis!"

Obviously, Omigato thought, the campaign to blame Tanis on a few traitorous *gaijin* had failed. That still didn't matter, fortunately, so long as his version of events here was all that reached Earth.

What was worrisome was the rebels' selection of Babel as the site of their demonstration. A pitched battle there might damage the sky-el. Any serious interruption in space elevator traffic would sharply cut into the planet's productivity. It would also end any possibility for terraforming Eridu, at least until the elevator could be repaired. If the damage was serious enough, the delay might be measured in decades.

Omigato was patient, but not *that* patient. His campaign, the campaign of the Men of Completion, had been so finely timed, so precisely forged and balanced . . . like the blade of a venerable Masamune katana. He'd expected that the rebel rising, when it came, would be in Winchester or one of the other cities in the south, not at Babel.

Much hung on the events of the next few hours.

"Since Tanis," *Chusa* Barton, CO of the 4th Terran Rangers, was saying, "we've had a dramatic increase in the number of desertions." His words were hard and curt, bordering on insolence. Omigato doubted that the man could be trusted and already planned to replace him. "Whole companies have simply walked off base, taking weapons, even warstriders, with them. There have been several skirmishes already when security personnel tried to stop them. . . ."

"Yes, but where do they *go*?" Omigato demanded. "These rebel battalions you tell me of, they cannot simply vanish into jungle! They need shelter! Food! Power! Air they can breathe! *Where are they hiding*?"

"We believe they are using outposts near the major population centers," a HEMILCOM staff officer said. One of the outpost symbols, a few kilometers south of Babel on the holographic display, grew brighter. "This is Emden, my Lord, constructed forty years ago for fungus prospectors in the Equatorial foothills. By triangulation and through computer simulations, we believe this facility was the staging area both for the attack on the monorail a few weeks ago and for the raid on Nimrod."

"And what has been done about it?"

"We have it under close observation from synchorbit, my Lord," a HEMILCOM security officer said. "We have iden-

·tified several people living there as probable rebels. When we—"

"Then *take* them!" Omigato exploded. "Or do I have to call in the Empire and show you how the thing is to be done? Take prisoners! Make them talk! They will know other rebels, leaders, hiding places! But *take them*!"

"It's not that easy, my Lord," a black-haired *gaijin* named Boudoin said. He was the commanding officer of the newly arrived Guard unit, the Centurians, and his image floated in space above the varicolored world with arms crossed, a dark expression on his face. "The civilian population is rapidly polarizing over the Tanis incident. Some support the Hegemony still, but AI projections estimate that sixty-five percent are siding openly with the rebels. They provide warnings of troop movements, shelter for deserters, supplies, recruits. Civilian workers on the military bases are leaking classified data faster than we can keep track of it. My staff believes that—"

"It is *quite* easy, *Taisa*," Omigato interrupted sharply. "Simplicity itself. You permit no civilian workers on your bases. You take hostages. You evacuate town domes and sequester their populations in holding centers. You shoot deserters. And if you can't maintain control, I remind you that the *Tokitukaze* alone has the firepower to destroy every habitat dome on the surface of this accursed planet! Is that understood?"

In the shocked silence, a staff assistant's voice sounded almost shockingly loud. "My Lord . . ."

"What is it?" Omigato was in no mood for interruptions.

"My Lord, please look at the realtime images from Babel. They . . . something is happening."

Omigato pivoted his point of view, staring at the mob scene illuminated in the empty space beyond the Eriduan globe like a theater stage. The crowd had grown still . . . almost expectant. A holographic public address screen had been erected, and Prem's image was towering over the mob, imploring them to disperse. Omigato's teeth ground with frustration. *He* would disperse them . . . and so thoroughly there would not be enough left to bury. But what . . .

At the mob's back, a warehouse door was opening.

Chapter 29

Article 10. Right of Revolution. Government being instituted for the common benefit, protection, and security of the whole community and not for the interests or emoluments of any one man, family, or class of men; therefore, whenever the ends of government are perverted, and public liberty manifestly endangered, and all other means of redress ineffectual, the people may, and of right ought to, reform the old, or establish a new government. The doctrine of non-resistance against arbitrary power and oppression is absurd, slavish, and destructive of the good and happiness of mankind.

—Article X
New Hampshire Bill of Rights
C.E. 1784

Katya consulted her internal time, then opened her tactical frequency. "Right. Let's go."

"Copy," Hagan's voice said in her head. "We're ready to move. Good luck, Katya."

"And you, Vic."

It was almost like being in the Thorhammers again. Katya was jacking her Ghostrider, and the striders flanking her included Vic Hagan and Lee Chung in a pair of RLN-90 Scoutstriders, and Erica Jacobsen in a Swiftstrider. The fifth machine was Roger Darcy's Fastrider, and for some reason that reminded her of Rudi Carlsson. She missed the impetuous Lokan and wished he were here.

Several hundred leggers were also gathered in that building, foot soldiers of the Rebel Network. One platoon had been fitted out with complete combat armor, but the rest were still wearing partial armor, or none at all. The rebellion had grown tremendously since Katya had arrived on Eridu, but it still was having trouble providing arms and equipment for all of its members.

The miracle was that what they did have had been successfully hidden from the Imperials and their Hegemony watchdogs. These four warstriders, for instance, had been shipped to warehouse 1103 in crates labeled MACHINE PARTS and stored there for the past week, awaiting this moment. It would not have been possible without the active, the enthusiastic, support of much of the city's population, including especially those like Simone Dagousset who were willing to tweak the government's computer network.

"You take the pods," she told Georg Lipinski, in the LaG-42's number two slot. "But if it comes to a fight, watch what you're shooting at. It's crowded out there."

"Iceworld," Lipinski said, his mental voice steady. "Easy feed." The kid had grown a lot in these past few weeks and taken on the stature of a combat veteran.

The sliding doors to warehouse 1103 were wide open now, and white light splashed into the dusty building interior from the city center outside. Beyond, a throng of civilians stood in a dense-packed mass, waiting in eerie silence. Katya could see some of their banners and slogans. ERIDU IS FREE! one crudely spray-painted placard read. She sincerely hoped that the wish could be made fact, though the odds were still against it. Against *them*.

Katya's Ghostrider emerged into daylight filtered through the broad transplas expanse of the largest Babel dome, leading the way into the town's central square where the people had gathered in a vast, shoulder-to-shoulder mass. They made way for the line of warstriders, but they'd been resisting for some time the loudhailer demands of militia and Hegemony troops to break up, to go home.

A line of Hegemony warstriders was arrayed opposite the mob, blocking the way toward the Towerdown dome and the base of the sky-el itself. Behind them, the holographic image of Governor Prem, five stories tall, implored the populace to disperse. Katya enhanced her view and read the unit emblems and designations on the silent row of Ghostriders, Scoutstriders, and one massive, three-slotter

Warlord. Chiron Centurians. Good troops . . . and not yet infected by the heady, antiauthoritarian air that had been filling the Eriduan domes for the past several weeks.

"People of Eridu," the enormously enlarged image of Prem was saying. "I promise you, your complaints, your dissatisfaction, your petitions have been heard! Return to your habs immediately. Otherwise, the government authority will have no alternative but to employ gas."

As the rebel warstriders entered the square, however, the Hegemony machines stirred and shifted nervously, as though wondering which side the newcomers might be on. Katya feared for the people between the two lines of giants. If a fight broke out . . .

Katya sought the Hegemony combat channels, her AI shifting through thousands of frequencies in a fraction of a second. There! She heard them talking—AI-coded, of course. "Join us," she said, speaking in the clear. There was a sudden, shocked silence. "Hegemony warstriders, join us! Or step aside and allow us to pass to Towerdown!"

"Who is this?" A man's voice, harsh with frustration.

"This is Captain Katya Alessandro of the Confederation," she said. She hoped she didn't sound as pompous as she felt. "Hegemony and Empire no longer govern here. Eridu is free. Allow us to enter the Towerdown dome."

She could see the entrance to Towerdown behind the warstriders and a line of Heglegger infantry. That dome had been heavily guarded throughout the past week, and if this rebellion was to have any chance at all, Sinclair's forces had to seize it. Besides the space elevator's base and power circuits, it housed the government-controlled transmitters and AI that connected much of Eridu with synchorbit. While government centers at Winchester and elsewhere possessed direct lasercom links with Babylon, the Hegemony's control of the planet's entertainment, news, and communications originated *there*, in Towerdown.

The biggest of the opposing striders, an old RS-64C Warlord, pivoted on its upper torso, the massive, blunt forearms housing megavolt particle cannons coming to bear on Katya's Ghostrider with unmistakable menace.

"Give it up, sweetheart," the voice replied, "before we squash you and your mincie friends here like bugs."

"Like you did at Tanis?" she shot back. "Another massacre? Start shooting and none of you will leave this plaza alive. *Let us pass!*"

The Warlord took a threatening step forward. The crowd, uncertain, wavered somewhere between panic and fury. Katya could imagine the sheer helplessness they would feel, faced by armored giants against which they were powerless. Some of them were shouting now, isolated cries, calling for the rebel striders to go ahead and attack.

She hesitated. Any overt force could trigger a firefight, and hundreds would die. She checked her internal time sense again. Sinclair had promised—

Yes! The vast image of Prem flickered, broke into dancing fragments, solidified once, then blanked out. In its place was a new figure, serene and cold and remote.

General Travis Sinclair, wearing an austere brown uniform with only a single star glinting at his throat to show his rank. The transmission, Katya knew, was being beamed into Eridu's communication system by hackers who'd managed to infiltrate the government's ViRcom network days before. She prayed they would be able to keep the tap open; *everything* depended on Sinclair's getting his message out now. The crowd, trembling at the brink of an all-out riot, grew still. Even the Heglegger troops around the perimeter turned to watch the screen.

"People of Eridu," Sinclair began, a simple and straightforward preamble. "As most of you know by now, the Eriduan Congress of Delegates has asked us to prepare a document advancing the New Constitutionalist position. We have done so. Congress has not yet voted to accept its provisions, but it occurs to us that, in a declaration of such import, in *events* of such import, a direct appeal to the people for ratification might best serve our cause. This is, after all, *your* world, and not Earth's. And, if you will it, it is your declaration.

"Therefore . . .

"We, the free peoples of a diverse and infinitely variable species, in order that our beliefs and the nature of our steadfast determination be set before the judgment of an informed and rational Humankind, do now publish this Declaration of Reason, establishing it as a covenant among those seeking relief from the burden imposed by Hegemony tyranny.

"A just and unemotional deference to the principles of reason demands that we explain our position clearly and without equivocation. Why should the rule of law given precedent by centuries of peace be called now into question? In explanation, then, we make these assertions:

"We hold that the vast distances sundering world from world and system from system serve to insulate the worlds of Mankind's diaspora from one another and from Earth, and that government cannot adequately bridge so vast a gap of time, space, and culture;

"We hold that the differences between mutually alien, albeit human cultures render impossible a thorough understanding of the needs, necessities, aspirations, goals, and dreams of those disparate worlds by any central governing body;

"We hold that the seizure of the wealth and property of our citizens on pain of imprisonment or suit is indistinguishable from armed robbery, that the forced servitude of our people on foreign worlds is indistinguishable from slavery, that the continued assimilation of diverse cultures into societal patterns determined by those claiming to represent popular opinion is indistinguishable from genocide;

"Further, we hold that human culture, economy, and aspirations are too varied to administer, regulate, or restrict by any means, but should be free, allowing each to thrive or fail on its own merits;

"That human rights derive neither from God nor from human government or institutions nor from precedent, but from a people's willingness to secure and maintain those rights for themselves;

"That every individual bears the responsibility for his own actions, and that personal liberty conveys no right to deprive others of life, liberty, or property; neither can what is regarded as morally wrong for the individual be considered morally right for government;

"That the only just role for government in human affairs is as defense against force or fraud;

"That when government no longer represents its people, that when government representatives advance their own interests at the expense of the people, that when legal attempts by the people to represent themselves and their interests and to redress the wrongs of the government prove ineffectual, that when government manifestly threatens the principles of individual liberty, then the people have not the right but the responsibility for reforming or, at need, changing that government. . . ."

There was more, a lot more, all of it following the same general thread, that people didn't have to let some amorphous and all-wise government think for them, but had the right . . . no, the *duty* to think for themselves. Katya wasn't entirely sure she believed all that was said. If there were no taxes—that line about seizure of wealth and property had caught her ear—how could the government keep open the trade routes between the worlds? If individual freedoms took precedence over public welfare, what was to stop someone from screaming "Fire!" in a crowded room? Or operating a groundcar or skimmer while a current trickled through the pleasure center of his brain?

Well, perhaps that line about individual responsibility covered that . . . but she still had the feeling that this Declaration of Reason was being just a bit glib on that point.

Nevertheless, she had a large, unyielding lump in her throat as she listened to the rest of the address, and she noticed that the crowd thronging the square was as silent and as still as if they'd been somehow suspended in time.

"We declare, therefore, that the Worlds of Man are and should be mutually sovereign, mutually independent of central authority, mutually free to pursue what they perceive as their own best interests, so long as those interests do not abridge the freedoms of their neighbors.

"And we further declare that the government of the United Terran Hegemony, having forfeited its right to govern through careless disregard of the needs and petitions of its citizens, can no longer be the legitimate and representative government for those worlds and peoples signatory to this contract, but that the said relationship between governed and governors is henceforth dissolved.

"It is the firm desire of the signatories of this declaration to live in peace with all men and all worlds, but we hereby pledge our devotion to the principles of individual liberty outlined in this document with a firm determination to uphold these principles in the face of coercion, intimidation, imprisonment, and death.

"To this we pledge our lives, our honor, and our trust as members of a common humanity."

What, Katya wondered, would the Xenophobes make of that? Nothing much, she decided, since concepts like "individual" and "personal" were wholly alien to them. She remembered again the Xenophobe's touch, and shuddered.

But the human members of the audience accepted the declaration with profound emotion. For long seconds after Sinclair's image had stopped speaking, there was silence . . . and then the square erupted in a thunderous ovation, in screams and cheers and roared approval. Scanning the crowd, Katya saw people on their knees in prayer, people in tears, people with their arms upraised and their eyes closed in a kind of ecstasy born of mass acclamation.

But others were in motion, surging *toward* the line of Centurian warstriders.

For one fragile moment, Katya thought that perhaps the Centurians were not going to fire, that the advancing crowd had caught them off-guard or that they could not bring themselves to fire on civilians. Then the Warlord's twin particle cannons thundered, twin bolts of blue-white light lashing the charging mob. Screams rose above the mob thunder, and Katya felt the icy touch of horror.

"Aim for their weapons!" she ordered. "Watch for the civilians!"

"Targeting!" Hagan yelled. His Scoutstrider's laser fired an instant later, striking the Warlord's left arm close to the shoulder joint.

Katya fired an instant later, wondering how many unarmed civilians would die in the ricochets of explosive rounds and the sweep of laser beams that would surely follow.

One of the Centurian Scoutstriders was trembling, then rocking back and forth as the crowd surged about its legs, pushing first one way, then the other. Its torso lashed about, its laser firing, scoring bloody, smoking paths through the sea of humanity before it, but then the mob hit it from the left like ocean breakers crashing against the shore, and the twenty-ton, three-and-a-half-meter-tall warstrider toppled over with flailing arms and a grinding crash.

Katya could hear the screams of the wounded over the roar of the crowd, but louder and louder came a thundering chant, a thousand voices or more picking up the theme and magnifying it: "*Ta*nis! *Ta*nis! *Ta*nis!" She caught a glimpse of the Scoutstrider's operator as he was hauled from his slot, but only a glimpse. He vanished beneath the crowd an instant later.

With infinite care she moved forward, fearful of treading on the densely packed, screaming, banner-waving mass of humanity before her. Both of the Warlord's particle cannons were smoking now, disabled by near-point-blank bursts of laser fire from the rebel striders. The other striders seemed hesitant to open fire, but a thick fog hung in the air . . . gas of some kind. *God, we've got to win this quick*, she thought.

Some Hegemony troops opened fire on the crowd and died. Some turned over their weapons without a fight and most lived. Some actually joined the crowd's roaring charge.

One Guard Scoutstrider shook off the spell that held its operator and fired some sort of close-in, shotgun-type weapon, a bursting shell that mowed down a column of civilians in a bloody, tangled mass. A bottle, flame streaming from its neck, arced through the air, struck the RLN-90 high up on its torso, and exploded in writhing flames. A second bottle followed, and a third, and then a rocket round from a shoulder-fired launcher streaked low above the crowd and struck the burning strider squarely in its side. The crippled machine kept trying to move, until several laser bolts from Hagan's machine stopped it for good. Katya waited for the pilot's ejection, but it never came.

The surviving warstriders were retreating now, unable to face the sheer, ferocious weight of Babel's civilian population. The Warlord broke to Katya's left, making for the south end of the dome. With few civilians blocking her path in that direction, Katya changed course and angled for an intercept.

The Warlord's high-velocity cannon, a squat dome-shaped turret mounted on the dorsal surface of its hull, loosed a buzzsaw burst of depleted uranium slugs that slammed into the Ghostrider and nearly smashed her to the ground. Lipinski, controlling the LaG-42's missile launchers, loosed a short-range ripple-fired volley of M-490 rockets that savaged the bigger machine's left leg and nearly brought it down. She locked onto a weak spot, a laser scar in the RS-64's armor near the leg actuator joints, and fired pulse after pulse of 100-megawatt laser energy into duralloy plate suddenly glowing white-hot. The left joint gave suddenly, bolts of lightning jaggedly caressing tortured armor as main power leads shorted out. The machine ground to a halt, and as Katya's Ghostrider moved closer, the crewmen ejected in a one-two-three sequence of smoke and noise.

It didn't help. The crowd caught them almost before their chute-slowed capsules finished bouncing off the pavement. Katya turned away, unable to stop what happened next, and unable to watch it.

"*Tanis! Tanis! Tanis!*"

She had never imagined a battle quite like this one.

Chapter 30

The first warflyers were man-jacked constructors and workpods equipped with maneuvering thrusters, indispensable for heavy construction work on the synchorbitals and other big orbital facilities. By 2250, forty-three years after the first military use of warstriders, orbital workpods were being armed for sentry and customs inspections. Slower and with less range than conventional space fighters, they have greater armor and endurance. Nonetheless, they have seen only limited use in combat.

—*Armored Combat, A Modern Military Overview*
Heisaku Ariyoshi
C.E. 2523

"They've just gone to General Quarters," Anders said over Dev's intercom circuit. "Looks like we have to do it the hard way."

Dev agreed. "Launch the warflyers."

Warflyers were little more than converted warstriders, with legs replaced by cryo-H tanks and strap-on maneuvering thrusters. The two DR-80 Tenrai craft—*Tenrai* was Nihongo for "Heavenly Thunder"—had been captured by the raid at Nimrod that rescued Dev and the other Terran Rangers. Each massed twelve tons—eighteen with a full load of reaction mass—and was essentially a small, self-contained spacecraft. They could not reach orbit by themselves, nor could they reenter atmosphere for a landing. Instead, they were carried to and from orbit in ascraft rider slots, just as striders were transported to landing zones on a planet's surface.

Silently in the vacuum of space, panels blew clear of the Moketuki's belly, spinning end over end as they drifted into the night. The DR-80s, secured by magnetic grippers inside the ascraft's riderslots, dropped free a second later. Just under fifteen minutes out from the Babylon orbital facility, Shippurport was visible only as a webwork of distant lights surmounting the razor-slash gleam of the sky-el. To Dev, it resembled a spider's web glittering with sunlit droplets of dew, indescribably delicate and beautiful.

The laser defenses hidden within that beauty must be targeting them at this very moment.

"Laser com functional," Simone reported. "We're linked."

Neither warflyer was manned, save for the Artificial Intelligences residing in their on-board computers. The odds were high that both craft would be destroyed in seconds. Instead, two of the ascraft's passengers, Harald Nicholson and Torolf Bondevik, had jacked in from their acceleration couches on the flight deck and were controlling the flyers through teleoperation.

Both of the former Thorhammers were Lokans, with experience doing this kind of work at Loki's Asgard synchorbital. They fired the DR-80s' main thrusters almost in unison, accelerating out from the shadow of the pirated ascraft.

"Quite a view," Nicholson said over the general frequency. "Sensors are recording a power-up zero-three-zero, plus zero-seven."

"Got it," Bondevik said. "Cloudscreen is armed."
"*Fire!*"

A bolt of light streaked from the central hull of one of the warflyers, followed a beat later by a launch from the other. The missiles, high-speed Starhawks, had a range of over one hundred kilometers. Though Imperial Starhawks could carry nukes, Hegemony weapons were limited to conventional warheads. These carried EWC-167 nanomunitions packs, and their twin detonations a moment later, a silent double flare of white light, released trillions of minute, nano-generated motes that gleamed in the sunlight like mirrored shields.

For centuries, engineers had searched for the key to the mythical "force field" of ViRdrama fictions. While numerous magnetic screens existed—such were vital for manned craft penetrating gas giant radiation belts, for example, or in the inner planetary systems of red dwarf flare stars—the magical defensive shield that could reflect lasers and charged particle bolts as well as nuclear missiles had remained a dream of science fiction.

Cloudscreens were the next best thing, however, for what couldn't be seen or tracked by radar could not be accurately targeted. Two hundred kilometers from the synchorbital docking port, the twin, silvery clouds slowly merged and continued to drift toward the port with a closing speed of nearly ten kilometers per second. Behind the cloud, the ascraft shuttle and the two warflyers accelerated together, pacing the cloud, hidden in its opaque radar shadow.

Lasers lashed out from the docked *Tokitukaze* and from small defensive turrets on the synchorbit facility itself. The beams left dazzling trails as they vaporized paths through the dust, but the cloud rapidly absorbed and dispersed each beam, while continuing to shield the attackers. Radar and ladar returned only the blank, silvery disks of the approaching clouds.

Missiles could have penetrated the cloud, of course, and used on-board AIs to identify and track the targets, but they could not be launched while the ship was docked. Orders were given to cast off from the port facility, but it would be minutes yet before the countless power and data links between ship and port could be secured. Meanwhile, the Imperial destroyer's missile tubes were blocked by the docking shroud, unable to turn their nuclear-tipped fury against the attackers.

And they had only seconds.

The cloudscreen swept across the port facility, a silent storm, the silvery dust already dispersing to transparency but packing inertia enough in each microscopic particle to scour painted numbers and insignia from duralloy surfaces, and sending spacesuited workers and workpods scurrying for shelter behind intervening superstructures. Transplas windows frosted over in seconds, and inside the synchorbital and aboard the docked destroyer, the drumming tick of hurtling dust sounded like the hissing roar of ocean surf.

The surf roar subsided as the cloud swept past, rapidly thinning, bound now at far greater than escape velocity for deep space. As the skies surrounding the synchorbital and the docked warship faded to transparency, the first high-explosive warheads struck.

"I see three other big Impie ships. What the hell are those?"

"Transports. Don't sweat 'em. Watch your closing rate."

"Copy. I've got the lead. . . ."

Dev listened silently to the ViRcommunications between Nicholson and Bondevik. It was hard to realize that both men were silently strapped into couches back on the shuttle's flight deck, and not actually aboard the two warflyers as they swiftly closed with the docked Imperial destroyer.

Each had loosed two more Starhawk missiles, these packing HE warheads, seconds after the cloud had engulfed the spaceport. Linking their cephlinks with the ascraft shuttle's AI, they'd computed accelerations, courses, and times with lightning speed and inhuman accuracy; the four Starhawks reached the *Tokitukaze*'s hull seconds after the cloudscreen began to dissipate.

"I've got a solid lock," Bondevik called. "Guiding home . . . *hit*!"

White light flared against the destroyer's port side. They were close enough now that Dev could clearly see the *Tokitukaze*, the forward third of its wedge-shaped length still engulfed by the docking shroud and the webwork of orbital gantries. Twisted fragments of wreckage spun across the night, and Dev could see the gantry frameworks rippling and twisting with the stress of the impact.

"Right behind you," Nicholson said. Dev saw the next missile, a minute point of light darting for the ragged, IR-glowing gap in the destroyer's port side. The spark flared, dazzlingly bright, then faded. "Damn! They nailed it. Switching to Two."

Dev's viewpoint was through a long-range, image-enhanced optical scanner aboard Bondevik's flyer. With a thought, he shifted his point of view to Nicholson's second missile. For a moment, he saw what Nicholson was seeing, the flank of the Imperial destroyer swelling with alarming speed, the ragged hole punched in her side by the first missile bracketed by target lock discretes, the flicker of numbers in one corner of the field showing the rapidly dwindling range. He had only a fleeting impression of the destroyer's sheer bulk, caught a glimpse of another soundless explosion to the right as Bondevik's second missile was taken out by a defensive laser battery. . . .

The hole in the *Tokitukaze*'s side expanded into a gaping cavern. Dev felt like he was hurtling through the cavern's mouth, sensed a tangle of wreckage and blast-twisted bulkheads ahead . . . and then his mind was filled with the staticky, hissing snow of a sharply broken ViRcom link.

His vision cleared with only a flicker of delay. He was aboard the shuttle once more, trailing the two flyers by nearly one hundred kilometers. Eridu's synchorbital facility had expanded to fill most of the sky ahead, a bewildering tangle of beams, struts, lights, tethers, storage tanks, and habitats. He could pick out the *Tokitukaze* now without enhancement. White fog—frozen air and water—was boiling into space from the double hit amidships.

A turret on the huge ship's dorsal side swiveled. "Power buildup," Anders warned. "I think—"

A gigawatt laser touched Bondevik's warflyer, and the chunky craft glowed white-hot for an instance before soundlessly vanishing.

"Here we go," Dev called. "Full acceleration!"

Nicholson's warflyer and the shuttle plunged toward the

Tokitukaze. The laser swung slightly, drawing down on the second flyer. Nicholson fired first, targeting the dorsal turret, which flared like a small sun.

And then the ascraft was so close that the destroyer filled the view forward, with the twisted and blackened hull plates centered dead ahead. Dev heard the *tic-tic-tic* of tiny, metallic fragments impacting on the ascraft's hull, could see the gigawatt laser turret pivoting for a third and final shot, and then Anders was firing full retros, decelerating the last few tens of meters on hard-driving pillars of white-hot plasma from the bow thrusters, the ship's squared-off prow plunging through tattered hull plating and twisted girders and burying itself in the destroyer's wounded flank like a thrusting knife blade.

Jacked into the shuttle's AI system, Dev did not feel the actual shock, but he knew they'd hit hard when both his vision and his data feed went out, leaving him literally in the dark. He broke his connection then, and woke up in the co-pilot's slot.

He had weight—a little, anyway, under a tenth of a G. Shippurport was far enough out-orbit from Babylon to provide a modest spin-gravity. He snatched up his helmet and gloves, grateful that the shuttle's hull hadn't been breached in the collision.

Actually, the shock had probably opened dozens of tiny leaks, but none serious enough to evacuate the ship suddenly. He pulled on the helmet, then donned his gloves and checked his seals. Simone and Lara were clambering out of their slots, and he helped them with their armor as well.

The *Tokitukaze* was an Amatukaze-class destroyer, 395 meters long and massing 84,000 tons. No single conventional warhead could destroy such a giant; it would take a nuclear warhead—which the rebels did not have—or a volley of subnuclear munitions—from more ships than the rebels could muster—to destroy her.

But she had to be taken out of action or the gains made by the rebels on the surface would be meaningless. The only alternative was to revive a form of naval warfare dead for six centuries. They would board and storm the giant warship in an attempt to reach her bridge.

Dev had researched their target carefully on the ground.

Her normal complement was around four hundred men, plus a marine company of 120, far too many for thirty rebels to handle.

Fortunately, they wouldn't need to. *Tokitukaze*—her Nihongo name meant "Fair Wind"—was in a friendly port, and though there was considerable tension on the planet's surface they could not be expecting an attack here at synchorbit. There would be a maintenance or caretaker crew aboard, fifty or less, plus perhaps half of the marines.

Odds of thirty to one hundred were still less than ideal, but the defenders would be scattered through different parts of the enormous ship, dazed by the attack, possibly trapped by warped pressure doors or by compartments opened to vacuum. Some would be dead; an instant before they'd rammed the bigger ship, Dev had actually *seen* several bodies pinwheeling through the night, blown out through the destroyer's ruptured side. The ship's slow and lackluster defense—only one main laser turret functioning with some fifteen minutes' warning—suggested that they had indeed caught the Imperial ship shorthanded and unprepared.

If they moved fast and struck hard, they might be able to reach the big ship's bridge, which was buried at her very core. He'd studied schematics of Amatukaze-class destroyers, and he'd selected the spot they'd rammed, briefing Bondevik and Nicholson carefully on their targeting. They'd slammed into the ship's number two cargo hold, port side amidships. The bridge was through one, possibly two bulkheads to the main portside passageway, then forward ten or twenty meters—*up* in the tenth-G gravity. Much depended on how far the twin HE Starhawks had penetrated.

The shuttle was half buried in the destroyer's flank now, its cargo hatch well inside the bigger ship. Power was out, so the rebels used hand cranks to winch the cargo hatch open, then spilled out into the Imperial ship, picking their way through the wreckage, weapons at the ready. By the time Dev and the others made their way back to the shuttle's cargo deck, most of the rebels had already debarked.

Dev, Simone, and Lara found weapons for themselves, then followed.

* * *

Omigato was no longer aboard the *Tokitukaze*.

As the battle had erupted in the Babel dome, his analogue had informed him of a discrepancy. Nakamura's shuttle was reported to be en route to Babylon—but Nakamura himself was still in Winchester, consulting with Nagai. The orders bore his personal ID authorization, but it had taken only a moment to call Nakamura personally and verify that he had most emphatically *not* issued orders for his secretary or his mistress to take his shuttle to Babylon.

That had been enough for Omigato, who immediately transferred his operations to HEMILCOM's war room, buried within Babylon's tangle of habs and synchorbit facilities. With most of *Tokitukaze*'s officers and crew scattered through Babylon or Shippurport, it made more sense to manage the battle from HEMILCOM's headquarters than from the destroyer.

In the meantime, he'd ordered *Tokitukaze* to go to General Quarters and given the command to destroy the incoming shuttle, which was almost certainly a diversionary raiding force, quite possibly a suicide attack, planned to pull his attention from the rebel attack on Babel.

"Intruders are reported aboard the *Tokitukaze*, my Lord," a voice said in his mind. "Efforts are being made to contain them. . . ."

And as he received bad news from his command ship, he was receiving worse from the officers floating weightless in the war room with him. He scowled at the war room's holographic display, as *Taisa* Theo Ramachandra, a staff tactician, gestured toward the miniature figures struggling across the Babel dome plaza. "Our forces have lost central Babel," he said. "With no room to maneuver, with conflicting and confusing orders about whether or not to open fire on civilians—"

"Never mind the professional critique of our blunders so far, Captain," Omigato said in Japanese. Everyone present spoke the language. "Tell me what we can do *now*?"

Ramachandra gestured, and the holoscene's scale changed. It showed now the Babel Plateau, one hundred meters above the chalk-white sea cliffs and rocks and the almost primitive village of Gulfport. The monorail line threaded through jungle to north and south. South lay the fortress complex at Nimrod; farther south still lay the suspected rebel encampment at Emden.

"We have Guard units raiding Emden now," Ramachandra said, his face and voice both expressionless. "They report capturing small amounts of equipment, a few deserters, but little of importance. It appears that the entire rebel force has been mobilized to coincide with the demonstrations inside the city.

"The First Chiron has been reinforced at Nimrod. A battalion of your Obake Regiment is en route via ascraft transport from Winchester and will arrive at Babel within two hours." Blue rectangles of light flickered and shifted on the three-D map as red numerals counted off the elapsed time.

"It is our belief that nothing can be done to save Babel," *Chusa* Barton added. His image was present as a holographic image; the man himself was with his troops on the planet. "Our assets within the city itself were too meager. However, we believe that the rebel military *must* come out of the city to defend it."

White rectangles flowed from the cluster of city domes, taking up positions south of the city, between Babel and Nimrod. They were clearly outnumbered by the Guard forces already near the city. As the ascraft arrived from Winchester, grounding on the defenders' flank and spilling nearly a full regiment of marine warstriders and armored infantry, the rebel forces were forced into a tighter and tighter pocket, pressed on two sides by government forces, with the sea cliffs to their left and the city dome at their back.

"If they do not?" Omigato growled.

"Then we assault the city, my Lord," Ramachandra said. "We take heavy casualties, but the city is wrecked, and, at conservative estimates, half of the population is killed." He paused, letting his words sink in. "Consider. The rebels depend for their existence on the goodwill and support of the local citizenry. Intelligence says that the civilian population has already sustained several hundred casualties in the fighting in the Babel city square. The rebels will not dare risk their local support. Their best strategy would be to leave the city in an attempt to gain freedom of maneuver."

Omigato nodded slowly. "Yes. I understand. In any case, whether they stay in the city or come out on the plain, they have no choice but to stand and die."

"Exactly, my Lord."

"What of this so-called Declaration of Reason?" a Guard general wanted to know. "It had a . . . an unusually powerful effect on the mincies. More than might have been expected."

"A stunt, nothing more," Omigato said with a confidence he did not quite feel. With the others, he had watched the three-D newscasts of the mob action after Prem's transmission had been overridden. The sight of a warstrider toppled by the crowd was . . . unnerving. "A propaganda ploy," he continued. "I believe the American military once referred to it as 'winning hearts and minds.' "

"We may have trouble with the local population if we lose their, ah, hearts and minds," Barton pointed out. "Especially since we have already lost our space support."

Omigato's blood ran cold at the implied insult. Almost, his hand went to the laser holstered at his side, but he forced himself to relax. Barton was a *gaijin*, a Hegemony barbarian, nothing more. He could not be expected to understand. Besides, he was forty thousand kilometers away, and any threat of force here and now would be childish, an admission of weakness.

The war room had gone death-silent at Barton's words, with every person present waiting to see Omigato's reaction. He surprised them by smiling.

"Regarding the *Tokitukaze*, gentlemen," he said slowly, "the vessel has sustained heavy damage and should not interfere with our operations here. Two additional Imperial warships, the *Gekko* and the *Shusui*, are en route from the outer system at this moment, with full complements of marines and sufficient firepower to destroy the raiders . . . and to support our operations on Eridu.

"As for Eriduan 'hearts and minds,' I urge you to leave that to the Imperial forces. By the time we finish here, every member of the population will be a devout supporter of the Hegemony and of the Emperor."

He did not add the obvious corollary: *Or they will be dead.*

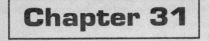

Chapter 31

*And what are the principles of combat? Control
the high ground, don't let the enemy on your flank.
Mobility, security, surprise. Fight because your warrior
brothers stand to left and right. Such are the constants
of human warfare, unchanged in six millennia.*

—*Kokorodo: Discipline of Warriors*
Ieyasu Sutsumi
C.E. 2529

A laser bolt scored the bulkhead behind Dev's head with a
hissing snap and he ducked, unable to return fire because
of the press of armored men ahead. The fight aboard the
Tokitukaze had none of the elegance of a classic warstrider
battle on open ground but was a cramped, ugly slugfest
between two groups of men almost totally blind to each
others' forces and positions. A grenade exploded ahead,
and Dev heard someone scream.

They'd burned their way into the main port passageway,
crowding into the ship's labyrinth of internal corridors. The
ship's own self-repair systems had sealed the breach behind
them before much atmosphere had been lost, but not before
most of the invaders were aboard and moving toward the
bridge.

The sounds of combat up ahead were louder now, more
raucous, more confused. There was another explosion . . .
and then an abrupt silence more unnerving than the crackling and hammering of combat had been. Dev pressed
forward . . .

. . . and stepped through forced-open doors leading to
the ship's bridge. It was a large, circular compartment
with a low overhead, hazy with smoke and ringed with

three-meter cylinders canted back from the central pit at forty-five-degree angles. Only a handful of the linkage tubes were occupied, Dev saw, and the rebels were holding three disarmed marine guards at gunpoint. Two more lay broken on the deck.

Dev took a quick glance around the bridge, identified the manual link console, and dropped his palm onto the interface panel. A second later, the pattern of lights glowing in the console's black acrylic surface shifted, greens becoming reds, and then the ship operators were waking up, unjacking, stumbling uncertainly from their tubes and into the waiting arms of the rebels.

Dev pointed to one young-looking Japanese officer. *"Kancho deska?"* he demanded. *Kancho* was one of several Nihongo words meaning "captain"—specifically, the CO of a warship. "Are you the commander of this warship?"

The man bowed stiffly. *"Hai!"* His rank tabs indicated he was a *shosa*, a naval lieutenant commander, probably third or fourth officer of the ship.

"Kancho deska?" Bondevik demanded, giving the initial *ka* sound a slightly different intonation, and the Nihonjin officer went rigid, fists clenched, face red. The way Bondevik had pronounced it, the question had become "Are you an enema?"

The other rebels laughed, and Dev had to shout to restore order. "Okay, enough, people! Leave them alone." He waved a gloved hand toward one side of the bridge. "Bondevik, Nicholson, Schneider, DeVreis! Those tubes over there are weapons links. Langley, Gomez, Tewari, and Koenig! Over there, those four tubes. They'll be engineering. We need shipboard power stat, and a lock-in to make sure no one cuts us off from an auxiliary bridge. Karposci, you're on security, any of those tubes over there. Anders, take helm. That one. Dagousset, find any terminal and go to work on the ship's AI. All of you now, jack in and get hot."

As the first group made for the link capsules, he turned, a little clumsily in his armor and the light gravity. "Belenko. How hard were we hurt coming in?"

"Eight killed, sir," a young rebel said. "Three wounded pretty bad. Michaels is with 'em now."

Dev winced. Eleven lost already out of his assault force of thirty.

"Okay. You, Abrams, and Kanavsky. Search and secure the prisoners. Use one of the compartments aft of the bridge. The rest of you, spread out through this deck. Roadblocks at the corridor intersections. We don't know how many bad guys are still aboard, and they're going to be gunning for us as soon as they figure out what the hell's going on. Okay? All clear? Jack it!"

The *Tokitukaze* was already powered up, with the first steps for switching to internal power preparatory to casting off already completed. The biggest danger the boarders faced was that someone in auxiliary control would isolate them from the ship's computer, leaving them high, dry, and helpless, but Dev was gambling on the fact that auxiliary bridges were rarely manned when a vessel was in port, and it took time to power them up and link them in with the ship's command systems. He watched for a moment, as men and women squeezed into the bridge link capsules, before removing his helmet and gloves, selecting a capsule for himself, and climbing in.

It was the tube the young *shosa* had been using, the one designated for the officer of the watch. He plugged the jacks into his sockets, touched the palm interface, and became the *Tokitukaze*.

Power thrilled through his being, power and purpose and a reason for living. He could sense the entire length of the huge warship, feel the damage in his side where the shuttle had rammed home. His view forward was blocked by the embrace of the Shippurport docking shroud, but behind it he could see the lights of Babylon spread across the sky like pearls on a string, and beyond that, suspended in space against the background stars, the cloud-wreathed, red-gold-violet glory of Eridu.

"Cameron on-line," he announced, the routines of his old ship-conning days returning with effortless familiarity. "Coordinate through me."

"Captain . . ." DeVreis said.

"Whatcha got, Paul?"

"Looks like two targets, inbound under free-fall at one hundred three thousand kilometers, bearing two-one-one, neg five-three. Power plant readings suggest approximate Kumano-class. They're hustling."

Kumanos. Frigates, massing perhaps fifty thousand tons each. Smaller than the *Tokitukaze*, but undamaged and more maneuverable. They would be trouble. "ETA?"

"If they maintain course and don't cut in their thrusters . . . make it eighteen minutes, Captain."

Almost a hundred kilometers per second. They *were* hustling.

"Weapons status?"

"Nicholson here. The spinal mount's shot, and the main dorsal gigawatt laser's off-line. Power failures in twenty-two percent of the megawatt point defense lasers. We have three other gigawatt turrets powered and green, though. Missile systems check out green, loaded, and ready."

"Good. Keep tracking. See what you can do about the PDLs."

Lara Anders cut into the network. "I'm reading green on all conventional thruster and maneuvering systems. We're go for release."

"Roger on that," Koenig added. "Looks like ship's systems have taken care of all leakage. ATM is steady at point nine-eight bar."

"Power coming up in the fusor packs," Onkar Tewari, an Earth-born Hindi, announced. "Cryo-H are secure and at full pressure."

Good. The collision had not vented their reaction mass into space.

"We've got about a platoon of marines coming at the front door," Anatol Karposci announced over the link network. "Plasma guns and rocket launchers. I think they mean business."

"Seal them off."

"Forward hatch is sealed. Boarding tube is released."

"I have the ship's AI on line," Simone reported. "I can't get at the codes for nuclear launch or the K-T drive, but we're jacked in on everything else."

"Easy feed," Dev said. He'd not expected to get the nukes. Those things were jealously guarded. And they wouldn't be needing to go faster than light. "Get to work on the mag grapples."

"Yes, sir."

That would be the tricky part. The magnetic grapples were not controlled from the ship but through the docking AI of Shippurport Approach Control. Simone would have to hack her way into the synchorbital facility's computer network to get them to release the ship.

"Captain? We have a demand from port security that we surrender and open the forward docking hatch."

Dev laughed. "Tell them we need Lord-high Omigato's permission for that. That'll keep 'em guessing."

He wondered if Omigato was still aboard the *Tokitukaze*. He doubted it. The Imperial *daihyo* would probably have gone where the action was as things broke loose on Eridu, buried somewhere in HEMILCOM's orbital fortress.

"Captain, this is Simone. I can't access the magnetic grapples—"

"Damn!"

"—but I *can* trigger the emergency explosive release."

"Outstanding! All stations! Report readiness for space."

"Engineering is go, Captain. Power up, thrusters standing by. You have maneuvering at your command."

"Weapons go. We're still tracking those bandits, now at one hundred one kay and closing."

"Maneuvering go."

"Affirmative. Okay, Simone. Do it. Now!"

An electrical signal flashed to explosive charges mounted at the base of each docking grapple. Soundlessly in vacuum, but with a dull, hollow thud that echoed through the passageways of the *Tokitukaze*, the charges detonated, releasing the destroyer's prow.

With nothing holding the ship, the centrifugal force of the synchorbital eased the *Tokitukaze* backward at a velocity of just over one meter per second. Koenig cut in the bow thrusters a moment later, and then they were falling free, clear of Shippurport and dropping into the night.

Nearly three hours had passed since the wild fight in the main Babel dome. After securing the Towerdown, the sky-el base, and the communications center, Katya had led the remainder of the rebel force out through the main airlock and onto the city plain.

They were standing on a broad hill almost a kilometer south of the Towerdown dome, a ridge named Raeder's Hill after Eridu's first governor. The view was spectacular, one hundred meters above a violet sea. The jungle circled in the distance, tangled and impenetrable save for the clear-cut slashes where monorails and roadways passed. At Katya's back, the sky-el speared the zenith, dwindling away overhead to a vanishing point lost somewhere in the depths of that green-blue sky.

Other rebel forces had been arriving all morning—from Gulfport, from Emden, from other outposts scattered across the equatorial zone, and even by monorail from as far away as Winchester and Boreal. Including the former Hegemony Guard warstriders that had come over to the rebel side, the Confederacy forces could muster thirty-three warstriders, plus something like eight hundred men with full combat armor, able to move and fight outside the city domes. Another two thousand, plus the thousands more of civilians who didn't even possess partial armor, waited inside the Babel domes, watching the overture to the coming battle.

"That was well done, Katya," a familiar voice said in her mind.

"General Sinclair! Where are you?"

An RS-64D Warlord ten meters in front of her turned and lightly raised its left arm. "Right here."

"But . . . you're not supposed—"

"Not supposed to risk my life?"

"The Network can't afford to lose you, sir."

"At this point, Katya, my living or dying won't make that much difference one way or the other. My analogue has been safely downloaded, just in case, and it knows all my contacts and codes. But now that the Declaration has been published, I'm just another striderjack."

"The Network needs a leader, General."

"The Confederation has all the leaders it will need. Right now, it needs men and women who aren't afraid to get their hands dirty. Right?"

Katya hesitated. "Yes, sir."

He shifted to the general command frequency. "Right, Alessandro! I'd like you on the right flank. Keeping an eye on the monorail."

"Yes, sir."

"Quillier and Sung, you're with me on the center. Creighton, you're on the left. Foot commanders, get your people well dispersed and well dug in. We're going to be counting on them to even up the odds a bit."

As Sinclair continued to rattle off orders, Katya turned her attention to the forest treeline, seven hundred meters to the south. A number of Hegemony Guard warstriders were already in sight at the bottom of the hill, secure in the knowledge that the rebels wouldn't start firing at them randomly. Ammunition, rockets and explosive shells, was too tight to waste it. She was tempted to try probing those ranks with her laser, but resisted the urge. All it would do would be to start a firefight now, before the leggers were in place. Well, if they were willing to stand around in the open waiting for the party to start, so was she. The cocky bastards even had banners up, she saw. Two stylized yellow stars and a centaur on a dark green background: the Chiron Centurians. She wondered if any of the people over there were New American Mech Cavs or 4th Terran Rangers, and what it would be like fighting someone in your own unit.

You ought to know, girl, she told yourself. *Just like Dev, all over again. The only difference is that this time you're trying to kill him before he kills you.*

She was suddenly very glad that Dev had joined the rebellion.

With brief, crisp orders, she deployed the striders in her squad, making sure they had at least fifty meters spacing between them and that their fields of fire overlapped. Chung, Hagan, and Jacobsen took up positions in a rough diamond pattern with her; Darcy, with his recon warstrider, went on the far right flank.

She glanced again into the sky. Where was the enemy's air? The rebels had a few ascraft—too few to challenge the government's air superiority. She'd expected them to use that advantage . . . one reason that she'd argued during the initial planning sessions that if they had to defend Babel, they'd be better off doing it inside the domes. She'd been overruled by Sinclair, however. They couldn't save Babel's population by killing them in the fallout from a strider-to-strider armored clash. Katya understood that, though she felt as though they were giving up one of their very few military advantages, the defensive cover provided by the domed structures. Out here on the open hilltop, they still had the advantage of position, but not of cover.

Sinclair had also overruled her on the suggestion that they try to summon the Xenophobes, using the code they'd imprinted on Katya's comel during her contact with the Self. "Katya," he'd said, "we need allies we can *trust!*"

And she'd not been able to press the point.

Explosions, many of them, set deep in the rock and repeating quickly, the comel had seemed to whisper in her mind after her return from the Xenophobe cavern. *Powerful magnetic fields, masses of pure elements grouped together. It will be felt. It is how Self tastes the interface, and what it hungers for. Self will come. . . .*

Dev had laughed when she'd told him. "How about that?" he'd said when he could breathe again. "Here we are stomping around on the surface of a planet in our warstriders, twenty, maybe forty tons of duralloy and steel and 'pure elements,' with magnetic fields in our skimmers and ascraft, explosions, noise . . ."

He'd laughed again. "Don't you see? Every time we used to gather all our striders together to go hunt for the Xenos, we were saying, 'Hey, guys! Dinnertime! Come and get it!' "

It wasn't as simple as that, of course. She thought that the "explosions, set deep in the rock and repeating quickly" ruled out the possibility that the Xenophobes would simply pop up in the middle of a battle. The sense she'd received from the comel had been of a deliberate signal, something that the Xenophobe would definitely hear in its deep lair, and respond to.

But Sinclair refused to even consider using the Xenophobes. "Too dangerous," he'd said, "especially this close to the sky-el. We'd be inviting disaster, bringing those things up on the surface anywhere near Babel."

Katya had understood, and in a way she'd been relieved. Ever since her return to the light of the surface, she'd tried not to think about those dark, close moments in the Xenophobe's belly, and she was not eager to see those crawling horrors again. Sinclair might be thinking of Babel and the space elevator, but she didn't want to bring them in because, she realized now, she was afraid for her own sanity.

One by one, the legger squads called in, reporting that they were ready. Robot guntowers had been deployed, trenches dug by constructors. Unfortunately, they'd not had time to grow any defensive walls.

In fact, they were still deploying the last of the troops when someone shouted over the general frequency. "Look there! More of the bastards!"

It was true. She'd counted five light Guard warstriders before, a single squad of LaG-17s and Ares-12s, clearly either a reconnaissance unit or a cavalry screen for troop movements farther back in the woods. Now she could see other light striders moving out from the trees, deploying in a long line of machines made hazy by the shimmer of nanoflage. Behind them, bigger, more powerful machines were lumbering from the woods, smashing their way clear of mushroom trees and thick foliage.

There were Ghostriders and Scoutstriders, of course, but she also saw the flat, twin-horned torsos of KR-9 Mantas, forty-two-ton medium assault striders with twin 100-MW lasers, missile packs, and automatic cannons. Behind them came four RS-64D Warlords, at least one Qu-19E Calliopede, and the ponderous, fifty-four-ton bulk of a Kr-200 Battlewraith. Skimmers spilled from among the trees, each carrying at least a squad of armored infantry.

The sight was shocking . . . and terrifying. Katya was counting striders as quickly as she could and had reached thirty-eight when Sinclair ordered all units to arm weapons and prepare to fire. The rebel defenders were outnumbered . . . and where their heaviest striders were three Warlords and four creaking Devastators, the enemy had at least twelve striders massing more than forty tons each.

Unless Sinclair decided to lift his restriction on Xenos or on retreats into the city, it was going to be a short fight, and a lopsided one.

A missile arced across the rebel lines, trailing smoke, striking behind the lines with a flash and a loud bang. With a roar like thunder, the government line advanced.

And Katya was fighting for her life.

* * *

His first crisis of command had been the problem of an unknown number of Imperials still loose aboard the *Tokitukaze*, men isolated in the aft part of the ship and more than able to mount an attack on Dev's handful of boarders, or worse, to tinker with the ship's drives or power source and leave the destroyer helplessly adrift.

The problem had been easy enough to solve. Seconds after dropping clear of Shippurport, he'd passed a warning to those of his crew not safely strapped into jacking tubes, giving them a chance to find acceleration couches, then applied four Gs of acceleration for over a minute. Anyone standing when the drives had kicked in would be on the deck now, probably with broken bones. Dev was gambling that anyone smart enough to find acceleration couches after that was smart enough to stay there. Periodically, he kicked in a short burst, just to keep his unwanted passengers aft cautious.

Now, Dev was looking back at Eridu, distant enough that Babylon and the space elevator were invisible, the world a peaceful-looking orb of brightly colored splendor. What was happening back there, he wondered? What was happening to Katya? He wished he could have stayed with her.

He sensed that his relationship with Katya had changed, though he still loved her. She'd drifted away from him in the past few months . . . or had he drifted from her? Hard to tell. Perhaps, when this fight was over, they could explore growing closer once more. He was willing, if she was.

If they survived. He didn't like thinking about that. The two Imperial frigates were less than fifty thousand kilometers away now, still well out of range, and *Tokitukaze* had begun maneuvering clumsily for an intercept. Perhaps eight minutes remained before the two sides came within extreme missile range.

Meanwhile, there was time for thought. Too much time.

Dev had always, *always* wanted to be a ship captain, a dream that went back to childhood and his unquestioning worship of a ship captain father. The sight of the Eridu space elevator from space as he'd backed the *Tokitukaze* clear had filled him with a sudden, an unexpected rush of emotion, of guilt that he'd not seen his father before Michal

Cameron's suicide, of understanding that this was what it must have been like, commanding an Imperial destroyer at the spaceside terminus of a planetary sky-el.

It was ironic, and it hurt to examine it. They'd called Michal Cameron a traitor because he'd destroyed the space elevator, stopping the Xenophobes of Lung Chi from reaching synchorbit and the refugee fleet docked there. Faced with a difficult choice and no time in which to choose, he'd acted. A hero.

Now Dev, once hero of the Empire, was committing treason, hijacking an Imperial destroyer to keep it from being used against rebel troops on the planet below.

I think you would've understood, Father.

For the first time in years, Dev wished his father was here to tell him what to do. He felt completely inadequate, jacked in as captain of a damaged ship, facing impossible odds. The original idea had simply been to keep the Imperials from using the *Tokitukaze* against the rebel defenders at Babel; now he was forced to take her into combat, shorthanded and with a hole in her side.

Imperial warships had large crews in part to provide frequent relief from duty, but particularly because more weapons links meant that greater numbers of teleoperated missiles, decoys, and sensor drones could be employed at one time. A jacker could only operate one missile at a time, and over typical ship combat ranges, that could tie up the operator through a large part of the battle. Dev had just nineteen men and women at his command, and nine of those were caring for the wounded or guarding prisoners or guarding the bridge. Four of those left were going to be busier than they could really manage handling the ship's maneuvering thrusters engineering, while Simone communed with the ship's AI and, perhaps most important now, kept watch on survivors of the Imperial crew who might now be burrowing into the destroyer's vitals, looking for ways to sabotage them.

That left Dev and four others, Bondevik and Nicholson from the old Thorhammers, Schneider and DeVreis from the 4th Terran Rangers, to handle all of *Tokitukaze*'s weapons.

It wasn't enough, not by a long shot.

Well, you always wanted to be a ship captain, he told himself wryly. *Now that you got your chance . . .*

In his mind, he shifted to Japanese, punning with the slippery word *kancho.*

Perhaps you're just an enema, and not a warship captain after all.

"Missile launch!" DeVreis warned. Dev saw it, a point of light bracketed in red by the ship's combat AI.

"Here we go, boys and girls," he said, his thoughts surprisingly steady. "Let's see just how much hell we can raise."

Chapter 32

When you try something on an adversary, if it doesn't work the first time, you won't get any benefit out of rushing to do it again. Change your tactics abruptly, doing something completely different. If that still doesn't work, then try something else.

Thus the science of the art of war involves the presence of mind to "act as the sea when the enemy is like a mountain, and act as a mountain when the enemy is like a sea."

This requires careful reflection.

—"Fire Scroll"
The Book of the Five Spheres
Miyamoto Musashi
Seventeenth century B.C.E.

The Hegemony warstriders advanced up the hill, struggling to cross seven hundred meters of fire-swept ground, leaning forward into the storm of laser, cannon, and plasma gun rounds as though pressing ahead in the teeth of a gale. Katya picked as her first target one of the Warlords, a dangerous strider with heavy armor and twin Ishikawajima charged-particle cannons. Three direct hits, and the big machine was still advancing, smoke curling from a ragged scar on its dorsal armor where one of Katya's shots had actually penetrated.

"Targeting!" Lipinski shouted warning. "On the left! Paint him!"

Katya snapped another laser bolt into the RS-64, then killed the pulse cutout, switching from hard-hitting punch to a diffuse beam. She kept the laser centered on the moving Warlord, tracking the vulnerable joints at thigh and hip. With a shuddering roar, the Ghostrider's left-hand Kv-70 weapons pack loosed a rippling salvo of rockets, shaped-charge warheads with laser-homing and impact fuzes. Tracking the backscatter of reflected laser energy, they slammed one after another into the Warlord in a succession of eye-searing flashes. Chunks of armor were blown thirty meters behind the lurching machine, which staggered, pivoted to the left, and then collapsed in a tangle of twisted duralloy legs.

Almost before she'd registered that she'd scored a kill, Katya's Ghostrider was slammed from the left, hard. Warning discretes flared across Katya's vision . . . *fire in section five . . . power failure in the primary energizing coils . . . pressure failure in the core housing . . .*

She dropped the LaG-42 into a crouch, twisting to the left to track her attacker. There . . . one of the Mantas, advancing up the slope. The KR-9 had just downloaded both 100-MW lasers into Katya's hull, and the blast had nearly stripped the Ghostrider's armor and holed the power plant.

Laser inoperative . . .

Weapons packs inoperative . . .

Recommend full power shutdown sequencing . . .

Override! They weren't dead yet! "Georg! Can you damp down that fire in section five?"

Fed by oxygen leaking from the life support reserves, that blaze could melt through to the main distributor circuits and maybe take out the AI logic as well.

"Working on it!"

"And bypass the secondary power feed to the Kv-70s!"

"You got it!"

A discrete flashed red to green. She had one missile launcher working again . . . and five M-490 rockets remaining in the left-side pack. Her chem-flamer was still fully charged, but that was a ten-meter weapon, knife-fighting range for a strider, and there were still friendly legger troops to Katya's front.

"Targeting!" The Manta was nearer now, forty meters and coming closer with a grim, step-by-step determination. Rocket fire and explosive high-speed cannon rounds were slashing into that flat, round hull, but it shrugged the fire off like rain and kept on coming. The ground beneath its heavy, flanged feet had been ripped and torn and churned into tortured hellground. "Fire!"

With her laser out, there was no way to guide the volley, but at forty meters she scarcely needed a smart-guided launch. Four of the five rockets slammed home, twisting one of the laser "horns" on the Manta's torso back and punching a hole in the glacis armor.

"Okay, boss! Fire's out!"

The temperature in section five was dropping. Power levels came back for the laser, though it would take precious seconds to build to full charge. Thirty meters away, a Fastrider loped past the slow-slogging Manta and stepped across one of the hastily dug front-line infantry trenches. Katya could see armored men scattering to avoid the machine's twelve-ton step.

Chin turret laser at seventy-five percent power . . .

It would have to do. Shifting her aim to the Fastrider, she locked in on the humped portion of armor that she knew shielded the pilot. The operator's jacking slot was always the most heavily armored portion of any warstrider, but LaG-17s didn't have that much armor to begin with. She tracked, slewing the Ghostrider's chin turret, then triggered the shot.

Armor exploded from the Fastrider's back, fist-sized chunks of shrapnel spinning across the slope. The strider took two more steps, hesitated . . . and then with a metal-rending groan it crumpled to the ground, burrowing its nose in churned-up earth. Katya swung back to loose another bolt at the Manta . . . and saw that it was withdrawing, *retreating* . . . and so were the other Hegemony striders. Eight of their machines lay scattered across the lower half of the slope, hulls ruptured, smoke billowing into the thin air and chasing its own shadows across the ground and into the forest.

"We got them on the run!" someone yelled, and several rebel striders started forward, firing into the retreating foe.

"Hold your ground!" Sinclair snapped. "Hold your position, damn it!" Let the government forces lure them into the jungle and the rebels would be cut to pieces. "All units, report! Who'd we lose?"

Three warstriders dead out of thirty-three. Two more badly damaged, but still fighting. Twenty-eight men KIA on the ground, all in exchange for eight kills, an unknown number of Hegleggers killed, plus several striders like that KR-9 hurt bad but still moving.

"Not bad, people," Sinclair's voice said, calming, reassuring. "We held 'em. We held 'em good!"

"I have movement on the front, range seven hundred . . ."

They were coming again, smashing out of the forest, some of them limping, some still trailing smoke from the last exchange, but all still coming.

Katya was already so tired she felt as though she was trembling, even though her LaG-42's reactions and movements remained iceworld-cold and engineer-precise. She was out of rockets, though, which left her with only the laser and about twenty antiarmor grenades, short-range weapons better for fighting infantry than warstriders.

And it didn't look as though the government forces were even thinking of letting up.

Gritting her mental teeth, Katya targeted a damaged Calliopede and downloaded her laser into its duralloy carapace.

"They're decelerating . . . must be three Gs," Bev Schneider warned. "They want to make it a stand-up fight."

Dev rotated his mental view of the ship dispositions, which showed the *Tokitukaze*, both frigates, Eridu and the Tower of Babel, and the sweeping, slightly curved lines representing ship vectors and orbits. The enemy had loosed a small cloud of missiles, now dispersing across the narrowing gulf between them and their prey. By shifting his perspective, Dev was able to see past the missile salvo and study the frigates themselves. According to the navdata glowing next to the tiny ship-silhouette images, they'd flipped over to present their sterns and were decelerating hard on fierce-driven torrents of plasma from their main thrusters.

Bev was right. In ship-to-ship combat there were basically two alternatives: sweep past the enemy at high speed, doing as much damage to him on the way as possible; or match course and speed with him, in effect moving in close and coming to a relative halt, pounding away with beam weapons, plasma guns, and missiles until he was dead or surrendered. The Imperial squadron commander had evidently chosen the latter.

According to *Tokitukaze*'s warbook, a Kumano-class frigate had a crew of 130, plus twenty marines. Those marines were intended as armed shore parties and for shipboard security rather than for ship-to-ship boarding actions, but the rebels' unconventional capture of the *Tokitukaze* would have alerted them to other possibilities, like crippling the captured destroyer and retaking her hand-to-hand. They'd probably been in touch with HEMILCOM and would know by now that there weren't many rebels manning her. They might even have guessed that some of their compatriots were still aboard.

In any case, it would make a hell of a lot more sense from the Imperial point of view to try to recapture the destroyer than to transform her into radioactive gas. Dead, Dev and the others would be rebel martyrs; alive, they would be rebel prisoners . . . and their mission a clear failure.

Even more than that, perhaps, was the question of *kao*, of face. The Imperial Navy had lost face when the *Tokitukaze* had been captured so easily. Some of that face would be restored if she were destroyed; far more would be won if she were recaptured.

That, at least, appeared to be the frigates' goal as they backed down at three Gs on columns of starcore-hot plasma. With the damage she had already suffered, and with only four men jacking her thrusters, the *Tokitukaze* was simply not a maneuverable vessel at the moment. A toe-to-toe slugging match was the best tactical approach Dev could hope for . . . and pray they weren't using nukes and pray the destroyer could stand up to a hell of a pounding, because otherwise those frigates were going to get off without a scratch.

Dev ordered the *Tokitukaze* spun end-for-end, and, after warning those of his people not jacked in, he engaged the ship's main thrusters. For long minutes, they decelerated at three Gs, slowing . . . slowing . . . and finally *Tokitukaze* began to accelerate again, heading back toward Eridu. He'd just made it a lot easier for them to match course and speed, an invitation saying "Come and get us."

Which was exactly what they were doing. They still had far more speed than the destroyer and were closing rapidly.

"Orders, Captain?" Torolf sounded nervous.

"Let 'em come. We're not going to outmaneuver them, that's certain."

"I've got an IFF decryption on them now, Captain," Simone said. "Definitely Kumano-class frigates, the *Shusui* and the *Gekko*."

"The *Sword Stroke* and the *Moonlight*, eh?" Koenig said. "Pretty."

"And dangerous," Dev pointed out. "If they decide to bombard our people from orbit, Sinclair won't have any defense."

Then there was no more time for analysis. The missiles, twenty-seven of them, converged on the *Tokitukaze*, and Dev ordered the point defense lasers linked over to the ship's AI. The Artificial Intelligence directing the ship's systems could act and react faster than any human, and with far greater precision.

The first phase of the battle was on them and past almost before they realized it. Eight missiles were vaporized as soon as they entered the *Tokitukaze*'s point defense envelope. Eight more were vaporized half a second later . . . and then seven more as one PDL short-circuited and failed.

Four missiles remained, on radar-active homing, closing on the ship too quickly to perceive. *Tokitukaze*'s AI was jamming on all combat frequencies and one missed, but the other three all had locked on to the highly reflective returns of the tangled ruin portside and amidships, where the ascraft was still embedded in the ruin of *Tokitukaze*'s flank.

Three missiles slammed home and detonated, one after the other in the space of two seconds; fragments of hull and ascraft shuttle spun into darkness. Buried in his cocoon,

Dev didn't feel the shock, but the cascade of systems failures and alarms flashing in his consciousness told him quickly enough that they'd been hit, and hit hard.

More missiles were coming, but Dev ignored them. It was the frigates he was concentrating on now, for both were reaching gigawatt laser range, but even as they slid inside the destroyer's targeting envelope, a pinpoint of light flashed between *Tokitukaze* and the frigates, then expanded into a shimmering sphere of reflected light, growing and drifting toward the destroyer at several kilometers per second.

"Main thrusters, full power, *now*!"

Tokitukaze lurched forward, accelerating slowly. Dev was watching the ever-shifting angles between the three ships and the cloudscreen, using the cloud's own movement to best position the destroyer for a shot. He suspected that the frigates had fired too soon.

They had, and they were lagging too far behind their cover. As *Tokitukaze* lumbered forward, Dev glimpsed the frigates in the cloud's shadow. Two of the ship's three gigawatt laser turrets could bear.

"Fire!"

There was no beam visible in the vacuum of space, no sound or other indicator of the torrent of energy unleashed across the void, but for a fraction of a second the *Shusui* shone more brightly than the local sun. "Hit!" DeVreis shouted . . . and then the *Gekko* was accelerating, pulling out from behind the drifting laser shield and loosing a salvo of laser bolts at the crippled destroyer.

Under the AI's guidance, all of *Tokitukaze*'s turrets that could bear swung and fired at the *Gekko*, but not before several tons of duralloy armor had boiled away and a cryo-H reaction mass tank had been holed and the destroyer's main thrusters had been cored by a beam that had sliced through the ship's vitals like a sword through a man's belly. For a moment, laser light shone from the *Gekko* as *Tokitukaze*'s beams raked her, but then the *Tokitukaze* was tumbling, nose-over-tail, completely out of control as the cryo-H superheated and blew out through the hull like a tremendous blast from a maneuvering thruster.

"Status!" Dev yelled. The stars were wheeling past his head, a complete rotation every few seconds.

"Main thrusters are dead, and I don't think we're gonna get 'em back," Langley reported. "We've got maneuvering still, and enough cryo-H. Gomez and Tewari are working on stopping our spin. They might manage it. We're losing air aft of frame ninety; that won't matter except to our Imperial passengers aft. We still have full power and all the weapons we started with.

"The bad news is we don't have our main thrusters. We can maneuver, but not accelerate with a delta V of more than a few meters per second. We're drifting in the general direction of Eridu. I'm starting a pool, folks. Will we miss the planet, skip off the atmosphere, or dig ourselves a nice hole?"

"What about the bandits?" Dev was searching the sky. They should be somewhere right about . . . there they were.

"I think we got them, Captain," Bev Schneider said. "No sign of life from either one."

"They're not necessarily kills," Nicholson added. "We hit them hard with a lot of juice. Probably vaporized every radio mast and antenna on their hulls, and most of their weapons mounts, too."

"As long as they're off our backs," Dev said, "and unable to help their friends on Eridu. Lara! What can you do about attitude control?"

"I'm slowing the spin gradually, Captain," Anders said. "We've taken a lot of stress amidships, and I don't want to snap her spine."

"Good thinking."

"Congratulations, Captain," Simone said. He could hear her smile over the link. "A successful ship-to-ship action, even if we don't get out of this in one piece!"

"Let's save the party until after we get this spin stopped," Dev said. Already, though, the wheeling of the stars had slowed. Eridu drifted gently across the heavens, then came to an unsteady rest. Indicators on the image confirmed what Langley had said. The *Tokitukaze* was dropping toward Eridu now in free-fall, though it did appear that they would miss the planet by a good margin.

Except for the maneuvering necessary to make certain they didn't slam into the space elevator, it appeared that the *Tokitukaze* was now out of the fight.

On the ground, though, things must be going hot and furious.

Dev wished he could be there with Katya and Hagan and the rest of them, wished at least that they were close enough to take a tactical feed from the ground and find out what was happening. The rebels must be fighting the fight of their lives right about now.

"Hey, listen up, people," he said suddenly. "Engineering! I need some numbers from you!"

"What?" DeVreis said. "You got an idea?"

"Maybe," Dev said. "How does this sound? . . ."

Three times now, the line of Hegemony warstriders had advanced from the woods, walking across the hellfire-blasted slope toward the rebel line. Three times they'd made it halfway up or a little farther before the sheer deadly volume of fire from the crest of the hill, the realization that if they kept pressing forward every one of them would be destroyed, forced them to back down. The slope was littered now with the smoking wreckage of warstriders from both sides. Katya did a quick count: Sinclair's forces numbered twelve warstriders now . . . fifteen if you counted three that couldn't move but still had at least one functional weapon.

Fifty percent casualties. The rebel line had already endured more than most warriors were ever asked to endure, and they'd held. She felt a furious, burning pride in their behavior, in the way they'd stood their ground, a pride that much sharper because she knew that the training she and the Thorhammers had passed on to raw rebel recruits was at least partly responsible for their good showing today.

But she wondered if pride was what she should be feeling, when the likeliest outcome was going to be death or capture for all of them.

What had happened to Dev? Laser fire had not dropped from the sky, scouring the rebels off the hilltop, so perhaps his mission to take the *Tokitukaze* out of the fight had succeeded. Earlier, there'd been a garbled report from Babel, something about the *Tokitukaze* leaving Shippurport . . . and something else about incoming Imperial frigates. Then nothing.

It was enough to wait and see what actually hit them without worrying about who-was . . . ghosts about which they could do nothing.

She thought again about the Xenophobes, about what might happen if they surfaced in the middle of a battlefield, then shuddered as she turned her mind away from the thought. Xenophobes, *here*. . . . No, she didn't want to face that. It was as though those subterranean horrors had replaced her old dread of closed-in spaces. At least they hadn't simply popped up when the battle had begun hours before, which meant that the Self was waiting for some specific and easily recognizable signal.

Would it be disappointed? Did it even understand such a concept?

"Lieutenant!" That was Darcy, off to the right. "I got movement!"

"What do you see?"

"Aircraft, incoming fast! I have five . . . six . . . no, eight aircraft, bearing one-eight-nine, range two-five. . . ."

"On your toes, people!" Sinclair rasped. "They're trying something different for a change!"

Somebody laughed over the circuit, but it sounded brittle, and Katya knew just how close to crumbling the rebel line was. Another good push, another few striders lost . . .

Then the ascraft were banking low overhead, the light of Marduk glinting from their wings. Chung's RLN-90 staggered as a bolt from the sky struck him, knocking his machine to the side.

"Fire!" Sinclair yelled. "Everybody fire!"

But there were too many of them, and too few rebel striders. The Hegemony warstriders were advancing for a fourth time from the woods, charging now with an almost joyful enthusiasm as the reinforcements from the south arrived over the battlefield. Katya could see a half dozen ascraft settling to the ground well out on the right flank, west of the monorail, and the death gleam of jet-black Imperial warstriders dropping from their riderslots and advancing on the rebel flank.

"On the right!" Katya yelled. "Imperial Marine striders on the right!" The trap yawned before her understanding now like an open pit. The rebels were trapped, trapped between

Hegemony, marines, the city, and the sea cliffs. Darcy's Fastrider was moving toward the right, blazing away with its laser, and then it was savaged by a pair of plasma bolts from the great, lumbering Katana that was pushing beneath the elevated monorail and advancing toward Katya faster than a man could run. She pivoted her Ghostrider and fired her laser, and that black armor seemed to drink the beam, absorbing it, dissipating it, and still the monster was thundering toward her.

The jaws of the trap were closing.

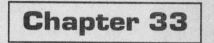

Chapter 33

In war, numbers alone confer no advantage. Do not advance relying on sheer military power.

—*The Art of War*
Sun Tzu
Third century B.C.E.

The *Tokitukaze* had made several course changes in the past half hour, as Eridu loomed larger and larger in the perceptions of her crew. On their original course, they would have missed the world by nearly fifty thousand kilometers—farther, even, than Babylon was from Towerdown—then looped into a wide, extended orbit.

They would be shaving the planet much more closely now, thanks to the course corrections they'd been able to make despite the damaged main engines. *Tokitukaze*'s AI had painted a concise and holographic picture of their encounter. By killing their speed and allowing the planet to turn a bit more, they could—with one course correction more—shift their perigee to a point just south of the space elevator and lower it to an altitude of somewhere between one hundred and five hundred kilometers. They would come in from the southwest, miss the Tower of Babel by between thirty and eighty kilometers, cross the equator over the Dawnthunder Sea, and loop on past the planet, entering a highly elliptical orbit with an apogee of about sixty thousand kilometers.

The uncertainties in the figures were due to the fact that the *Tokitukaze* was not an entirely predictable spacecraft. Large pieces were missing, and her AI was having difficulty assessing her exact current mass. Worse, once they hit atmosphere, it was impossible to predict exactly what she would do. The AI was vectoring them to skim Eridu's upper atmosphere, perhaps two hundred kilometers above the surface, but they could easily skip higher . . . or plunge deeper.

In any case, they would have a few precious seconds when they were in the sky above the fighting at the Babel Towerdown. If the fight was still going on at all, they might be able to throw a little of *Tokitukaze*'s considerable firepower on the side of the rebels.

"Captain?"

"What is it, Simone?"

"We're picking up the IFF and automatic call-sign IDs of the various units around Towerdown," she said. "It's all going through the ship's AI and, well, I could give you a direct feed on the tactical situation."

Dev considered. They would have only a few seconds above the enemy forces. No human could react, aim, and fire with any kind of accuracy in such a brief space of time, not even with cephlink-boosted reflexes. Only the superfast optical circuits and electronics of an AI could juggle so much data in so little time.

"Hang on a sec," Dev said. He was watching the dwindling handful of seconds left until the final course change. Three . . . two . . . one . . . there!

Silently, invisible plasmas stabbed into space at precisely calculated angles, slowing the *Tokitukaze* slightly, nudging her a bit closer to her target, and incidentally orienting her so that two of her three gigawatt lasers were facing the planet.

Maneuver completed. . . .

Twelve minutes now to perigee.

Eridu filled most of Dev's forward view, a vast globe of red and gold. He could make out the coastline of the Dawnthunder Sea now, and the convoluted twist of the Babel promontory. There were a lot of clouds. He'd not thought of that. Would they even be able to see the battleground? Jack that feed when we reach it. Was that the monofilament-thin gleam of the space elevator? Yes . . . he could just make it out where it caught the light of Marduk astern.

The falling ship shuddered, skipping on the first tenuous fringes of atmosphere. The erratic and unpredictable bouncing their weapons platform was about to suffer would not make this any easier, might well make it impossible.

"Simone? Go ahead. Give me a full tactical feed. And link all weapons through the AI."

Dev was braced, but the waterfall of data flowing through his cephlink was more than he'd ever tried to handle before. His view of Eridu was wiped away by the torrent. Shapes, lines, and mathematical formulas flickered and glowed in the complex depths of his virtual world. Eridu was *there* . . . its gravitational field *so*. . . .

In his mind, he could see each unit, Imperial, Hegemony, and rebel, as colored masses, could see each individual *warstrider* as a tiny figure highlighted against that war-blasted terrain. God of battles, were they too late? It looked as though a heavy Imperial Marine assault unit had just touched down on the rebel flank and was closing in for the kill. Dev could see only about a dozen rebel machines on their feet . . . no, fewer than that. And with the forces that closely involved, it would be damned hard to kill Imperials without hitting rebels.

Tokitukaze's path past the battlefield, her speed, altitude, and the reach of each of her weapons, were sensed rather than seen, a shifting interplay of mathematical calculations.

He could sense, too, the lightspeed flickerings of the AI's thought processes somewhere just behind his own reasoning. In a way, the direct cephlinkage with the computer had made that computer a part of Dev's own brain. He did not have to explain or calculate. He merely conveyed impressions . . . We need to hit *here* . . . *here* . . . *here* . . . but don't get too close *there* . . .

. . . and the ship's Artificial Intelligence calculated the best way to give Dev what he needed.

Seven minutes.

"We should tell them we're coming," Torolf suggested over the link. They could all see at least part of what Dev saw, picking up the feed from him, though they didn't have the godlike sense of having the ship's AI as a kind of extra hindbrain.

"Who?" Bev asked. "Our guys?"

"The Heggers and the Impies. Maybe take some of the heat off our people."

"And maybe get shot out of the sky," Tewari said.

"I doubt that they could touch us," Dev said. His own words sounded remote, like someone else speaking. "Anyway, their radar has probably been tracking us for an hour now." A thought occurred to him. "Anyway, we should announce the first official unit of the new Confederation Navy!"

There was a chorus of assents to that.

"You know," Koenig added, "we really need another name for this bucket. Somehow, the Confederation destroyer *Tokitukaze* doesn't quite make it."

"What's *Tokitukaze* in Inglic?" Torólf asked. "Ah . . . *Fair Wind*. Not bad, I suppose. . . ."

But Dev was remembering his first night with the rebels, after his rescue from Omigato.

He knew what the ship's name was, and he knew he didn't have to poll the other rebels on his decision.

Instead, he told Simone to open HEMILCOM's general com frequency. Transmitted in the open, every military unit on Eridu, rebel and government, ought to pick it up.

"Attention! This is the Confederation destroyer *Eagle*," he announced. "Imperial Naval forces in the Chi Draconis system have been eliminated."

Well, a slight exaggeration. The *Shusui* was still on a hyperbolic free-fall to nowhere, but the *Gekko* had apparently made some repairs and was making for Babylon. It didn't look like she was going to be much of a threat, however. Dev suspected her weapons and targeting systems were down.

"In the interest of ending further bloodshed," he continued, "we suggest that all government forces cease immediately all offensive operations and open negotiations with the local Confederation forces. . . ."

The refrain of Lorita's song repeated in his head, over and over.

> *For the Eagle has landed. Tell your children when.*
> *Time won't drive us down to dust again.*

Not strictly true. *Eagle* couldn't land, even if she had full thruster and maneuvering control, which she most certainly did not. He studied the rapidly evolving patterns of color unfolding on his mental viewscreen. There was the space elevator, ahead and slightly to the left. They were lower than expected. It looked like perigee would be about ninety kilometers.

"We're getting a reply from HEMILCOM, Captain," Simone reported. "In the clear. They're telling us to surrender. And I'm getting a simultaneous transmission to Hegemony units on the ground. Orders to continue the attack. Also in the clear."

"They want us to hear," Nicholson pointed out. "They're calling our bluff."

"They probably figure we couldn't unlock their nukes," Dev said. "Or else that we wouldn't dare trigger them that close to the space elevator. We'll show them what some computer-assisted conventional firepower can do."

Two minutes. The *Eagle* shuddered through thickening air, her outer hull glowing cherry red at her nose and the leading edges of her hull. Jagged bits of wreckage and hull metal peeled back from the hole in her side, then exploded into fiery bolides.

At the last moment, the ionization layer surrounding the hurtling vessel nearly ruined everything, blocking radio transmissions both from the ground and from HEMILCOM, and for a critical few seconds Dev and the computer both lost sight of their targets as they lost their data feeds.

Then the *Eagle* hit a denser layer of atmosphere and skipped high, like a flat stone skimming calm water. The ionization dissipated, the data feed was back.

And the last seconds ticked away to the moment when

Babel would be above the horizon and in range. *Five . . . four . . . three . . .*

The Imperial warstriders had engulfed the rebel right flank. Darcy had gone down, his Fastrider riddled by plasma bolts and laser fire and the *slam-slam-slam* of explosive cannon rounds. Katya didn't know if he'd ejected or not. The marine striders were behind her now, between her and the dome, and she had no time for anything but raw survival.

Hagan and Chung had their Scoutstriders next to her LaG-42; the three were virtually back to back now as the enemy closed in from three sides. The main rebel line was leaking like a sieve as Hegemony striders crested the hill at last, and black-armored infantry gunned down the fleeing rebel troopers.

The sky turned white.

For a long moment, Katya didn't know what was happening. She knew only that her optical sensors had been burned out and her external microphones had been knocked out and something like an earthquake had just slammed the bottoms of her Ghostrider's feet and knocked the machine over on its side. As her optics came back on-line, she was groggily aware of the canted horizon savagely backlit by what looked like a rapidly moving, pulsing pillar of fire. Eridu's odd mushroom-shaped trees were being plucked into the air and shredded, and with them went bits and pieces of combat machines and troop carriers and whole warstriders. The ground was continuing to hammer at her LaG-42 as though the planet itself had just woken up and was pounding at her like an irate tenant pounding for quiet on the ceiling above him.

And then the light, that glorious, dazzling, blinding light, was gone. Dust continued to swirl through the air, mingled with bits and shreds of vegetation. An instant later, it was starting to rain.

Katya was still dazed. *Strange,* she thought. *A moment ago there wasn't a cloud in the sky.*

Self could feel the vibrations from the interface between Void and Rock.

For some time now, it had been sensing disturbances, magnetic and seismic . . . there, but it was difficult to be certain that this was the human's signal.

But then, suddenly, there was no doubt. Pressure waves rippled through rock, one following the next in a pounding, hammering succession not unlike the shocks that had accompanied the cessation of the far-Self. Tendrils reaching through kilometers of rock twitched, anticipating Rock becoming Void in an agony of radiation flux . . . but then the vibrations were past. Dimly, dimly, Self sensed Something Else, a center of intense magnetic, radio, and thermal emissions sweeping through the Great Void quite close to the interface.

That was the signal. Widely spaced elements of Self triangulated on the precise epicenter of the shock waves. It was there, not far from the tempting savor of pure elements that extended from the interface and far into the Void.

Self gathered its strength, surged up toward the Void. . . .

The government forces broke and ran.

The actual target point for that unprecedented bombardment from space had not been on the front lines, for that would have destroyed rebel and government forces alike. Instead, the barrage had swept across the Hegemony's rear-area muster point, a group of clearings not far from the monorail line where they'd grouped their personnel carriers and repair vehicles and stockpiled the ammunition and repair parts they would need to fight a major battle. Several Imperial ascraft had been grounded there as well, those that were not in the skies over the battlefield, as well as the marine field commander's headquarters.

Most of the Hegemony reserves were destroyed outright. Every ascraft in the sky was clawed down by the greater-than-hurricane winds that briefly swept across that hillside with a force great enough to set the sky-el itself vibrating in a slow, ultralow-frequency ring that would not totally damp out for days.

As for the warstriders fighting atop the hill, many were banged up a bit, and one Hegemony pilot was killed when his Swiftstrider was impaled by a tree trunk, but they suffered relatively little direct damage. The marine and Hegemony striders had had enough, however. Once they'd learned their rear area logistical support had been wiped out, they elected to break off the fight and pull back to the fortress at Nimrod.

The politicians could wrangle all they wanted to. It was no part of a striderjack's duty to slug it out one-on-one with an enemy destroyer.

Many of them never made it. They were withdrawing in good order down the Babel-Nimrod road when a volcanic fountain of rock and debris spewed into the sky fifty meters in front of them. Seconds later, before they could react, before they could fully appreciate what was happening, the Xenophobe appeared.

Part of the problem was that the vast, tar-black, liquid-rippling thing in front of them was totally unlike any Xenophobe any of them had ever seen. Instead of the usual snake-form combat machine, this appeared to be a vast and gelatinous mass, a writhing, seething, living sea that engulfed the lead warstrider whole clear to its hips. The pilot was screaming mindlessly by the time the cloud of nano disassemblers wafting off that deadly sea's surface began to eat through to his slot.

Some of the Imperial striders managed to make it into the jungle to either side of the road, blundering ahead through nomad trees and anemone plants until they were helplessly trapped by the dense press of vegetation. Most of the Hegemony striders, unwilling to face the horror ahead and less than pleased with the desertion of their Imperial comrades, reversed course and returned to Babel. Many eventually joined the rebellion.

Self contented itself with absorbing a number of the metal-and-ceramic constructs, some trapped unmoving beside the path, others cut off by the quicksilver flow of its pseudopods.

Sadly, it found no other Self to communicate with. It found several humans and approached them, caressing them in an attempt to open a dialogue, but none possessed the biological communicator that the first human had worn as part of its outer covering. None wanted to speak with Self.

It hesitated for a long time then, sensing the overwhelming presence of pure metals, of humming magnetic fields, of the towering, massive glory that seemed to rise from Rock clear into the Great Void.

Then it bubbled to itself and backed away, flowing back down the tunnel it had warped through the rock. There was too much about humans that it did not understand, much about this interface zone at the ragged edge of the Void that was unpleasant. It would return to the comfort of Rock, there to wait its next human contact.

It wondered if humans would want to talk with it again, and what they might have to say.

Chapter 34

God forbid that we should ever be twenty years without such a rebellion.

—Thomas Jefferson
C.E. 1787

When Dev entered the Government House hall, the party was already in full swing. He remembered the last party he'd attended—the Kodama affair on Earth—and grinned. This one was a lot more . . . comfortable, though it was louder, rougher, and considerably more boisterous.

"Dev!" Koenig yelled from halfway across the quite large room. "Dev Cameron!" Someone started applauding, and then they all were doing it, clapping and whistling and cheering. Dev grinned and saluted, and then the noise and music were going again. Dev, wearing the newly designed brown-and-tan dress uniform of the Confederation Army, accepted a drink from a grinning Vince Creighton and started to make his way through the throng toward the far side of the room.

He spotted Lokans Vic Hagan, Harald Nicholson, and Erica Jacobsen in one corner, laughing uproariously with a cluster of Eriduan colonists and Newamie Mech Cav striderjacks.

In the middle of the room an impromptu square dance had started, with Lorita Fischer—as always, her red headband in evidence—providing the Scottish-sounding skirls of a fiddle tune on her mentar. Simone and Torolf were two of the dancers, thumping noisily about the square more or less in time to the music.

Most of the people present were in uniform of one sort or another, though the rest wore anything from the plain, rugged tunic and trousers of the typical frontier colonist to a few ambassadorial types in gold-trimmed capes and shoulder cloaks. Those last were Hegemony observers, and Dev wondered what they were going to report when they returned next week to the Hegemony Council. The Confederation was doing its best to present the revolution on Eridu as a fait accompli, something that the Hegemony and the Imperium would be better off simply accepting, rather than continuing with what would certainly be a long and destructive war. The Confederation had plenty of friends on Terra. Maybe . . . maybe there would be no more fighting.

Somehow, Dev doubted that things would work out that conveniently. A lot of good men and women had died on both sides of the lines in the short, sharp fight over Eridu, and many more would die before Hegemony recognized Confederation. The Empire would view the loss of one of the Shichiju worlds with alarm, a loss of *kao*, a first crack in the wall of an old and crumbling house. Other worlds were certain to join with Eridu in secession: New America and Liberty, already rattling their chains and proclaiming their freedom; Loki, its ravaged economy just recovering from a two-year struggle with the Xenophobes; Rainbow, from whence had come recent reports of sharp fighting between American colonists and Imperial marines. *Dai Nihon* would fight to preserve the old order, to keep the old house from falling down, even though the war, inevitably, would tear the Hegemony apart.

Well, maybe it was time for the old to give way to something new. Watching the animated people in this room, remembering the painted, pampered mannequins at Pulau Kodama, Dev wondered if there wasn't something cyclical in the need to give the cosmos a good shaking every so often, especially when civilization gave up the hungry, questing edge of the frontier for the comfortable familiarity of decadence.

Sinclair, resplendent in his new brown-and-tan uniform, was talking to two visiting diplomats. Dev had met both of them earlier. One was Manchurian, a *fu kuan* from the refugee colony on Chien V, a survivor of the Lung Chi disaster. The other was a striking woman, two meters tall, her skin ebony black, her hair, even her eyebrows, a startling, silvery white. Her name was Sheria, a Swahili word meaning "Justice," and she was a Network representative from Juanyekundu. Her white hair, he'd learned, was a dominant genetic trait among her people, who had carved a home for themselves on the innermost world of a flare-prone red-dwarf star.

The Confederation leader was gesturing as he spoke, thrusting repeatedly with his fist. Dev could almost read the words on his lips, the familiar refrain. *Diversity*, Sinclair was saying. *Mankind's survival lies in his diversity, not in the iron rule of a stagnant government from a distant, backwater world.*

If Eridu's fate as a free world had yet to be determined, at least the fate of the people trapped atop in Babylon was decided. The synchorbital facility was to be turned over to the Confederation next week, and those who wished to return to Earth or elsewhere would be permitted to do so. The negotiations had been carried out with Governor Prem, who spoke on behalf of both HEMILCOM personnel and the Imperial subjects. The Imperial *daihyo*, Yoshi Omigato, unfortunately had slit his belly in the traditional manner shortly after word of the disaster at Babel reached him.

Dev wondered what had hit the *daihyo* harder, the defeat on Eridu or the loss of his ship. The former *Tokitukaze*, now the *Eagle*, flagship of an infant rebel navy, had barely managed to limp into a higher orbit after its brief, fiery pass above Babel, and it had been forty hours before an ascraft from Babel had been able to match orbits and take off the crew—together with forty-seven bruised and battered Imperial crewmen. The *Eagle* would need repairs, lots of them, before she could fly or fight again. The rebels were carefully keeping her true condition secret from the Imperials during this impromptu truce, pretending that she was still a potent force in the Confederation arsenal.

God, but we need ships, Dev thought. *If we can't get them somewhere, the Imperials are going to trample us right into the ground.* The need for warships was, arguably, the single most pressing need the Confederation had at the moment . . . though the needs for trained soldiers, for weapons, for warstriders, and for AIs of every type were all clamoring for attention as well. But ships! They could not control their worlds without control of the space around them, and they could not coordinate the activities of one system with the next without control of the space lanes between them. At the moment, all they had were a handful of surface-to-orbit ascraft, a few merchantmen like the *Saiko Maru*, and the armed hulk that they called *Eagle*.

Dev was scowling, when he felt a touch on his arm.

"Katya!"

She smiled at him. "You were looking grim," she said. "Trouble?"

"Nothing a five-hundred-ship navy wouldn't solve. I was just wondering where it's all going. Where *I'm* going. This has all been . . . kind of sudden."

She laughed. "A month ago you were still the Empire's fair-haired *shiro*."

He grinned. *Shiro* was Nihongo slang for "white boy," a racial epithet. "Something like that."

She took a sip of her drink and looked around the room. "I know what you mean. I don't know about you, but I feel . . . at home. Doing something I believe in, with people I believe in."

"You can't ask for more than that, can you?"

"I can ask what you're doing tonight."

He raised his eyebrows. "You want to give us another chance?"

"We can try. No promises. But as long as we're finally on the same side . . ."

"Hey, I'd much rather serve in *your* army than the Emperor's. You're considerably prettier than he is."

"And more forgiving."

"Yes . . ."

"Ah. There you two are!"

They turned at the new voice. "General Sinclair!" Dev said. "Thank you for inviting us."

"Hell, I couldn't very well *not* invite the guy who pulled my tail out of the fire at the Battle of Raeder's Hill, could I?" He looked at Katya. "Have you asked him yet?"

"No. Haven't had a chance."

"Asked me what?"

"Got an assignment for you. If you want it."

Dev set his empty glass down on a passing tray and raised his eyebrows. "This doesn't involve pirating Imperial destroyers, does it?"

"Not quite. I'm leaving for New America in a few days. For a meeting of the Confederation Congress of Delegates."

"Your Declaration," Katya said, eyes lighting up.

He nodded. "We'll be proposing it to the delegates from twelve Shichiju worlds as the basis for secession from the Hegemony. If they like what they hear, well, it's a beginning. . . ."

"How does that involve us?"

Sinclair grinned. "Son, the Confederation is going to need all the help it can get. All the *friends* it can get. I'd like you two to be ambassadors at large . . . for the Xenophobes."

Dev blinked, stunned. "You want us to represent . . . the *Xenophobes*?"

"They can't represent themselves. Not yet, anyway."

"It's just you, actually," Katya added. She sounded embarrassed. "He asked me and I said no. I don't think I could."

"I have something else in mind for this young lady," Sinclair said. "I'm hoping to open friendly relations with the DalRiss as well. She will speak for them at the Congress."

This was all happening too fast for Dev. "I'm not sure what to say."

"Say yes. And come with us to New America. Help give rebirth to an old idea. To *freedom*."

In the background, the square dance had broken up and Lorita was singing "Hope Eyrie" again. Dev caught the words again that had arrested him during his first evening of freedom.

From all who tried out of history's tide,
Salute for the team that won.

And the old Earth smiles at her children's reach,
The wave that carried us up the beach
To reach for the shining sun. . . .

The old America had faltered, centuries ago, but somehow it had managed to break free of Mother Ocean and scrabble a few meters up onto a wet and empty beach. Now, the descendants of those first pioneers were opening a new frontier. A frontier of new promise. New hope.

New friends, even, though they were very strange friends, difficult to understand in the alien ways they looked at the cosmos. Maybe that was part of the evolutionary trek, though, learning to see the universe in a different way.

For the Eagle has landed. Tell your children when.
Time won't drive us down to dust again.

"Absolutely, General," Dev said. He exchanged a look with Katya, who nodded and smiled. "I'd say we need all the friends we can get."

Terminology and Glossary

AI: Artificial Intelligence. Since the Sentient Status Act of 2204, higher-model networking systems have been recognized as "self-aware but of restricted purview," a legal formula that precludes enfranchisement of machine intelligences.

Alpha: Type of Xenophobe combat machine, also called stalker, shapeshifter, silvershifter, etc. They are animated by numerous organic-machine hybrids and mass ten to twelve tons. Their weapons include nano-D shells and surfaces, and various magnetic effects. Alphas appear in two guises, a snakelike or wormlike shape that lets them travel underground along SDTs, and any of a variety of combat shapes, usually geometrical with numerous spines or tentacles. Each distinctive combat type is named after a poisonous Terran reptile, e.g., Fer-de-Lance, Cobra, Mamba, etc.

Alya: Naked-eye star Theta Serpentis (63 Serpentis) 130 light years from Sol. A double star with a separation of 900 AU (5 light-days), Alya A is an A5 star, Alya B an A7. Alya B-V is the homeworld of the DalRiss, who know it as GhegnuRish. Alya A-VI is known as ShraRish, a DalRiss colony.

Analogue: Computer-generated "double" of a person, used to handle routine business and communications through ViRcom linkage.

Annaisha: "Guide." Term for Imperial liaison officers who coordinate military or political activity between the Empire and Hegemony military forces.

Ascraft: Aerospace craft. Vehicles that can fly both in space and in atmosphere, including various transports, fighters, and shuttles.

Beta: Second class of Xenophobe combat machine, adapted from captured or abandoned human equipment. Its weapons are human-manufactured weapons, often reshaped to Xeno purposes. They have been known to travel underground.

Bionangineering: Use of nanotechnology to restructure life forms for medical or ornamental reasons.

Cephlink: Implant within the human brain allowing direct interface with computer-operated systems. It contains its own microcomputer and RAM storage and is accessed through sockets, usually located in the subject's temporal bones above and behind each ear. Limited (non-ViR) control and interface is possible through neural implants in the skin, usually in the palm of one hand.

Cephlink RAM: *Also* RAM. Random access memory, part of the microcircuitry within the cephlink assembly. Used for memory storage, message transfer, linguistics programming, and the storage of complex digital codes used in cephlinkage access. An artificial extension of human intelligence.

Ceramiplas: Plastic-ceramic composite used in personal armor.

Charged-Particle Gun (CPG): Primary weapon on larger warstriders. Including proton cannons and electron guns, they use powerful gauss fields to direct streams of charged subatomic particles at the target.

Chiji: "Governor." Specifically, the Hegemony governor of Shichiju worlds. Usually (but not always) an Imperial.

Coaster: Intrasystem, low-cost space transport, usually for cargo, although sometimes passengers are carried. Cramped, old, and uncomfortable, they are characterized by brief periods of high-G acceleration and deceleration at either end of the journey, with a long interval of zero-G "coasting" between.

Colonial Authority: Hegemonic bureaucracy charged with overseeing government, trade, and terraforming of the human-inhabited worlds.

Commpac: "Communications package." Long-range communications unit that plugs into both temporal sockets and is worn behind the head. It permits long-range communication and can serve as a modem to planetary computer networks without a direct palm interface.

Compatch: Small radio transceiver worn on the skin and jacked into a T-socket. Allows cephlink-to-link radio communications.

Compscam: Using computer networks—especially non-AI systems—to illegally divert money, equipment, etc.

Cryo-H: Liquid hydrogen cooled to a few degrees absolute, used as fuel for fusion power plants aboard striders, ascraft, and other vehicles. Sometimes called "slush hydrogen."

C-socket: Cervical socket, located in subject's cervical spine near the base of his neck. Directs neural impulses to jacked equipment, warstriders, construction gear, heavy lifters, etc.

DalRiss: Nonhuman intelligence first contacted in 2540. Native to Alya B-V (GhegnuRish), they are highly advanced in biological sciences, relatively backward in engineering and metallurgical sciences. Compound name reflects use of Dal, a gene-engineered organism, as "mount" by Riss ("Master").

DHS: Directorate of Hegemony Security. Joint military-civilian bureau under Imperial overwatch tasked with internal security in both civilian and military sectors.

Dracomycetes mirabila: Fungus harvested in jungle lowlands of Eridu, the source of a drug used for memory enhancement.

DSA: Deep seismic anomaly: Seismic tremors associated with subsurface movements of Xenophobe machines.

Durasheath: Armor grown as composite layers of diamond, duralloy, and ceramics; light, flexible, and very strong.

El-shuttle: Saucer-shaped pressurized chamber ferrying passengers and cargo up and down the sky-el. The passenger deck has seats for up to a hundred people, with jackplugs and a recjack library.

Embedded Interface: Network of wires and neural feeds embedded in the skin—usually in the palm near the base of the thumb—and used to access and control simple computer hardware. Provides control and datafeed functions only, not full-sensory input. Used to activate T- and C-socket jacks, to pass authorization and credit data, and to retrieve printed or vocal data "played" inside the user's mind. Also called 'face or skin implant.

E-suit: Environmental suit. Lightweight helmet and garment for use in space or hostile atmospheric conditions.

Fukushi: Imperial welfare program that provides Level One Implant technology, free housing, and ration subsidies to dependent citizens.

Fusorpak: Power unit carried on board most striders and large vehicles. Uses tanked slush hydrogen as fuel.

Gamma: Third type of Xenophobe combat machine, usually relatively small and amorphous. Apparently a fragment of a Xenophobe Alpha, animated by one or more Xeno machine-organism hybrids. Its surface consists of nanodisassemblers, making its touch deadly.

Glowglobe: Magnetically suspended lighting element, programmed to hover in place and produce light chemically on command.

Greens, Greenies: Political descendants of the Green Activist parties of the twenty-first and twenty-second centuries. Generally pro-environmental, anti-expansionist.

Grennel: Common name for a freshwater bladder plant harvested on Eridu. It is the source of a drug useful in treating impotence.

Guntower: Unmanned sentry outpost armed with various energy or projectile weapons. May be automated, remote-controlled, or directed by an on-site, low-level AI.

Hab: "Habitat," home, though it usually refers to a structure used primarily for recreation or entertainment rather than a dwelling.

Hegemony: Also Terran Hegemony. World government representing fifty-seven nations on Earth, plus the Colonial Authorities of the seventy-eight colonized worlds. Technically sovereign, it is dominated by Imperial Japan, which has a veto in its legislative assembly.

HEMILCOM: Hegemony Military Command. Local military command-control-communications (C^3) headquarters, usually based in sky-el orbitals. Coordinates military operations within a given sector.

Hivel Cannon: A turret-mounted rotary cannon (the word *hivel* comes from "high velocity"). Similar to twentieth-century CIWS systems, it fires bursts of depleted uranium slugs with a rate of fire as high as fifty per second. Usually controlled by an onboard AI, its primary function is anti-missile defense. It can also be voluntarily controlled and used against other targets.

Hotbox: Strap-on rocket or scramjet booster. Small modules allow striders to softland after an airdrop or provide jet-assisted boosts for navigating rough terrain. Larger modules provide surface-to-orbit thrust for aerospace transports.

Jacker: Slang for anyone with implanted jacks for neural interface with computers, machinery, or communications networks. Specifically applied to individuals who jack-in for a living, as opposed to recreational jackers, or "recjacks."

Kanrinin: "Controller." Device that plugs into subject's T- and C-sockets, allowing almost total motor nerve control by others. Used to handle or transfer prisoners.

Kansei no Otoko: "The Men of Completion." Nihonjinn faction at Court and within the Imperial Staff dedicated to cleansing upper levels of Imperial civilian and military organizations of *gaijin* influence.

Kokorodo: Literally "Way of the Mind." A mental discipline practiced by Imperial military jackers to achieve full mental and physical coordination through AI linkage.

K-T Plenum: Extraspacial realm at the hyperdimensional interface between normal fourspace and the quantum sea. From Nihongo *Kamisama no Taiyo*, literally "Ocean of God." Starships navigate through the K-T plenum.

Kuso: Japanese word for "feces." Not a Japanese explicative, it is used as such by Inglic speakers.

L-LOS: Laser line of sight. Straight-line path clear of interfering smoke, dust, or other obstruction along which laser communications can be established.

Loki: 36 Ophiuchi C (Dagstjerne) II. World 17.8 light years from Sol, currently undergoing terraforming by colonists of Scandinavian descent. Place names taken from Norse mythology, including Asgard (synchorbital), Bifrost (skyel), and Midgard (Towerdown). Capital: Midgard. Language: Norsk-Lokan, a dialect of Norse.

Lung Chi: DM+32° 2896 (Chien) IV. World terraformed by colonists of Manchurian descent. Overrun by Xenophobes in 2538.

Magflitter: Personal air transport, flown through interaction with a planetary magnetic field.

Nangineering: Nanotechnic engineering. Use of nanotechnic devices in building or in medicine.

Nanits: "Nanotechnic units." Molecule-sized or smaller programmable machines.

Nano-Ds: Nanodisassemblers. Xenophobe weapon, delivered by mag-accelerated projectile or through contact with a specialized appendage, consisting of billions of submicroscopic machines programmed to disassemble molecular bonds. A high concentration of nano-Ds can cause several kilos of mass to disintegrate into its component molecules within seconds.

Nanoflage: Nanofilm on military vehicles designed to transmit colors and textures of vehicle's immediate surroundings. Selectively reflective, it does not reflect bright light or motion.

Navsim: ViRsimulation used in ship navigation.

New America: 26 Draconis IV. Frontier colony 48.6 light years from Sol.

NOI: Nippon Orbital Industries, manufacturer of cephimplants and other DI (direct interface) equipment.

Null: Person possessing no cephlink hardware and unable to engage in financial transactions, interface with computers, or engage in useful work. Large numbers of Nulls on Frontier worlds and even in some areas on Earth constitute a growing and problematical lower class.

Prebiotic: A world similar to Earth in the distant past, before the evolution of life. Possessing primitive atmospheres carbon dioxide, water, methane, and ammonia, they can be tailored through terraforming techniques to eventually develop Earthlike environments.

Quantum Sea: Energy continuum reflected in "vacuum fluctuation," the constant appearance and reabsorption of vast quantities of energy on a subatomic scale. Tapped by starships operating within the K-T plenum.

Rank: Terran Hegemony ranks are based on the Imperial Japanese rank structure, though the English terminology is preferred in common usage. A rough comparison of rank in the Hegemony military, as compared to late-twentieth-century America, is given below:

Enlisted Ranks

U.S. Army/Marines	Imperial Military
Private 2nd class/(no equivalent)	Nitto hei
E-2 Private/PFC	Itto hei
Superior Private/(no equivalent)	Jotto hei
E-3 PFC/Lance Corporal	Heicho
E-4 Corporal/Corporal	Gocho
E-5 Sergeant/Sergeant	Gunso
E-9 Sgt. Major/Sgt. Major	Socho
WO Warrant Officers (CWO)	Jun-i

Commissioned Ranks

U.S. Army/Navy	Imperial Military
O-O Cadet	Seito
O-1 2nd Lieutenant/Ensign	Sho-i
O-2 Lieutenant/Lieutenant (jg)	Chu-i
O-3 Captain/Lieutenant	Tai-i
O-4 Major/Lieutenant Commander	Shosa
O-5 Lieutenant Colonel/Commander	Chusa
O-6 Colonel/Captain	Taisa
O-8 Major General/Rear Admiral	Shosho
O-9 Lieutenant General/Vice Admiral	Chujo
O-10 General/Admiral	Taisho
O-11 General of the Army/Fleet Admiral	Gensui

Rebrief: From "RAM-edited briefing." Originally a means to update RAM-loaded information by rewriting cephlink-stored data. Now means downloading fabricated data into a subject's RAM for purposes of interrogation or brain-washing.

Recjack: Using implants for recreational purposes. These uses range from participation in ViRdramas to shared multiple sensual stimulation to direct stimulation of the hypothalmic pleasure centers (PC-jacking).

Riderslot: Opening in an ascraft or other transport's hull designed to receive striders. Usually equipped with grippers, magnetic locks, and autoplug ICS and datafeed connectors.

Rogan Process: Nano construction technique, named after inventor Philip Rogan, employing assemblers and any plentiful raw material. Through "RoPro"—or "RoProduction"—walls, buildings, roads, and any similar large structure can be "grown" out of rock and earth quickly and cheaply.

SDT: Subsurface deformation track. Path through a planetary crust previously used by Xenophobe underground travelers. Rock once turned plastic by intense heat and pressure offers subsurface "highways" more easily traversed by subsequent Xenos.

Sekkodan: The Imperial Scout Service, tasked with exploring and cataloging new worlds, as well as operating high-speed courier ships between the worlds of the Shichiju. Its members wear green uniforms and it is considered to be a civilian bureau rather than a military unit.

Schiz, Schiz Out: Slang for mental breakdown brought on by jacked shutdown of mental activities for a protracted period of time, or through severe mental stress during linkage.

Sempu: "Whirlwind." Shotgunlike antipersonnel weapon firing shot connected by strands of monofilament.

Sensphere: Tennis-ball-sized gold sphere held against palm implants. Creates a pleasant, mildly stimulating, and erotic tingle through the interface circuitry.

Servot: A robotic, general-purpose servant.

Shakai: "Society." The elitist, upper-class culture of Imperial Earth.

Shichiju: Literally "The Seventy." Japanese term for the seventy-eight worlds in seventy-two systems so far colonized by Man.

Shishino Chi: "The Lion's Blood." Imperial equivalent of the Purple Heart.

Silicolubricant, Silicarb: Greasy black silicon compound used to reduce friction in interior working parts.

Sky-el: Elevator used to travel between a planetary ring and the surface of the planet. A cheap and efficient way of moving people and cargo back and forth from surface to orbit. Earth has three sky-els: Singapore (Pulau Lingga), Ecuador (Quito), and Kenya (Mount Kenya). New Earth has two. Other worlds have one. Some, such as New America, have none.

Slang (profanity):

> **dreamjack:** Military slang for a very good or much-desired assignment.

> **easy feed:** Slang expression for "No problem" or "That's okay."

> **gok, goking:** Sexual obscenity. From the Japanese *goku*, "rape."

> **Heggers, Hegleggers:** Military slang for Hegemony foot soldiers.

iceworld: Military slang for "Stay cool. I'm cool."

I'm linked: "I'm with you." "I'll go along with that."

jackin' Jill: Girlfriend, especially as a casual RJ sex partner.

mincies: Military slang for civilians. From the Japanese *minshu*.

nullhead: Stupid. Empty-headed. By association, crazy. Also, people without jacks, unable to interact in technic society.

odie: "Let's odie" means "Let's do it, let's move." From the Japanese *odori*, "dance."

staticjack: Mild curse. Expression of disgust or amazement.

straight hont, the hont: The truth. From the Japanese *hontono koto*.

Slot: (1) Linkage module for human controller. Warstriders have one, two, or three slots; a three-slotter strider has places for a commander, pilot, and weapons tech. (2) Space for equipment aboard a transport. Ascraft have "slots" to carry four or six warstriders. (Slang) By popular usage, a place for a person in an organization, e.g., a "slot in the infantry."

Synchorbit: That point, different for each world, at which a satellite has an orbital period exactly matching the planet's rotation. Planetary sky-els rise from a world's equator to extensive constructions—factories, habitats, and other orbital facilities—in synchorbit.

Synchorbital: Facilities built at synchorbit.

Tacsit: Military slang for "tactical situation."

Teikokuno Heiwa: "The Imperial Peace." The Pax Japonica.

Teikokuno Hoshi: "Star of the Empire." Imperial medal for supreme service to the Emperor.

Teleop Weapons: Long-range missiles operated by weapons technicians at remote locations. Control can be by radio or—to avoid battlefield jamming—laser or a molecular fiberline unreeled behind the projectile.

Tenno Kyuden: "Palace of Heaven." Seat of Imperial government, located at Singapore Orbital.

T-form: Terraform. Converting an existing planetary atmosphere and environment to one that supports humans.

Thermal: Military slang for any infrared sensory device or scanner.

Towerdown: The base of a sky-el tower, a busy terminus for freight and passengers.

Transplas: Synthetic building material, transparent and very strong.

T-socket: Temporal socket. Usually paired, one on each side of subject's skull in temporal bone above and behind the ear. Used for full-sensory, full-feedback jacking in conjunction with an AI system, including experiencing ViR, full-sensory communications, and computer control of ships or vehicles.

Universal Life, Lifers: A widespread, moderate "green" movement dedicated to preserving alien ecosystems.

Vacwalls: Walls or bulkheads holding pressure against vacuum.

VCH: Vehicle cephlinkage helmet. Allows direct human control of warstriders, ascraft, or other military vehicles.

Internal leads plug into the operator's temporal sockets, while external sockets receive leads from AI interface.

ViR, Virtual Reality: Made possible by cephalic implants, virtual reality is the "artificial reality" of computer interfaces that allows, for example, a human pilot to "become" the strider or missile he is piloting, to "live" a simplay, or to "see" things that do not really exist save as sophisticated computer software. An artificial world existing within the human mind that, through AI technology, can be shared with others.

ViRcom: Full sensory linked communication. Linker enters a chamber and plugs into communications net. He can then engage in conversation with one or more other humans or their computer analogues as though all were present together.

ViRdrama: Recreational jacking allowing full sensory experience through cephlinkage. Linker can participate in elaborate canned shows or AI-monitored games. Two or more linkers can share a single scenario, allowing them to interact with one another.

ViRnews: Also ViRinfo. Jack-fed informational programs permitting viewer interaction and questions with programmed "guides."

ViRpersona: The image of self projected in virtual reality dramas or communications. Clothing styles and even personal appearance can be purchased as a cephlink program, much as someone would buy new clothes.

Warstrider: Also strider. Battlefield armor on two or four legs, giving it high mobility over rough terrain. Generally consists of a fuselage slung between two legs and equipped either with two arms mounting weapons or with interchangeable weapons pods. Sizes include single-slotters (eight to twelve tons), dual-slotters (ten to thirty tons), three-slotters (twenty-five to seventy tons), and special vehicles such as armored personnel walkers that carry large numbers of troops.

Whitesuit: Slang for Hegemonic naval personnel. From their dress uniforms, which are white with gold trim.

Who-was: Rumor, scuttlebutt. Corruption of the Japanese *uwasa*.

Xeno, Xenophobe: Human name for the life-form that first attacked the human colony on An-Nur II in 2498. So-called because of their apparent hatred or fear of other life-forms. Investigations within the Alya system in 2541 proved Xenophobes are machine-organic hybrids evolved from fairly simple organisms billions of years ago. They are defined by their technology, much of which has been borrowed from other civilizations.

Yukanno Kisho: "Medal of Valor." Imperial decoration awarded in ten orders, or *dans*, for bravery in the line of duty.

Japanese Words and Phrases

Baka: Foolish, stupid, or silly.

Daihyo: Representative. In twenty-sixth-century usage, the Emperor's representative to a government or local military force within the Shichiju.

Dan: Order or ranking.

Fushi: Eternity, immortality. Era-name of current emperor. 2542 is the year Fushi 85.

Gaijin: Foreigner, specifically a non-Japanese.

Gokuhi: Secret.

Kancho: Depending on how you say it, "warship captain" or "enema."

Kao: Face.

Kichigai: "You're crazy!"

Ko-tori: Bird.

Mon: A family badge or design.

Nimotsu: Baggage. *O-nimotsusan* ("honorable baggage") refers to passengers aboard small and Spartan couriers and packets.

Obake: Black Goblins. Regimental name for 3rd Imperial Marines.

Sashimono: Military banners bearing the *mon* of the commander.

Sen-en: One thousand yen (*en* in Japanese).

Sensei: "Master." Title of respect for the teacher of a given discipline.

Sheseiji: "Bastards." Related to *shesei*, "posture" or "attitude."

Shoko: Military officer.

Tatami: Floor mat.

Tenno-heika: Formal title of address—"His Majesty, the Emperor."

BIO OF A SPACE TYRANT
Piers Anthony

"Brilliant...a thoroughly original thinker and storyteller with a unique ability to posit really *alien* alien life, humanize it, and make it come out alive on the page." *The Los Angeles Times*

A COLOSSAL NEW FIVE VOLUME SPACE THRILLER—
BIO OF A SPACE TYRANT
The Epic Adventures and Galactic Conquests of Hope Hubris

VOLUME I: REFUGEE   84194-0/$4.50 US/$5.50 Can
Hubris and his family embark upon an ill-fated voyage through space, searching for sanctuary, after pirates blast them from their home on Callisto.

VOLUME II: MERCENARY   87221-8/$4.50 US/$5.50 Can
Hubris joins the Navy of Jupiter and commands a squadron loyal to the death and sworn to war against the pirate warlords of the Jupiter Ecliptic.

VOLUME III: POLITICIAN   89685-0/$4.50 US/$5.50 Can
Fueled by his own fury, Hubris rose to triumph obliterating his enemies and blazing a path of glory across the face of Jupiter. Military legend...people's champion...promising political candidate...he now awoke to find himself the prisoner of a nightmare that knew no past.

VOLUME IV: EXECUTIVE   89834-9/$4.50 US/$5.50 Can
Destined to become the most hated and feared man of an era, Hope would assume an alternate identify to fulfill his dreams.

VOLUME V: STATESMAN   89835-7/$4.50 US/$5.50 Can
The climactic conclusion of Hubris' epic adventures.

THE CONTINUATION
OF THE FABULOUS
INCARNATIONS OF IMMORTALITY
SERIES

PIERS ANTHONY

FOR LOVE OF EVIL
75285-9/$4.95 US/$5.95 Can

AND ETERNITY
75286-7/$4.95 US/$5.95 Can

RETURN TO AMBER...
THE ONE *REAL* WORLD, OF WHICH
ALL OTHERS, INCLUDING EARTH,
ARE BUT SHADOWS

ROGER ZELAZNY

*The Triumphant conclusion
of the Amber novels*

PRINCE OF CHAOS   75502-5/$4.99 US/$5.99 Can

The Classic Amber Series

NINE PRINCES IN AMBER 01430-0/$4.50 US/$5.50 Can
THE GUNS OF AVALON   00083-0/$4.99 US/$5.99 Can
SIGN OF THE UNICORN   00031-9/$4.99 US/$5.99 Can
THE HAND OF OBERON   01664-8/$4.50 US/$5.50 Can
THE COURTS OF CHAOS   47175-2/$4.50 US/$5.50 Can
BLOOD OF AMBER   89636-2/$3.95 US/$4.95 Can
TRUMPS OF DOOM   89635-4/$3.95 US/$4.95 Can
SIGN OF CHAOS   89637-0/$3.95 US/$4.95 Can
KNIGHT OF SHADOWS   75501-7/$3.95 US/$4.95 Can

There are places on Earth
where magic worlds beckon…
where the other folk dwell

TOM DEITZ

takes you there…

DREAMBUILDER
76290-0/$4.99 US/$5.99 Can

SOULSMITH
76289-7/$4.99 US/$5.99 Can

STONESKIN'S REVENGE
76063-0/$3.95 US/$4.95 Can

WINDMASTER'S BANE
75029-5/$4.50 US/$5.50 Can

DARKTHUNDER'S WAY
75508-4/$3.95 US/$4.95 Can

FIRESHAPER'S DOOM
75329-4/$3.95 US/$4.95 Can

THE GRYPHON KING
75506-8/$3.95 US/$4.95 Can

SUNSHAKER'S WAR
76062-2/$3.95 US/$4.95 Can